W9-BAS-666

ROCKIN' THE BRONX

Also by Larry Kirwan

Memoir
  Green Suede Shoes

Novel
  Liverpool Fantasy

Plays
  Mad Angels, A Collection of Plays

Songs
  The Songs and Stories of Black 47

LARRY KIRWAN

A Brandon Original Paperback

First published in 2010 by Brandon
an imprint of Mount Eagle Publications
United States of America:
c/o Dufour Editions Inc, PO Box 7, Chester Springs PA 19425
Ireland: Dingle, Co. Kerry, Ireland and
England, Scotland and Wales
Unit 3, Olympia Trading Estate, Coburg Road, London N22 6TZ, England

www.brandonbooks.com

ISBN 978-0-863-22418-8

Mount Eagle Publications/Sliabh an Fhiolar Teoranta receives support from
the Arts Council/An Chomhairle Ealaíon.

2 4 6 8 10 9 7 5 3 1

Cover design: www.davidriedydesign.com
Typesetting by Red Barn Publishing, Skeagh, Skibbereen
Printed in the United States of America

For my sister, Ann Kirwan, 1962–2009

PROLOGUE

There were times when the pain ripped the heart right out of me. Though, to be truthful, when I was out on the town with the lads or cavorting with some young one, it rarely cost me the time of day. Still, all it took was the snatch of a song or a hint of her perfume on some passing dolly-bird, and up its ugly head would rear, and the whole bollocksy business would begin all over again.

Pain was one thing, pain in the arse quite another, and it was no simple matter separating them when I'd have to beg bilious auld Paddy Begley down the pub for a fist full of fifty-pence pieces to stick down the gullet of the pay phone.

"Ah, you're ringin' the quare one again, so you are?" A twisted sneer would light up the cute hoor's cash-registered face as he rolled the coins one by one over the counter before announcing to all and sundry, "Wouldn't you think his nibs here would have enough sense by now—and her off livin' the high life in the Big Apple?"

This papal bull would be greeted by a torrent of winks, sniggers, and a slew of variants on, "Oh now, he'll learn soon enough, won't he?" Then I'd be forced to slither flame-faced, Sahara-tongued, but bantam-cock defiant past the humps of all their fat behinds lined up like clay pigeons ready to be blown the hell out of there just as soon as they'd spent their dole money on Begley's pissy pints and watered-down spirits.

After one such encounter, I found myself down the harbor, standing in line outside the thrice pissed upon telephone box, pawing like a young bull, while some auld biddy argued with her up-the-pole daughter in London. With tears streaming down her face, Mammy dearest staggered out of the smoky, smelly sweatbox shielding herself from my expected censure. She needn't have bothered. I wasn't looking next nor near her, just wondering if the dilapidated bastard behind me would be able to decipher my own pending tale of unmitigated woe.

I dialed the long number while Packy Mooney's battered, blue, barnacled trawler inched around the near headland, lights bobbing in the soft swell of the violet April evening. I could recite those digits backwards by now, and why wouldn't I, and they clattering around my brain morning, noon, and half the endless night?

I focused on the islands, waiting for the first ring: our islands or, rather, hers. Truth be told, I'd never paid them much heed until she started raving about them. Purple they were in the gathering dusk; purple they'd be out there too with the heather up beyond your calf, thick and scraggly as a tramp's beard. I'd even hired mackerel-stinking Mooney to take us out there for her birthday and pick us up on his way back from the fishing. Gannets and gulls swooping down on us while the oily fisher-lads made cracks in their culchie accents about Romeo and Juliet, as if they'd know Willy Shakespeare from the back of an abattoir wall. But I didn't give a continental hoot if they said high mass, for I'd have six glorious hours alone with my Mary just as soon as their collective snot-noses puttered over the edge of the moody, blue Atlantic.

And finally, peace; no one to slag or pass a word of censure, not a snigger, nor a sneer, not even silence—just the metronomic gush and swish of the waves across the slimy black rocks. We'd got right down to business. Clothes off, Docs unlaced, then knee deep into the heather like two panthers going at it, not a bother about the prickles or the idiot wind howling above us. Scratches would heal, but time was a treasure we could rarely afford, for I could never have enough of her silky ways. And so I touched and teased her to my heart's content while lunatic hares bolted from marauding stoats. Shoulder to shoulder, mouth on mouth, I kissed her until she winced, while mice squealed as a hawk swooped down from the tail of a will-of-the-wisp wind. Life pulsing along as it always does out there—hunting, killing, living, lusting, and begetting—but all we felt was the achy moistness of the renegade love we felt for each other.

But little ever stayed steady with Mary. Without the least warning, she had grown moody and anxious, scanning the horizon for Mooney's boat before the afternoon had barely settled in, her raven-rinsed hair shrouding those grayish green eyes. I never knew a body who could sit so still, so concentrated, so oblivious of anything she deemed outside the scope of her interest. At first, I tried to mollify her, go along with her whims, suffer her scorn in the hope of coaxing her back into good form; for she could change like the weather, and the right word or line of a song could banish whatever misfortune she was harping upon. Eventually, I wearied of listening to my own cajoling, so there we sat, twin balls of misery peering out through a kaleidoscope of showers, mists and flashes of naked sunshine.

She had no thought of making love again, though she

touched me from time to time as though granting a petitioner some forlorn consolation. But whenever I'd try to hold her, she was all quicksilver diffidence, until late in the day she caught sight of some seals slipping and sliding over the seaweedy rocks and wondered if there might be a *selkie* amongst them. At that, she turned to me, the heather blazing in her eyes, all lips and teeth, until she became soft and silky and herself again. We were almost undressed when we heard the shout from the boat that had crept up unnoticed in the gathering wind and whispers of our private pornographies. Before I knew it, we were back on board, hot, bothered and unfulfilled, with Mooney's pollocky lads smirking and counting the pieces of heather stuck to the back of her skirt.

Then the phone was pealing in my ear, and my heart was in my mouth. What time was it in America? Had to be two in the afternoon. She should be well awake by now, but you never knew. Said she worked in a bar and didn't get home till all hours. Often times she'd sound out of it even at six in the evening. Jesus, did they never let up boozing over there in the Bronx?

The melodious ring tolling on and on: how different from the tuneless dissonance of its Irish equivalent. And on and on some more, a soundtrack to the impatience of the hawking, spitting, muttering bastard awaiting his own turn outside the box. At least she's sparing me the bloody answering machine. Talk about a real pain in the neck— mouthing into it like a bloody jackass, not knowing what I was saying or who might be monitoring my stuttered syllables of longing. Wanting to scream aloud that the heart was leaping out of my chest from the pure love of her, that I couldn't live another second without her two arms wrapped around me and her knee between my legs, but instead just running out of breath and limping to my usual flat-footed finale: "Well, I'll see you then, when I see you, I suppose . . . toodle doo." *Toodle doo,* how are you! I can just imagine her Yank admirers breaking their balls tittering over my Paddy-pathetic *toodle bloody doo!*

Then the ringing choked in mid-tone. I was so taken aback I barely remembered to press Button A. With a metallic clatter, the coins plunged into the pile of cash below.

"Mary?" I inquired into the staticky silence.

Not a peep out of her.

"Is that you, Mary?"

Then I heard it: the catching of a breath and its release, slow, sure, and shrouded with an infinitesimal hint of menace. With the phone crushed into my ear, I listened as if my life depended on it. Somewhere in the Bronx, someone listened back.

We clung to each other until whoever it was hung up. And then, the fidgety bollocks waiting outside rapped on the glass, but his words were swept away in the wind and the wildness of my own thoughts. Nothing left but to slam down the receiver, kick open the door, startling a clique of scavenging seagulls, storm off to the pub, and confront all the knowing, leering, creeping-Jesus, I-told-you-so looks with glass after glass of warm whiskey until I didn't give a flying fuck about Mary or the seven seasons of heartscald she was inflicting upon me. But down all that bitter Jameson's evening, the brooding Bronx silence I'd gone toe-to-toe with was never far from mind, and I had little need of a clear head to divine that all was not well with my love in America.

CHAPTER ONE

Pale faces, puffy eyes, tripping over ourselves living a lie, grief restrained under lock and key, the ache of goodbyes stashed aside, false smiles, deep sighs, Christmas won't be long acomin', then home again, hope again, until then again. Duck into the bog if you feel a breakdown gathering steam; no point in making a show of yourself; bad form when all is said and done. One sudden unsuspected outburst could break the bank and send even the hardest of chaws reeling off the deep end into unmitigated bawling. And what the hell does that profit anyone? You still have to get on that bloody plane, go back to Brooklyn, Dorchester, Philly, Chicago, Buffalo, Cleveland, and all the other south sides of the soul across the pond. Not a thing in this earthly world to be gained by losing your cool and causing a Paddy-outa-here meltdown.

Instead, take the hard man route: balls to the wall, belly up to the bar, we've been through a whole lot worse, and we'll get through this one too. Just straighten your back, suck in your gut, and hold on for better weather. In a week or so, this will all be history, and you'll be settled back into the old routine, nibbling away at the American dream; just got to make it through this God-awful morning that you've been dreading ever since you stepped off the plane from Kennedy.

So, c'mon now, lads, get them pints into you. More where that came from! A vodka and white for you, Bridie? Good girl yourself, and did you get the auld ride at all when you were home? Ah sure don't I know—I'm a terrible man! Couldn't bring me anywhere, could you? Still and all, you're looking top notch yourself, girl, with that Sligo suntan plastered all over you.

And so it goes, each one supporting the other lest they lose it and sink the whole bloody ship, people without a whit in common seven days of the week in the US of A, now bosom buddies in Shannon Airport lounge on the despairing eighth. For, it's no small task putting a good face on matters when the bottom is caving out of your already homesick stomach and your whole world is splintering apart at the seams.

I strolled into this maelstrom of repressed anguish, untutored in emigrant etiquette, my own twisted soul too anesthetized to even notice the stir I was causing. How could I know that the cardinal rule inside the departure lounge is, *don't stand out?* Fit in like crazy, look like everyone else, keep your head down and, for the love of Christ, button your lip and heart for fear you'll get the both of them smashed into smithereens.

Heads turned slyly to study this apparition from *Top of the Pops* descended to earth to mingle with mere mortals. Black jeans and jacket, sky blue shirt, combat boots, guitar slung over my shoulder, Clash LPs stuffed beneath my oxter, hair oiled back pre-army Elvis—a dark angel come to roost amongst the tweeds, twills, and gabardines of these Bronx and Southie cowboys.

Who the hell does he think he is? Yer man Geldof or the big

grinnin' Blackie from Thin Lizzy? A couple of days luggin'
buckets of wet cement will soften his cough.

Still, there was something comforting about this boozy
oasis with its polished wood, gleaming brass, and fag-burned
carpet. Reminded me of the hotel lounge back home where
my father had religiously tossed back his whiskey and sodas.
After the teary drag and drain of goodbye to my mother,
things were looking up, and a hair of some kind of the dog
would be far from out of order.

I found a spot at the bar and nodded to the bustling
white-shirted barman, a singular being who appeared to
possess the power of looking straight through his customers.
Coming to terms with the fact that reeling in a drink might
take more time than tact, I let my bloodshot eyes drift across
the sparkling bottles and wrestled with a desire to reach over
and pour one the hell down my sandpapered gullet. Instead,
when ignored one time too many, I inquired, "Any chance
of a drink round here?"

With an indifference that would do justice to a Parisian
maitre d', the shark-faced, beady-eyed guardian of the stick
strode by, nose in the air. He'd be damned if he'd even
entertain the notion of serving some young punk who wasn't
fit to wipe the boots of Big Tom or any other self-respecting
Country and Irish star.

Still, as luck would have it, a seat opened, and I parked
my weary rear end; I tossed the LPs on the counter, catching
the nonchalant eyes of Strummer staring back. What would
the Great White Punk do? But it was hard to picture the King
of the Clash in this particular situation.

In fact, it was hard to concentrate at all; my mind began
to drift through all kinds of scenarios until I was yanked

back into the vortex of my mother's goodbye. Should never have let her drive me to the airport in the first place, nor snarled at her to get back in the old Vauxhall, go home, and spare me her unrestrained misery. But there was no way I could have taken her into this vale of alcoholic heartbreak and have her dissolve in abstinent puddles all around me. Bad enough that her husband had wasted away less than three Christmases ago, now to lose her only son! Jesus Christ, give a man a bloody break.

"This is on the quare fellah with the cowboy hat down the corner."

I looked up as a pint of Guinness sailed under my nose. The barman already had his back turned, but the cowboy in the corner was giving me the most casual of once-overs. Though masked behind reflecting shades, there was something vaguely familiar about the cut of him—bedecked in a long-fringed suede jacket, a mass of greasy golden curls streaming down around his dandruffed shoulders. In a synchronized move that Jimmy Dean would have died for, he lowered the shades for an instant, lifted pint to lip and raised his eyebrows to the good God in heaven as if to ask why he, in all his coolness, had been landed amongst this crowd of woebegone arseholes who wouldn't know an Allman Brother from a Christian one.

The cowboy's shades shot back into place leaving me to struggle with the memory of a pair of watery green eyes, forever shifting even as they cast you as an extra in their ongoing movie. With some foreboding I raised my own pint in salute. The Guinness was sour and landed on my stomach like a bucket of horseradish tossed into a septic tank. Jesus, talk about an American wake the night before! How many pints had I downed, with matching shots to boot? I shuddered and held onto the counter for ballast. But the cowboy was beckoning me down to an empty stool in the corner. What choice was there with the price of a pint binding us? And so I staggered down the bar like a constipated juggler, balancing suitcase, LPs, guitar, and Guinness, while dodging the broad backs of what seemed like every emigrant navvy and nanny west of the wild majestic Shannon.

"Ah, sure you don't know anyone now, do you?" Despite the laconic smile, there was an accusatory tone to the cowboy's voice. "Hey, man, don't tell me you forgot the day your auld lad's bull broke out of the far field and mounted five of Moloney's heifers?"

I did indeed remember and who had left the gate open into the bargain.

"Nicky Hore?"

"The one and only. And do you recall the boot up the hole your father gave me when he sent me on me way without the three days' pay I had comin'?"

I remembered that too, and the money Moloney owed that was wiped off the slate on account of the rape of his Sabine heifers. The tale had spread like wildfire: cars, tractors, and motorcycles pulling up to ogle the young bull and marvel at his feat of passion.

How could I forget Nicky Hore from beyond the mountain, arseless and damn near shoeless, the snot flowing from his well-fingered red nose, nails the color of the bog he strode out of, a figure of hilarity to the teenaged sophisticates who congregated outside the chipper. I tried to reconcile him with this tall, confident cowboy sneering at me from behind Ray-Bans. How many years since the mountainy boy had badgered my father for a job until the old man had agreed, if only for a screed of peace. I recalled only too well his conniving ways; and how could I forget the envious glances cast at my own school blazer and patent leather shoes? But more than anything, I harked back to the young bull's exploits, one of many disasters that drove my father headlong into the hotel bar to hide behind whiskey and sodas until there was sweet damn all left of his health or the farm.

"I heard you skipped to London."

"Aye, what else was there to do and me without a seat in me trousers!"

I caught the veiled accusation and remembered why they called the snotty kid Arsehole. But the memory of my father's failure summoned its own store of bitterness: the whispers of pity on the Main Street at his approach, the giggles and taunts after he'd passed.

"But I didn't stay long." Arsehole lowered his voice conspiratorially and looked over his shoulder.

The bile was gnawing at me. I would have liked nothing better than to stride away from this memory. But the very thought of moving my gear back down the bar was exhausting, and so I sighed, "Why is that?"

"Sshh." Arsehole raised an index finger to his eye and whispered, "Connections, man."

"What, eh . . . kind of connections would you be talkin' about?"

Arsehole frowned at this lack of discretion. He pointed his finger towards the far window; all, it seemed, would be revealed there. I, however, could identify nothing more illuminating than a car park.

"Up North, you eejit! The Rah, man, the IRA! Do you want me to shout it to the four corners of the room?"

I could easily have taken Hore for a drug dealer or a pornographer, but an associate of the hard men up North?

"Now drink your pint, man, and let the matter rest," Arsehole cast a withering glance around the bar, "until we're on safer ground." Whereupon he took a massive gulp, belched loudly, and set the glass out for a refill.

I took a fair old swig of my own pint, noting that the sourness was less pronounced. The Guinness had even achieved a certain agreeable neutrality of taste, while its soothing darkness seemed to be banking, if not damping, the fires that roared down in the netherlands of my stomach.

"Two more please," I advised the passing barman.

"Put that money back where it came from and don't take it out again in my company," Arsehole barked and intimated to the somewhat impressed barman that he should pull two of the finest pints that he was capable of. Then, with concentration that would have done justice to John Wayne on a Saturday night in Laredo, he set to rolling a cigarette from a pouch of suspicious smelling tobacco. When our two pints were near drained, without looking next nor near me, he confided, "I was stood down by the Army Council in Belfast and sent to the States on matters of a confidential nature."

I too now stared straight ahead but nodded knowingly, as if such a thing happened by the hour in my own neck of the woods.

With the smoke drifting from his nostrils, Hore added, "They needed a sleeper."

I held my counsel and nodded sagely.

"My time will come." Hore drained his pint.

I continued to look into the near distance, no great chore since the Guinness was now kicking in big time. In fact, its dark magic seemed to be working wonders all over the bar. Voices, once slack, were now animated and knocking spots off any remaining formality. The general hum was increasing, and what only minutes previously had been a disparate bunch of craw-sick emigrants was now a lively soirée of hard men with dancing eyes and seasoned women accustomed to their lies, collectively throwing the devil to the wind. Players and Marlboro were being passed and lit, fumes and plumes of comforting smoke rising to the rafters, rounds called like they were going out of style, and memories of loved ones banished, not to be rerun until some desperate night on an unmade bed in Brooklyn or the Bronx, with only the rattle of the D train for company.

In or around the third pint, I began to feel at one with the company. All brothers and sisters now, we'd be out of there within the hour, off to seek fame and fortune in far Amerikay, and to hell with the stragglers left behind in their lace-curtained contentedness. These were my people—the conquistadors, the adventurers, the cream of the crop off to seek a new life. The rest could rot behind and keep the home fires burning. Let the Rah blow up the whole bloody place, run the Brits out of Belfast, and chase them back to Birmingham or Bolton or wherever they came from in the first place. My tribe had more pressing things on their minds, and as soon as that big 747 lifted off the runway, we'd be history on this rainy little island. And so we laughed and joked with abandon, and many the slap on the back for the lads and big blustery hugs for their sisters. A freckled-faced giant, his Guinness-stained shirt wide open, toasted the whole congregation and roared, "Last one out of the country turn out the feckin' lights. *Slán leat,* Charlie Haughey!" Everyone raised their glasses and roared their approval, and the craic revved up way beyond ninety.

Arsehole smoked his own rolled cigarettes with great deliberation and took little interest in the surrounding hullabaloo. Then, from out of the blue, he reiterated, "They needed someone they could trust for a mission of the greatest importance."

I wished to Christ I still smoked. The heroes in the old movies always lit up at critical moments and took meditative drags before delivering monosyllabic non sequiturs. Lacking that option, I counted to five and curtly noted, "I see."

Still and all, much as I tried, I couldn't restrain my curiosity. "But what exactly do you do?"

"Do?"

"Yeah, like how do you make a livin'?"

"Oh, I'm well looked after, man, have no fear on that score." Arsehole nodded with some gusto. "But just so no one would be gossipin' about me, I do a bit of personnel management . . . consultancy, like."

"In the Bronx?"

"What makes you say that?" He rounded on me suspiciously.

"Seems like everyone is heading there."

"Where else would they be goin'? Boston? Chicago?" He sneered, then sighed as though the mere mention of such backwaters was a drain on his spirit. "Isn't Bainbridge the dead center of the known universe for every Paddy with half a hole on him?"

He thereupon hailed the passing barman and ordered a couple of large Jameson's to be accompanied by two more pints.

As I dutifully reached for my wallet, Arsehole dug his fingers into my arm. "Did I not tell you to keep your money in your pocket?" He looked at his watch, at first casually, and then with the barest hint of concern. When he drained the whiskey, he shuddered and his upper lip twitched. He took a reassuring sip from his pint, wiped the froth from his lips, then stuck out his hand. When we shook, his mouth softened into a smile. Something of obvious import had passed between us, although for the life of me I couldn't tell what. Then he turned back to the bar, apparently satisfied that I was a man who could be trusted with matters great, if not small.

Over by the window, at a table full to collapsing with glasses, people were calling for quiet. They made little dint in the proceedings until a wiry man with a bulbous nose and a head of flaming red hair stood up and yelled out a command that all had heeded in school: "*Ciúnas, a chairde Ghaeil.*"

A young countrywoman rose hesitantly as the room hushed. Her coarse black hair was swept back off her forehead and held somewhat in place by a mother-of-pearl headband. Though in her early twenties, she dressed in the manner of a convent girl: pleated gray skirt, white blouse, and a dun cardigan. Her eyes were of the deepest cobalt blue and sparkled like the water off the islands on the sunniest of days.

As if she were a statue of the Virgin, the red-haired man reverently lifted her from the ground and placed her on the banquette. Her family and friends waited in a deep silence that spread like eiderdown over the room. She closed her eyes and halted a long moment, then began to sing, at first quietly but with increasing confidence as the song came into its own. Her voice was too rich for one so young. It caressed the words like the gentle wind that eases down from the mountains on its lazy way to the sea. It would curl around a particular phrase, wrapping it in tendrils of vibrato, then cast it aside and dance over the syllables of another, sometimes skipping beyond line or tempo, but always laying bare a meaning that I had never before gleaned from the old song.

You may travel far, far from your own native home,
Far away o'er the mountains, far away o'er the foam,
But of all the fine places that I've ever seen
There's none to compare with the Cliffs of Dooneen.

Take a view o'er the mountains, fine sights you'll see there.
You'll see the high rocky hills on the west coast of Clare.
The towns of Kilkee and Kilrush can be seen
From the high rocky slopes round the Cliffs of Dooneen.

That mountain wind now sifted through the room, bringing with it a truth too naked to be denied. The veneer of hardness and devil-may-care flippancy that had enveloped the emigrants began to crack, and a gray tide of sadness swept in. The girl's face, though ruddy by nature, waxed luminous and I, for one, saw the cliffs as if in a mirror. I witnessed other things too that I had tried to banish: my mother, well clear of Limerick traffic, heading home to a house full of ghosts. I even saw Mary peering out from the girl's cobalt eyes, and I remembered exactly why I was going away and how it was immeasurably too late to turn back.

People were humming along with the song, and the sound brought to mind a summer's day I had spent in the bog up

near the mountain. Off in the distance I had heard the
rumble of thunder and, on a high harmony, the drone of a
hive of bees. At first, the combination had been comforting
but, as the storm gathered, it grew ominous; I had felt odd
and ill at ease, and now it struck me that I had been listening
to the echo of my innocence departing. For, the week before,
I had noticed Mary outside the chipper.

Even on first glance, there was something particular about
her. The paleness of her face was accentuated by the delicacy
with which she applied her make-up. Unlike the townie girls,
she didn't slather it on like tar on a pebbled road. There was
thought behind every stroke. In fact, there was a quiet
deliberation to all her actions.

On that first day I couldn't tell if her eyes were green or
gray, but her pre-rinsed hair was no mystery; dark brown
and streaked with chestnut, it cascaded over the black leather
jacket, straying well below her shoulders. She wore her skirt
just above the knees, but not at an impractical height for a
girl who lived out on the mountain and had to cycle in more
days than not, while the seamed black nylons, though
fashionably ripped, clung to her well shaped legs and slid down
into gleaming Doc Marten boots. Everything was so well
thought out, or so it appeared.

She had noticed me studying her and held my stare until
I looked away. Small though the town was, I couldn't
remember seeing her before. Had she done a stint in London
or Dublin and come back remade and ready to lord it over
the locals: a queen bee to the drones outside the chipper? Yet,
she seemed oddly displaced, never quite fitting in, though
accepted by everyone in the way that those with a hint of
beauty always are.

But then when I finally risked a timid hello, it was as if I'd always known her. She could finish any of my sentences but was often content to listen, with that vaguely mocking smile but all-understanding eyes that invited the deepest of confidences. Within weeks, I had changed my hairstyle, clothes, attitude, ambitions, the very way I perceived myself.

Consumed by grief at the passing of her husband, my mother didn't notice until it was way too late. My marks at school hit rock bottom as my obsession with the strange girl from out the mountain deepened. Swept away were the widow's hopes of a settled life in law or accountancy, to be replaced by a mania for music and coolness. And right before her eyes I metamorphosed into a punky anti-Christ wrestling with the demons of first love.

I drained my pint and Mary faded back behind the singer's opalescent eyes. The girl had taken a long deep breath, the only one to do so in the room. She cast her head to one side, and the errant strands of hair slid off her face. Her skin glowed beneath the harsh glare of the lounge lights, and I saw that what I'd taken for innocence was really a mask for an odd intensity. She placed the fingers of one hand to her ear for tuning, closed her eyes again, and sang the verse that we all dreaded:

> *Fare thee well to Dooneen, fare thee well for a while,*
> *And to all the fine people I'm leaving behind,*
> *To the streams and the meadows where late I have been*
> *And the high rocky slopes of the Cliffs of Dooneen . . .*

The mood darkened. The song had exposed, then cut deep into the raw nerve of emigration. The ache of separation flitted across faces, etching them with webs of worry. The warm glow of the drink chilled to the gnawing anxiety of cumulative hangovers; the naked ceiling lights now beamed far too brightly.

Still we listened spellbound while the song circled back inexorably to its final haunted beginning.

You may travel far, far from your own native home,
Far away o'er the mountains, far away o'er the foam,
But of all the fine places that I've ever seen
There's none to compare with the Cliffs of Dooneen.

The girl held the last long note in a breathy vibrato. It drifted off into the waves that beat against the cliffs in foam and spray, before heading once more back out across the Atlantic to be washed up on the uncaring shores of Jersey, Cape Cod, or Long Island. Her voice faded away into a long silence.

The room erupted in applause, friend turned to stranger and complimented the girl, and wasn't that the finest version of the song they'd ever heard? Some compared it with past performances of Christy's in Brooklyn or Brookline or even Doolin itself, and the talk turned to other songs and other nights, but something had fled and could not be recaptured. And so we turned to our drinks, ordered last rounds, and grimaced when the whiskey clawed at the dull edge of despair.

But where was Arsehole? I hadn't noticed the cowboy slip by. Still I couldn't fail but catch the tinny inevitability of the official warning: "Last boarding call for Flight 113 to New York."

The Bronx contingent drained their glasses, while those heading to Boston sighed, stretched their legs luxuriously, and bid relieved farewells. Still time for one last pint, or even two if they got a move on.

I slid down from my stool and negotiated the floor. The barman smiled and handed me a minutely notated bill.

I winked back at him. "Arsehole's lookin' after that."

"Who?" The bartender squinted back.

"Your man with the cowboy hat that was here just a minute ago."

"This is your tab, young lad. The two of yez have been here drinkin' all mornin'."

"No problem. He'll be back in a minute."

"Well, then we'll wait for him, won't we?" He leaned across the counter, daring me, pleading with me, to do something stupid like run for the plane.

The last of the New York travelers snaked by, eyes averted. The Boston crowd was quieter too, but I could feel them all homing in on this conflagration in the making.

One of them, a tall Connemara man, swaggered up to the bar and threw an empathetic arm over my shoulder, "What's the matter then?"

"These two boyos think they can drink all day and then pull the old 'me friend is settlin' the bill' trick."

The Connemara man nodded his appreciation of the seriousness of the matter. "Ah now, it's probably all a misunderstanding. Sure, aren't you travelin' on the same plane with your mate?"

"I think so," I replied, "but I haven't laid eyes on him this six years."

"Oh yeah?" The barman sneered. "Yez looked very comfortable together."

The Connemara man leaned way across the counter and

draped his other arm over the barman's affronted shoulders. Then he turned back to me, "You know the best solution to this whole thingmejig?"

I hadn't a bull's notion.

"Just pay up now and settle with your mate on the flight. And everyone will live happily ever after."

"But look at the size of the bill." It was approaching three figures. There'd be sweet damn all shillings left by the time I got to the Bronx.

"That's not my problem," the barman growled. "Weren't the two of yez callin' rounds like there was no tomorrow?"

Oh Jesus, the sheer disgrace of crawling home without even having made it out of Shannon! How could I even dream of facing all the *I told you so's* down at the pub?

Then the door of the lounge slammed behind one last drunken straggler, and the glass-partitioned corridor that had earlier been throbbing with travelers was empty. There was nothing for it. I dug deep into my pocket and threw a sufficiency of banknotes on the counter.

"Good man yourself!" the Connemara man slapped me on the back.

The barman counted out the notes and pocketed the little that was left over. Wiping the slops from the counter as I bolted for the door—guitar, suitcase and albums all a jumble—he shouted after me, "You'll dance to a different bloody tune over on Bainbridge."

chapter two

Whatever about tunes, I was hotfooting it to a host of different drummers. In manic succession, Horslips, Zeppelin and The Kilfenora Ceili Band tumbled out of a battered jukebox and ricocheted around sheet-rocked walls before pulverizing my last few functioning brain cells.

At least, I was still standing. A far cry from Arsehole slumped over the bar, mouth wide open for the entrapment of flies, poseur's hat on a level with pint glasses, blond tresses splayed out like Venus Half Shell-shocked.

Not that I could even see the bastard, for the bar was three deep with Paddies positively pulsing with desire for instant ossification. Most of the male clientele had not seen home since dawn and still wore the dust and sweat of construction like a badge of honor. The ladies, however, had hastened to their apartments from a hard day's nannying; now freshly showered, shaved, and anointed with sundry unguents, they were decked out to kill in their employers' last year's fashions. Alas, much of this beautification was wasted on the lads who were so tanked they couldn't tell a Ford model from a Ford Cortina. Still, romance lurked in the air, though it was running a distant third behind stale sweat and tobacco fumes. Trays loaded with drink were off-handedly dispatched to gossiping groups of comely maidens, while a playful slap on the posterior was not deemed politically incorrect provided it was delivered by the calloused hand of a halfway decent suitor.

All in all, there seemed to be a Byzantine etiquette afoot that I could not quite put my finger on. Then again, it was hard to zero in on the mechanics of this meat market since the whole frenetic scene was barely illuminated by a horde of plastic shamrocks flashing in and out of time to the ever-changing jukebox beat. The remains of last year's Christmas lights added a lonely cheer as they blinked their nostalgic way over posters of Farah Fawcett, Glasgow Celtic, John XXIII, Big Tom, and The Boomtown Rats.

Were all pubs in New York as dark and dizzying? So unlike home, where one automatically knew one's place. What were they hiding? Hardly the charm of the bartender; scarcely five feet four, with white shirtsleeves rolled up to his bulging muscles, he gazed out scornfully on this roiling scene as though appraising a herd of badly castrated bullocks.

Even the beer was different. Ice cold and with less body than an anorexic flea, it struck you on the forehead like a cat-o-nine tails before dive-bombing into a frigid pool somewhere down around the base of your skull. It appeared to have little such effect on the other communicants, who imbibed it with such gusto it was a wonder they didn't get down on all fours and lick the spillings off the floor.

Then the needle of the jukebox caught in a groove, throwing Bob Marley into an unplanned dub of, "We're jammin', we're jammin', we're jammin' . . ."

The room throbbed with this ganja incantation until the barman roared out above the tumult, "Kick that fucker for me, will you, Paddy!"

Paddy, animatedly discussing Derry's chances of making the Ulster final, hoofed backwards with all the viciousness of a mare put upon by some scrawny stand-in stallion. Mister Marley abdicated with a screech to be succeeded by "Dancing Queen." This ditty caused mild pandemonium amongst the fairer sex, and a stray elbow nearly sent me sprawling when four Leitrim ladies hit the boards and proceeded to displace more cubic feet than even their formidable tonnage warranted.

Wiping the splattered beer from my leather jacket I marveled at the sight. The same ferocious foursome would languish in the corner of any self-respecting pub back home before making a show of themselves in such a fashion. But out here in the wild Northwest of the Bronx, it was apparently every woman for herself—beauty, poise or breeding being no drawback when it came to flaunting what you got.

Throwing his figurative hat into the ring, a carpenter— his belt weighed down by hammer, nails, and chisels—let forth a whoop of unbridled optimism and barreled into them; whereupon, one of the lovelies, without even a flicker of an eyebrow, slammed her shoulder into his chest, hunching him to hell and high water off the floor.

"You are a dancing queen!" the no-nonsense lovely echoed Benny and Björn, thrusting her fist skywards as though she had just netted a near-impossible goal for Manchester United.

"Good girl yourself, Bridie!" another of the foursome bellowed in sisterly solidarity.

The man of wood accepted this setback as part of some fair, if painful, mating ritual and staggered back to the bar for liquid fortification and a reappraisal of tactics.

I'd never felt so weary. Lapsing in and out of jet-lagged consciousness, I sagged onto the edge of a rickety table, around which two cement-caked laborers were arguing vehemently over a dozing diva of indeterminate age. They put little pass on me; then again they might not have noticed King Kong either. The dispute dragged on like Donegal drizzle until the lady started into outraged wakefulness and swept glasses and bottles from the table.

"I'll be fucked if I ever wipe another rich baby's arse!" She exclaimed.

No one gave a goddamn, her admirers least of all; nor did anyone stoop to pick up the shattered glass that crunched beneath the feet of every passer-by.

Then again, the whole country seemed to be built on a grid of argument and acrimony. It had been one bloody thing after another since the Aer Lingus jet bumped down at Kennedy Airport: delay, hassle, disagreement, compromise, and then have-at-it all over again.

After racing the length of Shannon and pleading for mercy from emigration, customs, and every class of airport bureaucrat, there was no sight of Hore on the plane. But I had been too embarrassed to mount more than a token search for the once arseless con artist.

"Holdin' up the show, boy. We'll be stuck in fuckin' Queens' traffic till the cows come home," one irate Cork man hissed as a matronly stewardess frog-marched me down the hostile aisle of the 747. It wasn't until I had claimed my suitcase at Kennedy that I'd noticed the Stetson bobbing off towards customs. Roaring like a lunatic at the rapidly retreating cowboy didn't do a whole lot of good either—merely gained me the attention of the security guards, and it was some time before I finally ran Arsehole to ground outside the terminal and lit into him.

Not that it bothered him much, for he merely inquired, "Where are you from, man?"

"What the hell do you mean, where am I from?"

"Obviously somewhere unacquainted with the great 'double-charge' racket, that's for sure certain," Arsehole sneered, nonchalantly rolling a cigarette in the palm of one hand while holding pouch and paper with the other. "Sure, isn't that knacker of a barman known the length and breadth of Ireland for pullin' the wool over decent Paddies drownin' their sorrows at Shannon Airport. There's not a man jack in the Bronx that hasn't been taken to the cleaners by that culchie Judas."

Thereupon, he lit his fag and took a long satisfying drag before sliding his arm around my still heaving shoulders. "Not to worry, man, there's a bed for you in the Bronx. Me minders will be picking me up here any minute."

Three rolled fags later, however, and now dripping from the heat and humidity, the cowboy called down the vilest of retribution on a "shower of no-good Irish Republican bastards" who would surely rue the day they left a sleeper of his caliber lounging around like a bloody tourist.

"We'll have to take a fuckin' cab, there's no two ways about it."

"How much will that cost?"

"It's but a hop, skip, and a jump."

"I said, how much will it cost?"

"Fifteen, twenty bucks at the most. But that's neither here nor there—this one's on me."

"Yeah, I remember the last time I heard that."

But the cowboy was already out in the midst of the lurching traffic, ignoring both me and a host of yellow taxis; he eventually waved a ramshackle green jalopy towards the curb. The gypsy cab shuddered to a halt, and a Rastafarian poked his head out through the passenger window. From somewhere in the midst of congealed dreads, a voice inquired in a patois so thick it made Peter Tosh sound like Henry Higgins, "Whey you goin', mon?"

"Bainbridge Avenue, the top of the Bronx, and no detours to see the fuckin' Statue of Liberty," Arsehole snarled.

The Jamaican took this caveat in stride. Flashing a set of gleaming white teeth, he cheerfully advised, "Get in, my brothers."

Arsehole tossed his bags into the back seat and, in his best Trenchtown imitation, replied, "Turn up that Marley, mon, and lively up yourself!"

Then slapping fives with his newly acquired sibling, he sank luxuriously into the passenger seat, imperially motioning that I should claim a spot amongst the luggage in the back. Whereupon, he closed his eyes and sighed, "Me belly full but me hungry."

With silky reggae throbbing, the cab blasted down the Van Wyck in the gathering darkness and near levitated over the Triboro Bridge into the bowels of the South Bronx, a huge spliff and forty ounces of malt beer passing like the Eucharist between us.

"This is the life, boy. You've no idea what's ahead of you," Arsehole exuded as we sped past acres of darkened warehouses interspersed with a moonscape of skeletal buildings and brick-strewn vacant lots. "Home of the brave, land of the fuckin' free."

I gazed on in silence, unable to put either sense or meaning to the dusky urban vista. So, this was America. It didn't look much like it. It certainly didn't feel the part. The hot air rushing through the four opened windows felt so wet and heavy you could damn near swim in it. I took to studying the faces in the careening vehicles we zig-zagged past; all ignored me save for a truck-driver who intimated that I go fuck myself.

The Rastaman's tresses and Arsehole's golden locks bopped in time to Mister Marley's magical groove even as my legs grew heavy, and my galloping brain gradually decelerated to the stately ganja tempo; so much so that when I closed my eyes, everything in my universe slid into soft synch with Family Man's pulsing bass.

Then out of nowhere the cab careened across two lanes and, to a screech of brakes and Arsehole's whoop of recognition, we veered off the highway. The terrain now took a turn for the better. We sped by rows of houses with small, neatly kept gardens, though each ground floor window was barred. Then with one last pedal to the metal, we blazed through a red light, across a tree-lined parkway, and up a hilly enclave with large apartment buildings drooping over the narrow streets. We rounded one last bend onto a well-lit avenue with many an Irish name blinking above a multitude of bars.

The cab skidded to a halt outside Murphy's Tavern, a dubious looking dive in sore need of a coat of paint. While I wrestled with our belongings, Arsehole disappeared.

"That be fifty dollahs, mon." The Rasta smiled.

"What do you mean, fifty dollars?"

His smile had barely frozen before it was replaced by an angry glare; my erstwhile Rasta brother reached beneath the front seat and produced a meat cleaver, ending all attempt at meaningful debate.

"Fuck you!" One of the laborers kicked out at the table, sending the remaining pints crashing to the floor.

"No, fuck you, boy! Take the stupid cow and be damned with it," his colleague replied.

"I want sweet fuck all to do with her fat arse, d'yeh hear me?"

"Then what the fuck are you goin' on about?"

I edged back towards the shelter of the jukebox just before the pint-sized barman leaped over the counter brandishing a hurling stick.

"I wouldn't ride either of yez for the exercise." The bleary-eyed nanny swept a half-filled pint glass from her lap.

Neither of her suitors appeared to be unduly dismayed by this rejection. Rather, they shoved each other and threw feathery punches, faces reddening from the effort. The barman snorted at such timidity and poked each of them in the ribs with the hurley. "Ah, for fuck's sake, lads, will yez give it a break," he pleaded; "every night, the same shaggin' argument! D'yeh know what the two of youse are like?"

When neither of them ventured an opinion, he shook his head in sorrow. "Two fuckin' stuck jukeboxes!"

"Ah will you shut your gob, you little dwarf," the nanny interjected. "I wouldn't let Saint Anthony on top of me if he drank in this knackers' whorehouse!"

"Listen, you," the barman cautioned in slit-eyed contempt, "keep a fuckin' civil tongue in your head, before I split you into two big slabs of pig shit."

With that threat off his chest, he spun on his heel to re-evaluate the two rivals who, though still glowering at

each other, had arrived at some form of détente. They did
not shake hands, as he proposed, but merely nodded sourly,
as if to suggest that they'd continue with this matter at a
more opportune time.

"All's settled then? C'mon now, lads, I'll buy yez one
meself." The urbane peacemaker slid his rippling muscles
around the two rivals' waists and drew them over to the bar.

"What about me, you little bollocks?" the nanny queried.

The barman swept around, his eyes blazing with the fury
of one who has suffered much and been finally provoked
beyond the bounds of human endurance. He brought the
hurley down on a Formica tabletop that buckled under the
blow. "That's it," he bellowed. "I've had it up to my fucking
tonsils with you and all your auld guff."

He cast the hurley to the four winds and, in one deft move,
grabbed his tormentor around the waist. He swung her like
a top, so that her back was to him, then hoisted her into the
air. "You're out of here! Jimmy, open up that fucking door,
good man yourself."

But the lady would not go easily into that dark night. She
grabbed a fistful of the bartender's hair in one hand and,
with the other, punched back over her shoulder. With her
dress well over her buttocks revealing an oversized pair of off-
white drawers, she kicked backwards with full intent of
gelding her oppressor.

"Let go of me hair, you fuckin' whore's melt!" the barman
keened, before digging his teeth into her shoulder. She reacted
with a cry akin to that of a stuck pig.

As they lurched towards the door, he raised his head.
"For the love of Jaysus, Jimmy, open the fuckin' thing wide
before she has the last hair pulled out of me head!"

But when Jimmy hastened to the door, he accidentally knocked his high-backed stool in the path of the approaching antagonists. There was a tremendous crash and much blasphemy as nanny, barman and stool intertwined and then collapsed to the floor. The patrons leaped for cover, unsure who would arise first from this tangle of metal and thrashing humanity.

"You fuckin' poxy cunt, there was no call for that!" The barman was first afoot, albeit clutching his crotch.

"Fuck you, and your deformed little mickey!" the lady countered in a tone intimating that there may have been more to their relationship than met the eye.

For an awful moment, the barman held his peace; then, with great deliberation, he rolled up his sleeves to reveal twin shimmering tattoos of a wonderfully endowed naked woman cavorting astride his bulging muscles. He spat into the palms of both hands and rubbed them together, his eyes glinting savagely beneath the winking Christmas lights.

"Keep that fuckin' door open, Jimmy!"

The lady, however, had extricated herself from the legs of the stool and was now crawling back towards the jukebox repeating the insult like a mantra.

"Where do you think you're goin,' you fuckin' mangy bollocks?" he demanded, while delivering a full-blooded kick to her formidable posterior.

She had just about gained the jukebox from which Bob Marley was cajoling his woman to "no cry," when the barman bent down and grabbed her by the head of hair and dragged her towards the door. The nanny clung to the leg of the broken Formica table and dragged it behind her.

"Let go of that good table, you scabby fucker!"

"Go on back to Roscommon with your little mickey!" the lady countered.

Stung by this insolence, he grabbed her under the arse and, with one last Herculean effort, hoisted her up onto his shoulders. "Jaysus Christ," he gasped, momentarily taken aback by the tonnage.

Spinning upside down above the concrete floor, the nanny let forth a howl of terror. But, with the door open, the little man was literally in sight of victory. With a mighty grunt he staggered out into the street and flung his screaming load into a heap of overflowing garbage cans.

"And don't even fuckin' dream of comin' back!" He wiped his hands on the seat of his trousers. The lady finally appeared to have given up on the prospect of a buy-back. Her dress up over her waist, she laid prone in the garbage bemoaning little mickeys, the county of Roscommon, and sundry other trials of life. Jimmy, a man for detail, offered her purse and loose change to the victor.

"And don't come lookin' for this piece of knacker thrash tomorrow." The barman flung the bag at her and pocketed the change. "Did yez see that?" He turned to the crowd framing the doorway. "She left with the little she came in with."

All legal niceties attended to, the respectful audience parted before him and Jimmy once more held the door open.

"Good man." The barman nodded his appreciation. But the words were barely out of his mouth when he stopped dead and gripped his head. With the adrenalin spent, the tears swelled in his eyes from the smoldering pain, and he turned one last time to the street.

"You're one fuckin' cruel bitch," he whimpered; but upon hearing murmurs from the crowd, he gathered himself and, to a man, stared them down. "Don't be believin' a word she said, do you hear me?" He didn't articulate it, but the threat of missing buy-backs was implied. Then, looking neither left nor right, he strode into the bar.

Jimmy hopped ahead and presented him with the hurley. He took it with a grave nod and strolled on like Wexford's Tony Doran after laying low the mighty Kilkenny back line— battered and bruised, every nerve end tingling, but with the ball lying safely in the back of the net.

I returned to my safe haven behind the blaring jukebox, unsure how events would unfold. But once the door slammed behind the last gawker, things returned to their unruly normal. Despite a few muttered oaths, the barman regained his scornful equanimity. Then Marley's woman cried one last time, making way for the sparest of bass lines followed by a peroxide voice walking on the moon.

It had been one of our songs, and it hurled me back across the Atlantic to the autumn night I had bummed us a lift back to her father's house on the mountain. Mary was more anxious than usual: scared of being late but dragging her feet at the prospect of going home. Things had "come to a head," she said but refused to elaborate. It was useless arguing. Besides, by then I had grown accustomed to her furtiveness, especially in relation to her family. I couldn't bear to just drop her off and leave, so we stood at the bottom of the dark boreen watching the tail-lights of the Hiace van pull off down the winding road.

"Run after it." She looked fragile under the brooding mass of the mountain, but I knew the darkness wasn't the problem; rather, it was the dim light oozing from the kitchen window.

"He'll have heard the van," she shuddered.

I opened my leather jacket and pulled her to the warmth of my chest, but there was something other than the mountainy wind ailing her. It struck me how little I knew about this girl who had come to mean the world to me. It was rumored around the chipper that she had gone to live with an aunt in England after her mother died, but returned after a couple of years when "things went sour." She rarely mentioned her stay in London or, for that matter, her father, who was solitary and disliked by any who knew him. No small wonder for he resembled the mountain itself: craggy, treacherous, and unforgiving. He barely acknowledged me on our few meetings, keeping his eyes glued to the ground before shambling off to the unkempt barns and rusty sheds that tumbled around the farmyard. But there was always the feeling that he was watching and waiting for the stranger to leave so that he might once more reassert himself.

I could taste her tears, and whispered that everything was going to be all right. We both knew it was a lie, so I held her for a long time—so long I almost forgot where I was. Then she kissed me in a way she never had before.

"I'll always remember this, Sean." She stepped out from my jacket and headed up the lane, picking her way carefully around familiar rain-filled potholes and ridges of gravel.

"Will you be all right?"

She didn't reply, nor did she look back.

I watched her slim figure fade into the darkness. Soon after, I heard the kitchen door open. The yellow light went out, and the house seeped back into the gloom of the mountain. Then an upstairs light was switched on and cast shadows across the small farmyard. A curtain was yanked over, and then only a dull glow held back the surrounding bleakness.

Seven miles to go, but I felt exhilarated strolling along under a racing moon. She had revealed another small part of herself. My patience had been rewarded, and soon there'd be no shadows between us. A mile or so from her house, I began to hum and then sing loudly about walking home from her place, walking on the moon. A jennet bolted across a field in a panic at my voice. I didn't care. I had my Mary, and that was all that counted.

Now Sting's words came back to haunt me. I strode over to Arsehole and yanked his cowboy head from the counter.

"Hore, wake up, will you. I need directions."

Not a peep out of him, no matter how much I shouted.

"There'll be no wakin' that fellah. Where is it you want to go?"

I fished in my pocket for the piece of crumpled paper.

"2702 Decatur Avenue." The barman read aloud as though it were the far side of Jupiter. "What, in the name of Christ, do you want to go down there for?"

"What's the matter with down there?"

"It's thick with spics and niggers. That's what's the matter."

The slurs were employed so casually I wasn't sure how to react. I thought of saying, "Fuck you, you Roscommon racist." Instead, I stammered, "Oh yeah, then how come me girlfriend lives there?"

"She's either got more balls than a pool table or she's black as the ace of spades."

"Actually, she's Irish."

"Actually, she's stupid. What's her name?"

"Mary Devine."

A couple of listening Paddies looked up.

The bartender fished some wet dollar bills from the counter and wrung them out before sticking them in his tip jar. He dropped his voice when he leaned towards me. "Do they know you're comin'?"

"I rang them earlier but there was a message saying they'd been disconnected."

"So I heard." The bartender rubbed his chin thoughtfully "You know, it's not the best of form over here to show up unannounced."

"I sent her a letter."

"And she wrote back?"

"No, but . . ."

"It's gettin' late. You'd be as well off stayin' here for the night."

"She'll be expecting me."

The barman noted the finality in my voice and took a bottle of Bushmills from the top shelf. He filled two small tumblers, pushed one forward, and raised the other.

"Give me that piece of paper." Grimacing from the shot, he drew a rough map, with much emphasis on streets to beware. "Leave your suitcase and the guitar here—the records too. Don't worry." He waved his arm at his clientele. "They wouldn't know The Clash from The Singin' Nun."

He shoved the case under the bar and the records behind the cash register. "You'd be a sittin' duck out there with all that shite hangin' out of you."

I drained the remainder of my shot but held on to my guitar.

He raised his eyebrows at my stupidity. "Don't stop for nothin,' you hear me! Act like you know where you're goin'—even when you don't. If you get lost, come back here. You can kip down the cellar."

"Thanks."

"No problem, Sean."

"How did you know my name?"

But he had already turned back to the cash register. Jimmy held the door open and nodded goodbye.

CHAPTER THREE

Then I'm out the door and I'm on my way
Welcome to the good old US of A
Down a pot-holed street that was a virgin one day
Before it got knocked up and renamed urban decay
The smell overwhelming
Piss and poverty out of control
Sirens screaming
Junkies dreaming
Hookers preening
Pimps screening
Kids old as Methusaleh
Checking you
Messing with you
Cursing you
Blessing you
"Hey, mire, what the white boy want
What he lookin' for
He whorin' or he scorin'?
Yoh, my man, over here
I got what you want
Got what you lookin' for."
The Bronx in all its elegance
Paranoia palpable

Don't look left, watch out on the right
Keep your head down
And whatever you do, keep moving.
But I could handle it
I could handle anything now
With that shot of Bushmills coursing through my veins
I was the man
I was walkin' with God.

All well and good with your mind afire from good old top-shelf Presbyterian whiskey, but would I remember a word of this rant in the morning? Would I even be alive in the bloody morning? If I could have just jotted the bones of it down in my notebook or even better hummed it into a tape recorder, I'd have had the makings of something that'd knock Bowie on his skinny arse. Fat chance of that when my pulse was throbbing like a Fender Precision, my feet hitting the pavement at one twenty a minute, too petrified to slow down and catch a breath for fear of keeling over.

I hadn't a bloody clue where I was; which was beyond mind blowing, because you could drop me off in the back-of-any-beyond in Ireland and I'd find something to hang my hat on: oak tree, mucky river, farmer's yard. But there was neither rhyme nor reason to that jangling jungle of broken glass, shattered buildings, and white-light take-outs; the whole damned place smoldering to high heavens in fumes of stale piss and jittery decay.

And what people! Lean and hungry, they shuffled, strolled, and staggered but, more often than not, lounged around waiting for life in all its possibilities to come ambling by. Some blocks pulsed with their presence, others trembled from their shadows—forever watching, sizing me up, sussing me out. I was the night's main attraction, and I might as well have been decked out in neon and mounted on a float, I was etched so clearly in all my innocence. And so they swallowed me whole through eyes like sieves, sucking me deeper into their sweltering miasma, closing in like night behind me, taking inventory of my guitar, clothes, sex, stroll, but most of all, the glaring paleness of my skin.

The drums never stopped: congas, kicks, timbales beating, pounding, chattering. If I wasn't so terrified I'd have been ecstatic, for I'd heard staticky whispers of this rhythmicity oozing from late night transistor radios. But it was a whole different kettle of fish when you're lost and lonely and within kissing distance of the wraiths creating this voodoo-chili soundtrack.

Had to pull myself together. What had the barman said? Always look like you know where you're going even when you haven't got a bull's notion. Easy enough for him, surrounded by a pub full of big country chaps with fists the size of shovels. Still, nothing for it! I threw my head back like the crazy taxi man in the pictures. "You lookin' at me? I said, are you fucking lookin' at me?"

"Oh Jesus Christ, I didn't mean nothing, Mister, honest to God. I was just whisperin' under my breath. Look as much as you like, sir, there's absolutely no charge. You want me to step off the footpath? Not a problem, sir, not a problem in this wide earthly world. I rather like slushing through this pile of rotting garbage. Adds a nice squelch and smell to my boots. Thank you very much, your honor, and no I don't have a light. Haven't smoked a fag since Christmas.

"What's that? Oh, Jaysus, no! I'm not calling anyone a

fag. It's a word for a cigarette back in Ireland. And, sure, how could you know? What would a fine big man like yourself be doing thinking about such a miserable, rainy little country? And yes, I absolutely agree with you, I am a total motherfucker. Everyone knows that back home. And it doesn't just stop with the mothers. Sisters too, brothers, goats, sheep, I take all comers. You nailed it right on the head, your lordship. And thank you so much for sharing that thought with me. And if you don't mind, I think I'll be on my way."

But when I was halfway down the block and safely out of earshot, "Fuck you and the scabby horse you rode in on, you big, long, black streak of misery."

Jesus, they'd never believe the cut of these people down in Begley's. I should import a couple—parade them in the front door. "How are they hangin,' Paddy? Meet me friends Otis and Leroy from the Bronx. Give them each a pint of your best porter and a ball of malt on the house. You'll get your reward in heaven, or sooner, if there's any auld lip out of you. And I wouldn't be calling these gentlemen black boogie boys either, like you do when you're watching Man United on the telly. You might end up with your balls wrapped up around your ear."

Oh now, wouldn't it be great sport to see these boyos draped over Begley's bar just like they do here on the bonnets of cars, arses big as ball alleys protruding onto the footpath. And always a crowd of them gathered within hailing distance of the public phones.

"Those wouldn't be coded rings now, would they, lads, for the trading of drugs and other illegal substances? I mean, I'm not as dumb as I look. I couldn't be, says you."

As for the women, though strange and lovely, it was hard

to ignore the mark of the cadaver already upon them. Back home they'd still be parading around in convent plaid, but on the shattered streets their eyes were already sinking like wet stones in their beautiful heads, skin taut against high cheekbones but loosey-goosey around their mystic-lipsticked mouths. Dressed to kill and quite ready to at the drop of a hat, they eyed me, sighed me, lured me over if I even glanced at their desolate splendor.

"Oh, I'd love to stop, girls, believe me nothing would suit me better, but not right now because, between you me and the four walls, I'm scared out of me bloody skivvies, not to mention that I'm on my way to rescue me long lost girlfriend. It wouldn't really be proper, would it? Just give me a couple of days, though, and I'll be back, when I get the lay of the land like."

"Yoh, my man, I got what you want, got what you lookin' for."

Oh, sweet divine Jesus, get me out of here alive and I'll go to mass every Sunday for the rest of me eternal days. Forget the Sunday? I'll go eight days a week dressed in sackcloth and ashes, me back flayed from the whipping I'll be laying on meself. I won't drink, do drugs, look at women, or play with myself for the next fifty years. I promise you, Jesus. You can trust me this time!

"Ah, no thanks, all the same." I stuttered to the tall young black man in the white fedora.

"Hey, my man, I got what all you Fordham cats be lookin' for. You stick my rock up your nose, that thing be froze beyond repose, you be so fine, in thirty seconds time, you be so high, oh me oh my, my shit the pride of the avenue, you know you want it to be havin' you."

"Ah no, I don't do any hard stuff myself, thanks very much anyway." I kept my eyes focused straight ahead, but this prince of the streets could sell pints of plain to Arthur Guinness.

"Hey, no problem, man, that's cool, so fine, a cat like you ain't down with no jive, I got smoke guaranteed to bend your brain, come here from Jamaica on a reggae wave."

"No, thanks very much indeed. I'm fierce into Bob Marley but I'm actually in a bit of a hurry. Most be trotting along, toodle doo . . ."

A small army of entrepreneurs had gathered, each one plying their wares. Despite the sticky heat, I began to shiver like a young willow. I needed time to think, to get the hell out of there as fast as my knocking knees would carry me, but I was way out of my league.

"Hey, my brother, don't waste your time, I got this little girl she be so fine, a virgin still you understand, fourteen year old, never known no man, been savin' herself, bidin' her time, till you arrive, make her change her mind, so, what do you say, my brother, my friend, you won't see her kind on these streets again."

It was now or never while there was still an opening in the closing circle; I strode through it, the words bouncing around me like billiard balls until a rare working traffic light brought me to a halt. The poet parked himself abreast, large brown eyes radiating deep pools of understanding; but back in their murky depths, a tiny electric eel of greedy violence was priming itself to rocket to the surface. No question about it, I was lost: This street sorcerer would have me for breakfast and lunch, with enough left over for the makings of a halfway decent dinner.

When the light changed, I plunged across the street, head down, barely dodging the gleaming hood of a yellow convertible that screeched to a halt centimeters from my hip. I vaulted to the sidewalk, almost tripping over a staccato stream of Spanish obscenities. But, at the least, I'd lost the poet.

Halfway up the block, curiosity won out and I turned. The wordsmith stood forlornly on the corner, the yellow convertible still blocking his way. He waved a futile "come back," but it was half-hearted and hardly worth the trouble. I was treading on someone else's turf, someone with yellow wheels at his beck and call, and muscle enough to put fear in a jerky rhyme-boy.

The streets were darker, quieter now, and the drums deepened to a more foreboding tempo. My heart slowed in sympathy, and a tepid sweat seeped out on my forehead. My shirt was soaked beneath the leather jacket, and I longed for a cool Atlantic breeze. Most of the streetlights had been shattered, yet I could sense a menace behind the tall stoops of the buildings. Deep plangent murmurs skulked around naked walls before floating out windowless frames.

I hurried towards the one functioning streetlight. It cast a warm, glowing circle, a haven from the anxious darkness; I could hardly wait to gain its safety. Hunching over the map, I tried to visualize where I might be, but how to tell with no street signs. All I could do now was cling to the thought of Mary waiting for me: her lovely eyes, teasing smile, the way she fit into the snug of my arms, kissing on rainy nights, her damp hair a shield around me, the secret warmth of her throat, the catch in her breath when she said my name.

"What you got on your back, white boy?"

I spun around to the sound of sheer hatred.

"A big gun for huntin' black man?" This was no rhyming poet—more like a couple of hundred pounds of baldheaded intimidation in a powder blue suit out for a night on the town and short about forty bucks.

"Actually, it's a Yamaha acoustic. I got it second hand in Dublin."

"You play the funk, boy?" For all his girth, the stranger moved gracefully, cutting off the space between the streetlight and the way back to Murphy's.

"The what?"

"Where the hell you from? Ain't never heard of the funk?"

The hatred was so exposed I froze dead in my tracks.

"Wha's a matter? Ain't never laid eyes on no black man before?"

"Oh Jaysus, surely I have. Aren't they—I mean—you people are all over Dublin these days. There's even a Nigerian doctor at the County Hospital."

Hatred's eyes narrowed even further.

"Actually, I know a bit of Hendrix too. Learned it off a fellah from Waterford."

"Yoh what?"

"Jimi Hendrix, your man from Seattle? The Experience, like."

"What the fuck you talkin' about? Give me that guitar." He reached out a huge hand, and I would have gladly obliged—from a twenty-yard distance.

"Don't you be fuckin' with me, boy! Gimme me here that guitar."

When he lunged I spun on my heel and ran, crashing

through a pile of garbage cans just beyond the circle of the light. The cans went down like ninepins, and a pile of rotten fruit spewed across the sidewalk.

"Motherfucker!" Hatred stepped on an overripe melon, and his right foot shot out from under him. He tottered for a second, almost righting himself before spinning one more time and toppling headlong into the filth.

"Oh, sweet divine Jesus!" I skidded on a bunch of putrid bananas, yet managed to hold my balance.

"My motherfuckin' suit!" Hatred wailed as he flailed around in a cesspit of stinking fruit. "Stop that white boy!"

I didn't linger to commiserate; I was already near the end of the block. I almost screamed with joy to see a cop car cruising past.

"Help!" I yelled at the top of my lungs. As if on cue, its siren exploded in an ear-splitting howl, while the spastic lights atop the roof cast the street in an eerie amber backdrop. I ran towards this oasis of white authority, but the car picked up speed. I chased it, crying out and gesticulating, first in hope, then despair, but was forced to leap aside when a fire engine, horns blaring in empathy, rounded the corner.

I raced alongside. A couple of grizzled veterans gazed out. One of them caught sight of me and my panic. His partner shrugged, his eyes hollowed from lack of sleep. Kid was obviously high as a kite, but he got his skinny rich ass over the GW looking for smack, and now he could haul it back to his daddy's big house in Fort Lee. Ladder Thirty-Three had its own problems with half of Kingsbridge goin' up in smoke.

And that was that. The engine sped through a stop sign and I slunk into a doorway, dreading the sound of large angry footsteps; but there wasn't a whisper, just the wail of sirens dying in the distance.

And then something caused me to look up. Though the sign was buckled, there was no mistaking "Decatur Avenue"! Oh sweet divine Jesus, what a break! It wouldn't be long now till I'd be clear of this madness and wrapped around my Mary. I hazarded a glance beyond the doorway; no crazy baldhead in view. But the bastard could be lurking in the shadows, waiting for me to stick out my big culchie ears.

I tightened the strap of the guitar, then sprinted out of the doorway and wheeled a sharp right onto Decatur. Zigzagging down the sidewalk past dealers, users, the walking wounded, and law-abiding etceteras, I tried to decipher the numbers on the darkened doors but to no avail. It wasn't until I surged past Jose's Bodega that I was able to fathom that the numbers were descending and I knew I was on the right track. I could almost feel Mary's arms reaching out to smother me in their warmth.

CHAPTER FOUR

I gazed up at 2702 Decatur Avenue. Though I had printed the address across a legion of envelopes, I had never even come close to visualizing the building's forbidding banality. At least, I assumed it was 2702, for the door itself boasted no number plate. Still, 2706 stood nearby, while a vacant lot dotted with weedy trees festered in between.

This disarray appeared to have little effect, for 2702 leaned haughtily backwards from the street. Still, the place had surely seen better days. A rusty fire escape clung to its bricky face, a foot or two of ladder dangling out of reach of all but giants and basketball players, its bottom rungs strung with barbed wire. The fourth floor platform was strewn with sheets, though it was hard to divine if they were out for airing or drying. The other tiers were empty save for a dead palm tree on the second, its fronds drooping ground-wards like the tresses of a hung-over hippy. The building may once have gleamed, but dirt, grime, and buckets of time had congealed to give it a nondescript puke-like complexion. A faded mural of Che Guevara—misplaced optimism still firing his eyes—gazed down on the potholed street.

Next to the steel-encased front door, an intercom system had been ripped out of the wall, its remains dangling from a couple of stripped wires. I studied the few surviving nameplates but could find nothing that even approximated Devine; and with that, the adrenalin that had been propelling me since Shannon evaporated. I leaned back against the heavy door, the jetlag nailing me to the front step. What now? Where the hell to turn? The door inched open under my weight. I peered into the hallway and was enveloped by a Bronx cocktail of stale piss and fresh poverty.

The door creaked shut behind me. I stood stock-still, all my senses aquiver, waiting for my eyes to adjust. Up on the first stairwell a naked bulb, caught in some slight cross breeze, chased shadows down bare corridors and out through the broken banisters. A few murmurs lingered, then choked, their silence limned by the rumble of distant distorted recordings and a squalling Spanish radio. Whoever was up there had heard me and now awaited my next move; he, she or whatever held all the cards. Still, I hadn't come three thousand miles to turn tail and run. To hell with them all! I seethed at my own tentativeness, reopened the door, and defiantly slammed it. Then I began to climb.

Each floor boasted its own distinctive cacophony: on the second, John Coltrane, Little Sparrow, and an Albanian drone sought the upper hand; but before I could analyze this psychotic brew, a flash of predatory eyes sent me scurrying up the next flight. The chattering staccato of salsa, trumpets ablare in brazen harmonies, mocked me, serenaded me; then like a drifting mournful echo, I heard Leonard Cohen's weary voice from behind a door on the fourth, and I knew my Mary was close at hand. I hurried across the sticky landing, but almost fainted when a figure solidified out of the shadows and blocked my way.

"*Que pasa, amigo?*" The man's voice was cordial enough.

Gaunt and squint-eyed, a red bandana creased his dusky forehead in a vain effort to restrain a shock of oily black hair. A silver crucifix glinted in his left ear. His smile revealed the absence of a front tooth before he floated across the landing, eyes laced with speed. But I moved even quicker. Sidestepping, I slipped past and hammered on the door.

Leonard dropped a couple of decibels, and an Irishwoman's voice answered in some annoyance, "What the hell is it now?"

"Open up, will you!" I pleaded.

"Listen, I got the shit round here," Squint Eye hissed. "You buyin'—you buyin' from me."

"Who is it?"

"Sean Kelly!"

"What's yoh problem, man?"

"I haven't the least problem—not a problem in the world," I stuttered, then shouted at the door, "For the love of Christ, does Mary Devine live in there?"

"Yeah, she does but . . . eh . . ."

"You messin' with me, man, I don't like that." Squint Eye lurched closer. One of his hands twitched as he gesticulated, the other was concealed inside his jeans jacket.

". . . She's gone away for the weekend."

"It's a Tuesday bloody night."

Only inches away from my face now, Squint Eye's hot garlicky breath was overwhelming. His whole body trembling, his pupils popping like organ-stops out of his skull. Then, in one fluid movement, he stepped back on his heel and whipped out a bayonet from inside his jacket.

"I cut you, man. I cut you bad," he whispered.

"Jaysus, there's no need for that kind of thing!" But the

words barely made it out of my parched throat. I leaned back against the door, the sweat oozing from every pore as Squint Eye twirled the long blade in a dreamy arc towards my Adam's apple. At first the point tickled; then it began to pinch.

"Maybe I just take your money, make life simple."

I couldn't have agreed more, but I was suddenly falling backwards, arms akimbo. I hit the floorboards on the seat of my pants but a foot in the shoulder kept me from toppling over. The door slammed and a young woman smashed a baseball bat against it.

"Keep off my landing, you feckin' bastard, or I'll split the head of you."

The room reeked of cigarettes, beer, and a faint tang of marijuana, but they were no match for the cheap perfume of the woman who stood poised as a cobra, muttering to herself, "One bloody thing after another."

She was wearing a Barry Manilow T-shirt above black panties, her face set in determination, as if certain that Squint Eye had the power to pass through the wall.

"I thought you'd be better lookin'," she remarked in a Mayo accent, her chest heaving from the exertion.

"I'm not at me best right now," I shot back, disapproving of the musical tastes of someone who couldn't have been more than twenty-five.

Somewhat less than svelte, she wore her curly peroxide hair at shoulder length and had large well-formed breasts. A surprisingly narrow waist seemed out of place above generous thighs and slightly thickened ankles.

"So," she inquired acidly, "do the goods meet with your approval?"

"I've seen worse." The compliment was apparently lost on her for she raised her eyebrows and winked. I arched my head backwards to behold a naked man.

"What about you?" the tall figure greeted me in a Belfast accent, soft at the core but spiked around the edges.

"Jesus Christ!" I ducked away a couple of modest inches. "Did you never hear about pajamas?"

The slim, muscular man clinically studied me before reaching down and jerking me to my feet. "You're a long way from pajamas now, Paddy."

Though his palm was hard and calloused, his fingers were surprisingly delicate. He rocked back and forth on his toes in the manner of well-conditioned athletes. Despite the lack of clothing, there was an innate dignity about him, yet it was spiced with an icy aloofness. Around six feet tall, he had fine black hair that drooped like Brian Ferry's across his forehead, until swept back by an impatient hand. A slightly large, though aristocratic, nose and full lips dominated his tanned face; but it was his pale blue eyes that commanded attention. They seemed flecked with mica and glowed with an odd mixture of curiosity and inner certainty. A small well-seasoned scar under his right cheekbone only served to highlight his overall handsomeness.

In his early thirties, he had the look of a man who had seen much of the world and generally disapproved of its carry-on. Added to that, he had a distinct way of finishing sentences that left the listener uncertain how to proceed; and in the silence that followed his last comment, my mind spun into action with the myriad possibilities of Mary and this naked Adonis living under the same roof.

"Will you put some clothes on, for the love of God?" the

woman mockingly beseeched. "The poor chap might think we were up to something."

"Be your lucky day."

"It would, indeed, with the size of that yoke winkin' at me."

"I'm Danny McCorley." He ignored her last remark and stuck out his hand. His grip was firm to the point of discomfort and I squeezed back for all I was worth. I had no intention of backing down for any of Mary's admirers.

He frowned and gave me one last piercing look before snapping at the woman, "Keep it down then."

"Keep it down yourself . . . if you can."

"Don't you ever think of nothing else?"

"I would and all, if there weren't so many distractions."

"The sooner you get a man for yourself, the better for everyone. Now, give my head some peace, woman, I have to work in the morning."

With that, he strode over to the far side of the room, threw himself into a cot, and pulled a sheet over his head, the interview apparently terminated.

"Isn't it awful what a girl has to put up with in this country?"

She had a point. The whole bloody city was out to lunch. Still, Mary wouldn't screw around, would she? But she'd made no mention of any Danny in her couple of cryptic letters. Never gave a description of the hellhole she lived in either. There was more to all this than met the eye.

At first glance, I couldn't put my finger on it, but the apartment seemed somehow out of whack, as if the parts were unable to come to terms with a definite whole. Still, it was a great deal more preferable to the stairway outside.

The Yamaha had not been smashed, as I had feared; the case had slid to one side when I fell backwards. One of the tuning pegs was loose, but that could be fixed. All in all, not a bad outcome.

"Just like that," the woman remarked irritably as I closed the guitar case.

"Just like what?"

"Your man over there buggers off to bed and leaves me to look after you."

"Ah, I don't think I'd be up to much of anything. I'm dead tired."

"Is that so, Mister Smart-Arse. Well for your information . . ." But then she waved her hand dismissively. "Ah, what am I doing? Wasting me time on another bogman."

She collapsed with a thud on the sofa and dug her face into her hands.

"What's the matter with you?"

"What's the fecking matter with me?" She looked up despairingly. "As usual, I'm the one left holding the baby."

Even through the fog of fatigue, I knew that the problem had to do with Mary and the naked Belfast man. "I don't know what you're talking about."

"No, *a leanbh,* I know you don't," she sighed.

I was close to telling her to shove her pity, but it was hard to concentrate.

"I suppose you'll be wanting a bed?"

"That cot there wouldn't be so bad."

"That's mine."

"The floor'll be fine so."

"You won't get much sleep on that with your man over there tramping about at the crack of dawn." She smiled for the first time, and her face softened. "By the way, I'm Kate," she said almost shyly, stretching her T-shirt down over her panties.

"Does everyone over here go around with their knickers hangin' down?"

She blushed. With the armor of sarcasm laid aside, she was pretty in a country kind of way. Her lips looked warm and rosy, and I knew that if I wasn't there on more serious business I wouldn't be long about sneaking a kiss at them.

She caught my drift and blushed even deeper. "The humidity wears you down," she murmured, and, at that quiet level, her voice reminded me of the stream back home on its way past the stepping stones. "After a couple of weeks you don't care much anymore."

"I'll be long gone by then. I've come to take Mary home."

She seemed ill at ease. For my own part I was getting horny, and no matter how hard I tried, my eyes kept returning to her black underwear.

That didn't escape her attention either and she tugged furiously on her T-shirt. "The quare fellah over there is a fine lookin' cut of a man, isn't he?" She tried to change the subject while reaching into a closet for a sleeping bag and spreading it on the couch.

There was something intriguing about her. Even when friendly she seemed on edge, her eyes darting this way and that. In fact, the longer I was there, the more the apartment itself seemed not only off kilter but totally out of its head. From a poster above a blocked fireplace, James Connolly gazed out. While across the room, on the other wall, a young Elvis sneered back. In an alcove near the kitchen, a small plaster statue of the Virgin Mary beamed at the two rivals. Oblivious to all this

clutter, his head exploding with psychedelic bric-a-brac, Jimi
Hendrix stared glassy-eyed out the window.

The room was divided into distinct fiefdoms: Over by
Danny's cot, it was as neat as a barracks except for a couple
of opened tomes lying astride two precisely packed bookcases.
In contrast, Kate's area exploded with clothes, make-up, and
romance novels. Mary's albums were strewn in a corner—Astral
Weeks, a couple of Nick Drake's and the ubiquitous Mister
Cohen atop the heap.

Part of the floor was laid with a ratty looking carpet, but
the boards had been sanded and stained in the open kitchen.
One corner of the table had been scrupulously cleared; the rest
was a jumble of unwashed dishes, beer cans and overflowing
ashtrays.

"The cleaning lady didn't show up today." Kate noticed
my appraisal.

Then Danny groaned in his sleep. She held her finger to
her lips. "Sometimes he talks . . ."

The Belfast man's face was creased in anguish, his lips
moving as if in prayer.

"What about?"

"All manner of things . . ."

I had a feeling that she wanted to say more, but it was
hardly my concern.

"What time will Mary be home?"

"Whenever she gets off work."

"I thought you said she was away for the weekend?"

"Did I?" She turned abruptly to a mirror over the sink
and fluffed out her hair. "Oh yeah, she's up in the Catskills."

"What's that?" I pulled off my boots.

"It's the mountains beyond Yonkers."

"She's skiing or something?"

"In the middle of bloody May?"

When I took off my socks the floorboards felt cool and soothing.

"Another Irish Einstein," she muttered at the mirror.

Hard put now to keep my eyes from drooping, I headed towards a closed door. "Is this the can? I'm only burstin'."

She dived in front of me. "It's over there," she said pointing at a door across the room. She was very close, lips parted and slightly trembling. I thought of kissing her and wondered if she'd mind.

"Hiding something in there?" I moved a little closer.

Her breath quickened and I could sense her vulnerability; still she held her ground. "Oh, just a couple of mortars and an anti-tank missile," she whispered, never taking her eyes from mine.

"Wouldn't surprise me with that fellow up on the wall." I pointed to the poster of Connolly.

At any other time I probably would have kissed her but she followed my finger and, with that, the moment passed. As I walked over to the bathroom I wondered if it would ever return. The door wouldn't quite fasten and slid open behind me. I was too knackered to care, even though I could feel her eyes upon me while I pissed.

When I came back out, I hung up my leather jacket and took off my shirt. "Jesus, I can hardly stand up I'm so tired."

After the chiseled hardness of the Belfast man I must have looked like a boy in the dim light: the hair on my chest soft as down, skin still smooth and creamy.

And yet she was reluctant to take her eyes off me. Finally, she cast a glance at her own disheveled cot.

I opened my belt and took off my pants. She blushed but still didn't look away.

The silence hung between us until the Belfast man turned suddenly in his sleep.

"Don't worry. I wouldn't get up on Marilyn Monroe right now."

"No. She'd be a bit on the moldy side."

"Am I safe with your man over there?" I threw an arm in Danny's direction.

"You never know your luck."

"Does he have a girlfriend?"

She evaded my eyes and didn't answer.

I knew there was a problem, and it would have to be faced and soon, but I was just too bollocksed. I pulled the sleeping bag over me and stretched out on the couch. "Anyway, we'll be out of here tomorrow." I yawned and took one last look around the room. "I hope Mary isn't too surprised when she sees me."

Kate sighed and turned out the lights.

chapter five

On and on I tumbled through the merry-go-round of my first sleep in America. In the midst of this helter-skelter, I could have sworn real figures peered in at me, though they were distant and distorted, as if viewed from the wrong end of a telescope.

Once I even sat up when startled by the howl of a siren, but the dreams were relentless and I was soon swooping in the lee of a south wind into Mary's farmhouse kitchen. Perched atop a smoky rafter, I listened to her father muttering about some "dirty little bitch." The gnarled farmer creased me with such a glare that I almost tumbled headlong into the fire; but just in time, I latched onto the whispering wind and was swept back out into the night.

High then over the dark hills of Munster and the inky black Atlantic to glide down on the spouting street poet before soaring past Hatred still brushing squashed melon from his powder blue suit. Up the shadowy stairs of 2702, I dodged a stream of Squint-Eyed curses to find safety on the couch. Just in time, for my mother bustled in on my delirium and tucked the sleeping bag smother-tight around my throat. When I kicked loose and tried to arise, she clung to me until pushed aside by a handsome olive-skinned man. Poised as a panther, his muscles rippling through a white silk shirt, the stranger studied me. Then Mary appeared wearing only a knee-length slip. She eased into the stranger's arms and raised a slender hand to caress his cheek before kissing him on the lips.

But I was already crash landing back at the bar in Shannon where Arsehole gravely advised me to stay at home, get a job, marry a virgin, beget two and a half average Irish kids, and keep the islands in view all year round. This advice had only begun to sink in when a naked Danny knocked Hore's block off, sending his spastic torso spinning into bed with Kate, who loudly declaimed that while she didn't give a damn what a man looked like, she did insist that he have some manner of a head on his shoulders.

Danny merely yawned at her distress and tucked a white T-shirt into dusty blue jeans; he thereupon lit a fag and took a drag, before musing, "What will be, will be. Not a bloody thing any of us can do about it." Nodding their agreement, my mother and father tangoed by in evening dress, only to shimmy right through the wall when Kate erupted from her cot complaining about headless men without the wherewithal to go down on her. She flounced around scattering clothes to the four walls until she managed to pour herself into a red summer dress, a size too small, and heels an inch too high. When she finally tottered to the front door and slammed it behind her, Mary floated over and lay down next to me. Then there was nothing but an exhausted void for a very long time until I found myself surfacing into a sun-drenched morning.

My eyes were glassy, a thin gauze softening the hard edge of reality until I felt her body. I was about to call out her name but hesitated. How to make sense of it all with the essence of the dream already speeding away? But what matter, the sheer delight that Mary was here!

She dozed on, lips parted, still not a line on her face. If she had lost weight it had done little to detract from her beauty: Her cheekbones were more defined than I remembered, skin even paler. Her shorter hair added to an overall look of maturity. The punky raven rinse now history, her natural brunette had reasserted itself with hints of chestnut playing in the sunlight.

I wanted to kiss her and hold her and tell her how I hadn't been the same since she left. But I knew I was treading on time, that when she awoke much would be different. No one, not even Mary, could take this moment away from me.

Outside, a horn blared and she moved towards me and laid her head on my chest. Her hair fell forward, concealing her face. I gathered the stray waves and moved them back, then noticed the dull welt just under her left ear lobe. It had not been there in Ireland.

She was wearing a dark fitted skirt and a long sleeved, low cut, white blouse. A delicate golden cross nestled on her breastbone. What roads had she traveled since shedding Doc Martens and shredded Clash T-shirts?

It didn't matter. I kissed her throat. She murmured something that sounded like Spanish and arched her neck backwards, the better for me to kiss her breasts. The strange-sounding words caught me off guard. She kissed me impatiently, opening her lips, but not her eyes; when I slipped in my tongue she responded with hers. I slid my hand inside her skirt, pulling her closer so that our hips touched.

But when she pressed against me, her eyes opened wide in alarm. She pushed me away and jumped back off the couch. Grasping the tiny cross for reassurance, she smoothed down her skirt with her other hand.

"Mary, don't you recognize me?"

She didn't, at first.

"Oh, God, you frightened the heart out of me."

"You surely knew I was here?"

"I saw you last night, but . . ." She looked beyond me as if for reassurance.

I followed her eyes towards an open door. The room inside was dark except for the crumpled sheets of an unmade bed. By the time I looked back she had gathered herself.

"You haven't forgotten that easy, have you?" I held out my hand.

She was hesitant but sat down next to me.

I pulled her closer to hide the hurt. Her hair had fallen in on her face; she made no effort to pull it back, though she did hug me.

"You feel so good," I whispered.

She kissed me gently on the cheek but moved quickly so that my lips brushed her ear.

"I've missed you so much," I said.

"I missed you too."

"You're sure?"

Outside, a truck revved up furiously.

"Sean?"

"Yeah?"

"What are you doing here?"

"I came for you."

"Just like that?"

"I had a feeling something was wrong."

She didn't answer, just dug her fingers tighter into my shoulder.

"Is there?"

Again, she chose not to answer, but finally sighed, "Oh, Sean, what am I going to do with you?"

"I can think of a couple of things right now."

She resisted a complete embrace, just rested her head on my shoulder.

"You should have written."

"I did, a hundred times . . . for all the good it did me."

"They rip off everything around here."

"You mean, your man out there with the squinty eye?"

She shrugged, the way a farmer might complain of a fox—a constant pest, but hardly something to get worked up about.

"I tried ringing but there's no phone anymore."

"No," she said, then added with some bitterness, "We had an argument about the bill so . . ." She stood up and straightened her blouse. Her hand instinctively reached for the cross.

"How do you live in this place, Mary?"

"What's wrong with it?"

"Jaysus, I almost got murdered coming here."

"There's a lot worse."

She walked over to the window and looked out but didn't open it. The room felt like a hothouse. The humidity was getting to me, sucking away what little energy I possessed. I could already feel a distance yawning between us, and spoke in a more accusing manner than I meant to: "There was a lot of rumors about you . . ."

She either didn't hear me or chose not to answer.

". . . You know what it's like back home."

"Yes," she finally murmured. "That's why I'm over here."

I felt guilty. What had I heard anyway—some sniggering down the pub, some gruff words of her father's that had been overheard and taken on a life of their own?

"Do you mind me coming, Mary?"

The sun must have moved beyond a stray cloud for a sudden ray of sunshine flooded the room. She looked fragile in the harsh glare.

"It's a bit unexpected."

"Apart from that . . . ?"

She had turned from the window and was staring in at the bedroom again. Something in there was bothering her. At first she strode over, but as she got closer her heels seemed to drag. Still she closed the door with some finality and leaned back against it.

"I want to know the truth this time, Mary." I couldn't take my eyes off her. No matter how many layers of detachment she wore back home, I had managed to pierce most of them with time. Now her very essence seemed different; it was the layers that were familiar. Then she smiled and my heart lifted.

"What do you want for breakfast?" She laughed at the practicality of the idea.

"You." I reached out and pulled her close.

She allowed the intimacy for an instant. "Someone might walk in."

"That never bothered you back home."

"A lot of things bothered me."

"You never said anything."

"Any time I tried . . . no one was listening."

"I was, Mary."

Though she stared in my direction, I had a feeling that she wasn't really seeing me. Then another cloud blocked the sun and she was suddenly decisive again. "Put your clothes on. We've a lot to talk about."

"Am I turning you on or something?" I stepped into my jeans and pulled on my shirt. My body felt stiff and weary, but I had surprisingly little hangover. "Mary."

She didn't answer.

"Who was that fellah last night?"

"Fellah?"

"You know who I'm talking about."

She strode over to the sink and began brushing her hair. Back home I loved to watch this ritual: What brush would she use, how many strokes, the way her gaze would eventually drift from impatience to a contented dreaminess. Now I could tell it was just a façade: She was avoiding my eyes.

"Your man that was bollocks naked."

"Oh, Danny." She laughed and threw back her hair over her shoulders.

"Yeah, Mister Universe himself."

"You seem very impressed."

"Jaysus, he could use that langer of his for a fire hose."

"And that's what has you worried?"

"Well, he's not exactly like one of the lads down the pub, is he?"

"No . . . he's not."

"It's no laughing matter, Mary. How come you're living with him?"

"Listen, Sean, enough of the inquisition." She swept a

couple of empty bottles from the table and dumped them in an overflowing garbage can. They clattered noisily to the floor. She winced but didn't bother to pick them up. "I don't expect you, or anyone else back in that stuck-up little town, to understand anything. I needed help paying the rent, and what he chooses to wear—or not—is his business. Now, where are you going to stay?"

"Stay?"

"Yes, stay! It's already full to bursting here."

"I don't believe you! I sell all me gear, come three thousand miles looking for you, and you have the nerve to ask me that?"

"Oh God! Now I'm stuck with looking after you too."

"Well, thanks very much."

She paced nervously up and down the room, her brow furrowed. "You'll have to get a job."

"That's the last thing on my mind right now."

"Well, how are you going to live?"

"I'll get by. Have no fear about me."

She rolled her eyes and continued her pacing. "Danny'll get you the start on the site. He's good like that."

"I don't want any charity from that bastard."

"I wouldn't go calling him that to his face. He can be a bit . . . edgy." She motioned to a smashed telephone in the corner.

I shrugged my indifference though it seemed he had one hell of a temper. It had probably happened after my pathetic phone call from the harbor.

"How much did you bring over with you?"

I didn't have to reach into my pocket to know the answer. She nodded grimly.

"Mary, listen to me, will you!" Her constant pacing was getting to me. On impulse I reached out and caught her just below the shoulder. She pulled away sharply and rubbed her arm through the sleeve of the blouse. She glared at me, but the words kept tumbling out for there was so much I wanted to tell her, "After you left, I stayed pissed for about six months. Then, one day it dawned on me—there's no future in being the David Bowie of Wexford."

Though her eyes were tearing, she began to smile. "Did you run out of my old mascara?"

"Will you quit the messing. I'm into a whole different thing now—more meaningful like."

"Oh God, you're priceless," she laughed.

"Be serious, will you! I'm writing all me own songs. They're absolutely brilliant."

She reached out and touched my cheek. "I never doubted you, Sean, even when they were all laughing at us."

"Laughing at me. You know what they wanted to do with you."

"That was all in your head, love."

The familiar endearment and the softness in her eyes almost took my breath away. Everything was going to be all right. I knew that now. She hadn't changed. It would always be just the two of us.

"Screw them all," I grinned. "We'll show them this time, right?"

"Everything is still so black and white with you, isn't it?"

"What's right is right, Mary. There's no two ways about that."

"There's a lot of grays over here, Sean." She turned away and walked to the window.

"I don't give a damn. I've got you and that's all that counts. Right?"

She didn't answer. Just lit a cigarette and blew smoke at the window-panes.

CHAPTER SIX

*M*ixing cement from dawn to dusk! Talk about unadulterated living hell. Shoveling that gray muck into buckets, then humping them up ladders to the lads pointing bricks above on the scaffold; arms dragging halfway out of their sockets, leaning your forehead into the splinters on the ladder for fear you'll topple backwards and break your arse on the concrete pavement. The hard chaws roaring at you, cursing and slagging you, unmercifully breaking both your balls and your heart, testing you, messing with you, checking if you're cut from the right stuff, or ready to down tools when the going gets tough and run home bawling to the comforting arms of your ever loving mammy.

Well, fuck them, and all that came before them! I point-blank refused to admit that every bone in my body was screaming "outahere;" nor did I let on that I was mere centimeters away from flinging a full bucket of that mucky shite in their stupid Neanderthal faces. But, more than anything, I would not give that shower of sheep-shagging culchies the satisfaction of suspecting that I was teetering on the very brink of breaking down and bawling my eyes out in front of them.

The site itself drove me to distraction with the noise and the clutter; and as for dust, I could barely think straight with the fine gray leavings of bricks and mortar clogging the very byways *of my brain. All I knew was that I had no choice but to persevere. If somebody was going to break, it would not be yours truly.*

Cement, of all bloody things, was my savior. On that first sweltering morning, Danny informed me in no uncertain terms that the gray dust was king and the man mixing it ruled. Though this unheralded laborer might be considered first cousin to a scabby leper, spat upon and scorned by masons, bricklayers, carpenters, and gangers, the site would come grinding to a halt without him. Along with tenacity and a back of steel, this warrior needed the discipline and discernment, if not the temperament, of a French chef. But first and foremost, he had to be aware that a blend of mortar was essential for those engaged in the fine art of laying brick or pointing, whereas Portland was your man in any less rarified endeavor.

When I inquired the difference, Danny looked at me as though I might have been short a few essential marbles. Didn't every Paddy in the universe know that not only was Portland coarser and less expensive, but it contained a dose of limestone that hastened the setting; thus it could be indiscriminately slathered on walls or floors by any moron. Whereas the finer, more expensive mortar was reserved for work only undertaken by master craftsmen. These Brahmin of the scaffold were assigned apprentices whose raison d'être, *apart from making tea and trips to the OTB, was to keep their masters' mortar moist like paste and ready for instant deployment between the bricks.*

I hastened to assure Danny that I, and all of my ancestors back to the noble ape, had indeed been privy to such sacerdotal knowledge, but what with the jetlag and the general uncertainty of my station, this treasured data had slipped my mind.

He appeared relieved that he had not been saddled with a total dolt, and informed me in hushed tones that three to almost one was the magic formula for a sound, but economical, mix of cement. I gravely nodded my appreciation that he would deign to share this secret of the inner sanctum with the lowly likes of me, and reassured him that under no circumstances would I ever divulge the fact that three loaded shovels of sand should be mixed with no more than one topped-off shovel of cement. He further confided that such thrift would accrue big bucks for our employer over the course of a year, leading to a bonus of a week's wages for the trip home at Christmas, if such an excursion was my desire.

He thereupon flung down a couple of hundred pound bags of cement in front of an Everest of sand, then watched like a hawk as I divested thirty heaped shovelfuls from this mountain and added ten loads of carefully topped off cement. With infinite care, he demonstrated how to mix these two elements—"back and forth, sideways-arseways"—until they had become an indistinguishable gray heap. He then bade me excavate a large hole in the center of the mound, so that its surroundings looked suspiciously like a sandcastle. When I mentioned this analogy he cautioned that, whatever one chose to contemplate, the shovel must keep moving, for time, as the hooker said, was indisputably money.

Into this hole you then tossed a lake of water and the real Zen of mixing cement began. With a couple of good whacks, you collapsed the inner structure without breaching the outer battlements. Next, slosh the whole kit and caboodle around like your mother's day-old porridge. Waste no time in admiring your work, he advised, but carve out little islands of the remaining quagmire and examine them closely for the least hint of dryness; then sprinkle out more water until the mess attained a consistent gumbo, not too runny, nor too sandy, or as he savagely observed,

"The motherfucker won't stick, and the pricks of owners won't pay their bills."

"But you're a far cry from finished yet, Paddy," he cautioned. "Now for the tricky part. Demolish your outer battlements and toss them into the stew; but on no account allow the bloody thing to go cavorting down the pavement. No, run around like Peter Power's pet otter erecting dams until all avenues of escape have been sealed off. Mix again like a martyr for another ten minutes or so; then sluice your shovel through the whole goddamn thing until your inner craftsman informs you that you've achieved the magical mixture."

He neglected to mention that the Brahmin atop the scaffold would by now be requesting one's presence in hushed tones such as: "Would you ever hurry up with that fucking cement, you whore's melt!" or: "Hey, shit-for-brains, what the fuck are you doin'—mixin' the goddamned thing with your bloody bollocks?"

So, in some alarm, you fill to the brim buckets that you can barely shove around, let alone carry. Then, up you storm the creaky ladder like a hound out of hell—the first couple of times, anyway. But as the morning wears on, you know you can't go one more step, but you do anyway. And when you're literally choking with dust, the tongue hanging out of you, what do you see but the selfish dickheads above passing a bottle of water around, but ne'er a drop for a stuck-up little queer like you who hasn't the decency to bend over and take his God-ordained, first-day-on-the-job slagging like any other self-respecting Paddy.

If that wasn't bad enough, the real humiliation came when they downed tools and sauntered off to the pub and never told you where this tabernacle of oblivion might be. Until Danny saw the look of dismay on your face and bade you follow him. And so, you repaired to the salubrious confines of the Blarney

Stone, where your comrades in dust were all tipping back ice-cold Buds and scarfing down big plates of greasy ham and cabbage and spuds and carrots, and not paying the least attention to you in your finely honed, solipsistic misery.

Not to mention that you stood a better chance of conversation with the barstools than Mister Universe, adrift in his own thoughts and unwilling to spare a grunt, let alone some manner of civilized small talk. Still you hung in there in your calcified gloom while the bogmen sniggered at you and auditioned various scabrous nicknames, the mere prospect of which caused the hair to stand on the back of your neck.

But oh, by Jesus Christ, didn't that first cold Bud taste like the nectar of the gods! Down it flowed through your parched windpipe where it congealed around the greasy ham and cabbage and spuds and carrots. And, by sweet sanctified Mary the Mother of our Redeemer, the second one hit the spot even more head on. By the third, you were a hair unsteady, but bulling for the fourth, when Danny abruptly stood up, whereupon all hands stumbled and rumbled and belched and farted their way back to the site for another round of dusty masochism.

In the long searing afternoon, the banter on the scaffold decayed into a heavy brooding silence: each man lost in his own hopes, regrets, and resolutions, longing for the blessed oblivion that the night would surely provide. You, however, had little time for such contemplation, what with having to hump endless buckets of medicated goo up the rickety ladder, the fear of God in you that you might miss a slimy step, topple over, and smash like porcelain on the swaying street below.

Three o'clock was the worst hour. With the sun burning holes in the back of your head, muscles locking, gut fermenting, *you'd hit the four fiery walls of hell. But hawk-eyed Danny beckoned you over. Wasn't he only dying for a cup of coffee, and would you ever run down to the bodega like a good man, and get one regular and, while you're at it, another for yourself.*

That walk in the shade was like heaven itself, and there was a blessed line ahead of you, and it took you twenty minutes to get back, your heart in your mouth that Danny would be making an eejit of you in front of the smirking ensemble. Instead, he sat you down in the front seat of the truck, blasted the air-conditioner, and made small talk about football and God knows what else. And you could barely believe it: the great gangerman, Mister Universe himself, chatty and more than halfway decent; and when he had sprinted back up the ladder, you saw that he hadn't touched a drop of his own coffee, and you were about to run up after him with it, such was your gratitude, but you kind of knew you shouldn't, and you didn't.

And then the shadows were deepening, the bogmen traipsing past and taking the piss out of you because you'd already started in on another batch of cement that wouldn't be "worth a heap of dried dog shit in the morning."

"Shut the fuck up!" Danny's eyes were like daggers flashing. "You live and learn, and which one of us didn't make an arsehole of himself the first day of his start!"

With that off his chest, he strode to the bar and was wrapped around the pay phone when you came in, and you didn't know what the hell to do with yourself, so you stood there like a spare prick at a wedding. Then a round was called and a bottle placed gruffly in your hand, not a word said; every eye averted but you caught the faintest glimmer of welcoming grins filtering across sunburned faces. And you wanted to cry, but that would hardly have been acceptable, so you shuffled off to the bog, smiled at your newly accepted self in the mirror, and blew your snotty nose and grateful mind alone.

On the sardine-packed D train home, you stood with Mister Universe, silent as the grave again and devouring some gynormous dog-eared paperback. What's auld Crime and Punishment *about anyway? you ventured, and that you love a good mystery yourself.*

"It's about life, boy, bloody life," he murmured, without favoring you with even the barest of glances.

Well, fuck him and his bloody big book about life! Down you sank on the metal seat and not only were you asleep by 125th but drooling on some poor Dominican lady the whole way to Kingsbridge where he had to pick you up and drag you out onto the boiling elevated platform. Almost cracking your skull descending the steel staircase, you traced his footsteps along some of the same streets that you fled through two days earlier, but now not one lousy denizen even gave you a second thought in your cementy jeans and dust caked T-shirt. Yet, at every Bud-fueled pit stop on the way, Tyrone boys and a host of other Northern blaggards gave you the once over, leaving little doubt that whoever traveled with the Master of the Universe was a fit object for curiosity. Then finally up the rarified stairs of 2702 you crawled only to slide into the scalding heat of a full bath, every sinew and bone in your body throbbing, exulting, then passing out simultaneously.

On and on it went, day after wretched day, a litany of blisters, bruises, calluses, and skin braising ever redder; but every hour you're coarsening, coating yourself with extra layers of sarcasm and disgust, until you're more of a prick than you ever thought possible.

Danny stands apart from all of us and he makes no bones

*about it. A prince of the scaffold, he rules his rickety empire with
an iron fist, and everyone gives him a wide arc. Which is just
about miraculous, because the bogmen make fun of everyone:
me in particular, but also bosses, cops, firemen, priests, whores,
faggots, Puerto Ricans, and blacks of all shades and sizes. Yet,
their voices drop to a murmur when he approaches, and they
never refer to him by name, only "yer man" or "the big fellah."
They have an odd kind of grudging respect for him, but it's
worlds away from anything you might class as affection.*

*I put it all down to envy, especially after I heard that he was
a star of the County Antrim team back home with a reputation
that stretched the length and breadth of Ulster; and isn't he now
the toast of Gaelic Park on Sunday afternoons, a da Vinci of
the football, with long legs, muscles to burn, and proud black
Irish looks to die for.*

*But there's another side of him that doesn't totally gel, a
certain coldness and even contempt for those around him and
the world in general. It's hard to put your finger on, because he
hasn't always been like that—you can tell from the surprised looks
of old friends from home when he brushes them off after a
cursory greeting. This disciplined frigidity clashes fiercely with
the natural charisma that oozes from him—the result being
that you always feel slightly uneasy in his presence. Still, I never
doubt but that's his intention.*

*There's something in his past, too, that's occasionally
whispered on the scaffold, especially when he's off conferring
with Big Boss Dennehy, who democratically treats every man like
a piece of shit. But whenever I try to listen, the conversation of
the bogmen trails off to be replaced by hostile glares. Of course,
I'm the Southerner or "Free Stater" as they derogatively describe
me and just "don't understand" the Northern world that they*

come from. If Danny is a problem, he's their problem, and whatever is in his past concerns them alone and isn't the business of some blow-in. Then again, on that crew of East Tyrone, South Armagh and West Belfast boys, pasts are rarely shouted from the rooftops for, from what I can gather, the British army would like nothing better than a little chat with any number of them.

Not that I'm burning midnight oil thinking about any of the bastards. No, it's Mary that's on my mind, for all the good that does me. She's always going just as I'm coming, or floating home when I'm staggering out. And sweet damn all explanation as to where she's been or with whom!

She's light worlds away from the girl I remember. Jumpy as a cat on a griddle at times, but more often than not mooning around like she doesn't know what day it is. Probably dreaming about Mister Universe and what they get up to when I'm passed out or absent. I know there's something going on. I just can't put a name on it. But oh, by sweet Jesus, I will.

I tossed the pen to one side and closed my journal. If nothing else, I might have a couple of songs or the makings of a story to show for all this bloody misery. I drained the can of beer. Writing was thirsty work, and the humidity was a scourge. Though well into my third week in the city, the heat still flayed me. I had stepped out of a cold shower only an hour previously, but my shirt was already sticking to my back. My jeans were perpetually plastered to my legs for, truth be known, I was still paranoid of displaying my milky-white calves.

Not so Danny, over by the window soaking up the cross breeze, down to cut-offs, a tank top, and bare feet; while Kate, barely covered by halter-top and mini-skirt, hulked over the far end of the table. She was up to her eyes in a Jackie

Collins paperback, sweating along in empathy with its panting characters. A smoldering Parliament dangled from her lower lip while wisps of blue smoke filtered through her frizzy hair.

I hadn't noticed the silence in the first week but it had begun to oppress me. Both Danny and Mary were deliberate speakers, and neither made any effort at small talk. Kate, on the other hand, could be effusive, especially with a few bottles aboard, but she tended to wax and wane with Danny's moods. And right now, Mister Universe was silent as a mummy, his attention riveted on the street. I considered a suitable icebreaker such as, *What the fuck is so interesting down there?* But the heat sapped any initiative. I strummed a few half-hearted chords on the guitar. Despite wearing gloves on the site—to the hoots of the bogmen—my fingers had become coarse and rigid. I skimmed along a couple of minor scales then launched into "Tangled Up In Blue;" but I was stiff as day-old concrete, all at odds with the grace of the tune. I overcame a flashflood yearning to smash the guitar down on the table and instead took another beer from the fridge.

"Shit!" I nicked my finger ripping the top off the can.

Danny didn't even glance around, but Kate clucked in lifeless sympathy when she caught me sucking the warm blood. She heaved herself up from the table, ran the hot tap, and bade me hold my finger beneath the stream. When the pain got too much, I yelped. "I tell you one thing: I didn't come all the way over here to get a degree in mixing cement!"

"What do you want with no feckin' green card? A job down on Wall Street?" She drew hard on the Parliament and collapsed back on her chair.

"I was better off back home on the dole."

"The dole is history." She tossed the romance onto the table and stretched her legs wide apart. My gaze lingered a moment too long on her underwear. She snorted her indifference and stubbed out the cigarette—only gymnasts, or horny young fellahs not worth the trouble could have sex on their mind in this weather. "Besides, you're in the home of democracy—everyone starts at the bottom."

"Aye, and some of us stay there . . ." Danny wheeled from the window to face the door. We turned too, but there was no sound from the landing. Eventually, though, we heard the shuffle of some lazy footsteps on the stairs and a key jiggled in the lock; it was some moments before Mary strolled in.

She was wearing a summer dress, with a print of black roses scattered over the soft red material. Despite the heat she wore a matching cardigan, its thin sleeves rolled down to her wrists. A faint sheen of perspiration glistened on her face, and the roots of her hair were damp around the temples. Eyes glazed from the climb upstairs, she warily took in the whole room. Stepping out of her heeled sandals, she bent down to pick them up. She looked fragile as a saint in a stained-glass window.

". . . While others get squired around in yellow Cadillacs." Danny's voice was dripping with venom.

Mary slowly rose to her full height and replied, "People in glass houses shouldn't throw stones."

"Some might go so far as to call that Cadillac . . . a pimp mobile." The angrier he got, the quieter Danny spoke and the more pronounced his Belfast accent until the harshness of "pimp" diluted to a soft "pump."

"You're the last one should be talking about any kind of perversion."

"If you've got something to say, woman, then out with it."

"I know where you go on weekends, and if I hear another word out of you, everyone else will too."

The flecks in Danny's pale blue eyes were glinting, and his lips curled into an ugly sneer. He seemed about to say something but instead stalked into the bathroom and slammed the door.

Mary looked like a cat after an attack, still bristling but with one life less to spare. She rounded on me, challenging me to question her. I found it hard to hold her glassy stare and glanced at Kate for support, but she just lit another cigarette.

"What the hell's going on between you and him?"

"Oh, will you open your eyes!" Mary gestured for a cigarette, and Kate handed her the lit one. She held it between trembling fingers. The smoke arced around her as the sweat streamed down her face and onto her cardigan. Her breathing was so shallow her body quivered and the black roses seemed ready to leap off her red dress.

"You're doing a line with him, aren't you?"

"For God's sake, will you ever grow up?"

"I asked you a simple question, Mary."

She stubbed out the cigarette. "I don't owe you or anyone else an answer." She enunciated each word, then strode into the bedroom, rattling the door almost off its hinges.

I glanced over towards the bathroom where Danny was loudly pissing. "Will someone tell me what the hell's going on around here?"

Though Kate had reopened the book, she was far from reading. "Why don't you write to Dear Abby?"

"Who?"

"Jaysus! Don't you know anything?"

"I mean she'll barely touch me."

"Pity about you. I haven't had a decent rub of the relic this six months."

"And that fellah in there running around in his pelt. You can't tell me there's nothing going on between them."

"You're so far gone you only hear what you want to—so why bother?"

"I'm getting to the bottom of this bloody thing once and for all." I was striding over to the bathroom when a very distinctive rap on the front door stopped me dead.

"Oh God, it never rains but it pours," Kate groaned.

"Aren't you going to answer it?"

"Answer it yourself. I'm sick to the teeth of the whole lot of you." She took an unladylike swig of beer before reaching across the table for her lipstick.

This time the rap was a shade more impatient.

"I'll open it myself, so." I stormed over and wrestled with the police lock, then flung the door open. A Puerto Rican man, his light brown skin gleaming in the fluorescent hall glare, stared back. He had both inches and years on me, and was dressed in a tailored tan suit, his creamy silk shirt open at the neck to reveal a powerful chest. He nodded formally. My bristling hostility seemed to bounce right off him even as an innate curiosity tempered his hard black eyes. When neither welcomed nor invited in, he stepped around me and entered the room.

"*Que pasa?*" he murmured to no one in particular.

Kate blushed and shyly motioned to the bedroom door.

"*Gracias.*"

He knocked quietly and closed the door behind him.

I could almost feel the color drain from my face. I was scarcely breathing as I made it over to the fridge. I opened another beer, but it tasted flat and metallic. When I slammed the can down, the foam sprayed all over the table.

"Bitch!" I was at her door and about to grasp the handle when my resolve evaporated; instead I laid my head against the coolness of the wall.

With the toilet flushing I didn't hear the door open nor Mary behind me, until she touched my shoulder.

"I wanted to tell you, but every time I looked at you . . ." her voice trailed off.

I shook her hand away like she had the mange. She stared at it as though it was some foreign object, then whispered, "I didn't want you to think he was replacing you."

Danny emerged from the bathroom buttoning his fly and nodding grimly. "So, the cat's finally out of the bag."

"Mister Sensitivity," Kate hissed.

"You should have told him the first night instead of making an eejit of the chap."

"Oh, blame me, is it? Why didn't you tell him yourself and you working with him?"

"I make it my business never to interfere with her 'neighborhood' social set."

"You got a problem with Latinos?" The stranger stepped out of the bedroom.

"No. Just you and the other trash out in the hallway."

"Better you go back to your own country, before trash teach you a lesson in manners."

"That'll be the rock you perish on, *amigo*."

Mary stepped between them. Neither appeared to notice.

It was just the two of them now with no love lost on either side.

"Is this what you really want?" I pointed at the stranger. When she didn't answer, I shouted, "I'm talking to you, Mary."

"Give it time, Sean . . ."

I stood my ground and waited, for when push came to shove back home she usually came to me. But as the seconds ticked on, I knew this time it would be different.

"I'll see you around," I nodded to her with what little nonchalance I could muster. I packed the guitar and threw some clothes into my father's suitcase. The familiar smell of the battered leather brought tears to my eyes.

"Where are you going?" She seemed surprised.

"I'll sleep on the streets before I spend another minute in this kip." When Danny blocked my way to the door, I gave it to him, "Get out of my fucking way."

"Would you ever catch yourself on? You wouldn't last a minute out there."

"The last thing I need is your help." I tried to sidestep but he wrapped his arms around me.

"Let me go, you bastard."

"I've had enough of your wee melodrama. Shut the fuck up!" He squeezed until I gasped for breath. Then he flung me up against the wall. "Now he stays or else I go." He pointed at Kate, "And she comes with me."

"A proposal! Yes, darlin,' yes!"

"Would you ever give it a fuckin' break!" Danny glowered at her before sneering at Mary. "Or maybe, you'd like to move your pimp in here full time?"

Mary anticipated the stranger's lunge. She grabbed him by the lapels but he kept moving, bearing her before him.

There was no hint of sarcasm in Danny now, no fear either, yet every fiber of his being was fixated on the menace before him.

But Mary had gained eye contact, and the stranger came to a reluctant halt. He shook her hands from his lapels and spat at Danny, "Someday, you go too far."

"That day can't dawn soon enough for me."

They continued to stare at each other, lips pursed, eyes narrowed, and yet a deal had been struck. There was no need for further talk, but Danny had to have the last word. "Until then, *amigo.*"

"Let's go, Jesús, please?"

There was no need for Mary's concern; the Puerto Rican had already recovered. He thrust his shoulders back as though casting off a load. Yet she kept eye contact with him even as she slipped on her sandals and straightened her dress. She never even looked at me when she walked by. We watched her open the front door and pass out into the hallway. Jesús nodded to Kate. Then he closed the door and a chapter of my life behind him.

CHAPTER SEVEN

It was getting on for July and blistering even by Bronx standards. The sky low to the ground, great big gray clouds hovering over the apartment buildings, not a breath of fresh air, everything sticky and grimy, pressure dropping, temperature rising, and if the thought ever mustered enough strength to cross their fatigued minds, New Yorkers wondered what the hell were they still doing in the godforsaken city.

Down at Scutch Murphy's air-conditioned emporium, such Yank concerns rolled off the Paddies like rain off a duck's backside. In fact, it was business as usual: reading the papers and watching the videos from home, jiving to quicksteps on the jukebox, arguing over games, memories, facts, and figures, drinking every last penny on the weekend, broke, sick, and disgusted again Monday, off to gut buildings or wipe rich babies' arses—the dreams of going home to open a chipper or get married evaporating down imperial pint glasses.

You've hit concrete bottom, Paddy, and there's no way out. Forget about the fields of Athenry, or any other haggard or briar patch on the green grassy slopes of Erin! Those smashed-up, stinking streets outside are your reality now. Wrap your head around that, me auld flower!

Then again, how bad is it? You can always borrow enough for the trip home at Christmas, score some fancy threads down the Deuce, hire a flash car in Shannon, roar up to the old homestead, a New York prince returned in all his finery to wipe the tears from his mammy's face, wolf down her salutary offering of rashers, sausages, and blood-black puddings, and listen with mouth suitably agape to all the parish pump gossip of who got married, who's up the pole, who did a runner to London, and what cute local hoor is raking in the punts over in Dublin, and weren't you twice as smart in school, but sure didn't you always have too much of the auld rebellion in you; until the clock tolls the sacred hour of social benediction when you swagger off to the pub with your younger brother and his suitably impressed cider mates and get jet-lagged, shit-faced, falling down drunk, arrogantly throwing around dollars like they were going out of style and refusing to pick your change up off the counter no matter how many times the robot of a barman shoves it towards you.

Then it's off to the disco to reignite old flames and sweep them off their feet with your bullshit about Manhattan high life: the models you're datin', the food you're atin', the cars you're racin', the money you're savin'; lie bald-faced that you wouldn't be caught dead living on their rainy little island again, and repeat the same rigmarole ten nights in a row until your pockets are poor-house empty and you're sick of the very sound of your own line of shite. When truth be told, all you want is to be the way you were back when people accepted you and didn't snigger at your Yankee ways. But it's a bit late in the day to turn back now, isn't it, Paddy? You've been and gone and seen and done and stretched way beyond yourself until you've well and truly lost your way and you haven't a snowball's chance in hell of fitting in back home again.

Like a ghost, I drifted through this netherworld of twisted dreams, nightmares, memories, and hard knock stories, lurching from drink to drink, day to day, heartache to hangover, my eyes red rimmed from tears unshed—surly, morose, and ready to offend at the drop of a hat, except in the hyper-happy hysterical hour between the fourth and sixth pint when everything made sense, and if it didn't who gave a flying fuck anyway? Invariably, though, somewhere in the midst of the seventh, life would reassert itself in all its squalid splendor, slapping me back in the face with a glimpse of bald reality. It was all downhill on the eight and ninth. Forget about the tenth: a succession of violent strobe-lit blurs through which I occasionally noticed I was being saved from my bollocksy behavior by Danny's muscle, Scutch's hurley, or Kate flashing an eye or tit at some drunk about to kick my belligerent skinny little arse.

Come morning, Danny would find me already awake and staring bloodshot up at the cracks in the ceiling, the hangover simultaneously pulverizing me and slithering across my dreams like a big slimy corpse.

I rarely saw Mary. On the odd occasion our paths crossed, she merely nodded and averted her eyes, anticipating the cold shoulder I was only dying to bare. But who was I fooling? I thought about her constantly, fretted, fawned, and fantasized over her, fought running battles with the little good sense I still possessed; so that when she closed the bedroom door I had to nail my feet to the floor to prevent myself from rushing in and begging her to run off home with me on the next Aer Lingus jet.

Nor was it pride that stopped me; I would have gladly cast aside its few remaining tatters. No, it was deeper: There was something foreign about Mary, an ineffable quality well outside my frame of reference that gave me pause. Though I blamed it on Jesús, I knew it went way beyond the bastard. Mary had placed some form of psychic glass wall between us: I could see and hear her but couldn't for the life of me touch her anymore. I had noticed the moody beginnings of this rift back in Ireland, but now that it was full in my face I could no longer explain it away, much less deny it.

Jesús had not returned to the apartment, but his brown skin, gleaming teeth, and steely eyes haunted me. The lean, muscled body taunted and reminded me that this was a man forged in the smithy of New York's streets, while I was little more than a trumped-up country boy swimming up a millstream in a panic.

Nor could I obscure the fact that Mary and Jesús were a couple. I had seen their glances, their casual intimacy, the way they locked eyes; all of this was fodder for my galloping obsession, and I shamelessly reran my imaginings of them making love until it took my breath away. For I remembered only too well our own intimacies, the gentle whispered longings that now tormented me. I had little doubt that she employed these same phrases with Jesús. This humiliation perversely repelled and excited me. I couldn't shake it and hated myself for dwelling on the details.

Why did she gaze on Jesús in such a different way? It had to be something lacking within myself. She had always looked at me with interest, humor, and even a poignant dreaminess that, at its best, now seemed barely a poor first cousin of love. Even at her most passionate, she often appeared distracted, as if waiting for something to happen or someone to turn up. There had been potential rivals back home: the chalk-faced fellah from Dublin, the married man who had given her lifts home, the showband singer. But all of these had eventually dissolved into passive, if troubling, memories. Not so, Jesús! Mary and he shared a hunger that I had never been privy to, and I instinctively recognized that while she had been a girl to me, with Jesús she was a woman.

This belief rattled around my head as I careened between deadening days on the site and liquid nights on Bainbridge. Anything could set me off: a thought, a word, but especially a song blasting from the jukebox. We might have both hated the tune or the sentiment, but it could resurrect a kiss, a glance, the touch of her hand, and in a millisecond I'd be right back with her, walking on the moon like a rolling stone with every little thing gonna be all right, until the awful reality would hit me that Jesús was the one she now clung to in such moments.

I'd stop in mid-sentence with Danny, Kate, Arsehole, or Scutch, close my eyes to dam the nascent tears or glare maniacally at the gleaming bottles behind the bar. After a while, the others got used to this nonsense, even raised their eyebrows at the first rumble of Sting's bass, Dylan's snarl, or Marley's Rasta incantations.

I drank to distraction, but the alcohol didn't seem to affect me as it did the other losers who littered the watering holes of the North Bronx. Many could barely remember the original hurt, so successfully had it been doused in a stream of frigid, pissy American beer. That didn't work for me. Just when I'd crossed the merry border of intoxication, up she'd pop like some Punchless Judy, and I might as well have been flailing at windmills as trying to banish Mary in all her incarnations.

My comrades in heartscald had little such problems: Down their heads would slide onto the counter where they'd lie in grateful somnolence until Scutch would bark, "Ah, Jon-Joe, for the love of Jaysus, would you ever go home like a good man and sleep it off. Mick! Paddy! Will you put this disaster in bed before he wakes the dead with his snorin'."

Jon-Joe would be stood full square on his two front feet where he would shake free from Mick and Paddy, order one for the road, another for the ditch, and then stumble off to an empty room throbbing with memories.

Danny, as usual, was in a league of his own. Though he could drink like a fish when the mood was on him, more often than not he'd toy with a couple of beers and answer questions with polite indifference. But like many stranded on Bainbridge, he had his dark side too, and when that surfaced even the totally inebriated would give him a wide berth. His fists would clench and mood darken until you'd expect the demons to come ricocheting out of his skull; then, halfway through a bottle, he'd push back his chair, toss some bills on the counter, and stride off into the night. Sometimes, he'd go back to Decatur, sit at the table devouring Dostoyevsky, or just throw himself into his cot and lie there, eyes burning holes in the ceiling, until the room would hum to the darkness of his thoughts. Other times, he'd just disappear into the night. Yet he'd always be back by six in the morning to make sure I was ready for work.

How odd then to hear a supple guitar figure rippling from the apartment as I trudged up the stairs. Danny had rarely even mentioned music, let alone that he played so well, thumb hard and steady on a 2/4 rhythm. The melody he hummed, though lush, was cloaked with an icy regret. It leaked through the door, brave and tough, full to the gills with flawed longing.

He seemed to be searching for a particular chord and repeated the same eight bars, loss melding with a smoldering anger. When he resolved the problem, his hum matured into a surprisingly sensitive tenor, surging upwards on a chorus before curving back around again on a dominant seventh, more intense with each reading.

The words meant little to me: They were of a private nature with mentions of the neighborhood and its characters; but their actual sound, combined with the vocal intensity, thrilled me. They cracked open a door, allowing a real glimpse of the streets outside. I could touch, feel, and smell vistas I'd previously sleepwalked through. It was a far cry from hearing Dylan or Mister Cohen for the first time: I had appreciated their songs, wondered at them, and eventually mastered them. But I'd never be a part of them. Whereas, I had little doubt that someday I'd add verses and choruses of my own to Danny's.

I had to get closer. Had to discover the root of these chords and words. I eased the door open. Danny was at the kitchen table, hunched over the Yamaha, jacket draped over the chair, boots sprawled on the floor, down to undershirt and black jeans. Between his shoulders, a small circle of sweat stained the bleached white cotton. He was locking with the rhythm, totally at one with the song.

I slid in the door, unbeknownst—didn't risk closing it. As if waiting for me, Danny began the mournful verse, always taking care to sneer at any hint of melodrama, balancing story and reality on a blade honed by hard-won experience.

The melody was an odd mixture of a plaintive Irish air made lively by the suggestion of a rippling tango. He repeated it a number of times, as if fixing the arrangement in his mind. I recognized the chords: sympathetic majors for the most part, with a minor second in place of a fifth to add an air of irresolution. I could imagine a trumpet counterpoint and almost whistled it.

The muscles on Danny's back were taut. He was auditing himself, substituting an occasional word to match the tune. Where had he gained the store of understanding to write such a song? What kind of life had he lived before Decatur? Where did he spend the nights he didn't come home? Did he sleep at all, or was he just another 4 a.m. angel brooding over the anxious city? And then he halted in mid-verse.

"Eavesdroppers never hear good of themselves, Paddy."

"I didn't know you could hear . . ."

"A bull elephant would have made less noise." He laid the guitar down on the table but made a point of not turning around.

I knew the feeling well. You're singing something personal, putting every shred of your soul on the line, then someone steals up behind and sniggers at your nakedness.

"I'm sorry, I didn't mean to . . . that song is only brilliant."

When he did turn, his eyes were on a slow burn, taking me apart by the seams. Finally, he whispered, "That's OK . . . Paddy."

"The name is Sean, in case you hadn't noticed."

He stood up, his eyes deepening with distrust. A tight, unpleasant smile creased the corners of his lips.

I was tired of the constant testing of all the things I was expected to understand. "Sean! Is that so fucking hard to understand?"

When his chest began to heave from suppressed laughter, I launched forward. But he saw it coming a mile, nimbly danced aside, and clipped me on the ear.

"You fucker!" I crashed into the table, trying to get at him.

"Keep your peace, man. I'm only messin' with you."

"Messin' my arse! You meant every word of it."

"You better grab a hold of yourself or one of us might get hurt." He guffawed as a right hook of mine missed him by centimeters.

"You fuckin' IRA bastard!" I lunged forward again, this time taking him by surprise with the dint of my fury. I grabbed him around the waist and we staggered across the room. He tried to regain balance, but a Harold Robbins tome underfoot was his undoing.

We skidded backwards and went crashing down on Kate's cot. With the crunch of a wooden leg fracturing, the unmade bed collapsed beneath us. Now that we were stationary, he used his strength to roll over atop me. Pinning me to the mattress, our faces were only inches apart.

"So it's IRA bastard now, is it?"

I could feel his heart beating, taste his cigarette breath. We were too close and the intensity scared the daylights out of me.

"Who's been talkin'?" His fingers were like pincers in my arms.

"No one, I was just messin' . . ."

"I said who's been fuckin' talkin'?" His lips hovered just above mine. I tried to push him back but it was useless.

"Jesus, Mary, and Joseph." Kate's scream startled both of us.

Danny leaped backwards onto the floor.

"What have yez done to me good bed?" She strode through the open door and yanked me to my feet.

"It's nothing. I'll fix it in a minute," Danny muttered.

"You will like hell. You'll fix it right now."

"Will you don't be makin' such a commotion out of nothin', woman."

"A commotion, is it? You're straddling that young fellah and in my bed too."

"I told you I'd fix it. Now shut the fuck up!" The icy harshness ripped her. She dropped to her knees as much to hide the hurt as to examine the damage.

"Kate, I'm sorry," he said gently.

She didn't move.

"Please. Let me take a look."

Her eyes were gleaming with tears. Then she noticed me staring and, by the time she stood up, she had recovered her usual bluster. "All the nights you could have hopped in beside me. I leave the house for a couple of hours and . . ."

Danny blushed and gathered a pile of books to take the place of the broken leg.

"And as for you, young fellah," she said, "you seem to have gotten over your heartbreak in a hurry?"

"It wasn't anything like you think it was."

"No?" She stood hands on hips, looking me dead in the eye. "Then what exactly were the two of you doing on top of each other, pray tell me?"

"It was nothin'—just a misunderstanding over a song."

"A song?"

"Yeah, and it was only brilliant." I pointed at the window. "All about out there."

"You mean that auld yoke about the Puerto Ricans? He never shut up with it until he did us all a favor and flogged his guitar."

"There, that should hold you up." Danny sat down hard on the bed. "I'll bring home a lump of wood tomorrow and fashion a new leg for you." Then he smiled. "But I wouldn't be getting up to any gymnastics in the meanwhile."

"Fat chance." She felt better at the resumption of their old banter. But when I picked up the guitar and played the D to G major seventh intro, she knew well that neither of us were paying her any heed.

"F sharp minor, E minor, A seventh," Danny ordered.

"Where did you get that from?" The chord sequence was deceptively simple and would have gained little traction back in damp and windy Ireland; yet, its restrained melancholia made perfect sense in the overheated clutter of the Bronx apartment.

"It's nothin' out of the ordinary."

"It has a nice feel though."

"Aye, it's its own thing. Resolve it on an E major, Sean."

It was the first time he'd used my name. The Northern burr added an odd urgency. I glanced up, but he hadn't noticed; his eyes were far away, reliving some memory he hadn't the least intention of sharing.

When the chorus finished and wheeled back to the intro, he beat an accompanying tattoo on the table. I finally relaxed into the flow of the chords, caressing them, stretching them beyond the ordered beat, sliding and shifting them around the pocket.

"Where did you get those words?"

He'd gone over to the window and was lighting a cigarette. He took a long drag and let the smoke curl out his nose. "I keep my eyes open."

But something had changed with the onset of the memory. He stared stonily ahead, all prickly diffidence again. Then he turned on the two of us, the old arrogance back in spades. "Not like the rest of you, getting cricks in your necks from looking back at Ireland."

"I'm not lookin' anywhere."

"You can't even see beyond your nose, boy."

"Meaning?"

"When you're not sniveling over your Blessed Virgin Mary, you're down the pub bawlin' in your beer with all the other plastic Paddies."

"You leave her out of this."

"Why should I? You obviously can't."

"Because she's none of your business."

"That one is everyone's business," he laughed bitterly, "especially those without green cards. She'll have us all back in Ireland if we don't keep an eye on her."

"She's mine, you hear me? I'll sort her out in my own way."

"You've a lot of growing up to do, Paddy."

"Sean to you."

A vein in his forehead was pumping overtime. "You may be a long way from home, kid, but she's even further."

"What's that supposed to mean?"

He looked to Kate for support, but she was conveniently smoothing out the pages of her squashed Harold Robbins.

"I mean, what did you expect her to do—wear a chastity belt?" he barked.

"I expected her to have the decency to tell me, instead of lettin' me come all the way over here to make a feckin' eejit of meself."

"You'd have come anyway."

"I would in my bollocks! I had young ones goin' mad for me over there."

"And was there any one of them with the beatings of her?"

"At least I'd be back with me own, not stuck in this madhouse of a fuckin' city."

"Your own won't be half what you think they are by the time you get back—if you ever do."

"Oh, I'm goin' back all right. And it won't be long, you mark my words."

He snatched the guitar from me. The top E had flattened; he tuned it as he spoke. "Those who have sense let time do the healing. The rest of us walk through walls and hope to Christ we come out the far side standing."

"Yeah, yeah, yeah!"

"If you're even half the man I think you are, you'll catch on soon enough, Paddy." He eyeballed me, reaming me, challenging me, before he shrugged, "But then again, maybe you're just another gobshite."

"Why don't you leave me the fuck alone?"

"Sometimes I ask myself the same question." He struck a sustained seventh and let it hang unresolved.

Kate closed the Harold Robbins and coughed as the chord died away. Then she strode over to the bathroom and ran a tap. The water spluttered at first, then roared into the sink.

"You're not the first Paddy to be dumped for a pair of black eyes." He hit a diminished chord and slapped at the strings to dim the sound of the running water.

"I may have to listen to your sermons on the job, but not around here." I had enough of his guff and headed for the door. "Put that guitar back in its case when you're finished with it."

"Oh now, you're a great wee man for the grand gesture, aren't you."

"Why don't you just go back to reading your James fucking Connolly?"

He punched his fist in mock solidarity with the socialist staring down from above the fireplace. "Listen, you came over here with a dream, and she's not part of it anymore. Now grow up and stop pityin' yourself!"

He dug into the tune again, this time bending the strings bluesily, a smoldering anger informing every note.

I longed to lose myself in the cool, comforting anonymity of the pub. But the song had me snared. I couldn't say the same for the singer. I wasn't even sure I liked him—a bossy bloody know-it-all Northern bastard at the best of times. But there was something about him that made me see things in a different way.

"You know . . . maybe, we should start something."

"What you got in mind, sailor?" he lisped.

"A band."

"I already tried the Paddy Rock thing down the Village. They found it . . . vaguely quaint but musically and intellectually insubstantial." He mimicked a pompous *Voice* critic.

"I mean right here—on Bainbridge."

"You mean Braindamage."

"Whatever you want to call it. Suppose we were to write about the Paddies and Marys up here—like your song except from an Irish angle?"

"Oh God, it's like listening to Mick and Keith." Kate emerged from the bathroom. She had taken off her top and was wearing only a bra with her skirt. I found it hard to drag my eyes from her cleavage. She had just splashed cold water on her throat, and the drops gleamed on her breastbone.

"We should be writing about the likes of her and the lads on the site. They'd eat it up."

"I wouldn't count on it. They're rather sensitive souls."

Kate pouted, then stuck her breasts out at him. "Oh now, you wouldn't believe the things I'd do for a Barry White from Belfast moanin' at me."

"Will you give my head some peace, woman!"

"Give me that guitar!" I swept a couple of empty cans off my journal and flicked the pages until I found the verses I was looking for. I knew I only had one shot to impress him. It had to be right. I ran the words silently against the chords and the traditional melody I'd been thinking of, then I let it rip. The song concerned a construction worker and a nanny sizing each other up in a pub. The verse was all over the place but the chorus locked like a fist in a glove.

"What do you think?"

He shrugged.

"It couldn't miss. I'm tellin' you."

Kate watched intently from her cot.

"Maybe," he said.

"So you'll do it?"

"I said maybe . . . But I've sweet damn all time for messing around. Do you hear me?"

"I won't let you down, man, I promise."

He lit a cigarette and strolled over to the window. "We'll see about that."

But his attention was once more on the street.

CHAPTER EIGHT

"**W**ill you pull yourself together, for fuck's sake!" His exasperation slit through the smoke and murmur of impatient conversation.

"I'm all right," I hissed back and bent down to recheck the volume on my amplifier. I even fiddled one more time with the bass and treble—anything but look out at what was glowering back at me.

And then Danny was spitting in my ear: "Listen, Paddy, just play the fucking chords—the songs will look after themselves!"

Not to put too fine a point on it, I was scared out of my shagging wits. And what chancer wouldn't be? Up on stage in the holy of holies itself, the Olympia Ballroom, pride of Kingsbridge and Jerome; a Mecca unto which every warrior of the scaffold hied and hithered from big skied Inwood, bounteous Bay Ridge, and hard assed Woodside, not to mention all points of the compass north of Fordham Road beyond the burgh of Yonkers, even up unto well-heeled Westchester itself. It was no rarity either to see Paddies from the swamps of Jersey, leafy Connecticut, or wild and wooly Upstate tripping the light fantastic across its slithery boards.

And though it was only a lowly Monday night, who cared that the advertised band from Mayo had failed to make it through Immigration? The joint was jammed to the rafters, and we, nameless and lacking a rehearsal, were there to rock their culchie world.

With two quick phone calls and some illicit promises, Danny had cobbled together an outfit consisting of him and me out front on guitars, flanked by Bugs Delaney on bass. Meanwhile, Ringo Shiggins, the hottest drummer on the avenue, glared disapprovingly at our three posteriors from behind his Ray-Bans, his mood having been honed to a refined edginess by a couple of lines of Colombia's purest. The fact that I had never even met either of these two hired guns did not appear to present a problem for the other three. Shiggins, in fact, had as yet to acknowledge my presence.

With a cryptic command to "watch me arse for the groove and me foot for the time," Danny had already led us through an hour's worth of standards. Ringo's jittery chin jutted upwards at such an angle that it was unlikely he could even see Danny's neck, let alone his backside or boot; and how Bugs could fathom groove or tempo at the rate he was murdering Heinekens, only God in his wisdom could ascertain.

I was the problem, no ifs, buts, or maybes. This was no singalong down in Begley's pub. The Olympia was the real deal—the top rung of the Paddy-ladder in New York City— and I had messed up the lyrics of "Rave On." Not that Buddy Holly up in high heaven or any of the patrons gave a flying fuck if I had recited the telephone book backwards rather than the hallowed words; no, the trouble was, I had frozen stiff as a board and stranded the assembled high kickers on the dance floor.

"Drink the fuckin' thing!" Danny was already counting

into "Peggy Sue" as Bugs thrust an opened hip flask in my direction.

The *poitín* tasted like a cross between rusty water and paraffin oil. It lacerated my throat on its madcap gallop down to the tips of my toenails. My stomach heaved, my hands began to sweat, and the room suddenly tumbled head over heels into strobe lights glancing, mirror balls romancing, plastic Paddies blinking, *céad míle fáiltes* winking on gallons of sparkling mascara daubed on the eyelids of nurses and nannies—Marys, Kates, and Annies—dolled up and drinking, dressed to kill, and looking for romance, or at least, a chance to dance with neighbors from Mayo, Kerry, and Donegal, Leitrim, Fermanagh, and Tyrone; while over at the bar, the lads sized up these beauties in all their glossy tonnage like so many heifers at a fair. A full day's hard slogging under their belts, but now freshly shaved and showered, already sloshed from sun and six-pack, these culchie Valentinos primed themselves for amorous encounters somewhere, anywhere, the far side of a platonic nature.

One of their number—a brawny blaggard from west of the Shannon, fists like hams, his shirt Coors-stained, tie askew, lack of socks, shoes scuffed, and a sudden flash fire blazing in his lobelia-tinted eyes—hectored the others: "Ah, drink up, for the love of Christ, will yez, lads! Just one more round of pints and shots, then c'mon now, boys, let's hit the boards, no better men, sweep them biddies off their feet! Straighten up now, Tom, will you, don't be makin' a show of yourself fallin' all over the place in front of everyone. Hurry up, Séamus, like a good man, and drain the fuckin' thing for the sake of Jaysus and His Holy Mother. Come on, lads, get your mickeys in motion, foot on the clutch, and put

her in gear before every last woman in the place is up to her
you-know-what in Dublin Jackeens, not to mention fawnin'
all over them greasy Albanians, and watch out for a knife in
the gut, I'm warnin' you, young fellah! How come they let
them shower of oily spics in a good Irish establishment
anyway? Ah, for fuck's sake, Mick, will you get up off the
floor and stop makin' a hunt of yourself! If you were back
home lampin' rabbits, there'd be no stoppin' you! Isn't the
night half over already, not a biddy taken down, and look at
the sorry state of you!"

Then murdering great big flat pissy pints of Bud and
Coors and shuddering from shots of rock-solid Presbyterian
Bushmills, the lads troop out on to the dance floor to a beat
they've jived to from Oughterard to Kiltimagh, Clifden to
Ballyvaughan. But it's too late, baby, just too late, for Peggy
Sue has skittered off home to Abilene, and we've already
segued somewhat clumsily into the reggae *riddim* of one of
Marley's magical mysteries. The Paddies are skewered
sideways by the reverbed crack of Shiggins' snare, brassy and
bold as a jilted biddy's slap in the face. This is not what the
doctor ordered and far from what they paid good hard-earned
dollars for! And how in the name of Our Lady of Knock did
it come to pass that decent Irish lads have to put up with
the roars and brazen yelps of a crowd of bowsies that should
never have been allowed up on that bandstand in the first
feckin' place?

But Danny had their number. As a band we might have
been fresh out of the oven, but he knew the rules and was
calling the songs in streamlined sets. Three fast so the ladies
could throw shapes and preen like so many fillies in a
paddock, followed by three slows for the lads to stagger over

and plaster big greasy third-trimester beer bellies against them. This familiar regimen kept the patrons occupied, if less than ecstatic about our choice of material and general cohesion. As soon as Danny sensed the mood deteriorating, he'd turn the like of "Hide Your Love Away" into an exaggerated old time waltz or whip "Satisfaction" into a quickstep that would have had the Glimmer Twins scratching their horny heads and heading for the hills.

At the corner of the bar, Arsehole watched our every move as though he were beholding the second coming. When we made a balls of "Suffragette City" or massacred "Into The Mystic," he raised his shades as though to reassure himself that he was indeed hearing such wonders in the sheet-rocked confines of the Olympia. Having confirmed this impossibility, he would then applaud like his life depended on it. And, when Danny and I sang my tune about the nannies and the lads on the site, he arose from his stool and roared "Bravo!" as though he were in evening dress at La Scala rather than jeans and tank top in a one-storied firetrap beneath the El on Jerome Avenue.

But eventually both steam and repertoire ran low and, in the break that followed, a low violent murmuring began to mature and surge towards the stage. Instead of countering with a chestnut, Danny launched into a Curtis Mayfield style vamp. I recognized "Freedom" instantly, for he had been consumed with this new tune back in the apartment. The rhythm was beyond my league. I just didn't have the chops to add anything but brakes to its skittering tempo. Luckily, it only took Ringo and Bugsy seconds to catch him and swing along with the funky meter; but the change was too drastic and the crowd scattered to the far walls—a capital offence in a ballroom of the wild Northwest Bronx.

And Danny knew full well he had blown it. He had eased
into the groove in liquid sixteens across the top of his wah-
wah pedal; but as the dancers fled and the floorboards became
more and more visible, he began to hammer like a navvy on
the one, dissipating all the Mayfield magic. The Funk fought
back, turning wooden and stiff, but he hung on like a terrier,
worrying and snapping at its heels. To add insult to injury,
the words fled him too, and he was reduced to bawling out
the title as if stuck in the quicksand of some strangled mantra.

Shiggins did his best to create space; he laid off the snare,
breaking the kick down to two quick adjacent eights at the
top of the beat and skimming sixteenths across the high hat
like quantized rain on a galvanized roof. Bugs caught the
drummer's design and locked in reggae style, fashioning a
sympathetic pattern by hitting the big note when it made
sense, laying off when it didn't. But Danny wanted neither
part nor parcel of some funky breakdown. He was back on
the rainy streets of West Belfast, pissed off and pugnacious,
ready for a rumble, him and him alone against the world.
And the world was ready and waiting when we stopped dead
on Shiggins' count of four.

"Get the fuck out of here with yer nigger music!" A
Galway accent ripped across the sudden silence, and many
a head nodded in agreement. Danny was bending down to
pick up his pint, the sweat dripping all over his new Strat.
He froze and the room iced over with him before he arose
slowly. I glanced around at Shiggins, coiled tight as a trigger,
his drumsticks clasped like missiles in his fists.

Danny scanned the room for the voice. A couple of
Tyrone boys from the site gave one another the nod. The Big
Fellah might be a first-class bollocks, but he would not stand

alone against a shower of Free State bastards. There was a ripple, then a general movement, as disinterested parties cleared the floor and sides were taken amongst those remaining. A lone bouncer at the door stepped forward, but seeing no reinforcements, thought better of it. The room cleaved seamlessly into a North–South divide. Antrim, Fermanagh, and Tyrone shifted to one side; Galway, Kerry, and Mayo took their measure from the other.

Danny had just stepped up to the microphone when I felt the sting of a flung drumstick in the back of my leg. Shiggins and Bugs must have been communicating silently, for at a crash on the snare the bass player dug into a plectrumed intro of "Brown Eyed Girl." Kate took to the floor with one of Danny's Northern crew. Her breasts bounced in time to the syncopated bass and kick drum as I caught the rhythm and called out, "Hey where did we go . . ." A couple of pairs of nannies began jiving, and by the end of the first chorus the boards of the Olympia were again black with dancers. Across the divide, the would-be combatants eyed each other, a rumble still a concrete possibility. But the call of booze and the chance of a stray ride proved stronger. Besides, it was still a Monday; there'd be other nights to sort out the rights and wrongs of this particular matter.

Danny gazed on defiantly. He had primed himself for combat and now, like a boxer with a bout postponed, he was all edge and denied anticipation. He wiped the rivulets of sweat off his guitar then deliberately thrashed the solo, much like Hendrix might have done when distracted by a toothache.

It was a long sullen night that often veered towards violence before the strobes ceased and the mirror ball froze.

Near three o'clock, we played the Irish National Anthem, and the remains of the crowd stood to attention. Back home, this duty had been dispatched perfunctorily and listened to with all the attention of the hung-over lads slouched against the door at late mass on a Sunday. To the Northerners present, however, the song was an affirmation of their right to a united Ireland. Eyes glowed and fists clenched when Danny vehemently sang

Sinne Fianna Fáil
Atá fé gheall ag Éirinn,
Buíon dár slua
Thar toinn do ráinigh chugainn . . .

and nary a whisper was hazarded by those of us from the South who cared little about such aspirations.

Shiggins cleaned his sticks, persnickety as a master butcher with his cleavers. He cast me the barest of nods. I had apparently passed his scrupulous muster, though he left little doubt that I had a long way to go before gaining real acceptance. Bugsy was already at the bar, murdering a large Jameson's, oblivion now beckoning.

Danny packed his chords and laid the sacred Stratocaster in its case, all accomplished in the same methodical manner that he packed his tools on the site. No praise, no admonishments, just move on inexorably towards a goal that he alone was privy to. I was exhausted and could have handled a little pat on the back; but seeing none was forthcoming, I leaned against the stage, sucked on my beer, and watched the few stragglers make peace with the fact that they would once more sleep alone. The nannies and nurses had long departed, taking with them any surfeit of glamour. Now, in the cruel glare of the house lights, the Olympia was revealed for what it really was: four sheet-rocked walls and a bare wooden floor strewn with bottles, glasses, and fag butts, and morning fast approaching.

Shiggins had joined Bugsy at the bar. There they waited for their pay: one thin as a rake and iced to the eyebrows; the other jowly from beer, his good looks now barely a memory. The drummer, oiled and coiffed, was dressed head to toe in forty shades of black; the bass player in proletarian denim swayed this way and that, his gut spilling out over his tightened belt. I was about to head over to them when a rising hubbub at the far end of the room caught my attention. Then above it, the shrill voice of a lady exhorting one of a group of gentlemen to, "Go on now, Patsy, put them pack of cunts in their places."

"No better fuckin' man!" one of them called back as he ambled towards the stage. Danny must have seen him approaching, for he purposely bent over to unplug his amp.

Patsy resembled the product of a night's fornication between a bandy-legged jockey and an unsuspecting jennet; a pop-eyed, ferret-faced little bastard. His crowning glory, a coal-black toupee, would have done credit to Elvis on a bad-hair day. The raven rug perched precariously atop a skeletal head sporting a mouth full of teeth, the like of which could have done double duty in a cemetery. These yellow tombstones were now gleaming dully under the houselights as he swaggered towards us, well the worse for a full night's intake of Powers whiskey. He wore the standard garb of every gombeen man who'd made and held on to a couple of thousand dollars: a checkered sports jacket, fawn trousers, white shirt, plaid tie, and highly polished brown shoes, all designed to show the boys back in the bog just how well he was doing over in the good old US of A. His companions followed at a respectful distance, yet more than eager to partake of the sport about to transpire.

"Are youse fuckin' serious?" he inquired of Danny's bent-over arse. I, apparently, was not deemed worthy of such august consideration.

Danny did not hazard an answer, intrigued as he was with the settings of his amplifier.

"Yez call that music?"

Although he had none of the vocal richness, there was something about his equine features that reminded me of Mister Ed. Because his entourage was grinning broadly, I allowed myself a smile at the memory of my father's favorite TV character.

"What the hell are you laughin' at?" He rounded on me.

"Go fuck yourself!" I replied.

"You shouldn't have said that, young fellah," Patsy's lady friend sniggered.

"Why not?"

"Because he's Patsy 'Alowishus' Murphy," she informed me in breathless tones that suggested it was only a matter of time before this hallowed personage once again took his place at the right hand side of his Father in heaven.

"I don't care if he's the fuckin' Shah of Iran."

"Well you should," she exploded hyena-like, "'cause he owns the feckin' place."

Patsy did a little jig of triumph when he saw my jaw drop. He then readdressed Danny's arse. "That shite yez were playin' might suit a pack of boogaloos! But, for your information, this is Jerome Avenue, not the middle of Harlem."

This remark caused the lady friend to double over with mirth; but it also initiated a serious case of the hiccups.

Danny rose from his crouch. With the briefest of nods, he signaled that I should button my lip before turning his full attention to the business at hand. Patsy leered back, never a good tactic with Danny, who could suck in anything you cared to throw at him and spit it right back at you. His look was cold and distant, but there was something in it of the hawk poised in mid-air awaiting the next movement of the rabbit.

Patsy betrayed a moment of foreboding, but the night's whiskey had clouded his native canniness. With an effort, he wrenched himself away from Danny's gaze and sneered at me, "I don't know who you are, young fellah, but I'd be more careful about your choice of partners. Right, Danny . . . boy?"

He lingered on the last word and stretched it out malignantly. Danny took a toothpick from his pocket and with great deliberation worked it between his front teeth. When he finally flicked it to one side, we all followed its motion across the boards of the dance floor.

"You know what, Patsy?" he smiled. "Someday I'm going to knock those false teeth of yours right through that second-hand toupee."

Patsy's lady friend hiccupped and her stomach rumbled in sympathy. "Excuse me."

"Shut up, you fuckin' cow." Patsy's hand involuntarily rose to his head, making sure that the piece was intact; then, one by one, he glared savagely at his posse. Fortified that no one was smirking, he swung back at Danny, "Go on, get out of here now."

Danny shrugged and turned to his amplifier. This must

have given Patsy further courage for he sneered, "I know all about you and your carry-on."

I didn't see it coming. One instant, he grasped Patsy by the throat, the next he had him spread-eagled over a table. Bottles and glasses smashed under the owner's bony behind, his bandy legs twitched high in the air. The toupee hung down around his ears, and he alternated between little squeals and long gasping wheezes.

None of the entourage dared intervene. Nor did I, until a sound brought me back to a Christmas Eve when I had come upon my father choking a turkey. Right before its neck broke, there was one last awful rattle of breath. I grabbed Danny around the waist.

"For fuck's sake, you're killing him!"

I might as well have been talking to the wall. He merely swiveled his hips away from me. I moved to the other side and hunched him full on the shoulder. It bounced off him harmlessly, but I caught a glimpse of Patsy's miserable little face turning purple. His beady eyes were fit to pop out of their sockets, the fear of God coursing through him.

"What are you doing?" I yelled.

But Danny's eyes, though flecked with mica, were blank and implacable. I looked around panic-stricken. The lady friend caught my glance and took a step forward, her hand thrust out; she was far from hiccupping now.

Danny pulled Patsy closer, the better to tighten his grip. There was an awful scraping sound as the bony butt kneaded into the glass and wood. I threw myself at Danny. He still paid me no mind, but I managed to grab him around the shoulders and swung him a couple of inches towards me. Then I kneed him in the balls.

He jack-knifed backwards and his fingers unclenched.
Patsy didn't move—just lay there, staring at the ceiling, the
froth seething on his lips. His tie had tightened like a noose;
I reached out to loosen it and didn't see Danny coming at
me. The punch would have taken half of my head off, if he
hadn't slipped in the spilt beer. Instead it glanced off my
skull. The stars did a tango before my eyes, and I keeled
backwards across the table, my fingers still on Patsy's tie,
dragging both him and his toupee in my wake.

I don't know how that rickety table held the both of us.
Luckily for me, most of the bottles and glasses had already
spilled off. Patsy was gurgling an act of contrition as my
vision cleared to find Danny towering above me, a Heineken
bottle in his upraised fist.

"Danny, it's me!"

But there was no life in his eyes.

"It's Sean, for fuck's sake!"

I didn't dare move. The bottle was still in striking
position, and I'd never been as scared. Patsy was mumbling
away to an impressive array of saints and virgins like some
prayer factory on overtime. It seemed an eternity before
Danny laid down the Heineken bottle and ran his fingers
through his hair. In the throes of divine supplication, Patsy
now seemed oblivious to him, inching painfully off the table
onto a chair, then down on all fours to the ground.

I lay there afraid to move until the life came back into
Danny's eyes. He reached out and pulled me to my feet as
if I had merely slipped in wet cement on the site. Not a
word of apology—though he did take note of Patsy's moans
and cocked his head for a better view. Almost as an
afterthought, he delivered a fairly serious kick in the behind

to aid him on his way, and without another word, picked up guitar and amp, and headed for the door. The entourage hopped to one side. He paid them no heed, merely nodded in a business like manner to Shiggins and Bugsy. All eyes watched the door close behind him.

Bald-headed and bedraggled, toupee in his fist, his arse cut and bleeding, Patsy crawled off towards the bar. His lady friend, now sober as a judge, reached down to help him, but he spat out a hoarse curse and continued on his way. The thought crossed my mind that I should solicit him for our pay, but the moment didn't seem quite opportune.

The jukebox must have been on some kind of timer, for Keith's inappropriate chords suddenly blasted forth at full volume. Patsy was being helped towards his office as I packed up and hurried for the door to Mick emoting "When the Whip Comes Down."

Up the block, Danny leaned against a street lamp. He was firing up a joint already, safely back behind his shades. My hand was still shaking when I took the offered toke. A cop car cleared the corner of Kingsbridge on two wheels, its siren screaming. We idly watched it speed off under the El, lights flashing and waited for the accompanying sound of a fire engine. There was no further squeal of brakes or clang of simulated bells, however—nothing but a throbbing silence broken only by the hum of gypsy cabs and the babble of voices as people entered and left the Greek diner.

I sucked in another deep drag and handed back the joint. "You could have killed him."

Danny blew smoke after the flashing lights. The vein had stopped throbbing in his temple. He seemed composed, though he did feign some surprise when I refused the joint. For my own part, I was trying to put two and two together and knew that, given the circumstances, an excess of grass would bring the total way beyond my usual five.

"I don't suppose they'll want us back next week," I ventured.

Danny ground the roach beneath his foot. The silence really got to me. Maybe where he came from stranglings were two a penny, but they were few and far between in my neck of the woods.

"You could have killed him."

"Nah, I was only muckin' around."

"He was fucking choking, man!"

For a moment he studied me, curious about my concern.

"He's nothin' but a piece of shite." He dismissed the incident, barely a trace of emotion in his voice and, without knowing exactly why, I could tell that this wasn't the first time he'd come close to taking a life. It was a sobering thought, and I didn't feel very good about it, standing there in the bloody Bronx on a humid Tuesday morning.

He could tell I had some major questions on my mind and he waited patiently. But in the end all I could do was whine, "What the hell are we goin' to do?"

"Do?" For once he appeared puzzled. "Have you learned sweet fuck all in the past few months?"

He spat on the ground and pushed the Bryan Ferry cow's lick out of his eyes. "Jaysus, you're as thick as a yard of good cement."

"I mean for gigs like?"

"Is that all you're worried about?"

"No, but it's a start."

"You do what you like, Paddy, but I'm not lettin' that shower of bastards run my life."

"It's only music, Danny."

"No! It's life, and don't you ever forget it. The minute you start thinkin' like them, it's over."

He glanced at his watch, then, without a word, strode off, swinging the amp and guitar like they were two parcels of feathers. Just as he was about to round the Greek's corner, he halted and yelled back, "Eyes on the prize, boy!"

Some of the diner patrons pointed at him through the window, but he ignored them. "You hear me," he roared. "Always eyes on the prize."

And with that he was gone. I picked up my gear and ran after him.

CHAPTER NINE

I was drinking myself silly. No two ways about that. It was also a rare evening there wasn't a bag of reefer on the kitchen table. I wasn't sure what straight was anymore, not that anyone paid much attention except James Connolly glaring down from above the mantelpiece, the neon sign from the bodega kindling some new-found fire in his revolutionary eyes. One night I lost it and roared back, "A pity about you!"

But not a feather did it raise upon him. The old bastard was obviously made of stern stuff, for he just kept right on staring.

I could have handled long-term obliteration; that would have been little problem. Instead, I'd come to on the couch in the pre-dawn darkness, my head pounding like the hammers of hell. As hard as I tried to banish Mary from my skull, it was a losing battle. She was locked in there for the long haul, rent paid, door slammed, key tossed in the depths of the slimy Bronx River.

If that wasn't bad enough, there was an eeriness lurking about the apartment that inevitably made its presence known around the second or third joint. It was hard to nail down, but I could sense it, even smell it and, once or twice, it brushed by my face scaring the living daylights out of me.

Connolly could feel it too. I could tell even though he always
kept his superior, socialistic, straight face.

I tried to rationalize what Mary had done to me, but it
was hard to put into any kind of perspective. What I could
do was focus on all the little mysteries back in Ireland. Her
disappearances, the strangers who came and went, her shifting
moods and silences, all began to weave themselves into a
threadbare cloak of deceit. I could have kicked myself for my
fawning faith in her. Now all the knowing smiles and leering
remarks down at Begley's fell into place. The whole town must
have been laughing at me. And what were they thinking now,
lounging over their pints, sneering at my predicament that,
no doubt, was being relayed back in minute detail on the
Paddy bush telegraph? My face would flush from
mortification in the dawn light, and it was almost a blessing
when Danny would arise and proclaim that we had "another
day above ground" to be grateful for.

Yet, unbeknownst, I was getting tougher and leaner,
physically at any rate. All trace of baby fat had been flayed
off my hide, and I was as mean and stringy as a tinker's
mongrel bitch. Emotionally, I was still fit to be hung out with
the washing; but I had finally hit bottom. The drink was the
only thing keeping me going, but even that was wearing thin
with its endless mornings after. I could see no light at the
end of the tunnel. Most times, I couldn't even see the bloody
tunnel itself.

Then one day I awoke to the mother and father of all
hangovers. The bloody thing just wouldn't give up. I'd been
so out of it on the subway downtown I'd even lost my hat,
and all through the morning the sun beat like the hammers
of hell on my face. I felt sick and faint and, instead of bending

to and mixing the gray dust, I often had to lean on the shovel
for support. Danny had noticed me stagger just after lunch
and told me to feck off home. When I informed him what
he could do with his pity, he got all narky and roared, "I told
you—go! The last thing Dennehy needs is another amateur
tumblin' off the scaffold."

I didn't have the stomach to argue with him, and besides
I knew he'd mark me down for a full day. I was seeing double
getting on the train but found a seat and recovered somewhat
in the air-conditioning. By the time we got to the Bronx, I
was on the mend and bought a couple of quarts to ease me
through the afternoon. A bit of shut-eye would sort me out,
I figured, and headed up the darkened stairs. I had little fear
of junkies anymore and, in my idyllic frame of mind, I'd
have welcomed a dust-up with Squint Eye.

I smelled it first on our landing. It reminded me of the
incense on evenings back home in the Franciscan chapel
when the boy and his mother received benediction from the
raised monstrance. When I opened the hall door, I heard
voices from Mary's bedroom. With that, all rosy memories
took a back seat. He was back. I couldn't face any more
humiliation and had my hand on the doorknob to beat a
retreat, when the spleen took control: *This is bullshit. I'm
paying rent here too.* Or more likely, in my refined masochism,
I wanted my face rubbed in it all over again.

The bedroom door was slightly ajar. I eased it open and
stepped into a hothouse. The curtains were drawn; all was
dark except for the anemic flutter of a candle close to
guttering, and even that was obscured behind a scrim of
frankincense. She was alone; yet I was certain I'd heard voices.
Even more surprising, she was on her knees in front of the

little plaster statue of Our Lady that had once graced the kitchen alcove. I'd never seen her pray before. Or was it prayer? I was trying to identify the words when she noticed me. Her eyes, large and glassy, instantly narrowed. She shoved something under the bed and hissed, "Get out!"

Then she was on her feet and shrieking, "How dare you spy on me?"

At my father's insistence, I had once bagged some wild kittens for drowning. The mother cat returned unexpectedly and flew at me as I plucked the last one from its nest. Mary's rage had much the same quality. When I reeled out, she slammed the door. With my head spinning, I sank down onto the couch, drained a quart of beer, then began another.

I awoke to find her staring down at me. She reached out to touch my face, though not in affection, more like reassurance. Her hair was wet and uncombed, her shirt and sleeves damp. She must have stuck her head under the tap. She looked lost and disconnected. I was about to reach out but there was no need. She sank down beside me, put her face in her hands, and cried softly.

I watched her shoulders barely heaving. My head was on fire, a thin shaft of pain drilling away behind my eyes. I wanted to comfort her but no longer knew how. And so I watched and waited.

The sobbing stopped. Something had caught her attention. I followed her eyes, but all I could make out were some shadows playing on the wall. A warm breeze was stirring the dusty white curtains; it even reached us on the couch, cutting its way through the humidity that blanketed the room. At every footstep in the hallway, her eyes would dart over to the door. I couldn't be certain she even knew I was there. Yet, when she spoke, it was in her old deliberate manner. "Do you have it inside you to forgive me, Sean?"

Oh, I did. And I had to almost bite my tongue from screaming it. Just that one simple question and all the weeks of pain and despair dissolved. Or did they? Some nagging little ache of caution remained. Maybe I was finally catching on to myself?

What was she thinking? I couldn't read her anymore, and I wondered if I'd always been humbugging myself; yet I knew she only had to look in my eyes and the game would be up. I needn't have worried. Her attention had turned to the window where the curtains were now flapping in the gathering breeze. Was she aware of the power she had over me? Or had she become so used to her dominance that she could turn it on and off like a tap?

I could feel myself slipping back towards her. I had to dig my nails into the palm of my hand to prevent myself from touching her. But I wouldn't give. I'd never let her have that sway over me again.

Did she know what I was thinking, for she laid the tips of her fingers on my fist? Her face was at its palest and streaked with tears; it was thinner than I'd ever noticed. A wisp of damp hair had strayed down over her lips. Back home, she would never have allowed that, always fussing with it, bemoaning its errant ways. She looked fragile as one of my mother's Dresden figurines, but I could sense a strange, new inner hardness, and I was wary of her.

She pried her fingers into my fist and made me unclench. But I wouldn't look directly at her.

"Sean, no matter what you think . . ."

"I don't think anything."

"I didn't want to do this to you."

"But you're doing it, right?"

She looked down at our two hands intertwined. I followed her eyes. It all seemed so natural—the touch, feel, shape, look—just like it used to be back home. Yet so much had happened between us. I wanted to snatch my hand away, but I only had strength enough for the bitterness in my voice. Besides, if I let go, she might stand up and walk away, and I couldn't bear that.

"It's not as simple as that," she sighed.

"Yeah . . ."

Someone passed in the hall. She turned abruptly. The footsteps took a long time to die out.

"I still have feelings for you."

I knew she did, though I had no idea what they were anymore. Had I ever known? Still, I could barely resist taking her in my arms and reassuring her that everything was going to be all right.

"I just want you to know." She swept back the offending strand of hair.

For some reason, that one small action unleashed all the hurt and anger. I pushed her aside and stood up. "What the hell are you doing with yourself, Mary?"

"What do you mean?"

"I mean, look at you!"

"You didn't used to be so judgmental."

"I didn't used to be so stupid."

"Don't get hard, Sean."

"What do you expect me to be?"

"You have every right to feel this way, but . . ."

"Yeah."

"I know I could have handled it better. But it's not just like it seems."

"Don't give me that shite! I mean, what are they going to say about you back in Ireland?"

"That I'm going out with a spic?"

"Well, he's not exactly one of the lads down the pub, is he?"

"Would that have made it better?"

I sank back down on the couch. I couldn't bear to think of her with anyone else, whispering the things she used to whisper to me. "Nothing makes it better."

She put her hand on my forehead. She always knew exactly where I hurt. If we'd been in bed, she would have run her fingers across my heart. "There are things . . . that you don't understand."

"We don't belong here, Mary. Let's go home."

The breeze had stopped, the curtains were still, and the shadows no longer played on the wall.

"Ireland's gone, Sean."

"What's that supposed to mean?"

She looked at me with an odd mixture of kindness and concern, all the while unclenching my fist. Then she held my fingers to her lips. "I do care about you. Whatever happens, don't ever forget that."

I buried my head in her damp hair. Despite the dousing, it smelled of frankincense and a hint of sweat. I didn't care—just to have her in my arms again, the warmth and familiarity, the perfect shape of her body, the way it molded exactly with mine. She nestled there but was already pulling away before the distinctive knock. I hadn't heard a footstep. The bastard must have crept up. He had probably even heard my begging.

"And this is your way of showing it?" I pushed her away.

She stood up and smoothed down her skirt. The wisp of hair had come loose again. She pushed it aside and hurried to the mirror hanging over the sink.

"It's Danny's football night. I thought . . . maybe the three of us could have a drink together." Her voice was almost matter-of-fact. She studied Kate's lipsticks, searching for the least garish before adding a hint of color.

"A fucking drink! Jesus Christ, I have feelings, you know."

She wasn't particularly vain, but when she took the effort to look into a mirror she gave it her full attention. She was engaged in damage control on her eyes when she finally replied. "We have to deal with this."

"No!"

Frowning in the mirror, she tied up her hair. She was about to wipe the perspiration off the back of her neck with one of Kate's towels but sniffed it first. Curling up her nose, she tossed it in the corner behind a garbage bag. She used a tissue instead and then absentmindedly crumpled it. "You'd better go out so."

"I've just bloody well come in."

"Then stay."

"And listen to you moaning and groaning in the other room."

She stopped and studied me before shaking her head almost in wonder. "I wouldn't do that to you, Sean."

Despite everything, I knew she wouldn't.

"This is the only way, believe me." She smiled weakly as if to give me courage.

He never smiled when he set eyes on her. Rather he examined her anxiously as if searching for something before enveloping her into his orbit. No one else mattered in those moments. It was far different than an Irish greeting: nothing the least off-hand or taken for granted. The sheer intensity left me with a deep sense of inferiority.

His suit, this time, was of a much lighter tan, even paling towards cream. The freshly ironed shirt was open at the neck—how did he always manage to look so cool in the reeking humidity? But his cologne was a hair too strong; he must have just applied it in the car. Cradled in his arms, he held a brown paper bag. This was uncharacteristic, I realized later, for he preferred to have his hands free at all times.

When she smiled at this anomaly, he shrugged and glanced across the room at me. I made a point of turning my back. Through the mirror over the kitchen sink, I could see them watching. She kissed him lightly on the lips and bolted the front door. Then they moved across the kitchen. She cleared some space, and I heard the familiar sound of a six-pack hitting the table. I didn't give a goddamn if he'd humped a case of champagne up the stairs. I had no intention of speaking to the bastard.

He ripped off the paper bag and opened a can.

"I don't like this no more than you do." His voice was higher pitched than I remembered.

"The least you can do is answer." She broke the silence.

Yeah, and say what? Thanks for shagging me girlfriend. And, oh by the way, how's the craic down in Puerto Rico these days?

"Well, seeing we're disturbing you, we'll just go into the bedroom."

They'd won, but he betrayed no look of triumph. He had that disconcerting way of staring right at you without saying anything. Irish lads never pulled that off, except for Danny, and his glare was invariably confrontational.

"As soon as I get some money, I'll be out of here like a shot." My own voice sounded high and squeaky. Maybe she had that castrating effect on both of us.

He nodded his understanding, then spread forth his hands in the gracious Bronx manner that signified: What can a man do? It was a gesture I would grow more familiar with.

Mary smiled. The ice had been broken. Such was her relief she might have kissed me had I not been bristling like a wild baldoon. She caught my drift and veered off into the bedroom. "I won't be long," she called back.

Jesús nodded that the situation was under control.

In my arse it was! I had no intention of making it easy on either of them. She left the door of the bedroom ajar, no doubt to make sure we weren't strangling each other. She must have pulled back the curtains earlier, for the sun was beaming in, window wide open. There was little smell of frankincense now, everything just bright and breezy and going her way as she dried her hair and dolled herself up for the big date.

I rifled the fridge, but my last quart was over by the couch—flat and warm. He motioned to one of his tallboys, beads of condensation dripping down its coolness, and not for the first time in my life did thirst whip pride. He intimated that I should store the others in the fridge. They both had the same casually magisterial way of getting people to do their bidding.

"You're John." He had some difficulty enunciating the "J."

"Sean."

"Juan," he nodded. "My brother's name."

I took a slug of the Schaefer and didn't try to stop the belch. He noted my bad manners.

"Dead." His tone was casual, yet I could see it cut him deeply.

"Listen, I'm sorry for your troubles, but they've sweet damn all to do with me."

"Was just a kid . . . like you."

"I'm twenty-one, OK?"

"That's what I said—just a kid."

He took a swig of beer and rolled it around in his mouth, as if tasting a good wine.

"He take the powder." He gestured, injecting his arm.

"You'll never catch me touching that stuff."

"That's what he say too," he laughed bitterly. "Take a man to use that shit—not let it use you."

"I wouldn't know, would I?"

"Not yet."

"Listen," I began, but he cut me off with a wave of his hand.

"Heard a lot about you."

"Well, that's the difference, isn't it? I heard sweet shag all about you."

She had taken a red dress out of the closet and was holding it up to the mirror. He nodded his appreciation.

"Irish always hard on themselves," he smiled. "Find a cloud in every sunshine."

"Bit of a philosopher, aren't you?"

He studied me when I drained the tallboy and took another from the fridge. He disliked excess. Everything about him was measured, even down to his manicured nails.

"It's OK a man be hard on hisself. But Maria . . . she is not strong."

"Her name is Mary."

"Her name is whatever I call her." He matched the intensity of my voice, his eyes zeroed on mine. "You go easy on her, you hear?"

"I don't need your advice."

"You stupider than I thought." His eyes flashed, but just as suddenly the mask of coiled indifference descended again. "Blind too. The girl got problems."

"I bet she has, hanging out with the likes of you."

"She had problems before I met her . . . but she mine now."

"You don't own her."

She had put on the red dress and was matching it with a light silk shawl that draped over her shoulders.

"Maria!" With a slight wave of his hand he beckoned her over. He didn't look up until she stood by his side; then he lightly brushed her fingers with his lips and murmured, "*Mi vida*."

When he let go of her hand she returned to the room— my humiliation complete.

"You were just a boy. Didn't know her."

"For your information, I knew her extremely well."

He rose from his chair, black eyes blazing. I thought he might strike me and knew that I was totally out of my depth.

"Don't you never speak like that again," he whispered.

I regretted what I'd said but couldn't admit it. He dismissed me with contempt and strode over to the window. His walk was assured, yet it reminded me of a panther: caged and padding the floors of a zoo. He studied the scene below in much the same manner as Danny.

"Streets bring out the worst in everyone . . ." Something

caught his eye and his voice trailed off. Then satisfied that it made some sense or logic, he shifted back from stalker to mere observer.

"My family from Boquerón, Puerto Rico." He exuded an old world authority when employing the Spanish place names, like some conquistador or grandee. "Lots of trees, the wind, ocean. A man can breathe." But all the pomp drained from him when he admitted, "Just seen the pictures."

He pointed into the bedroom. "Someday me and her gonna go there. Check it out."

"Send me a postcard."

"I do that," he smiled.

"Wexford." He rolled the word on his tongue, and I could tell that he lacked comfort with things unfamiliar. "The big waves come crashing in on the islands. Wind blowing in your hair, salt spray on your face."

The words seemed otherworldly, the description memorized, with even a hint of Mary's accent, and yet he could touch its essence. A seed of home was blossoming in the concrete of the North Bronx, and I didn't like it one bit. "She talk about it late at night. Talk about you too."

"In bed, no doubt."

"Don't do no good to crucify yourself."

"Nothing does any good."

We were silent for a while until I slammed my beer down on the table. "Ah, Jaysus!"

At first I didn't understand his surprise. Then it dawned on me. "What the hell are you doing with a name like Jaysus anyway?"

He looked at me like I was the crazy one.

"Your man with the big beard up in the sky?"

He frowned, dismayed to be at a disadvantage with someone he considered his inferior. It was a chink in his armor that I would remember.

"This whole city is stark raving mad! Fellahs going around calling themselves Jesus." I laid it on thick but he didn't smile. I didn't give a damn. The booze had kicked in; I was feeling better about myself and pointed to the fridge. "Get me another one of them beers, will you?"

He bowed almost imperceptibly and reached in. But with a flip of his wrist he flung the can directly at me, making me scramble to catch it before I was struck. Mary must have sensed the change, for she emerged from the bedroom. "What are you talking about?"

Her hair was still up but drawn back off her face by matching silver combs. She was wearing heels—worlds away from the young punk back home.

"Oh, contemporaneous religious practices." I mustered every last iota of irony.

"Men!" She raised her eyebrows but never lost sight of Jesús.

She had discarded the dress for a black skirt and a red silk blouse that hugged her arms and figure. Despite the heat, she wore a cameo on a black velvet choker around her throat that should have looked overdone but somehow didn't. Her make-up, as ever, was perfect: mascara highlighting the paleness of her eyes.

But looks, to Mary, were incidental. She accepted the admiration more out of duty than any satisfaction. Then, tiring of the scrutiny, she motioned to the door. "Ready?"

He flashed the barest of smiles and touched her arm. She recoiled, then quickly gathered herself. Yet something had passed between them. He frowned and was about to say something, then thought the better of it and gently took her elbow. This time she accepted the gesture, and when she linked him it was in the formal manner of a married couple.

"Catch you later, bro." He nodded to me.

"Good night, Sean," she barely turned her head. "Sleep tight."

"Yeah." I cracked another beer. "Or maybe I'll just wear earplugs."

chapter ten

We were in the thick of the dog days. Heat like I couldn't believe, the air thick and soupy, curried by a faint acidic tang. Was it the reek of the decomposing city or just plain old stale sweat? The hum, click and clatter of fatigued air-conditioners supplied the ongoing soundtrack to both our dreams and waking hours. Yet these monstrosities clung only to the sills of citizens and the legal. The rest of us, undocumented or unfocused, jacked our windows wide open to suck in any rustle of a breeze caused by bus, truck, or even God, undoubtedly perspiring along in empathy somewhere up there in the weary clouds. Who cared if that draft was tarred with diesel fumes and the stink of uncollected garbage? And for that matter, was there a sanitation strike afoot? No one could be sure since the pick-up trucks rarely roved down Decatur Avenue at the best of times. And few read the local rags, for what had Yank life to do with us unless you were the rare one like Danny, who was into Reggie Jackson, or Arsehole who made a big show of carting the *Village Voice* around every Wednesday. Who in their right mind gave a damn about the Bronx anyway—definitely not the boys down in City Hall dancing jigs to Ed Koch's fiddle.

Gasoline Gomez cared. And he was out and about day and night torching apartments, bodegas, abandoned buildings, and all manner of houses of worship. What was his angle? What revenge was he seeking? Or was he just another head-the-ball rejoicing in the crackle and glow of his own pyromania?

And everywhere the sound of drums: Mad conga players, sweat cascading off their naked torsos, thumped out relentless interlocking rhythms. You could ignore them for hours on end; then they'd catch you unawares on a one-and-four and shake you until your ribs rattled. Street corner prophets, adamant that we were approaching the end, mouthed their warnings as we trudged by. They needn't have wasted their voices. We all knew something had to give. The infinitesimal center that remained was caving in by the hour, and there was a natty dread in the air that an exhausted era was hurtling to a close.

Where did these drummers get the energy? The rest of us could barely make it to the bodega for the Arctic beer that was our sustenance. On and on they pounded: mad voodoo priests shielding our block from the evil eye of Señor Gomez. It was easy enough to pass out from the booze, but deep sleep was rare; yet no one complained, for the adjacent streets were littered with charred buildings. Bad as it might be to live in a fetid tenement, far worse would it be to lay down in a city shelter with every manner of drug addict and pervert roaming the corridors.

If the drums held the bottom, then the fire engines owned the high preserves as they careened willy-nilly up the pot-holed hills and around dead-end bends. It was a rare hour that you didn't hear the whine of one of them in the distance. Meanwhile, law and order was something spouted about by pundits and politicos in the *News* and the *Post*—

silver haired men like Mario Biaggi who occasionally
popped his head into Gaelic Park. But who paid them any
heed? They were as distant as Carter and Reagan posturing
on TV—two cardboard cutouts full of toothy smiles and
plastic promises droning on down in distant DC, wherever
the hell that was.

Just keep the lid on—that was the order from on high.
And the street knew it. Junkies, whores, and pimps no longer
bothered hiding their wares and tares from patrol cars always
speeding by to somewhere else, lights flashing, hopes dashing,
sirens howling, while inside the boys in blue scowled out at
the world, just trying to stay alive for one more tour in the
hope that someone downtown had noticed their application
for transfer to Staten Island, City Island, any bloody island
as long as it was oceans away from the only borough on the
mainland.

Amidst all this, Paddy and Mary Illegal Immigrant
soldiered on. Born and bred in temperate Tipperarys of the
body and soul, seventy-five degrees was beyond heatwave to
them. But the days braised away in the nineties while nights
rarely dipped below a stifling eighty. Few bothered with air-
conditioners, for that would be an admission of permanence.
*Ah sure, won't September soon be upon us. Then just make it
through till the Christmas and you won't catch hide nor hair
of me in this hellhole next year.*

And so they made their exhausted way down Kingsbridge
and Bainbridge to the subway in the dewy dawn, oozing
sweat and promises never to suffer another summer in this
sauna. Twelve hours later, caked in dust and denial, they'd
trundle back in sweltering sardine cans better known as the
D and 4 trains. Despite frigid showers, they'd be dripping

again by the time they made their nightly pilgrimage to the coolness of the alcohol emporiums that dotted the avenue.

Scutch Murphy's was no better nor worse than any of them: a bit on the rough side, but you got what you paid for. No questions asked, even fewer answered. Don't break the chairs, puke on the floor, or go beyond an acceptable level of ball-breaking, and you got your third or fourth on the house, depending on the wee man's mood. And, after a couple of quick pints and some minutes spent with arms upraised before the mother of all air-conditioners, you felt almost normal again. Another pint or two and you were in perfect calibration with the comfortably numbing immigrant ambience, nary a thought wasted on the alien streets outside.

And without even realizing it, I had taken to plowing the same furrow as everyone else, for I knew deep down in my heart of hearts that in a matter of months I'd be home. I wasn't going to waste my best days in the blistering Bronx with the rest of the losers; I'd stay just long enough so that the lads down in Begley's wouldn't fall over themselves when they saw me snaking through the door, red-faced and bare-arsed, with my hand outstretched for a free pint and a limitless supply of I-told-you-so's. In my own addled mind I was unique, a cut above everyone else. But truth be told, I was too much of a moron to see that Scutch's was jammed to the rafters with fellow illusionists, each with their own reason for not going home, all of them as valid as my own.

Back in the apartment on Decatur we were adrift: nothing anchoring us, not a green card to our names, and Mary getting weirder by the day. It wasn't that she was avoiding me, more like not really even seeing me. On her brief excursions to and from her room, she'd nod as if to say, "Oh there you are," while I stood stiff as a board, bristling with self-piteous indignation, and more righteous than the Rev. Paisley himself back in East Belfast.

She came and went as though night and day were part and parcel of each other. But there was something even more troubling: when the door cracked open, I'd often glimpse her kneeling in front of that little plaster statue of Our Lady. It wasn't so much that she was praying, more like seeking to meld every molecule of her being with the Virgin's blue and white indifferent stillness. What was she thinking of doing— becoming a nun? Might as well for all the action I was getting.

She paid little heed to Kate: a watery smile here, a cursory nod there, or a barked order if the blackness was on her. Yet it was clear that there once had been affection between them. Kate, in her turn, seemed exhausted with the whole state of affairs; odd in itself, for she had a tongue as sharp as a chisel and usually took no nonsense. She treated Mary like a sister who had been led astray: She didn't blame her, nor hold Jesús responsible, although I had little doubt that he was the snake in the grass.

Danny, too, bristled around Mary, yet gave her a wide berth. They never spoke and, on his arrival, she'd bolt for her bedroom as if the oxygen was being sucked from around him. He would stare after her and shake his head. It was a stand-off between them; both knew more about the other than they cared to say, and I just couldn't bear to ask. The lies were bad enough; the truth might have been unbearable.

Besides, I had enough on my plate. Danny ran that building site like a drill sergeant. Everything had to be to his specification, and he had no problem putting in sixty hours a week if called for. He expected the same from the rest of us, though he made sure we got double pay on Sunday with time off to attend mass for those who cared about such things.

But occasionally out of the blue he'd just disappear, not a word to anyone, although he must have kept Big Boss Dennehy informed, for that fish-eyed Antichrist would roar up in his big car, just so everyone knew we were still under surveillance. Eventually, Danny would stroll in, shades on, walls up, and not a word of explanation. Not that anyone was stupid enough to inquire, for he'd be in a foul mood that would spread through the site and even permeate the gray dust swirling around us.

Kate dreaded the nights of his vanishing and could tell when one was at hand. He'd be on a short fuse, and you could feel the storm mounting. It was often a relief when the clouds finally broke. He was unpredictable, though; some evenings he'd just head for the bleachers down Yankee Stadium for, though he didn't care a great deal about baseball, he had a thing for Reggie Jackson and his rebellious nonchalance. Then, depending on how Mister October was hitting, he might head off on a solitary drunk and ramble home eventually. You'd come out of a deep sleep to find him staring down at you with that strange disturbing intensity. How long had he been looking at you? What was he after? But before you could put any of your scattered thoughts into words, he'd be off to his own cot and dare you intrude.

He knew Kate worried about him and, more often than not, would murmur a few words to let her know he was safe. Other times he'd be less thoughtful and wouldn't show up until it was time to stir me from my slumbers. He never said where he'd been, and neither of us was stupid enough to inquire.

Until one furnace of a night, the air scarcely breathable, it was late and still, nothing moving but the odd mosquito rousing you from your drowsiness. Mary had gone out. I knew all her moves by now. When she dressed to kill, she was with Jesús and would not return. When she took little care, I didn't know where she went except that she would crawl back at a late hour. I took to creeping into her bed on the dolled-up nights. Though the hurt was powerful, I couldn't resist inhaling her memory. Neither Danny nor Kate made any comment and, in the end, as with many things in the Bronx, what began as a diversion ended up an obsession.

With the windows and door to her room wide open to capture any phantom cross breeze, I was dozing in and out of anxious oblivion. Despite the ever-present rumble of the night outside, I could hear Kate tossing in her cot. I knew she was in her usual state of provocative half-nakedness because I had taken a peek on my way to the bathroom. There was a lusciousness about her that could cause any man to catch his breath, and I was no exception. Still, it didn't take rocket science to recognize that she was fretting about Danny as she studied the ceiling and pretended not to notice me pretending not to notice her. Though we'd shared the same apartment for a couple of months, I was still turned on at the sight of her in panties, no bra, and a tight T-shirt. No matter how much nonchalance I affected, I was forever on the verge of crying out, "For Jaysus sake, girl, can I just get one good look at you, then I'll be off to bed with meself." She wouldn't have given a toss, but I couldn't find the words;

and after all, wasn't I supposed to be the broken-hearted martyr, with no thought of such things?

To add to the equation, I had begun buying dime bags of my own weed from the dealers on Decatur and was playing so many solo mind games, I wasn't sure if a simple look was the only subject on my agenda. So, like all good potheads, after my second not-so-necessary trot to the toilet, I smoked another joint to try and make sense of my dilemma.

I must have drifted off into one of those dreamless marijuana conk-outs, for I didn't hear any doors opening nor notice lights being switched on. Then, from a distance but approaching like a 747, I caught Rory Gallagher's roar inquiring what was going on all about town and how come everybody was trying to put the kid down? I arose in terror off the bed and fumbled for my jeans. For all I knew the cops were in the kitchen, and I had no wish to arrive back at Shannon Airport clad only in my skivvies.

Out in the front room, the beer cans were shivering on the table from the sheer volume. To add to the cacophony, the Ukrainians downstairs were banging on their ceiling. I could barely think from the combination of Rory's bluesy bawling and the pot thick as treacle jamming up my synapses. The scene was so surreal I had to blink and re-focus, for over by the stereo Kate was on her knees hugging Danny's legs and apparently yelling at him, though I could only surmise this by the contortions on her face. Danny, oblivious to her entreaties, was bent over the receiver trying to coax either more volume or a better performance from Mister Gallagher. There was a sudden violent screech of the needle across the disc and an even louder roar: "You've broke me Rory, you fuckin' bitch!"

After such volume, the silence trembled in the room; then, one last barrage of ceiling thumping from below, and nothing. We'd come through the many rings of a hurricane and were now becalmed smack dab in the center of its third eye.

"What are you doing?" My voice sounded surreal.

Kate looked back in surprise, but Danny didn't answer, so busy was he swinging at her with one hand, the other hanging limply at his side.

"Oh, I'm just down here saying a decade of the Rosary," she screeched from her knees, breasts heaving as she dodged the off-balance hooks and uppercuts. "What do you think I'm doing, you feckin' eejit? I'm getting' the head beat off me."

"What's the matter with him?"

"He thinks he's Muhammad Ali! Will you get over here before I'm kilt."

For a better grip, Danny had yanked her T-shirt up around her ears, exposing a first class view of a freckled back and the rims of two lovely breasts.

"Ruined me fuckin' Rory," he repeated in disbelief.

Vainly hanging onto his knees and attempting to shelter her breasts, Kate howled from inside the thin material. Though in serious fear of getting clobbered myself, I bent closer for a better view.

"Will you grab him by the good hand" she shrieked, for he now had her by the head of hair.

"What happened to the other one?"

"He broke it on some bouncer."

"Objection, your honor!" Danny cried out, now swaying even more as he ducked away from my cautious efforts to restrain him. "No hand of mine laid a finger on the gentleman in question."

He then laughed uproariously, pulled me in close and laid a big slobbering whiskey kiss on my cheek. Having loosened his grip on her T-shirt, Kate raised herself up onto her haunches and again grabbed him around the hips. The three of us staggered then swayed across the room where we finally gained steady ground next to the table.

"It's his feckin' guitar hand too," I groaned.

"It's me bloody wankin' hand. You'll have to do the honors tonight, Kate."

"Oh, would you ever shut up, you big lug." She disentangled herself and, to my dismay, pulled down her T-shirt, all the while snorting and shaking the sweat off herself like a young filly after a good gallop. She grabbed a hold of Danny's injured hand.

"Aaaghhhh! Will you go easy, woman!"

"What did you do with it?"

"I hit the bastard with the business end of a Heineken bottle, but he had a jaw like a slab of granite, and I twisted the bloody thing."

"Are you mad? You could have cut your hand off."

He shrugged that these things happen and should not be blown out of proportion.

"Why?" she persisted.

"He called me a bad word."

"He's a bouncer. That's what they pay him for."

"Then he better try a safer line of work."

"What did he call you?"

"No matter. He won't do it for a long time, his jaw will be wired so tight."

"It must have been something desperate altogether, with the language I hear out of the two of you."

"You'll hear soon enough." His mood lurched to a rank bitterness. "It'll be all over Braindamage tomorrow."

He was crackling with so much resentment I backed off.

"I'm sure people have a lot better things to talk about." Kate tried to close the subject with some small talk but it was too late.

The whites of Danny's knuckles almost popped through his fists as he held onto a kitchen chair. He fixed us both with that black implacable gaze, and then in a violent whisper: "Oh, they'll make time for this all right."

Without warning he kicked out at the chair and it lifted across the room, putting a dent in the wall just below the poster of Elvis. I ducked as he swept every last can and bottle from the table. When he roared, it came from someplace I didn't want to know about.

"The bastards!" He dropped to his knees and began to pound both fists into the floor. "The fucking bastards!"

I didn't know what to do. In fact, after the initial shock, I was embarrassed. Not Kate. She ran to him, but it was of little use. Whatever he had let loose wasn't about to be bottled and corked again. It broke through in one long feral moan. She took his head and held it to her breasts, spoke soothingly to him, while I wished the room would swallow me up and spit me out of there. Still, I was afraid to leave her alone with him.

For a long time she just rocked him and spoke like my mother did when nursing the calves at home. His head moved limply in motion with her. I was about to sneak back to bed when he jerked back into life, pulled her to him, and kissed her fiercely on the mouth.

It was all her dreams come true, yet hardly how she'd envisioned them. Her body was taut as he raised both of them to full height. His hands were everywhere, and he was holding her so tight I feared she might break.

She gathered herself and began to reciprocate. That was enough for me. I tried to edge my way past them, but they were already staggering to the bedroom. They didn't even bother closing the door, just collapsed on the bed. I was amazed it didn't buckle. He almost ripped the T-shirt off her, and I don't know how she unbuckled his belt.

I couldn't take my eyes off them, then finally came to my senses. I considered going out in the hallway but didn't fancy a half-naked run-in with Squint Eye. Finally I figured that if I could turn off the kitchen light, they could do whatever they pleased.

I must have looked ridiculous tiptoeing over. But just as I got my finger on the switch, they stopped. I froze too, my arm outstretched, afraid they might think I was spying. Then he whispered something and I strained to listen. She must not have heard either for she said, "What?"

He murmured the same words, but again I failed to decipher them. She drew back then struck him hard across the face. She didn't even bother to pick up her T-shirt. Just bounded back off the bed and ran bare-breasted out of the room.

I don't think she even saw me, but I caught a glimpse of her face. It was a cruel thing, for all hope had been drained. She threw herself into her cot and pulled the sheet up over her head; still, I could hear the muffled sobs.

Danny didn't move. Nor did I, trapped there in the shame of it all. He picked himself slowly up from the bed and walked over to the opened window. His figure silhouetted against the streetlight, he lit a cigarette, fingers trembling. Then he took a deep long drag, the sirens screaming outside and inside his head.

chapter eleven

The band was causing a bit of a stir on the avenue. Nothing to write home about, just word leaking out that a bunch of heads was playing whatever the hell they liked. It wasn't that we were doing anything particularly original—more a matter of approach. What we lacked in finesse we made up for with fury. If none of the other musicians broke a sweat, we tossed off buckets. While everyone else did their best to copy the bands back home, we did our worst to sound anything but like them.

The punters still hated us with a passion, but we wore their disgust like a badge of honor, soaking it up and spitting it right back at them. Now at every gig a new person or two would show up, at first because they'd heard we were messing with Marley or The Clash; but, after a couple of weeks, they'd latch on to one of our own songs and, oh sweet Jesus, wasn't that just nirvana!

Arsehole was the bedrock of our support. There wasn't an Irish music head in the Bronx that he wasn't on first name terms with. He'd arrive early, grab the best seat at the bar, and then slap fives with wild looking men from Mayo mad for Captain Beefheart, farmers' sons from Kerry who knew every word Tom Waits had ever growled, or shirty Orangemen from Hyndford Street who adored the very cobblestones Van had pissed upon. He dragged black-nyloned *cailíns* away from their Nick Drake records and petitioned bovver-booted skinheads to vent their agro on the only band in Paddyland with balls enough to have a run at the Specials or Prince Buster.

All of these musicos had one thing in common: they drank like fish. Thus, it wasn't long before bar owners ignored the regulars and their litany of complaints. Even more to the point, we drew women, who in turn drew men who didn't give a rat's ass if we played polkas or Presley, Strummer or Stravinsky. Swordsmen all, these boyos had only one thing on their minds; through them the word spread like wildfire along Bainbridge that any man with two legs and something between them stood a fighting chance of getting the ride at our gigs.

Danny and Shiggins were our drawing cards in the ladies' department. From behind their shades they exuded cool. I struck few sparks, grinning away like a hyena at my good fortune to even be in a band, while Bugsy was never sober enough to promise much in the realm of sexual fantasy. The other two were like lightning rods, though it was a rare occasion that they'd even bother to nod at their admirers, let alone engage them in the few couplets of conversation it would take to procure a knee-trembler out in the alley.

Danny hadn't said a word about the night with Kate, yet it hung like a dead fish between us. She had slept in the following morning, the sheet still over her head, and when we got home that night there was a note saying that she'd be spending the weekend downtown caring for her charges. Such an absence wasn't unusual and, though we both caught the significance, neither of us felt called upon to make comment. Danny carefully refolded the over-scented paper and stored it with the Con Edison bills. When she returned well into the week, they were civility itself to each other, everything cool and just so—except that it wasn't. You could almost feel the hurt throbbing across the room between them.

For my own part, I was going through a brusque, if still thorny, stage with Mary and mostly dealt with her through Kate. Danny had long since stopped talking to the love of my life and treated me like her legal guardian, to be delegated to in all matters concerning the sound running of the apartment.

It was a strange scene; there was no two ways about it. But I suppose it was a case of better the devil you know than the one you don't, and besides, there was always a six-pack or a couple of joints to seal the cracks. Fatigue was another solvent: With the band playing a couple of nights a week, there were times when it was hard to tell whether I was literally coming or going.

If he was on edge before, the incident with Kate added fuel to Danny's fire. In an odd way this was to lead to a change in the band's dynamic. He withdrew more both on and offstage, leaving a space for me to step forward, try new songs, loon about, or preen to my heart's desire. Although he had a style and sound all his own, Danny was never the most technical of guitarists. It's just that he brought a certain flair to everything he did and approached each challenge as if he couldn't lose. With this in mind, I began to wonder if there wasn't a foot or two of clay pounding around Gaelic Park on Sunday afternoons. He had many skills, there was no denying that, but they were powered by a naked drive and sheer force of character. Consequently, his was a jarring presence that tended to heighten awareness of your own shortcomings. Though usually unintentional, this caused a lot of resentment, but it was just that he set impossibly high standards for himself, while what others did or thought was of little consequence to him.

Except for me! He was constantly amazed at my ability to prevaricate and was a perpetual thorn in my side, always badgering me to "better myself." Kate looked on in wonder and not a little envy, but I squirmed under the attention. I could tell his concern was well meaning, but there was a proprietary element that caused a vague discomfort.

He now channeled whatever was ailing him into music. It wasn't that he played louder, but the intensity was palpable, and his unconventional electric lines snapped like whiplash across the sheet-rocked walls of every pub we performed in. A fellah from Fermanagh could be prancing by valiantly chatting up some lassie from Longford when his stream of blather would be cut to ribbons by one of Danny's flash floods of distilled fury, leaving the couple beached and speechless, wondering what the hell had hit them.

Indifferent to opinion at the best of times, he now didn't give a brass farthing if the crowd loved, hated, or simply ignored him. I had no idea what he was trying to dredge up, but you could almost see the sparks spraying from his fingers up and down the neck of his Strat. He did lose interest—or was it faith—in his voice though and would often impatiently motion me forward to sing his numbers. At first I hesitated, not wishing to dull his thunder, but I learned to anticipate his need. The best times were when we would jump on a line together; then he'd curl his voice up or down a third or a fifth and glide around me in a manner I'd never heard before.

Every note he played onstage made sense, but you had
to be ready at all times to jump with him or fall on your face.
Shiggins and Bugsy had his measure. They knew that feel was
your only guide: Find the pocket of his groove, then be
careful not to skitter backwards off its greasy edges. You
could feel him flinch when he began some familiar run.
Furious with himself, he'd do anything to break free from its
shackles. It mattered little that the line might have worked
wonderfully only the night before; this was a new day and
called for a different tack. Still, I never doubted that he was
working his way through some old heartscald that the
incident with Kate had only exacerbated, but I had no idea
what that was.

Although he wouldn't have admitted it in a million years,
Shiggins was moved by the music that Danny was dragging
out of himself. Like a pointer with his ears cocked, he reacted
to every nuance: slowing down, speeding up, creating holes,
driving the beat, gliding on sixteenths, spinning on eights,
pounding on fours, turning in tandem on a dime with
Danny's jagged solos. They never acknowledged each other
onstage, never shared a drink off, but they were made from
the same stern stuff and shared some kind of intuition that
was foreign to me. Nevertheless, I became a musician by
listening to their interaction.

Although Shiggins didn't become any friendlier, he took
to instructing me. By the barest of nods, he prodded me
forward or held me in line. Whenever I got messy, he would
crack his ride cymbal a hair louder and, with a withering
glance, make me focus on the space between his kick and snare.
He'd been around the block musically, polished his chops
down in Manhattan, and returned to the easy money of the

Bronx the better for the experience. He was a big fish in a small pond but going nowhere fast until we knocked on his door. He knew bands like the back of his hand and understood full well that this stage wouldn't last long. We'd go beyond ourselves or burn out. Still, he recognized a real shot when he saw it, and he'd be damned if he'd let an amateur like me mess with the magic.

Bugsy drank his way through the whole thing, anchoring us to the floorboards and never putting a foot wrong despite his pickled brain. He had begun to speak to me in his quiet way about women, football, and all the casual things that men murmur about in bars. There was a bit of normality in him, unlike the other two, who stood apart during the breaks, lost in whatever relentless worlds they occupied behind their shades. Until one night, out of the blue, after we'd finished a set with a particular caterwauling jam on a Marley tune, he let me have it in his Killarney accent. "Will you, for the love of Jaysus, boy, listen to the fuckin' music, instead of wankin' all over the bloody thing."

"What are you talkin' about?" I countered, nonplussed at the ferocity of this assault.

He threw me a stare lined with daggers, then turned away and muttered something into his bottle.

I was thrilled with just being able to improvise around Bob Marley's magic, and it took me some moments to get beyond my self-infatuation, but I knew this was important.

Bugsy hated any kind of confrontation and instantly regretted his statement. He seemed to shrink before me, but I wouldn't let it go.

"I asked you a question, man." I grabbed him by the shoulder, but he shook my hand off.

He was furious, and I saw him as he must have been before the bottle became his universe. Perhaps it was the dimness of the lights, but the puffiness seemed to drain from his face as he spat out, "You're so fuckin' full of yourself, aren't you?"

And then I saw myself as he must have on so many nights: a preening bantam cock, thrilled with the fact that I could strut around the stage, with no thought to listen to the lines that the others were laying down, always just dying to slather my own brand of shite all over the mix.

He put his bottle to one side, a rare thing. He was breathing heavily, and I knew this unaccustomed frankness was hard on him. In true Paddy fashion, I'd never asked him how he'd ended up on Bainbridge, why he'd left his lovely mountains and lakes so far behind. In that moment I knew that he'd never make it back: These battered streets, dingy apartments, and sheet-rocked dancehalls were the only home he'd ever know. He pissed away his money as quickly as he earned it, and unless there was one hell of a funeral collection, there'd be no box for Bugsy going back to Killarney courtesy of Aer Lingus. He'd await his Maker's judgment while pushing up daisies in Woodlawn cemetery.

Did he read that in my eyes? Or catch a glimpse of my own hurt and confusion? He had so much talent—was so much a better musician than me—but something had gone wrong, and now he was stranded on the avenue. His talent would always guarantee him a living, and the bottle would douse whatever hurt was holding him back, but his options were fading fast behind him. He sighed and was about to bury himself beneath some banality about football or the *craic*; instead he halted in mid-swing on his stool, then very tentatively reached out and grasped my elbow.

"Quit your fixation with the notes, man! Listen to the holes," he whispered, "and don't be filling them to the hilt like some culchie down the site. Leave them spacious and open, fit for a very king to fall into."

He stared at me and nodded until he was certain that I understood. Then he stuck his hand out and waited until I grasped it. His fingers were long and thick, the tops callused, but the flesh was like porcelain, cool and alcoholic smooth. Then he called for two shots of Powers and became his amiable self again, arguing with the bartender about the relative merits of Mick O'Connell, Din Joe Crowley, and the Kerry football team of '69.

No one had ever put it to me like that before, and for the first time I realized that music is as much about what you leave out as you put in. Was that the way with life too, and, if so, why didn't Bugsy take his own advice and go running home before it got too late? Was there a greater lesson for me to be learned as well? Was I heading down the same tramp's heartbreak as the Killarney man, and would I be sitting in some bar on Bainbridge ten years hence, anesthetizing myself with great big shots of lukewarm Powers?

I was still pondering this scenario as we lugged the amps and guitars into the apartment. Perhaps that's why I didn't notice Danny's mood. He was lighting one cigarette after another and stubbing them out after a couple of puffs until he finally burned himself with the hot ash.

"I suppose she told you," he said, licking his finger.

"What?"

"Don't act so stupid."

"Listen, it doesn't matter to me."

"Sean, don't do this, man. I'm trying to straighten things out between us."

'There's no need." I stood up from the table, but he dragged me back down.

"Don't you know what I'm trying to say?"

"Listen, I don't want to get involved in anything between you and Kate."

"Me and Kate, my arse! Are you that out to lunch?" He lit another cigarette and blew the smoke back across his shoulder. Then he locked eyes with me in that particular way of his where you couldn't look away.

"I'm gay, Sean."

He might as well have said he was the Abominable Snowman.

"I'm a queer, a homo, a faggot, whatever you call it in your neck of the woods."

I reddened to the gills. I could still feel the touch of his fingers on my arm. "Then what were you doin' with Kate?"

"Using her—what do you think?"

I couldn't think anything. To the best of my knowledge, I'd never met someone of that nature before, except for a couple of transvestites down the Bowery; but those fellows were wearing dresses and lipstick. Danny was a football champion, the pride of Gaelic Park. Jesus Christ, he was the bloody gangerman on the site! He had to be having me on.

"You want to know why I was usin' her?" he murmured.

"No! Not in the least."

"No, I suppose you don't." He took another long drag of his cigarette. This time he blew the smoke right at me. "Anyway, it didn't work."

"No?" I didn't know what to say except that I wanted this

interview to conclude with all due haste. He didn't say anything. Just stared at me until finally I was forced to inquire, "How come?"

"It's hard when you've had the real thing."

"Jaysus!"

"Jaysus is right! You should try it yourself sometime. You never know . . ."

"No bloody way! I mean . . ."

"You mean you're not a faggot, right?"

What the hell do you say to a question like that? I don't know how long he left me twisting in the wind before he began to provocatively leer at me and then laugh uproariously at my discomfort. "Relax. I'm not going to hop over the table and bugger you . . . yet."

"But what are you going to do?" I finally asked him.

"Do? Oh, I'm going straight down to the vet and get meself fixed! What the fuck do you think I'm going to do?"

"I mean . . . you know what they're like up here."

He took one last drag then let the smoke seep out through his nostrils. "I know what they're like everywhere, Sean."

He wanted me to say something, but I was still reeling and the silence was pounding between us. Eventually, he shrugged that it made no difference, but it did, and it cut me to the core. A moment had passed, and a wall—of my own building—went up between us.

He nodded his understanding, his eyes still fixed on me. "You're sure you still want to do the band thing?"

"Yeah! I mean, why not?" I was so relieved I positively jumped at the change of subject.

"They'll be talking about you too."

"Me?"

"With us living together and all."

"And all what?"

"Well," he smiled, "they might think you're me little rent boy."

"Ah no, sure look at me. No one would ever think that I'm a . . ."

"The David Bowie of Wexford?" he lisped, raising his eyebrows.

"Fuck 'em!" They could call me what they liked. Danny was my mate, and if he wanted to bugger Gerty Murphy's goat, that was fine with me. I was no holy molly from the bog that would head for the hills at the mere mention of such perversion.

"I wouldn't with yours, boy." He stood up and held out his arms to hug me, but when he sensed my embarrassment, he backed off and stuck out his hand. It was something lacking in me and again I felt it deeply, but he seemed to understand, and so we shook on the matter. Then he yawned. Whatever had gone down was already fading away behind him.

"You're all right, Sean. Just don't bend down for the fake soap."

"The what?"

"Jaysus." He threw himself down on his cot. "If you get any greener, you'll turn into a cabbage."

He was asleep before I could find the words to answer him.

CHAPTER TWELVE

When it rained you would be in mind of home with the south wind sweeping up from the Atlantic drenching the countryside. Then again, rain in Ireland was common as dishwater and could commence at the drop of a hat; in the Bronx, it required fanfares and days of anticipation. With the sky threatening to collapse under the pressure and your nerves on end, you finally understood just what the Temptations were singing about.

Then, with a merciful crack of thunder, the heavens would open, and the rain would ricochet like silver bullets off the parched streets. Through rivulets and ravines, it would sweep the garbage into drains, flooding whole intersections where urchins could splash to their hearts' content. Young men in tank tops who had been listless for days would nod towards bedrooms, girls would loosen their hair, shrug their soft shoulders, and follow them, while old men lit cigars and remembered times when the rain fell for them. And when the storm had passed, for a few brief hours the sun would pour down like honey on the resurrected flagstones of Decatur Avenue.

But soon foreboding clouds would return and with them the sweat, the grime, and the unanswered questions. Then I'd think about Danny and wonder what made him tick. Why was he just so much beyond my frame of reference?

Part of it was the difference between Northern lads and those of us from the South, and this disparity was being exacerbated daily by the talk of hunger strikes emanating from the British prison camps of Long Kesh and Armagh. To us, from the Republic, it was something we read about in the papers, troubling but not really our concern; while to those born under the Unionist jackboot in the North, it was an ongoing reality that one could be interned for years at the whim of a juryless court. Some of the lads on the avenue had already been inside; more had bearded and emaciated friends and relatives "on the blanket" refusing use of any prison facility until their political status was restored. To the casual outsider, we Paddies all looked the same, talked the same, but there was much more than miles separating us.

Even the shallowest of them had a better handle on the world. What would be a simple stroll for us in Dublin or Galway could prove an existential adventure in Belfast or Derry, where one could be thrown up against a wall by a British soldier waving a cocked gun and screaming that you were nothing but a dirty, stinking Irish bastard.

Discrimination of that nature could happen to the least political of people in the North. But I knew deep down that Danny had been more involved than most: He had the mark of it on him. Not that such experience made him stand out in certain bars along Bainbridge, but there were also things about him that didn't add up. Republicans who should have been friendly were merely respectful, while others were sullenly hostile, though more often than not behind his back.

One telling point was that, despite his reputation and skill with the football at Gaelic Park, afterwards in the bar he quickly gravitated towards Kate and myself rather than mix with his teammates. The only one he seemed to have any time for was Big Boss Dennehy, the cash muscle behind the Tyrone team, but even that relationship seemed more dutiful than friendly. With a curt nod, Dennehy always sent over a round of drinks but never joined us. This didn't trouble me, for there was a coldness to the man that gave me pause. On top of being a law unto himself on his various building sites, he was rumored to be sending large sums of money back to the North, with little of it earmarked for his retirement fund.

Such matters were rarely spoken aloud on Bainbridge, though they were sometimes murmured at four in the morning. Of course, there were eejits like Arsehole who would rave about their weekly phone call with Gerry in Belfast or having broken bread with Martin on their last trip home to Derry. But everyone knew that was Arthur Guinness or Adolph Coors doing the talking. Then there was Danny and his ilk. It was hard to put a finger on it, but small talk subsided when they approached. There was a solitariness and a stillness about them that was discomfiting to outsiders. They had seen and done things that we did not wish to think about. Even if we were to step beyond propriety and question them, we didn't seem to possess the appropriate words for the occasion.

Danny, on first impression, seemed all muscle and brain, but it didn't take an eternity to fathom that he was really a cluster of contradictions. Although he had moments of abandon, compared to the rest of us he was careful of both himself and the walls he built to keep his distance. Most Paddies had trouble coming to terms with Yank ways: Illegals, particularly, tended to cluster together in familiar pubs for company and reassurance. Danny was different, more like a warrior, at home in any arena. And yet the chinks in his armor could be glaring.

For though he was adventurous, he was also a creature of habit. No one had more regard for the sweaty, sardine-can subways. Even after the fare was doubled, he claimed it was the best sixty cents a man could spend, and he was as familiar with Coney Island and Ditmars Boulevard as any of our turf in the Bronx. Still he was compulsive, and dare anyone trespass on his sun-drenched spot on the downtown platform of the Kingsbridge station! He'd throw open his *Daily News*, hum "I, Me, Mine," and nudge the intruder to one side until he alone stood bathed in the golden halo of light caused by a puncture in the roof overhead.

But just when you thought you had his number, he'd do something totally off the wall, like the time he breezed in after an all-nighter and dragged me out of bed. It was a rare day of rest, yet nothing would do but that I throw on some clothes and follow him over to Bainbridge. I could smell the Bushmills seeping out of him as I strove to keep in stride. Then without warning, on the corner of 205th, he dropped to his knees and groped through the cracks in the sidewalk before cupping a little red flower in the hollow of his hands, smiling like he was greeting a long lost friend and jabbering away about seeing the universe in a grain of sand or some such Sunday morning balderdash. I was mortified at what people must be saying about the two of us going mental over a little weed not even the size of a self-respecting daisy.

Most of the time, though, he walked with a purpose, neither glancing left nor right, aware of everything but betraying no apparent interest. Though I was usually beat after my day on the site, I took to accompanying him, less for the exercise than to get away from Mary and her moods. Some evenings he just liked to ramble. On others his mood would be black: heading somewhere, but only after he had come to terms with whatever was gnawing away inside him.

On one such occasion outside the Armory on Kingsbridge, he stopped to light a joint. With the ganja pluming around us, we took in the scene: a cop car snaking by with bigger fish to fry, an ambulance screeching up to the Veterans Hospital, a couple of early evening black whores staking out premium spots beneath the El, a solitary Paddy in overalls, tools dangling from his belt, full to his truculent gills, and bouncing off the stream of decent Ricans homeward bound from their daily labors.

Across the street The Gallowglass stuck out like a sore thumb, its thatched cottage exterior nestled between bodegas and fast food joints—a last, lonely Irish outpost of 1950s emigration defiantly holding it own against the graffitied Latino tide sweeping up over the Concourse. Danny studied the pub with all the intensity the Soviet army might have devoted to Hitler's bunker.

"What do you want to go in there for?"

He didn't reply, nor did I pursue the matter. I had come to terms with his habit of prevaricating if he suspected that an answer might be of the least importance to you. I took another toke and turned around to marvel at the architectural folly of the Armory—all towered and slit-holed for the loosing of arrows in an age when every cheap hood north of Hunt's Point had access to weaponry that could blow it to smithereens.

"All they're missing is the pigs in the cabbage patch." Danny nodded at the thatched roof of the pub as he ground the roach beneath his heel. Then, without even looking at me, he loped over Kingsbridge with no regard for either his own safety or the roars of the gypsy cab drivers.

He was already nearing the door before I took my life into my hands and ran after him. Seated on a stool in the vestibule, a red-bearded man of some girth blocked his way.

"What about you, Danny?" The doorkeeper used the Belfast greeting, albeit with a Bronx twang. With penetrating blue eyes beneath wavy red hair, he resembled a battle-hardened version of Christy Moore and possessed all the authority of the singer, with not a little of his attitude. Something in his demeanor hinted that he might not be exactly imbued with a peace and love outlook in political affairs. He did seem a shade perplexed at the sight of Danny, though his natural cool wasn't long about returning.

"Fair enough, Benny, and yourself?"

"I'm fine, considering . . ." Benny let the last word hang; both nodded slightly in appreciation of what was left unsaid.

"Any word from home?" It was a reflexive question, and Benny immediately regretted it.

"Oh yeah," Danny snapped. "Joe Cahill was on the phone this mornin', and Martin sent me a birthday card. What the fuck do you think?"

I pulled on my dumbest face and stared anywhere but at Benny, who was reaming me even as he disapprovingly shook his head at this obvious breach of discretion.

But Danny was having none of it. "Am I welcome or not?"

Benny heaved a long sigh then reached out for Danny's shoulder. "You know you're always welcome with me, lad."

"I didn't ask that."

Benny withdrew his hand as if it had been singed. A fire
engine raced down Kingsbridge across Jerome heading for the
Concourse; beyond the inner door of the pub, a fiddle sawed
away above the clatter of a banjo. The windows of the
vestibule had been painted black save for one pane directly
behind Benny's head. In between posters for Republican
causes, a number of scrawled notices had been taped to the
daubed glass.

With the siren fading, I studied these as nonchalantly as
possible while they eyeballed each other across the narrow
space. Danny's breathing, though still even, had modulated
to a quicker tempo. Benny wheezed away on his stool,
soaking up the younger man's icy rage.

Just when I thought the very ceiling was going to blow
off, Benny turned away and peered through the clear pane.
Satisfying himself on some score, he faced Danny again:
"You've no call to be so hard on them; you'd have done the
same yourself."

Danny made a point of ignoring him—just focused on
the large leg still blocking his entrance. Benny now turned
his full attention on me.

"He's sound," Danny snapped. "He's with me."

"That's what you said the last time."

Danny stiffened and straightened to full height. It brought
to mind the time a Tyrone boy had shown up for work hours
late, a smell of drink off him that could have blinded you.
When reprimanded he murmured something under his breath
and was beaten from one end of the scaffold to the other for
his troubles. But Benny was sober and made of sterner stuff;
he returned Danny's scowl with compound interest. Some
point having been made, his leg dropped like dead weight.

"Keep a cool head, lad," he murmured as Danny strolled past and flung the door open.

The vestibule must have been expertly soundproofed, for now the instruments danced over the hum of voices. A thick cloud of smoke and the comforting smell of freshly pulled pints oozed out. My eyes watered and I tried to follow, but Benny's leg was already back in place. With his eyes on full bore, I panicked. Danny must have sensed what was happening for he swiveled around, but Benny's leg dropped again. It had only cost him a moment to take my measure.

By the time I joined him at the bar, Danny had already ordered.

"What was that all about?" I asked.

"Benny's all right. It's the others . . ." He cast a hooded glance down the end of the stick where Dennehy was holding court with a number of severe looking young men, their clothes still dusty from the back laneways of rebel South Armagh. A couple of them recognized Danny but instantly averted their eyes. Taciturn as ever, Dennehy raised his glass a centimeter or two in our direction. Although I'd often bumped into him around the site, he'd never acknowledged me; now he betrayed the slightest hint of amusement at my presence.

The room was dimly lit, the air layered with stagnant banks of pale blue smoke. Large beams of dark timber held up the ceiling, while others ornamented the off-white walls. A framed poster of an old piper hung over an open fireplace, while here and there a fiddle or concertina had been nailed to the beams. The room was full to overflowing and swayed with the melded sound of many conversations going at once. Above this dull rumble, a button accordion joined the fiddle and banjo. The box player added heft to the melody, going note for note with the fiddler, occasionally adding a trill or a couple of grace notes at the end of a line. The tempo quickened as the two players skipped along in rough unison, both of them masters of slightly different versions of the same tune. Plodding along in their wake, the banjo man did his best to hold them in place, but they were having no part of this delaying tactic. They disdained to even glance in his direction, but locked inward stares across a bottle-filled table. The sweat stood out on the banjoist's forehead; then with a muttered oath, he let them have their heads as they hurtled into the second section of the reel. He gained on them again during the first couple of notes, now accepting as gospel their blistering tempo and even hustling them along like a dog out on the mountain rounding up a couple of errant sheep.

The conversation in the room surged with the speed of the tune, and every foot was tapping. I could sense anticipation in Danny. He slapped his thigh in time, eyes closed, head nodding. How quickly he could shrug trouble behind him. Whatever had gone down in the vestibule was already history.

"Watch this," he said to me without turning.

"What?"

"Over there." He opened his eyes and reverently pointed to the corner where the musicians were sitting. "That's Johnnie Crowley."

A decrepit-looking old bastard was wolfing down a sandwich, a fiddle balanced on his knee. He appeared to be either stone drunk or mentally challenged, his lids drooping over a pair of addled eyes. The crumbs from the sandwich fell into his gray, stringy beard, a fact that seemed to cause him no concern. Nor did he appear in the least impressed by the efforts of the other musicians. Rather, he devoted his full attention to the fast disappearing ham, cheese, and mayonnaise concoction, washing it down with great big draughts of Guinness and surprisingly dainty sips at a tumbler of whiskey. Not having a full complement of front teeth, he spat out a couple of offending crusts on the table and wiped his mouth with the sleeve of his jacket. When the last crumbs were devoured or discarded, he yawned mightily, displaying a mouth crowned with an array of off-white stumps. Only then did he put the fiddle to his ear to check the tuning. With the other three players roaring down the stretch, he raised his bow, and all eyes in the room turned in expectancy.

His first note was a long quivering G, and it clashed with the reel that had now resolved into a series of sympathetic movements around its signature key of D. He let the note bend and waver precariously, a quarter-tone or so above and below the irresolution. It lingered leeringly in its dissonance, seeming to fondle and then kiss the other three instruments, much in the manner of an old man touching up a schoolgirl. Though the note was intimate to the extreme, despite its intensity it was delivered dispassionately with barely a flicker of interest in Crowley's rheumy eyes.

The room caught its collective breath and began some hermetic countdown that I had no notion of. There was a sudden roar and a scattering of "Up on your bike" and "Good man yourself, Johnnie!" and, before I knew it, the other three musicians had modulated as one and torn off into a new reel in the key of G. For the first round, all four played in unison, but Johnnie soon tired of this drudgery. He began to dance around them, and I swear the air changed. With dainty licks and ornamentals, he tripped across their melody like a ballerina, pirouetting ahead of them, allowing them to catch up, then lingering in their wake, before leapfrogging gaily into the lead again. As yet he had barely shaken the glaze out of his eyes, but they soon began to sparkle.

He suddenly peeled off into some wild improvisation, a reel unto itself, that meshed in counterpoint with what now seemed like the mere foundation the other three were laying. I could see the strain in their shoulders as they sought to concentrate on their own lines and not get carried away by the majesty of the melody that Johnny was spinning all around them. The banjo player's eyes were almost popping out of their sockets, and he was cursing furiously as he tried to not only stay snapping at Johnnie's heels but keep the other two in some kind of order.

Round and round they went, four mad steeplechasers at a point-to-point, leaping over and through fences, the finish pole in sight but still so far away. Johnnie's stamina was amazing; he now had the others by the reins and was pulling them home all on his own. The room erupted as they rounded the last bend, sweat flying off his three minions, the ghost of a smile creasing the master's lips. In the last few yards, he slowed down, then gathering his disciples around him, they stormed across the line in tandem and came to a sliced halt.

The room quivered with the strangeness of silence. Johnnie sighed. He seemed disappointed to be back in the land of the living and picked up the couple of discarded crusts from his sandwich. He sucked away indifferently and didn't even tip his hat to the roar of the crowd. I heard Danny yelling, and only then became aware that I was matching him in volume. We were both banging our fists off the bar, and we were two of the most restrained in the room.

Despite all this elation, I felt an ineffable feeling of discomfort. Sure enough, when I turned round, Benny was studying us from the door. His frown was far from malicious, yet I felt a sudden fear for Danny, beaming away and for once off guard, a rare innocence burnishing his natural wariness. When I looked back, the door was closed again, and Benny's red locks were visible through the pane of clear glass.

I spun around and, sure enough, Dennehy was staring in the same direction. I felt certain that Benny had just silently communicated with him. The big boss instantly caught my eye and favored me with one of his frigid appraisals before lingering a moment on Danny in all his vulnerability. He left little doubt that I was an outsider who had no idea of what I was getting myself into.

"That's what we need for the band," Danny interrupted.

I wanted to tell him about Benny and Dennehy, stammer out a hundred questions, warnings, whatever, but I didn't have a clue how to begin without seeming irrational.

He caught something in my mood, glanced down the bar and then over at the door before shrugging his indifference.

"Do you hear me?"

"What's that?"

"Johnnie!"

"You can't be serious?"

"When did you ever hear music like that before?"

"Sure, they'd laugh us off the stage."

"Don't you think they're pissing themselves anyway?" He gripped my leather jacket: "Wearing that yoke in the middle of the summer and the boots on you like some biker down on Christopher waitin' to get his arse reamed."

I must have turned pale for he softened a bit. "Listen, Sean, I know it's been a tough station, but it's time you caught a hold of yourself."

"What are you on about now?"

"You and your bloody Mary!"

"What about her?"

"She's got you stuck in a fuckin' time warp."

"That's a load of shite."

"Can't you see what's going on?"

"I can see everything." But, adamant as I was, forty shades of doubt were clattering around inside my skull.

"Yeah . . . everything you want to see." He snorted and took a long gulp from his beer. After he had savored it, he shrugged then threw his arm around my shoulder. "Listen, whatever about her, there's only one way you and me are going to make it out of this kip and that's by being ourselves."

"I thought that's what we were doing?"

"Yeah. Half-arsed and hopin'. There's a hundred bands down the Village that can play us under the table; but there's not a one of them has the makings of what we have." He punched me right on the heart. "And they surely have nothin' the like of that."

He motioned towards Johnnie, and we watched this mountainy man drain his Guinness, the drops of the brown stuff meandering down his jaw.

"He's as thick and shiftless as the rest of them." Danny's Belfast burr was all but unintelligible now. "But he's got lightnin' streakin' around inside him, and we're the right goms if we don't ride it the hell out of here."

I finished my Heineken and took another from the bar. But it would take more than Dutch magic for me to imagine the likes of Johnnie Crowley in a rock and roll band. His old black suit clung to him, shiny and creased from wear and tear; by the cut of it, he might well have bought it back in the '50s. The thing was so old, it had already been in and out of fashion a couple of times and was overdue another reprise. His gray hair drooped in screeds over the collar and festooned his shoulders and upper arms with a fine dusting of dandruff. Though his shirt appeared the lightest shade of tan, I had the impression that it may originally have been white, while his tie, gleaming like black leather, was mere polyester and caked with grease. I tried to visualize him standing up straight, but I wouldn't have even bet on him having legs if a pair of filthy sneakers weren't protruding from under the table. Still, there was no doubting that the gentleman in question had a certain timeless quality. It would have been risky to hazard an opinion on his age: he could well have been a worn-out forty or a youngish looking sixty.

Then he recognized Danny and waved us over. A sly calculating scrim was already descending across his features, and his whole body had sunk into an anticipatory crouch. I was well familiar with such looks; they still haunted me from the fairs and cattle marts I attended with my father before he and the farm went under.

"Jaysus, he thinks it's the fucking Who come to hire him," Danny groaned.

"How does he know?"

"I mentioned it to Bugsy—more fool I!"

The memories of the humiliations that my father had endured swept back. He'd never been a match for the gombeen men he was forced to haggle with. Ashamed of his lack of skill, he'd leave me to attend our few scraggly bullocks while he repaired to a pub for the bargaining. A couple of quick whiskeys made the inevitable defeats more palatable.

"But will he play with us?" I was well aware that traditional Irish musicians hated the very thought of rock and roll.

Danny ordered two large Gold Labels and appraised Johnnie. "That fucker'd play with the Queen if she spread her legs far enough."

He shook his head in dismay at the task before him. "We do need him, right?"

"As long as you know what you're doin'."

"When the fuck did I ever know that?" He threw back his shoulders and headed across the room, dodging lithely through the crowd, the whiskeys held aloft. "I'd better find out the going rate."

"Stay where you are," he called back. "This'll be like cornerin' a rat. One does better than two."

She startled me. Even though she only gently touched my shoulder, I still had Benny at the back of my mind. She stepped back, unsure of herself, and I could tell she had been screwing up her courage. The shy smile betrayed her, but was soon masked by a studied indifference, an Irish woman's first line of defense. I wanted to reach out and hold onto that smile, cherish it until she had need of it again.

"I didn't mean to . . ." she began.

"No, it's all right . . ."

"I shouldn't have . . ."

"No, honestly . . ."

I shifted from one foot to another, rifling for words to

put her at ease. We were alike, hopeless at the small talk it takes to get beyond the first hurdle.

She was wearing the same mother-of-pearl headband, but her forehead seemed even higher. A worldlier woman would have known that this only heightened her vulnerability. Such innocence was the snare that drew me in.

Again, we spoke at the same time though she was a fraction ahead.

"I just wanted to say . . ."

"Can I buy you a drink?"

The absurdity of the situation struck me. Jesus, I was no pimply adolescent. I should have been able to string a couple of sentences together.

"What are you laughing at?" she demanded.

"I don't know. I suppose I'm laughing at myself."

"You don't remember me, do you?"

I could only wonder why I hadn't thought of her in the last months. Her song at Shannon would have turned my world around at any other time. A sadness welled up inside of me when I considered all I had lost and what I'd become.

I had a crazy notion that she could read my mind and gauge what I was feeling. It wasn't invasive as when Danny gave you the once-over, taking stock of the very springs and wheels that made you tick. Her probe was soothing, reassuring as a breeze off the river on a summer day.

"I remember you like yesterday," I said.

She took note of the expression. Then, to mask her discomfort, she looked for the bartender. He was a particularly sour-looking yokel with a hangdog face more fitting for a basset hound or an undertaker. But for her he broke into a beatific smile, the like of which you'd see on a statue of St. Francis of Assisi as he beholds the birds shitting on his outstretched arms.

"The usual, Noreen?" The words flowed out of him like chiseled silk.

The name was old-fashioned and out of currency in my part of the country, but I liked the ring of it. It reminded me of dark country nights and candlelight. Then I remembered my manners and almost tore a hole in my pocket dragging forth a handful of bills. The barman crinkled his nose at my audacity.

"We look after our own here."

Before I could protest, he had topped a bottle of coke into a glass, slapped it down on the counter, and was already pouring two pints of Guinness at the far end of the bar.

"I don't drink," she said.

"What are you doing in a pub then?" I was surprised at the edge in my voice. But it didn't seem to bother her; she merely pointed over to the table where Johnnie and Danny were laughing to beat the band. The hard bargaining had obviously not yet begun.

"Oh, the music," I answered my own question. Then held out my hand: "I'm Sean."

"I know. I asked Danny last week."

"You did?"

"He didn't tell you?"

"He never tells me anything."

"That's Danny," she smiled in fondness. "And you know my name."

She looked down at the bartender, who beamed back at her and then flashed an *I've got my eye on you, boy* look at me.

She sipped at the coke and frowned. Her eyes, still the deepest of blue, did not sparkle like back in the airport, perhaps because she was struggling to find the right words, for she was hesitant when she spoke. "I was worried about you back in Shannon."

"I didn't even know you noticed me."

When she smiled again her eyes did light up. "It would have been hard to miss you."

She laughed at my confusion. I had been trying to remember the sound of her singing voice; it was quite unlike the gentleness of her speech. The laugh was much more akin, strong but melodious. It curled around you like the heat from a turf fire, warming you and making you feel good about yourself.

"Do you always wear the leather jacket? It's fierce hot in here."

First, Danny, now her. Maybe I was a few pence short of the full shilling.

"I mean the guitar and the punk records . . . they were all calling you Geldof."

She considered this the height of hilarity. I would have much preferred Strummer or Dylan. Then again, such a comparison wasn't so bad coming from a shower of culchie arseholes whose musical boundaries would never stray past Abba.

"What did you think?" I tested the waters.

"I felt bad for you."

This wasn't quite what I had in mind either, and I shot her a hard look.

"I didn't mean it like that," she said.

"I would hope not."

"I meant . . . you were the only one there not crying."

"I didn't notice too many tears on the other gobshites," I lashed out at her.

"Everyone was crying for someone—on the inside."

I shrugged. To the best of my memory, I hadn't been a ball of laughs either.

"Everyone except you," she added.

"I might have cried for my girlfriend if she hadn't been fucking around with someone else."

She lowered her eyes at my coarseness. A golden Claddagh locket dangled from her throat; some letters had been engraved on the heart. When she looked up again, I was trying to decipher them. She thought I was staring at her breasts and blushed.

"Anyway, I have to go now," she said. "I'm glad you're OK."

"Wait! Would you . . . some night . . . like to go to the pictures?"

She giggled like a schoolgirl. "They call it 'the movies' over here, Sean."

She held out her hand. It was all so formal—another brush off. But when she squeezed I felt a neatly folded piece of paper. The room began to hush as she made her way over to the musician's table.

Danny and Johnnie were in the midst of some animated negotiations, but they too looked up. Johnnie appeared to make some kind of sweeping final demand. Danny shook his head in disbelief but reluctantly offered his hand. Johnnie winked at him, then spat in his own palm and they shook. As Danny stood up, I could see the conniving smile writ large across the fiddler's face.

The room was totally silent by the time Danny reached

my side. He didn't see me pocket the piece of paper across which a phone number was written in copperplate. Then Noreen began to sing.

Oh, the trees they grow high, the leaves they do grow green
Many is the time, my true love I have seen
Many is the hour I have watched him all alone
For the bonny boy is young but he's growing.

Oh father, dear father, why have you done me wrong
To go and get me married to one who is so young
For he is only fourteen years and I am twenty-one?
Oh, the bonny boy is young but he's growing.

Daughter, dear daughter, I've done you no wrong
For I have married you to a great lord's son
He'll be the one to care for you when I am dead and gone
Oh, the bonny boy is young but he's growing.

And so early in the morning at the dawning of the day
We went into a hayfield to have some sport and play
And all the things we did there, I never will declare
But I'll never more complain of his growing.

At the early age of fourteen, he was a married man
And at the age of fifteen, the father of a son
At the age of seventeen, his grave it was green.
Cruel death had put an end to his growing.

I'll buy my love some flannel and I will make a shroud
With every stitch I put in it, the tears they will pour down
With every stitch I put in it, my tears like rain will flow.
Cruel life has put an end to his growing.

CHAPTER THIRTEEN

It was nice to think of someone else for a change, to wonder what she was doing, where she came from, where she was going, but most importantly was I on her mind as much as she on mine? At the peak of my optimism this seemed far from unlikely; after all, she had given me her number. But I also roamed amok through a maze of tortuous speculation on her failure to accept my invitation to the pictures. This ranged from compassion for her obvious deafness to visions of her crouched by the phone, poised to scream, "Go out with the likes of you? You've got to be off your rocker, mate."

I was in no hurry to call her. Quite apart from the fear of rejection, I hadn't noticed a cinema in our neighborhood. In fact I wasn't entirely certain where Decatur Avenue lay in the grand scheme of the city. I knew it was in the Bronx, give or take the guts of an hour's subway journey from the site in Manhattan. Like every other Paddy, I could identify the Empire State and the World Trades, though I was unlikely to have any dealings with either unless I happened to be slathering cement on them. Of course, I knew every crack in the sidewalk around Bainbridge and 204th Street and could have strolled blindfolded from one of thirty or so establishments to the next. I was also familiar with the names of the various Blarney Stones, Treaty Stones, and every other Stone that we frequented around Dennehy's sites and could find my way home from them in varied states of consciousness, but that was about the extent of my geographical orientation.

When I, as nonchalantly as possible, inquired of Danny if he ever went to the flicks, he reluctantly allowed that such things could indeed be viewed down on 42nd Street, but he cautioned that one should leave one's wallet at home, on no account fall asleep, and that he personally wouldn't be caught dead at such an assembly. He did concede that each man had his own tastes in these matters. I hesitated to inquire what "these matters" might allude to, for he was studying me keenly. I did get the impression, however, that we were laboring under some misunderstanding and wasn't sure that I should risk a first date with Noreen down on Forty Deuce.

My recent conversation with the lady in question also led me to suspect that I was somewhat out to lunch on an emotional level. Back in Ireland, I had been of the opinion that, while I was relatively sane, those around me were whacked out of their skulls. But I had little doubt that I had crossed a line and was now as out there as anyone else, for I was habitually either shooting my mouth off or instead languishing in the depths of catatonic despair. To add insult to injury, I felt very much at home in either state and was reluctant to initiate an advance that might send a nice Irish girl howling for the hills. And so I bided my time, figuring that a couple of days—or even a week—of reflection might help regain me some kind of foothold in the land of the modestly sane.

Still, Noreen's now dog-eared piece of paper assumed iconic

stature in my life. I transferred it from overalls to jeans and back again, and often scoured my pockets for it on the site. Once on the D train, I was sure it was lost and spread my worldly contents—crumpled dollar bills, plectrums, lottery tickets, and a lonely Trojan—out on my lap until Danny hissed, "Are you out of your fuckin' mind?" I looked up, my face more crimson than any beetroot, to find the whole carriage studiously avoiding the eyes of such an obviously deranged person. After that, I scribbled out copies of her number and hid them behind the poster of James Connolly as well as in various nooks and crannies around the apartment and the site.

Despite this, Mary was ever on my mind. I hated seeing her and yet fretted in her many absences. I always awoke when she came meandering home in the depths of the night. It didn't matter how tired I was, just hearing her footstep in the hall gave me spasms of sweet torment. I'd lie there in the sweating darkness, dig my nails into my arm for fear I'd cave in and beg her to lie down alongside me and my despair. Then when her door would shut, I'd toss and turn until the dawn and Danny's inevitable hand on my shoulder. During our rare evenings home, rather than look her directly in the eye, I'd stumble around like a blind man. Everything she did took on cosmic proportions, and I minutely analyzed her cryptic mumblings in some vain effort to judge my current status in her standings.

Then one morning she had already shuffled by before I even noticed her. I was so shocked I called out hello. This must have taken her by surprise, for when I inquired how she was doing she stammered, "I'm all right, Sean . . ." Then, before drifting on about her glazed business, she added in a hollow voice, "I suppose."

Her bed was tossed, and I was amazed that I hadn't heard her come in the night before. I wanted to dance a double-jig and scream in triumph that, no matter how much she had hurt me, I was finally getting over her. Then I saw her willowy figure bent over the kitchen sink—fragile and alone—and the thought struck me that she was probably going through some private hell of her own. And with that, the old yearning came flooding back, and it was all I could do to stop myself from gathering her in my arms and swearing to protect her from whatever might be amiss.

But there were other times when the hurt eased sufficiently for me to compare her with Noreen, although this was no easy task for they had all the similarities of chalk and cheese. Where one had a translucent inner calmness, the other was all dark turbulence and mystery. I longed for the former but was enmeshed in the latter. Still, there were days when I could romance myself into thinking that I might be happy with Noreen. Jesus, talk about putting the cart before the horse! I didn't even know her last name; for all I knew, she could have been trying to sign me up for Alcoholics Anonymous or a berth in a moderately priced asylum. On and on, I would fantasize about her, but the foundations of these dreams rarely withstood the fear of losing Mary forever.

This would be hammered home whenever I'd see her with Jesús. Always cordial, if removed, he went out of his way not to grind my nose in the shame. But despite my studied indifference, the fluency of their body language would send me packing off to the pub, there to seek solace in snorts of Jameson's amidst the unvarnished pearls of wisdom dropping from the lips of Scutch and Arsehole.

Such was my dithering I might never have called Noreen

if she hadn't shown up for our second gig with Johnnie Crowley. The first, while not an unmitigated disaster, was at best anti-climactic. Gone was the smirk of confidence; the decrepit fiddler seemed to shrink under the constant spotlight and shuffled self-consciously around the stage when not playing. He probably hadn't even rosined his bow standing up since winning successive All Ireland championships back in the unspecified mists of time. He did perk up in the final set and, when given his head on a set of jigs, left us all trailing in his considerable dust. But he chafed under the strictures of a set beat, and the tunes didn't catch fire until Shiggins abandoned all pretence of bringing him to heel. The question remained: Could this unruly force of nature play with a band or was he forever destined to blow the ceilings off the back rooms of pubs. To which Danny answered, "That maniac will play the bollocks off Hendrix if we put the right petrol in his engine."

By the night of our second outing, word had spread along the avenue that the great Johnnie Crowley was hooking up with the Pack of Tinkers. The name was an insult spat at us by an outraged barmaid and, for want of any better suggestion, it stuck. With Patsy in Ireland recovering from his humiliation, his partners at the Olympia had booked us back. The room was jammed, though more to see us fall on our faces than to behold any musical epiphany.

Once again, the scrutiny intimidated Johnnie. Under the white lights he almost evaporated within the folds of his greasy suit, and we plodded along uneventfully. The fact that he hadn't bothered to show up for our lone rehearsal was still vexing me when I saw Noreen waltz by. My mood was helped less by the fact that her partner appeared besotted by her than that she failed to pay appropriate attention to me floundering around in my artistic miasma.

"That auld bastard is blowin' it on us," I whined when Johnnie fled to the toilets at the end of the set.

But Danny was locked in conversation with Shiggins, unusual in itself; then they actually shook hands before the drummer spun on his heel and hurried after Johnnie.

"What was that all about?"

"There's more ways than one to rosin a bow, Paddy," Danny muttered.

"What are you talkin' about now?"

"That fiddle will dance to a different tune this set." With that, he turned to polishing his guitar, sphinx-like as ever when a lesser mortal such as I wished to get to the bottom of something.

"Aren't you going to say hello?"

She surprised me again. No besotted partner waltzing her by—no headband either. Her dark hair framing her face, she smiled, and somehow everything fell into place. Without thinking I slid my arm under her cardigan and pulled her close. She laid her right hand on my shoulder as though we were dancing. Perhaps we were for I wasn't aware of anything except the lilac smell of her hair and my own heart beating against her breast. I don't know how long we stayed like that, mere seconds perhaps, but when she finally drew back a link had been forged. Did I buy her a drink? Ask her out to the pictures again? I don't know and it hardly mattered, because from then on every time I stepped off the stage, she was waiting for me.

I wanted to sing and dance and take all the solos just for her. I barely noticed that Johnnie was sneezing like blue thunder

and sweating like a pig when the lights came up, for I had
Noreen's cobalt eyes fastened on mine, and I entertained no other
desire but to mainline my way into her heart. I had to show
her that the Pack of Tinkers could swing the house in a way
that mere Traddies could never dream of. But before I could
even get warmed up, Johnnie shattered all my notions. After
one last tremendous *ahtishoo,* he did a little jig of anticipation;
then, in great sweeps of melody and flourishes of improvisation,
he swept up and down the neck of that fiddle until the very
rafters were rattling and roaring from the storm he was weaving.

The crowd stood gape-jawed as we rolling stoned and
fought the law, then got up and stood up, before Johnnie
dispensed with all formalism and catapulted us into the "King
of the Fairies." It even took Shiggins moments to figure what
madness the fiddler was conjuring, such was the intensity and
profusion of grace notes and ornamentals exploding from
his fingers; but in the midst of the gale the drummer
hammered down a thunderous four on the floor while the
rest of us scurried to identify the myriad keys that Johnnie
was running riot amongst. On the second go-round, Shiggins
added a sixteenth on his high hat, whereupon Bugsy threw
caution to the wind and plucked a harmonic on his G-string,
allowing it to hang until the end of the line, when he plunged
down in a perfect series of triads to hit the floor again on a
one. A crack on the snare every eight kicks, and we had
entered some kind of crazy Rocksteady Céili heaven. Danny
struck a lofty sustain and held it, occasionally modulating up
a fifth to sound like a cross between Ladder 33's siren and
David Gilmour ripping off Curtis Mayfield on speed. So fast
was the tempo, it was all I could do to lay down a skanked-
out chord, laced with vibrato, at the top of every bar.

And all of a sudden we clicked, and every cynical bastard in the Olympia knew it. With a whoop that might have been heard back in Dingle, a giant Kerryman grabbed a red-headed woman from Donegal and swung her to the four points of the compass. A space cleared as they rocketed off a ring of onlookers, but when each of the felled rose to their feet, instead of settling scores, they grabbed a partner and attempted to outdo the wild duo in their whirling. With the whole floor swirling like dervishes, the Tinkers had arrived, and the Bronx had never seen their like before.

And later that night, I was kissing Noreen in a darkened doorway and telling her all the things I hadn't whispered to a woman in a long time. And she was listening and kissing me back until our two bodies ached from the pleasure. And there was a madness in the night that made even the brutal streets sparkle with delight, and the eyes of every passer-by gleamed in at us, banishing all our misfortune and swearing that we were made for each other and that nothing in this wide earthly would ever tear us apart, while my head still spun from the lilting madness of the music that Johnnie had wrenched from his fiddle. Indeed, if either of us had looked up we might have seen a drunken *pucán* doing a half-set atop the Kingsbridge Armory, for Johnnie's magic fingers had unleashed on the Bronx his majesty, the lascivious, lugubrious, and highly unpredictable, King of the Fairies.

CHAPTER FOURTEEN

S he must have been at the front of the train, for I hadn't noticed her getting off at Kingsbridge. Had Danny been with me, I'd have been up there too. He was intent on maximizing every second: striding like a sergeant-major up the platform in Manhattan so that we'd be positioned to stroll right out the gate when the doors opened in the Bronx. In his absence I tended to dawdle down by the entrance and board whatever car happened to screech up next to me.

I raced up the avenue after her and was just about to yell out, but something about the purpose in her step gave me pause. In general, she tended to gaze in shop windows and meet the glance of anyone who cast an eye at her; now she was all business, head down and bulling for home.

We hadn't seen Kate in some time, although she called Scutch's every week to let us know that she'd be staying downtown "another few days or so" looking after the children. She had our schedules down pat for she always managed to get me on the phone. I always felt weird telling Danny later. But he never betrayed a flicker of emotion nor inquired further about her. She even sent a money order for her share of the rent to the pub. Scutch had a thing for Kate, and they were close in an odd kind of way. She had obviously given him instructions, for he'd bide his time until Danny had gone home before handing over the letter. This was always accompanied by a questioning look, but I never rose to the bait.

Although I couldn't for the life of me fathom why, it seemed that Kate somehow blamed me for her rift with Danny. And here I was trailing her down the hill through the little park that housed Poe's cabin, the resident junkies staring past me through vacant eyes. The lights were on in the windows of the surrounding apartment buildings though it was barely six o'clock. The leaves on the few scrawny trees had turned brown, some were already dancing around my feet, and I hadn't broken a sweat in a month nor longed for an Atlantic breeze.

Had I even thought of home? When was the last time I'd called my mother to recite the lies we shared, though I knew she believed none of them? When was the last time I'd dashed off a letter full of exaggerations and wishful thinking? It had been months since I'd looked up at a street sign or studied a subway map. Now I padded these concrete canyons like a native, stepping around the garbage and the people, barely noticing hands held out for loose change and the hard luck stories behind them. I had dealt with few of the immigrant rites of passage with any kind of grace; in truth I had barged straight through them without a thought for anyone but myself. Yet, somehow, I had reached the other side. But if I was a rougher and readier person than the innocent who had landed at Kennedy at the beginning of the summer, so too had I little trouble staying just far back enough from Kate so that she wouldn't catch sight of me out of the corner of her eye.

If I hadn't been so familiar with the particularities of her figure, I would never have recognized her, for she was sporting a flame-haired wig that, even to my untutored eye, had been out of style since the dawn of disco. Nor did it take a *fashionista* to divine that she had stuffed herself into the couple-of-sizes-too-small discard from her Manhattan employer. Though I couldn't see her breasts, I had no doubt that they were peeking out over the top of her ruby red dress since every Puerto Rican male, from *Papi* to pre-pubescent, was expressing unalloyed enthusiasm as she clip-clopped by. I could hardly fault them; I was fixated on the glory of her derriere as it shifted and shaped beneath the slinky silk material. All things being equal, I was one up on my neighbors for, having shared close quarters, I could speculate with some authority on the color and cut of underwear she would choose to match such finery.

When we turned onto Decatur, I was only yards behind and torn as to whether I should follow her quietly up the stairs and perhaps confirm my lingerie speculations or buy a couple of six-packs. Thirst and a nagging degree of chivalry won the day. By the time I reached our landing, she had already entered the apartment; the door, however, was still cracked open. I was just about to barge in and welcome her home when I heard Danny drag the words out of himself: "I'm sorry, Kate."

"For what?"

"You know."

I was stranded, with my tool bag in one hand, two six-packs dripping beneath my oxter, and an eye roaming around the back of my head in case Squint Eye might light upon me.

"I'm no different than I was before. . . ."

"Yes, you are," she interrupted him. "I used to be crazy about you and there was some small chance, but now . . ."

"For Christ sake, woman, I'm doing me best."

"Your best is it?" she spat out the words. "You don't have a clue, do you? How proud I used to be at Gaelic Park with the man of the match coming over and talking to me. Me! That no one else bothered about except when they were after a cheap feel. All the girls green with envy, and me keeping meself pure for you in case you'd see the light some day. And, even if it was a bunch of humbug, it was still brilliant, 'cause I never had anything like that before. I mean look at me!"

She must have flung something because I heard cans scattering across the table and hitting the floor. One by one, they were picked up and tossed into the garbage before Danny replied, "You're worth a hundred of them any day of the week."

"I'd have walked through walls for you . . . but sure, what's the use?"

"Don't give up on me, Kate."

"Give up on you! What are you asking me?"

"I'm not asking you anything. It's just . . ."

"It's just what, Danny?"

"Ah, Jaysus . . ."

It wasn't a scream like on the awful night, more a low moan of nothingness that was almost drowned out by a shuffle of movement. She must have taken him in her arms, for her next words were whispered: "It's OK, pet, it's OK."

She should have left well enough alone, gone on cradling him. Instead, she whispered, "I know, Danny, *a stór*. I hear you talking in your sleep."

"What are you on about?" His voice was suddenly jagged with the raw edge of the Belfast streets. "What did you hear, woman?"

"You're hurting me, Danny."

"What did I say?"

"Nothing, I swear."

"You're lying—just like the rest of them!"

"I'm not. Just . . . stuff about Morgan."

"Shut up!"

"I didn't mean anything by it, Danny, I'm sorry."

"Shut the fuck up!"

"Don't, please . . ."

I couldn't take any more. But by the time I staggered in the door making a big show of having had a few drinks and slamming down the two sixes on the table, Danny was on the way to his usual spot by the window while Kate was by the sink trying to lend some shape to her flattened hair. The red wig lay in a heap on the table, its many curls crumpled and awry. They both knew I'd been eavesdropping, but neither made an attempt to go along with my Olivier.

Trapped in the smoldering silence, I wondered how two people so close could be at such cross-purposes? Who else did they have but each other? They were now all I had too, what with my mother halfway around the world fading so quickly I could no longer summon up her face in any clear likeness. Rooted to pedestals on either side of the room, they were my ballast. Without them I would float away. As though I were a child of divorcing parents, I wanted above all else to bring them together: sit them down at the table, split my six-packs until we were easy again with each other, then stroll down to Scutch's and get blasted like the old days. The old

days, my arse! Five months ago, I didn't even know the two
of them from Adam, and there was a lot I still couldn't put
my finger on. No wonder my world had neither shape nor
make to it.

But Kate was back. That was something in and of itself.
Despite the hurt and the strained silence, she soon began to
putter around the apartment, reclaiming her space like some
great displaced tabby: sniffing around Mary's room, cocking
her nose at yesterday's incense, laying out voluminous jars and
tubes of ointments, unguents, powders, and perfumes on the
rim of the kitchen sink.

Brooding away at the table, hammering down beer after
beer, I knew that it was within my power to bridge the gap
between them. I'd never bothered doing such a thing before—
had always watched from the sidelines, a perennial hurler on
the ditch. I had failed to reach out to my mother in her
pining grief; nor had I spoken up in Nolan's Hotel Bar while
my father's life dissolved into tumblers of whiskey. I'd even
allowed Mary to disappear for days on end without
demanding what the hell she was up to.

Around the fifth or sixth beer, I thought about Noreen
and some kind of levee broke within me. I told them how
she made me feel new again, how I lit up in her presence,
and how the fractured stars above the Bronx glittered in her
eyes. I spoke of the simple things that moved me: watching
her brushing her hair and mooring it with combs or
headbands; the care she took to match earrings with whatever
colors she was wearing; the gentle way she touched my face
when a cloud of sadness threatened; the taste of her lips and
skin; and how she would invite me over when her roommates
had gone to the pub; how we would lie shoulder to shoulder

in her single bed, the way we touched each other through our clothes and, sometimes when the heat of the night became too much, how we would undress and go so far, but no further.

At first, they thought I was mad and bade me hush, for none of us had spoken in such terms before. But the more I blathered on, the greater the relief and, as the night settled in, they drew closer and finally sat at the table. Kate produced a bottle of rum, while Danny foraged beneath his bed for some cans of Coke to mix with it. They were forced to face each other and, even if the hurt remained, we became our own family—fucked, flustered and far from home though we might have been.

We did not throw our arms around each other, shed tears, and swear eternal friendship, for we were Irish and left that class of thing to the Yanks. But we did exult in the warmth of our own company and the sparks of friendship that we struck off each other, and all because I had opened up for the first time in my callow life. It wouldn't be the last occasion, I swore to myself. Though it still might cut me to the quick whenever I thought of Mary, things were looking up. The Tinkers were rockin' the bejaysus out of Bainbridge, I had a girlfriend who cared, and a brother and a sister to share secrets with. And on certain nights, with the King of the Fairies beaming down on us, even the concrete fields of the Bronx sparkled beneath our feet.

Was it then that Danny broke the news that Arsehole had managed to get a rough tape to a Steve from RCA through some Paddy doorman down in Manhattan? Or was it the occasion he told us that Steve thought we had "potential"? I'm pretty sure it wasn't the night he cast off all his Northern reserve and proclaimed that the great man himself would be coming up by limo to catch the band in the Olympia. It's hard to remember for there were many such intoxicating evenings during the magical rise of the Pack of Tinkers.

CHAPTER FIFTEEN

It was a long fall and it seemed like winter would never come. A cold front might threaten for a day or two, but the last gasps of an Indian summer would inevitably rout it. Still, as the nights grew shorter, you could feel a nip in the air and tell that some change was at hand. Strange exotic leaves from the nearby Botanical Gardens rustled down Decatur out of whack with the rude grey street; but in the end, the Bronx levels everything and, all in good time, they clogged the drains and added to the sludge that lapped around the rotting bags of garbage.

News from the North was troubling. Conditions in the prison camps had been deteriorating, with more internees refusing to avail of even the most basic of facilities. And now some of these blanket men with their long scraggly hair and hollowed out eyes had begun a hunger strike in filthy Long Kesh, though the newspapers promised that it was only a matter of time until the British compromised and granted them a renewal of political status. All along Bainbridge the drinkers muttered behind their glasses, and the Tyrone boys did not share the media's optimism or hold their breath for signs of British reasonableness.

I barely noticed. I was consumed by the band, with any time to spare devoted to Noreen. She wasn't continually on my mind in Mary fashion; rather she was a warm presence stored away for a daydream or a rough moment, always there when I needed her. Bugsy said that's what girlfriends were for—to be the backbone of their men and not cause all manner of bother cavorting around. He did warn that men had certain obligations too, but that seemed to provoke a memory that saddened him, and I had sense enough to let the matter rest.

Word had spread about the Tinkers, and we were playing four or even five nights a week, though there was a combustible element to the outfit: Most nights Johnnie would show but, from time to time, there'd be no sign of him.

"It's just the nature of the beast," Danny said one evening while we waited onstage. "It's hard to bottle lightning. We'll just have to muck along without him."

And we did. Confidence does that for you—that sense you get when you finally know where you're going, even if you're not sure how you're getting there. On top of that, the focus had turned to our own songs, and Paddies were now showing up to hear about themselves, their thoughts, and concerns; sometimes you could even catch them mouthing the lines of choruses.

We'd branched out from the avenue and were often to be seen in Dennehy's van barreling across the Triborough Bridge to Woodside or Bay Ridge. Arsehole, our self-appointed manager, was even fielding inquiries from as far away as Jersey and Connecticut.

Sleep was now a rarity to be eked out in naps on the subway or during the few sacred hours between the end of the gig and Danny's six-in-the-morning hand on my shoulder. Yet I never had such a spring in my step. Who needed sleep when the biddies were beaming at you, and lads who hadn't given you the time of day now nodded and murmured in your wake, "That fellah is one of the Tinkers."

It was all down to Johnnie initially, but the rest of our boats rose on the swelling of his tide. Ideas that you might have suppressed for fear of being laughed at seemed not only possible but practical. Songs that I considered too personal now sat nicely within the arc of the fiddler's dazzling musicality. Each player marked out his own space, delighting in the lightning sparked by the others. Danny was exporting sheets of controlled feedback from his new Vox 440 amplifier, allowing Johnnie's fiddle to glide over, under, around, and between these gales of shifting dissonance. But it was Shiggins and Bugsy who molded and then held the whole quivering equation together, tightening the beats within ever-greasier grooves until the very walls of the pubs shook to their syncopation.

If I was on the pig's back, I was also oblivious to much of what was going on around me. Still, I was shocked to see Danny replaced by a lesser player in a big match at Gaelic Park. It didn't surprise me that he promptly quit the Tyrone team, for he was uppity and took offence easily, although there may have been more to it than met the eye. Unusual for two men who rarely spoke above whispers to each other, there was a blazing row between himself and Dennehy that even the walls of the site-office couldn't contain.

"You were warned to keep your nose clean," Dennehy roared.

"Stay the hell out of my business."

"You are my bloody business, and them fellahs are only troublemakers. We don't need any splits at a time like this."

"I do what the fuck I like and when I feel like it!"

"And you see where that got you!"

"Yeah, in this shite hole—when you could have me doin' what I do best!"

"Them days are over!"

"For you maybe! But I'm not going to rot here forever."

"For the love of Jaysus, lad, there are some only dyin' to send a bad word home about you."

"They can't do any worse than they've done already." Danny's voice had lowered and I, as well as many of the bogmen, had to strain to hear Dennehy's final chilling words.

"You, of all people, know better than that."

I didn't tell Kate the full story, but she must have read between the lines, for the color drained from her face, and she began the tuneless humming that accompanied all crises. Still, after a while she seemed almost relieved, as if something had come to a head and was better dealt with that way. She said that it was just as well that Danny was taking a rest because the poor chap had been wrestling with gland problems for a while and didn't need to be traipsing his arse off around Gaelic Park for people the like of Dennehy, who didn't appreciate him anyway.

I didn't feel so positive. Apart from the chill in Dennehy's voice, football was part of Danny's identity. It provided part of the authority that kept him head and shoulders above the bogmen. Take that away and would they be as willing to bend to his will and close ranks behind him in an emergency? Few liked him, most admired him, but what about the handful who did neither? Would they be as eager to deal with his arrogant ways and cocksure manner now that the big boss had publicly demonstrated his disapproval?

Despite my fears, there was no perceptible change in Danny's status on the site or elsewhere. Yet from that point on he kept even more to himself and would mostly sit in with Kate on our nights off, reading, curling licks on his Strat, or staring out the window. He'd be long asleep by the time I got in from Noreen's.

On one of those nights, I put no pass on their absence, for they occasionally took a late stroll to the diner. Then I remembered that Kate was babysitting downtown. I figured I'd wait up for Danny; I wanted to discuss the type of set we should play for the guy from RCA. After a couple of beers I got worried; he had looked a bit pale of late, and only that morning I'd seen him strain to lift a sack of cement.

Though I was pretty knackered, I threw on my army jacket and headed down to Scutch's. It was a relief to see Danny ensconced there amongst the stragglers, and I realized, though we'd been much in each other's company, we hadn't had a heart to heart of late. He gazed up blearily but called for a couple of Powers when I sat down next to him. He looked thin and a bit fragile, but that wasn't so odd considering the all-nighters we'd been pulling. It was his eyes that troubled me, dull and motionless. To top it all, he was dead drunk.

"It's over," he said, and I almost fell off the chair. Jesus Christ, we hadn't even played CB's yet, let alone the Mudd Club or Max's.

"What are you talkin' about?"

"I said it's fuckin' over." He wheeled away in disgust.

Just like that, Mister Universe calls it quits, and that's the end of the Tinkers? No bloody way! I lit into him for his selfishness and was in the midst of a rant when he leaned into me and threw his arm around my shoulder. His face was touching mine, and I was nervous at the intimacy, especially with the whole bar looking on. He was reeking of whiskey and, for an awful second, I thought he might kiss me.

"They got their man," he whispered.

Out of the corner of my eye, I could see Scutch mouthing some words. There wasn't even a murmur from the stragglers. "Strawberry Fields" faded off the jukebox, to be replaced by the saxophone intro of "Whatever Gets You Through the Night." I was thinking I hadn't heard those songs in a while when I finally deciphered Scutch's lips: "Lennon." He then drew his finger across his throat.

"Come on now, Danny," he cajoled above the jubilation of the song, "Sean will get you home."

"You take me bloody money all night and then throw me out?"

"No one's throwin' you out, man. You have the early start in the mornin'."

"Then give us another round!"

"No! Go home to bed, for the love of God. I've had enough meself."

There was a murmur of protest from the stragglers.

"That's it! Jimmy, turn off that feckin' television and pull down the shutters."

With that he cut the jukebox and produced the hurley. I hadn't even noticed the TV running with the sound muted. I caught one picture of a familiar building opposite Central Park before the screen went dead. A cold blast of air surged into the silence when Jimmy opened the door; then a chain was yanked and the first steel shutter came clattering down. When Danny tossed back the remains of his shot, Scutch put away the hurley but stood ready for action, arms crossed, his tattoos glowing through the white nylon shirt. His face was fierce but distressed; Lennon's murder had affected the little man too.

Indeed, it had disturbed the whole company: Boozers who couldn't have named a Beatles tune for the life of them shouldered an extra layer of care. It wasn't just the music or anything the Liverpudlian had stood for; it was more the pointlessness and sheer randomness of the act that rankled, allied to the anxiety that one more rickety pillar of their uncertain existence had been sledge-hammered from beneath them. And so they glowered into their beers, pissed to high heaven with Danny and the world in general for upending their nightly excursion to oblivion.

Unconcerned with their plight, Danny staggered out the door with no word of farewell. A couple of times he stumbled into the garbage, and I had to grab onto him. Either he had lost weight or I was getting stronger, but I had little trouble holding him up. Still, there was a dread to the night, for he mumbled to himself like some old ciderhead the whole way home, finally refusing to mount the stairs at Decatur until I heard out his drunken raving in the piss-stained hallway.

"You don't understand, Paddy." He poked his finger in my chest, spraying me with spittle, his eyes now commandeered by a mad certainty. "You're like all the rest of them. You think nothin's connected. But it is, man, just open your eyes. You and your Mary, me and the Cause, Dennehy and the leadership—Johnnie Lennon and his music was one of the few good things that held us all together. The pig is on a roll, I'm tellin' you. You don't know sweet fuck all about him because you've never had to deal with the bastard! But he's got his man in the White House now. You may laugh and snigger at Ronnie Reagan, but mark my words, this country will dance to a different jig yet. By the time he's finished, the world'll be turned arse over elbow."

He stepped back from me, incredulous that I couldn't comprehend what was so obvious. In truth I was only half-listening, humoring him in the hope of getting him upstairs and into bed as quickly as possible. But certain of his words stuck in my brain and left me the far side of uneasiness.

The next morning, there was no hand on my shoulder; in fact, it took me a good minute to wake him. He looked awful, his face bleached and drawn. I tried to persuade him to stay in bed, for all the good that did. Instead he huddled in the passenger seat of the van and insisted that I drive, though I didn't have a license. Bad enough, but then he bade me cruise down through Harlem past the Dakota, though half the cops and cameras in New York were gathered outside. I felt a bit of a fake when we blessed ourselves; though I loved Lennon and, like the rest of the city, was staggered by the sheer randomness of his murder, the world didn't seem a whole lot different without him—just emptier and a bit grayer. As for the dream being over, that was all very well for those who had achieved something but I still had bucketfuls of my own ambitions to attend to.

When Kate came home that night, she lit into me for letting Danny out of bed. She called in sick herself and ordered him to stay home too. To my surprise, he did as he was told. After a couple of days' rest, the blush returned to his cheeks. He didn't mention Lennon again, though the whole town was abuzz with the shooting. Still, I could tell it never strayed far from his mind. He had sensed something that I had no notion of and it was eating the heart out of him.

On the morning of the day that RCA Steve was to grace the Olympia, Danny's hand again did not shake my shoulder. Maybe he needed the day off himself, but I wasn't complaining. When I finally surfaced in the early afternoon, the long sleep had worked wonders and I felt like a new man. It was a glorious day—cool, bright and flinty—nothing to do but rehearse at the Olympia. The mood within the band was keen and optimistic, not a nerve out of place. Shiggins' last words were, "Remember, lads, it's us that's auditioning him." Danny had some last matters to discuss with Arsehole, who was taking the train down to Manhattan so that he might later cut a bit of a figure while emerging from Steve's limo.

A cold front was seeping down from Canada, and there was a touch of ice in the air on my way back to Decatur. Holiday lights were blinking from stores, and even the poorest of apartment windows were decorated with some sort of sparkling cheer. There was an odd beauty to it all, and I felt a sudden, unexpected surge of empathy for the battered streets around me. Then the thought struck that it would be my first Christmas away from home. Would my mother kill the turkey as she always did? Sit down at the table for her solitary meal, or would she even bother—just take a plate in her lap by the fire? The guilt smothered me, and I knew I should go home and be with her, but that might compromise my getting back to the Bronx. Besides, there were gigs to play, and what if things went well with RCA, and now there was Noreen to consider. It was too much. There'd be time enough for such thoughts later. I had to keep my mind locked in on the Tinkers and the task ahead.

The skeleton of a half-moon perched over the rooftops,

while across the Concourse the last golden breath of the sun gave way to the frozen night. For a few moments in the soft twilight, the great thoroughfare looked as it must have when first constructed: a monument to ambition and grand dreams before the garish tide of graffiti and decay turned it into the nightmare it had become. The elderly, the abandoned, and those with children hurried home, their heads down, a night to kill stretching ahead. As soon as darkness closed in, the old street of dreams would revert to a no man's land beset by hair-trigger turf and smack wars. I pulled up my collar, for the wind was swirling on every corner, and passed on. I had an urge to hear the warmth of Noreen's voice, but there was a line of people outside the public phone.

Mary was in the kitchen, a pile of her clothes tossed over a chair as she matched colors with Kate's lipsticks; no doubt she was going out with Jesús. For once, I didn't care.

She didn't seem to be much bothered either, for she casually let a skirt fall to the floor before stepping into another. Despite my affected nonchalance, it would have taken a stone not to observe her slim figure. If she had lost weight, she had done so proportionately. She was wearing a thin blue cardigan with the sleeves rolled down, but it was unbuttoned and, without meaning to, I glanced at the tiny birthmark above her left breast. She smiled and I caught a hold of myself—standing there like an idiot ogling her, my leather jacket still buttoned up, the sweat pouring off me from the steaming heat inside the apartment.

"I'm glad you and Jesús have become friends."

"Oh yeah, we're absolutely inseparable."

"At least, you don't hate him?"

Actually, I hadn't been giving him a lot of thought. I

should have just gone about my business, but old habits die hard, and I couldn't resist snapping, "Two can play your game, Mary."

She crossed her arms over her breasts, her eyes all at once brimming with tears. "Sean," she whispered.

At another time, I might have run to her, but she began to shiver; it seemed so out of place in the steaming heat. To my surprise, she walked over to the window and threw it open. A breeze unsettled the curtains as she leaned back against the poster of Hendrix. She looked even paler next to the wash of psychedelia and, even at a distance, I could make out tiny goose bumps. She seemed otherworldly, and I couldn't take my eyes off her.

"Everything is not the way it looks."

I barely caught her words and turned away, for I felt I was intruding. Then I saw her fancy clothes piled on the chair again; Jesús would be arriving soon. I made no attempt to hide the bitterness. "It never was with you."

"Someday, I'll explain it all to you, Sean."

"Someday is for other people."

I took off my jacket and, without thinking, laid it on her clothes. We used to do that all the time back home, mix and match our Clash T-shirts and leather. But these dresses and skirts were an eternity away from Strummer and the girl I knew. I grabbed the jacket and flung it across the room— anywhere but next to the clothes she wore only for him.

"Don't get hard, love. It doesn't suit you."

The use of the endearment cut me to the quick, for what currency did it have any more?

"I'm going to survive you," I snarled. "Someday, you'll be just another memory."

"When did you start writing country songs?"

At another time, I might have smiled, for she always knew how to puncture my pretensions. Instead I stared down her affection. But she had already let her skirt slide to the floor and was searching through the pile for another.

"Put on some clothes, will you."

"It's nothing you haven't seen before."

"Yeah, but I never want to again."

She studied me for some moments. Then she reached out and touched my cheek. She was so close it hurt.

"Don't you, Sean?"

I could smell the incense in her hair. She moved an inch closer than she should have before murmuring, "At least, we're still friends."

"I'm not sure I'd use that description." I tried to be casual when all I really wanted to do was crush her to me.

But she had already moved away, humming to herself as she tried on a black fitted skirt. It was a song by the Cure that used to mean something to us, and yet, for the life of me, I couldn't place it.

"I hear you have a new girlfriend."

"Good news travels fast."

"Do I know her?"

"I somehow doubt it. She's not very fluent in Spanish."

"What's she like, Sean?"

What's she like—what's she like? The words ricocheted around my brain, but I didn't want to share her with Mary. Didn't want to mention Noreen's name. Didn't want to hear it trip off Mary's tongue. But most of all, I didn't want to compare them. Was I ashamed of Noreen? Why did other women always come up short against Mary? After all, she had screwed me royally, and here I was pleading for more. Still, I knew that there would always be things between us that I could never share with anyone. Things we had done together, things I might never do with anyone else. She knew that full well too.

"Tell me, Sean," she persisted.

"Well, she's blonde, a bit taller than you. Slimmer, but . . ." I motioned to my chest because she had once confided that she would have liked fuller breasts. "She has nice lips, a beautiful smile, and . . . someday I'm going to fuck her on that couch like you and your Spanish bastard!"

She shivered again and unconsciously massaged her arms. "Sean, I'm scared."

"Oh, go fuck yourself. You made your bed, now you can lie in it."

"Can you do me a favor?"

"No."

"Please?"

"Don't you have ears? I said, no!"

She stood motionless as the steam from the broken radiator valve sizzled and heightened the silence between us. Her eyes raced from pleading to hunted, then hung a sudden u-turn through calculating to end up at a calm but icy resolve. "Come out with me tonight," she murmured.

"Are you crazy? The fellah from RCA is coming up to the Olympia."

"Just for a drink."

"No!"

"I promise you, it won't take long."

"What's Rudolph Valentino going to say?"

"He's taking care of his kid."

"His kid? Jesus Christ, you've made a right mess of your life, haven't you?"

There were footsteps in the hallway; then a guitar case was balanced against the door. She had already grabbed her clothes and dragged me inside her room before a key turned in the lock. She put her finger over her lips, and we listened as Danny hurried to the bathroom and took a long relieving piss. She was nestled so close I could feel her shivering beneath the thin cardigan.

"I've got something to do down the Lower East Side, and I can't go on my own," she whispered.

"That's your problem."

She edged even closer and dug her fingers into my arm; she didn't let go until I lowered my voice. "I've got to get my head together for this gig."

"We can take car service and be right back."

"Where the hell are you getting money for car service?"

"Sean, you're the only one I can ask."

She looked at me with all the hope and pleading that I could never refuse, and I knew I was only fooling myself.

She knew it too. She smiled like she used to when we shared secrets. She slipped on a skirt, smoothed it down, and then ran a brush through her hair, never once taking her eyes off me. I glanced at my watch—still over four hours until the first set. Even with traffic, there was no way we'd take longer than three.

"I've got to be in the Olympia by ten o'clock."

"I swear you'll be back well before then. Let's go." She dragged a large black pocketbook from under the bed and slung it over her shoulder. Then she took one last glance in the mirror and grimaced at her pouting lips.

Danny was at the table wrestling with a set list. He looked up sharply when I came out of her room.

"I'll be back soon." I avoided his stare, grabbed my jacket, and headed towards the door.

"Where are you going?"

"I've got to get some strings."

"What's she doing? Riding shotgun?"

Mary was nudging me forward, and I felt like a pawn between them.

"I'm asking you a question."

He had risen from the chair, his body taut as he leaned towards us, his two hands gripping the edge of the table. She pushed me once again but I spun around at him. "Listen, we might be in a band together, but I'm not married to you."

"Yet," Mary whispered and opened the door.

"For Christ sake, don't be late. This guy won't hang around," he shouted, but we were already on the landing.

"You should watch that one," she said, while we took the stairs two at a time.

I felt sick to my stomach, but I don't think she even heard me reply, "He says the same about you."

CHAPTER SIXTEEN

I never knew what hit me. One minute I was standing in a doorway down on Avenue C, the next I was being hustled through a hallway and flung up against the wall of a foul smelling, dimly lit room. The pain was so bad I wanted to drop to the floorboards, but a black man in a navy windbreaker held me by the throat while pressing a small snout-nosed gun into my temple.

"Mary!" I cried out. He whipped back the gun and brought it down so close to my face that it brushed the stubble on my chin. Without a flicker of emotion, he signaled that I would do well to zip my mouth for the foreseeable future.

Any time I wobbled from the fright and faintness, he tightened his grip; when my eyes closed, he intimated that I keep them open. Though he never slackened his gaze, he betrayed little interest. I might as well have been a less than scintillating sack of turnips in need of balance. I never doubted that this man could kill me and think little of the matter.

After some minutes his grip slackened, and I became more aware of the throbbing in the back of my head. My collar was damp and sticky, and I prayed that it was sweat. I struggled to block out the smell of piss and stale dampness, but my stomach began to heave, and I was in mortal fear of throwing up. Should I tell him and risk a beating or let the damn thing spurt out and take my chances?

He must have sensed my thoughts, for he thrust me even closer to the wall and stepped back a tad. Now I could clearly see the gun he still pointed at me: So small and cartoon like, and yet one squeeze of the trigger and my brains would be splattered all over the puke-colored walls. Then the music began. Swaying and samba-like, it wasn't until the guitar entered that I recognized Santana. The black man smiled knowingly. Without moving my head, I followed the sound to a slit of light leaking from under a door. She was in there with someone.

With the pounding at the back of my skull worsening, I tried to piece together what had happened. Mary had been fidgety and unable to sit still in the livery car. I felt relatively relaxed as the driver made good time down the thruway and across the Third Avenue Bridge onto the FDR. Besides, it was one of those pristine New York nights when you fancied that you could even see stars dangling over the emerald city. The half moon had shed its veil and cast a milky sheen down the length of the East River. The water shimmered in stillness except near the 59th Street Bridge, where a lone tugboat sliced perfect waves that danced fandangos against the pylons. We didn't speak above the chatter of the Spanish radio station. She was hanging on tightly to her pocketbook, fixated on the winding highway, oblivious of the stark beauty. I wondered about her agitation and kept an eye on the speedometer; at the rate we were traveling, I might even have time for a nice soak in the bath before the gig.

My mood darkened somewhat when we veered off the FDR onto Houston Street and raced beneath the towering bulk of the projects. The driver ignored a red light and sped around the corner on Avenue C just in front of a screaming ambulance. Avenue was a rather pretentious designation for a laneway gouged with potholes, the tenements on both sides teetering in on top of it. Most of the street bulbs had been smashed, and what light there was leaked out from a succession of ratty bodegas. The driver wove his way gingerly down the center of this rutted track despite the occasional oncoming gypsy cab.

Mary bade him halt at the corner of 5th Street and fished in her jacket pocket for the fare. But when some lounging Puerto Rican men edged over to the window, she screamed at him to take us a couple of blocks further. In a staccato stream of *Nuyorican,* he fired back that he had a fare waiting on Fordham, and what was the *señorita's* problem? She replied, in an Irish-tinged version of the same dialect, that if he cared to go home with a tip he'd better shut the fuck up and do exactly as the *señorita* said. To which the driver shook his head in disgust. Still he took care to accelerate away from the men.

"Get out!" she barked, before the cab had even halted, while reaching over and shoving some notes into the driver's fist. The Puerto Rican men were already sauntering up the avenue towards us.

They were still over a block away, but my feet felt nailed to the sidewalk. Though I was well used to the slums of my own neighborhood, this part of town reeked of a new malevolence.

"Hurry up!" Mary shoved me in the back.

The driver had pulled off but something spooked him,

for he suddenly swerved around with a screech of tires and was now approaching us again.

"Let's get out of here!" I yelled.

"Are you fucking mad?" She dashed ahead of me towards a doorway.

I hailed the driver but he sped past, wildly gesticulating at some parked cars. I tried to follow Mary but slipped on a half-broken pane of glass. Attempting to right myself, I did a tango on the kerb, the street cascading around me in a swirl of graffiti, metal shutters and stained concrete. The Puerto Rican men had now broken into a gallop, and I lurched towards the doorway. I was just inside when a blaze of pain seared through the back of my head.

I followed the black man's glance towards the door. He smiled when it was thrown open and the music blared into our room. A man's voice, cajoling at first, rose in pitch until it cut across Santana's velvet groove.

"You better if you know what's good for you!" There was no mistaking the nasal threat. I barely glimpsed a tall thin man in a Yankees cap before the door closed behind Mary. Her hair was disheveled, her lipstick smeared; for an instant, she didn't move, then she wiped her mouth with the back of her hand.

"Are you OK?" I risked a whisper and flinched, but the black man had lost interest and was staring at her too. She didn't answer, just drifted over, her eyes glazed. She reached out but couldn't quite bring her fingers to touch me.

The black man leered at her, then casually pushed me away and walked towards the closed door. Without his support, I felt faint again.

"Come." She said, tears streaming down her face.

And then we were out on the avenue. The half-moon was milky again, or perhaps my vision was blurred. I was shivering, though the night did not feel as cold as before.

I'm not sure how we got to St. Vincent's. I stumbled at one point, some rough hands picked me up, and Mary discovered the wound on the back of my head. I recall her sobbing in a taxi, then arguing with someone on a busy street while she held me stationary. Everything in the hospital, however, is etched in aspic. The poor, the lame, the blind, the injured, the overdosed, the strung out, the near lifeless and catatonic, all demanding attention from a couple of overworked nurses, one of whom declared in a broad Mayo accent, "And it's not even the feckin' weekend yet!"

Mary was fierce as a lioness demanding attention. Whenever I tried to speak, she shushed me and fumed, "Don't let these culchie bitches know you're Irish." So, I held my tongue, even through the nightmare of a Nigerian intern ripping six stitches through the back of my head. The pills only partly dulled the pounding; still they kept me dopey enough to miss most of the taxi ride back to Decatur.

It was while climbing the stairs that the dread hit me. Had I been in better shape, I might have scurried back down the steps rather than face Danny. Mary must have shared my apprehension, for she steeled herself before throwing open the door and nudging me through.

"Where the fuck have you been?"

The pent-up frustration burst like shrapnel across the room, though I must have looked pretty rough, for Danny did a double take before moving menacingly towards me. "You little bastard! You just blew the one chance we had to get out of this kip."

"There'll be others," I mumbled, trying to steady the swaying room.

He clenched and unclenched his right fist while the small vein above his eyebrow beat like a hammer. It mesmerized me as the true enormity of what I'd done sank in. He wanted to hit me; I wished he would and get it over with.

"Not with me there won't."

I could have cried, for I knew he meant it. I stepped right into his face. If he'd only hit me, there was a chance he'd reconsider. But instead he wheeled on Mary, and all the bile flowed out. "You fuckin' bitch! Your handwriting's all over this."

She shrugged wearily.

"Leave her alone." I tried to summon up some authority, not an easy task when your voice sounds like it's leaking through the tail end of a megaphone. "She took me to the hospital."

"She should have fucking left you there!"

The little color that remained was draining from Mary's face. I could tell she wanted to run into her room and slam the door on all of this. It would have been better if she had, for I found it hard to deal with Danny in her presence.

"She's been through enough," I said.

"I know exactly what she's been through. The question is—why don't you?"

"Shut up, you!" Mary spat at him.

"If you don't tell him, I will."

She didn't flinch but went right at Danny, though he had five or more inches on her. "What's keeping you?"

When he didn't speak, she sneered, "Because you know what he'll think of you by the time I've finished."

Danny was seething. He opened his mouth to lash out at her.

"Go on," she goaded him, then very quietly added, "Morgan . . ."

His hatred was so raw I was deathly afraid he might strangle her. The strength was seeping from my knees and I could feel myself swaying, but I managed to murmur, "We were mugged down in the city."

"While you were buying strings, no doubt."

"We were checking out a pub for some gigs. We had a drink, then . . ."

"Here, pull the other one." Danny made a crude gesture.

"That's what you'd like, wouldn't you?" Mary sneered.

"You went all the way down the city for a drink?"

"Yes, just like you go all the way down to Christopher Street."

"I don't go down there for just a drink, baby."

"I know you don't."

"That makes us two of a kind. But he's different. Keep him the fuck out of your hellhole." He strode off to the bathroom and slammed the door. The blood was roaring inside my head, my eardrums pounding. I groped for a chair and sat down.

"Thanks," she murmured and laid her hand on my shoulder—more to steady me than out of any affection.

"For what?"

"For sticking up for me."

"Jesus Christ, Mary, what have you got us into? I can still feel that gun."

"I told you already, there was never anything to worry about."

"It was sticking in my bloody head."

She made a gesture belittling this unnecessary melodrama.

"That black fellah never stopped staring at me the whole time," I said.

"You're alive aren't you?"

"What do you know about it? You were in the other room."

"Yes, I was in the other room," she whispered bitterly; then a sudden panic swept her face. Cursing quietly, she dropped to the floor and groped inside her pocketbook. After a moment, she cast a huge sigh of relief and sat back on her heels. She ran her free hand across her forehead and wiped away the sweat.

A cop car howled by outside as it swerved around the corner; then the siren choked, and she froze until it began blaring again. Eventually it faded back into the soundtrack of distant traffic and the shouts of the dealers on the corners. She swiveled away from me, but I caught the flash of green that she clutched in her fist. She peeled off some bills and stood up. With a glance over at the bathroom door, she slipped them in my hand.

The bills were new and stuck to each other; they took time to count. "Nine hundred dollars?"

"I paid for the hospital too," she added as if I was being ungrateful. "That was well over a hundred."

"Why are you giving it to me?"

"Because you were the only one who'd come with me."

"That's nearly a month's wages."

"You earned it, didn't you?"

"But how did you get it?"

"That's my business."

When she saw my look of hurt, she sighed, "Sean, just take it. I paid for every penny of it."

Then Danny flushed the toilet and she was all business again. "Put it away and keep your mouth shut—especially to Jesús."

Even as I slipped the money in my pocket, I knew I was crossing a line. That being said, there was something I just had to get to the bottom of.

"What were you doing in that room, Mary?"

"You wouldn't want to know."

"Yes, I would."

"No, you fucking wouldn't!" Her voice rose in shrillness just as Danny strode out of the bathroom.

"Tell him," he said.

Those two words stripped away all her masks. I'd never seen her so helpless. She glanced over at me for help.

"Tell him," Danny shouted.

She gripped on to the table for support, and who knows what she would have said had the key not turned in the lock. There was a moment's grace before the door was pushed open. That was all it took for her to regain some composure. I don't know whom she'd been expecting, but it certainly wasn't Kate clutching a bottle of champagne, much less the weedy stranger behind her. Both of them must have heard Danny. They paused in the doorway and, in those seconds, I saw us as we must have seemed to others: Mary, drawn and haggard, her eyes alternately dazed or electric. The streets had worn her down, and she was all a jingle-jangle of frayed nerves and feverish resolution. The clothes that she had once worn with taste and flair looked garish—there was no joy in them—while the make-up that had once heightened her looks now served only to highlight her fretfulness.

And why hadn't I noticed Danny's uniform before? Many men on Bainbridge wore blue denim jeans and jackets with white undershirts, but they did so casually. Danny's shirt hugged his chest so closely you could see the outline of his nipples. Nor was his jacket a twenty-dollars Levi afterthought; it fit so well it might as well have been tailored by Brooks Brothers. He had the beginnings of a tight moustache; though subtle, it was as studied as any on Christopher Street. But if anything, he was more a mix of contradictions than ever. For all his primping, a large part of him still spoke of the harshness of West Belfast, and he carried himself with the air of one who had measured himself against the British army: dangerous, canny, and just a little off-center. Now he was burning holes in this stranger who was standing just that extra centimeter too close to Kate.

And what of me? I had landed at Kennedy a wannabe Joe Strummer, full to overflowing with all manner of romantic notions. Most of these had long since fled with the humidity, while both my face and spirit had coarsened from long days on the site and endless nights in the pub. What remained? I wasn't even sure I wanted to know.

"This is Arnold," Kate said defiantly, dragging him forward a pace.

What the hell was she thinking, wearing heels when she was already an inch or so taller than him? He must have been shortsighted, for he peered into the room, vainly attempting to bring the assembled clutter into some kind of focus. He was slight and undistinguished, though not without the confidence that a good weekly paycheck and a tailored suit bestows. His one distinctive trait was a pair of full lips that he was now pursing in puzzlement. He was losing his hair and, though less than thirty, seemed of another generation. But it was more than that: Coming from such a dissimilar class and background, he might just as well have beamed down from a different galaxy.

I examined him with guarded curiosity and Mary gave him a relieved once-over, but Danny was bristling with a mixture of disdain and unconcealed hostility. Either the poor man was genuinely out to lunch or no pushover, for he soaked up the full gale. Kate squeezed his arm for reassurance and edged even closer.

Where did Danny come off with such an attitude? What right had he to any hold on Kate? He had spurned her, turned her away, and now he was quivering like some ode to hurt pride. Wasn't it bad enough that Kate had been seared and would always love him, without twisting the knife? Wasn't it sufficient that, both literally and figuratively, he was head and shoulders above this shortsighted little man? Or is love always so prideful and inconsiderate, disregarding of any kind of morality or fair play?

But I was a good one to talk! Why did I continue obsessing about Mary despite all the hurt and hopelessness? I had a girlfriend who cared deeply for me, who could banish most of my misfortune with her soothing voice and lips and hair. All I had to do was stagger out of this maelstrom of contradictions and run to her. What had I in common with this woman across the room swaying slightly as though caught in some psychic cross-breeze, all the while kneading her nails into her palms? Was I in love with a memory? Or was the memory itself just a figment of an overheated adolescent imagination?

"Arnold P. Levinsky," the stranger announced with a

booming voice that belied his physique. He stepped towards
me, hand outstretched. My own felt calloused and coarse
next to his tapered fingers. I blushed and mumbled some kind
of halting welcome.

Mary smiled wanly, barely registering his presence; he
might as well have been some inconsequential ghost flitting
through the room. The ghost studied her intently. She still,
quite obviously, evoked some aura of mystery and frazzled
beauty.

Danny made no effort to step around the table but rather
gazed down stone-faced at this lesser being. Arnold waved
cheerily, either missing or ignoring his categorization.

"He just wanted to make sure I got home safe," Kate
said; then added with forced cheer, "I warned him the
cleaning lady didn't come on Thursdays."

"You should have seen my room at NYU," Arnold breezily
declared, while navigating his way around my discarded work
clothes and a couple of Danielle Steel tomes.

"Anyway, it's time for you to get back to civilization. I
don't think they've ever seen a Porsche up here." Kate had
taken him by the arm and was shunting him towards the door.

"It's used," he confided while passing me. "Got it for a
song."

"Good luck," I replied, less out of conviction than to
break the brooding silence.

Arnold smiled, making the best of a bad situation. Still,
he was nothing if not assertive. At the door he took Kate in
his arms. Though he had to rise slightly on his toes, he kissed
her full on the lips. At first she was flustered but, noting
Danny's smoldering disapproval, she dug in with gusto.

"Whew," Arnold exclaimed after some torrid seconds.

I winked back, though surreptitiously; I was in enough deep water with Danny. As Arnold struggled with the police lock, I called out, "Watch out for . . ." But I wasn't quite sure how to describe Squint Eye.

"It's OK. He's got a brown belt in karate." Kate blew a kiss after him before closing the door. Then she sashayed over to the table and shrugged at Mary. "Well, he's no David Bowie or Hayzoo Christi, I suppose."

"He seems," Mary searched for the right words, "nice . . ."

"He has his moments. What do you think of him yourself, Sean?"

"Eh . . . he looks sound enough."

"Ah, will yez give me a break? Don't I know he's a bit scrawny? But sure isn't he a man with a couple of legs and something halfway decent to hold onto in between them!"

She had aimed this at Danny but awaited an answer from me. I knew I had heard his name before and that he had something to do with her employers. "Is he the fellow with the big ears you were talking about?"

"Jesus, you'd think you were talking about Paddy Doyle's donkey. Sure isn't that his brother, the lawyer! This man's a dentist." She slapped out at me and caught me on the shoulder. Though it was only playful, I felt dizzy again. I swiveled to keep her directly in front of me. I had no wish to explain the missing hair and the stitches in the back of my head.

"Well, he's no Burt Reynolds or Robert Redford, but sure isn't he like all of yez? He improves with a couple of drinks."

Forgoing the bottle of champagne, she took a full slug of an opened can of beer. It must have contained a cigarette butt, for she croaked in disgust and spat mightily into the sink. "Jesus Christ! Did you never hear of ashtrays?"

She rinsed her mouth out from the tap then studied us.

"Anyway, I'm sure yez are dying to know all. Hasn't he been giving me the eye this last couple of weeks. So, this morning when I took the two children out to his mansion in Hempstead, they were barely set in front of Mister Rogers when he leapt on me and ripped the clothes off me back!"

She turned her attention to the champagne and wrestled with the cork, grinning to herself as she dwelt on some lurid detail or other. My own mind was still full of Mary in that room downtown. I wanted to drag her into the bedroom and get to the bottom of the whole business. But fat chance of that now, so I opened a beer and said for want of something better, "I hope you put up some kind of resistance."

"I did like fuck! After the drought I've been through with the likes of that queer fellow over there . . ." She pointed accusingly at Danny. "Not to mention Scutch Murphy who goes into a coma from the drink before he even gets your bra half off. Resist, is it? I tell you one thing, that chap will sleep sound tonight!"

Then the cork popped and slammed off the kitchen wall.

"Sweet Christ!" she squealed, grabbing some cups from the drainer. "Besides he's in love up to his bushy eyebrows, and he's circumscribed too. Did you ever do it with a man like that, Mary? It's simply gorgeous."

She ran gamely from one to the other of us, pouring till the bubbles brimmed over the rims of our cups. "Make no mistake about it! This boyo is my meal ticket, my green card, and my regular bit of the other all wrapped up in one. Mrs. Arnold P. Levinsky—it's got a grand ring to it, hasn't it?"

Mary was shivering again, even though beads of sweat were oozing from her forehead.

"You'll have to turn Jewish," she murmured gamely.

"I don't care if I turn into the seventh bride of Frankenstein as long as I don't have to wipe another rich baby's arse—barrin' it's one of me own. I think I'll have two, no maybe three—two boys and a girl—just to please me mother. Now would yez ever drink to me health and get them long faces off of you."

She poured another dollop into her cup. "And as for you, Danny boy," she stared him down, "if you ever get yourself cured, I can always use a boy toy out in Hempstead."

With that, she burst out crying.

CHAPTER SEVENTEEN

It was the worst Christmas of my life. I had thought that nothing could out-gloom the one after the passing of my father. But to some degree we'd been prepared for that and, even if my mother was in tears at every memory, there was always the town to bolt to with its familiar customs and faces. No such luck on Bainbridge where the hymns rang hollow and the lights winked to an alien beat; not to mention, who absconded with the holly, plum pudding, and mince pies, and replaced them with Yule logs and Charlie Brown's Christmas Special? But more than anything, why weren't we home where we belonged? Heartbreak straddled the avenue and strained the faces of the stranded. The pubs were half-empty, Bing Crosby groaning from the jukebox broke us apart, while the memories of Christmases past threatened to do our heads in.

Drink was the only constant, and we attacked it with a new ferociousness. The mean rafters of Scutch's rang with forced laughter as we named those who would have to be smuggled over the bridge in Buffalo on their illegal way back. Weren't we the wise devils to stay put, and what was all the fuss about anyway? Wasn't the *craic* on Bainbridge as good as any in Belfast or Belmullet? But it was all baloney. There wasn't one of us who wouldn't have risked hellfire for the chance of being home that Christmas Eve.

Shook to the roots and shivering with hangovers, Christmas day itself was anti-climactic. For most it was a turkey sandwich for dinner at the Greek's, then more drinks to ease sick stomachs as the feast of Saint Nicholas slowly ticked away. By the 26th, mercifully, it was all over. No Saint Stephen's Day dances, Wren Boys, coursing the greyhounds, or visits to relatives! Rather, get your arse straight back to work, Paddy, for Dennehy's cement needed mixing, a buck had to be made, rent to be paid. I, for one, was not complaining. Christmas on Bainbridge was just another twist of the emigrant knife with one saving grace—it was over almost before it had begun.

I would have totally gone to pieces, had it not been for Noreen. Sweet Noreen, always ready to welcome me into her bed when her roommates were out. There she'd hold me while I raged against the world and the bad hand it was dealing me. To soothe my heartache, she'd lilt a Gaelic lament in my ear; and when I awoke, the world rarely hurt quite so badly.

It was during this time that I came to know her in all her odd beauty. Alone of us, she never let the concrete fingers of the Bronx coarsen her. I often wondered why she had ever left her lovely Kerry mountains? The rumor was that she had been badly used by an older man—a fiddler of note—but the subject was off limits. Any kind of prying was politely discouraged. Without it ever being said, she made it known that you took her for what she was and no more. Yet, there was a stillness and a certainty to her that made you long to glimpse beneath the surface, but she resisted this fiercely and, in the end, you complied. It wasn't that she was a total innocent or without her wiles: She knew that there was a magic to her voice that couldn't be matched on the avenue and held her head a little higher on that account. In the way of all attractive women, she wasn't unaware of her looks either. Yet, there was a rare completeness to her. It was as if she was content with the portion of perfection that she'd been allotted, so why search for more.

She was looking for someone who would complement her, an equal with whom she could build a life. I can only speculate on what she saw in me, for I had all the stability of a sack full of kittens. All through those dark days, she held me close and soaked up every ounce of self-pity that I threw at her. She encouraged me to reveal the shame I felt for betraying Danny and the Tinkers, but also allowed me to vent my rage at them for failing to understand my predicament. After all, how could I have let Mary down in her moment of trial? Though she would often stiffen at the very sound of that name, she never chided me; instead, she urged me to purge myself of any remaining poison that might lie dormant.

But there were matters between Mary and me that Noreen had no knowledge of, secret places we had explored that Noreen had no notion of, nor interest in.

Her roommates had a sense of that. They never liked me and were suspicious I would lead her astray; while to me, they were a couple of know-it-all culchie bitches who could never appreciate a cosmopolitan the like of myself. My moments with Noreen were always limned by their comings and goings, and they took keen delight in barging home early from the pub and rousing me from the warmth of her single bed.

And so I'd crawl back to Decatur at two or three in the morning to find Mary pacing the floor, sometimes oblivious but, more often than not, grateful for any kind of company now that Kate spent most of her time with Arnold. Danny, if there at all, was always conveniently asleep. Perhaps, it was our bonding down on Avenue C but, in a weird way, we had grown tighter again or, at least, more reliant on each other. With her having fewer visits from Jesús, I fancied that there was some rift between them. Despite my gathering closeness to Noreen, I began to daydream that there was still a chance for us, and on my drunker nights when I slyly alluded to such a resurrection, Mary never quite slammed the door in my face.

Not so, Danny. He only spoke when absolutely necessary. Nor did he rouse me any more in the morning. In fact, I was forced to buy an alarm clock, for on the first day after our row I would have slept right through the afternoon, had Mary not insisted on taking me to Montefiore to have my wound dressed. Since I was now a bricklayer's gofer, there was no longer a need for me to be totally subject to Danny's eagle eye. Still, his chilly distance was noted and led to a general lessening of my stature in the Byzantine pecking order of the site.

The word had spread along Bainbridge about my betrayal. The Olympia had been jammed, all hands ready to shout for the home team. RCA Steve, his entourage, and Arsehole had descended from the limo to much awe. They had awaited my arrival through a couple of rounds of top shelf vodka. In the end, the Tinkers had been forced to take the stage, for after all there was still need of a night's dancing. But the band had sounded desultory and deplete; if I was not the strongest liquor in the cocktail, I was apparently the straw that stirred it. After an hour or so of Arsehole's excuses, Steve and his posse had retreated to their limo, never again to show their faces on the wild side of the Triborough Bridge.

In typical Irish fashion, the Tinkers said nothing to me, good, bad or indifferent. We had taken a week off to savor our expected triumph and to leave time available should we be summoned down to the RCA studios. And so, some of the edge had worn off by the time we got together for our next gig in the Olympia. I'm not even sure I'd have shown up if Noreen hadn't locked steps with me to Jerome and Kingsbridge. As it turned out, I need not have feared any cold shoulder, for Danny was a no-show, and the Tinkers hit the stage a member short for the second gig in a row. I then understood how they must have felt, for I was lost without him. After a couple of lackluster tunes, the crowd reverted to ignoring us in the way of the Bronx, and we meandered to a halt at closing time, demoralized as a bunch of bullocks after a day's rain.

I did step up to the plate and call a rehearsal for the following Monday night. I even had balls enough to leave a note on our kitchen table requesting the pleasure of Danny's company but, when neither he nor Johnnie materialized, Shiggins excused himself; then Bugsy and I got rightly shit-faced until Noreen was summoned and shoveled me home by car service.

I couldn't believe it. All our dreams, hopes and hard work gone up in smoke because I had tried to do the right thing. Well, I wasn't going to get down on my knees and beg the bastards to put the band back together. It would be their loss, not mine. Let them stew in their own failure. All I needed was enough bucks to get home then build some kind of small recording studio. If my songs worked in the Bronx, they would surely move heads in Dublin, London, or anywhere else people took music seriously. I wasn't beholden to a bunch of stuck up, coked up, drunken musicians, gay or straight. I'd seen the light, and no one was going to extinguish it on me again.

That was my party line, and I stuck to it heroically through a week of nightly tears in my beer and dehydrated mornings spent languishing on the couch. In the midst of this, I received word from Dennehy and Company that my services would no longer be required on the site, leaving my circle well and truly squared. Fuck them all, was my response. Let them mix their own bloody cement. I had the nine hundred bucks stored behind James Connolly's poster. That would buy me some breathing space. As my father used to say, there were more ways than one to skin a cat.

Though I was still deeply troubled by the incident downtown with Mary, a seed of some sort had been planted; money now insinuated itself into all my reasoning. I was no idiot. If I was stuck in the center of capitalism, better adapt. When in Rome and all that bullshit. Connolly glared down at me, but that was his problem. Where had all his socialism and sacrifice got him? Only head-the-balls like Danny put their store in the old revolutionary's dated dreams.

Money was the key. How much more convenient to posit that Jesús' power over Mary stemmed from financial rather than erotic roots. What would he be without his big yellow Cadillac? And wasn't he the fountainhead of her hundred dollar bills? Take all that away and he wouldn't be such a big man.

With the Tinkers gone, I had time to think—maybe too much. Despite all Noreen's attention and my feelings for her,

I could still be cast into the seventh sewer of depression at the mere thought of someone else touching Mary. I never questioned the sanity of this dichotomy. Instead a crazy seed of reasoning began to rattle around my skull through a maze of its own making: If I could only come into some decent cash, then I could smash the spell Jesús had woven around her. The nine hundred dollars she had given me assumed mythic proportions. Score that amount ten, twenty times a year, and all my needs would be taken care of. Maybe I wouldn't go home at all. Just head down to Bleecker Street with my Yamaha, cause a stir at the Bitter End or one of those folk joints, and have a dozen Steves lining up to sign me. Mary, of course, would be there waiting for me, or Noreen, or the Queen of bloody Sheba for that matter.

If I was confused I was also cagey. I might not have known what Mary was up to in that room on Avenue C, but delivering drugs for Jesús was at the heart of it. I also figured that if I approached her head on for an introduction to the business, she'd turn me down. Having analyzed the situation from left, right, and center, I felt confident that if only a little more brain power was put into the planning, then the whole operation could be carried off in a decidedly more discreet, not to mention painless, manner. And so I floated the notion that, should the occasion arise, I'd escort her again. She never acknowledged my offer, though a certain speculation crept into her eyes, and there I allowed matters to rest.

I wasn't prepared for the change in Jesús when he finally showed up again on Decatur. Gone was the suave prince of the streets decked out in cream suits and smothered in cologne. Of course it was January and he was wearing an army jacket against the icy wind, but there was more to it. His face was pinched, eyes jagged with fatigue; he was edgy and suspicious, and any good will he had harbored towards me had evaporated.

They had been arguing when I entered, which only added to my smugness. Trouble in paradise was just hunky-dory by me. She was more wired than usual, though I knew she had slept deeply, for I had checked on her around dawn. After a cursory nod, he curtly refused the beer I offered, leading me to believe that this was not the best time to inquire about employment opportunities. Indeed, I would have buggered off to the pub had it not been for the sheer satisfaction of marking their uneasiness with each other.

"So you want outa here?"

He took me by surprise. Still, I recognized an opening and leaped at it.

"Yeah, I'm going home, build a studio—record my songs."

"Same with all you *blanquitos*," he sneered. "Can't wait to get here, then you dyin' to get out."

I'd never heard him use the derogatory term before, though it was common enough on the streets. He was testing me but I had no intention of rising to the bait. "What's to keep me? The band's broken up and . . ."

"You should never have come in the first place," Mary snapped.

"I could say the same for you," I fired back.

"Some of us had no choice."

"Always choice, girl!" Jesús pushed back his chair and paced the floor, once more a jaguar behind bars. "Question is—do you have the strength to make it?"

"When I need a lecture from you, I'll ask. OK?"

"You know what I'm talkin' about, boy?"

"Leave him out of this!"

"Why? He gonna find out sooner or later."

"Shut up!" She then turned to me with a sickening smile. "Sean likes me the way I am, right?"

"I don't know what either of you is talking about."

"That's 'cause you don't got eyes to see!" Jesús laughed bitterly. "Go home, *jíbaro.*"

The strange word hung in the air. I could tell I was being insulted, just couldn't be sure how badly. My pulse was throbbing where the stitches had been removed. I knew I was playing with fire, but I gave it one last try.

"Cut me in for a couple of months and I'll go home."

"And her and me live happy ever after—that the plan?"

"I'll be out of your hair."

"More than one way to arrange that, *chingón.*"

Mary shuddered at the sneering vehemence he invested in the word. "For God's sake, he just wants to make a little money." She slithered over to him, but he raised his palm, warning her to keep her distance.

"That what you said too."

She halted in mid-step, and he strode past her to the window. Taking a deep breath, he gazed out on the street, not a muscle moving. "I got enough problems."

"I'll pay you back every penny," Mary said.

"Ain't just the money. Street think I'm losin' it."

"It won't happen again, Jesús, I promise."

"No . . . it won't." The old resolve returned, and with it a spring to his step. He came right up to me. "Go back to playin' your guitar, boy. This is a man's world."

"What about her?"

"I watch her back. Who watch yours?"

"I just need enough to build my studio. That's the deal!"

He grabbed me by the jacket and yanked me to within centimeters of a headbutt. "I make the deals! You mess with me, you make a big mistake."

I could smell the remains of day-old cologne on his face before he threw me to one side as if I had infected him. "You hear that too, Maria? No more!"

He spun around. Neither Mary nor I had noticed Danny's entry. Under an opened trench coat, he was dressed in downtown blue denim, if anything his white undershirt clinging even tighter. His hair tightly cropped, moustache sculpted and full, he was handsome as ever, even if he had shed some pounds since I'd seen him. He was carrying his old tool bag, although, from his manicured appearance, he had spent the day far from the site.

As Jesús took Danny's measure, his nostrils flared. Almost imperceptibly Danny nodded back. "What's this then? Three's company, four's a crowd?"

The Belfast sarcasm seemed as alien as his accent, but Jesús got the intent. I searched for words to defuse the situation, but Mary beat me to it.

"I see you're fitting in well on Christopher Street. It's a wonder you come back up here at all."

"And miss the pleasure of our little narcotic get-togethers?" He flipped his tool bag on the loaded kitchen table. A half-empty beer can splashed on me, another on Jesús, who moved so quickly he caught Danny by surprise. One hand gripped his denim jacket, the other thrust a long, thin blade towards the base of his throat.

"Go ahead." Danny might as well have been talking about the weather. "Do us all a favor. Right, Sean?"

Jesús' eyes betrayed only the zeal of a craftsman who has done his job well, until Danny spat at him: "What's keepin' you? Do it, you bloody spic!"

It took Jesús a moment to control the shake in his hand. This was not lost on Danny; he smiled again though the blade now pricked his throat, at first reddening it until a tiny bead of blood gleamed on his skin.

"I'm way beyond you, man," he said very quietly, "and you know it."

Jesús glared back. Then, in one movement, he let go of the jacket, shoved Danny backwards, and slipped the blade into the fold of his army jacket.

"*Vámanos,*" he signaled to Mary. "There's a smell in here."

"Yeah, and you know who it's comin' from," Danny replied.

Jesús halted on his way to the door but chose not to answer.

"One last thing, *amigo,*" Danny said, and the word was loaded with derision. "You hurt anything that's close to me . . ."

"You know where to find me." Jesús was already opening the door for Mary.

As she passed through, Danny added, "Yeah, and so do a lot of other people."

Then it was just the two of us. Danny flicked at the bead of blood with his index finger and examined it. He took a couple of ice cubes from the fridge, wrapped them in a towel and held it to his throat. He grimaced at the smell, holding the towel well away from his white undershirt.

When I felt a cramp in my leg, I realized that I hadn't moved for minutes. I shifted weight then took a slug of beer. "He could have killed you."

"Someday, I'm goin' to let you in on a big secret."

"For Christ sake, Danny, what the hell are you up to?"

"I might say the same for you. Dennehy let you go?"

"Who cares? I had enough of his shite."

"Don't mess with Dennehy, Sean. He's in a different league than you."

"Fuck him, the arrogant little prick!"

"You don't have a clue, do you? Not a bloody clue." He sighed and tossed the towel into the sink. Then he came right up to me. "Whatever about Dennehy, those two are bad news, man. Stay away from them."

"I'm not doing anything with them."

"I know well what you're doing." He slapped me on the shoulder. "I just can't believe you're such a fuckin' eejit. People get killed at their racket."

"I can look after myself."

"Like hell you can! What's your mother going to say when you come home in a box?"

"You're a fine one to talk, considering what you were up to in Belfast."

"That was for a cause, man!"

"Fuck you and your cause." I stuck my finger up at the poster of Connolly.

"Don't you ever do that again, you little Free State bastard!"

It was his ultimate insult, and he glared at me with disgust. But I'd had enough of all of them and their advice.

"You keep out of my life. It's none of your business."

"No," he sighed. "It's gone way beyond that."

"I've got to do something. I'm going crazy over here."

"Go home then."

"A failure?"

"Alive!" he shouted at me.

"No way!" I threw open the fridge door and found a tallboy. When I flicked the top off, the foam rose like a fountain. I didn't bother to wipe it off, but just let the cold suds run down my fingers onto my sleeves. "When I go back, I'll have bucks in my pocket—not another Paddy Yank bumming drinks down the pub."

"Then you better get down to the site tomorrow and beg Dennehy to take you back."

"There's other ways, Danny. We could go in this together."

"I don't want to hear that shite from you! There's only one way to make honest money—you get up in the first light of the mornin' and work your balls off all day."

"Just like you, right?"

He searched for the right words then just shook his head.

"You do it your way," I said quietly. "I'll do it mine."

I had placed my beer on the table. As in the old days, he reached out for it, knowing that there was little likelihood of finding another in the fridge. He raised the can to his lips and drank deeply, but then pulled it away as though it were poison and began to pour the remains down the kitchen sink.

"What the hell are you doin'?"

"You don't need this right now."

"The hell I don't!" I grabbed at the can, but he held on and pushed me away as the remains flowed down the sink.

"Grow up, Sean." He tossed the can in the overflowing garbage and rammed down the lid before turning to me. "Listen, I won't always be there to watch your back."

"I don't need you. I've got this city sussed. Either you beat it or it beats you."

"Will you for Christ sakes listen to me! You think the Virgin Mary's goin' to be wearin' black when you're stretched out in the morgue? No way! She'll be too busy linin' up the next sucker."

"You leave her out of this, you hear me!"

"You're messin' with my head, man! Get rid of her! She's the root of all our problems."

"Don't you talk about her like that, you dirty queer!"

The slap wasn't hard; still I felt wobbly from the shock. Through the tears, I could see that the pain etched across his face hurt a great deal more than the sting in my ear.

"Don't say that. Anyone but you."

For a moment I thought he might cry, but he gathered himself quickly enough. "Look at you. Even the music's gone." He pointed over to the corner where my guitar case was gathering dust.

"Leave me alone!"

"She's sleepin' with him. Don't you hear them in there?"

"Shut up!"

"Do you want to know what she does with him?"

"Shut the fuck up!"

He put his arms around me and drew me close. "I'm only doing this to help you, man. You know I wouldn't harm a hair on your head."

He drew me closer until I thought he might kiss me.

"What are you doing?"

"It's OK."

I broke away from him. He stood there with his arms outstretched. "No, Sean, it's not like that."

But it was. I ran for the door, screaming back at him, "Keep away from me, you hear me! You keep the hell away from me, you fuckin' faggot!"

CHAPTER EIGHTEEN

Three days later I was in Miami. Not the Beach of the golden sands and the flowing palm trees, but a run down, twenty bucks a night, hooker motel ringed by a buckled concrete car park and crawling with all manner of insects, rodents, pimps, whores, transvestites, welfare refugees, and stranded retirees.

Jesús wouldn't have touched me with a forty-foot pole, but one mule got busted and the other, rather ominously, "fell down a stairs." On no account would he use "brothers," Latino or Black; only a *blanquito* in a suit could carry his dope. Wouldn't use "sisters" either, and though Mary fit the complexion requirements, she wasn't exactly high on his list after her recent debacle. He was hard set not to hold his nose when he finally gave in to her pleading and threw me the gig. But as soon as I was anointed he got right with the program: Stuck a wad of cash in my hand and dispatched me to Gimbel's where I was to purchase a dark suit, white shirt, sensible tie, shoes, socks, and anything else that would help me look "real American."

He even accompanied me to the barbers where I traded the remains of my punk credentials for a straight back and sides. My mother would have been over the moon at the sight of me: a living, breathing cross between a penguin and an insurance salesman.

By the time he and Mary dropped me at LaGuardia the following dawn, I could have passed for another young subaltern in Ronald Reagan's all-conquering conservative army but for the fact that my briefcase contained two brown envelopes crammed to the hilt with hundred dollar bills.

Contrary to his fierce admonishment, I was first in line when the bar opened and tossed back a beer to steady my shaking hands. I needn't have bothered. No one cast a look except to marvel at my suited formality in the midst of so many Hawaiian-shirted vacationers. At Miami Airport I gelled a little easier with the Latino businessmen in their tailored finery, but I almost buckled from the humidity when I stepped out of the air-conditioning and hailed a taxi.

"What you wanna go there for, man?" The driver scratched his head, obviously questioning my sanity as I marveled at the fronds of the palm trees already limp in the noonday heat.

I was inclined to agree when I arrived at *La Hacienda* and had to line up behind two stoned hookers and their somewhat impatient clients. The ladies were in the process of haggling with the day clerk, an aristocratic Cuban in an immaculate white linen suit who, even in this mundane transaction, managed to betray his undying antipathy for Uncle Fidel.

Whatever about his politics, he had little need of a tutorial on the economics of the early afternoon sex trade. After he had dispatched these somewhat haggard-looking lasses to the boudoirs of their choice, he surveyed me over his pince-nez.

"Good morning, Señor."

"How's it going?"

"It is as ever . . ." He adjusted a golden cuff link and spread the delicate palms of his hands in a gesture of resignation ". . . when one is far from home."

"You can sing that." I almost bit my tongue at this voluntary surrendering of information.

He took note of my consternation, then, with a deep sigh and an even more fluid hand gesture, intimated that he understood both the nature and sensitivity of such matters before inquiring, "Now, how may I be of service to you?"

"Eh . . . I'd like a room?"

"Such a wish is easily granted. However, we have many rooms at your disposal."

When I didn't rise to the bait, he continued in cultured but slightly accented English, "Some with ceiling mirrors, others with waterbeds, and in some cases both. There are also king-sized four-posters that come with certain—how should one phrase it—attachments?"

He halted, apparently unwilling to exert more energy until he gauged the nature of my preference.

"Attachments?" I repeated, tightening my grip on the briefcase.

This action did not escape his notice, and he gave it, then me, a thorough once over before carefully enumerating, "Handcuffs, bonds, stays, whatever your preference."

Jesus Christ! What class of knocking shop had they sent me to? I must have reddened, for he averted his eyes to ease my embarrassment and murmured, "On the other hand, we also have at our disposal a number of chambers suitable for a couple bound by the vows of matrimony."

He shuffled some papers in front of him, then, without raising his eyes, confided, "There are many ladies—and their escorts—who prefer a more formal and dignified setting in which to . . ." and there he decided to discreetly let the matter rest.

"I'm actually just in town solo—for a sort of eh . . . vacation. Check out the museums, art galleries, that kind of thing," I blurted out.

"Ah, a cultural expedition, as it were?"

"Yeah, catch a show or whatever . . ."

"I see. And how long will La Hacienda be favored with the pleasure of your company?"

"Well . . . that depends."

"On extraneous factors?" He darted a look at my briefcase, and I realized I was sweating despite the sub-zero temperature created by a giant rattling air-conditioner that occupied a considerable portion of the lone window.

"Yeah, the weather and such like . . ."

The phone rang. He hesitated and seemed uncertain as to how to proceed. On the fourth ring he nodded his apologies, picked up the receiver, and listened intently without taking his eyes from me. Finally, he answered in a mellifluous string of Spanish sentences, worlds away from the staccato *Nuyorican* exchanges I had become accustomed to around Decatur. Yet I had the distinct impression that he was somehow addressing my presence. The disturbing thought struck me that perhaps I had been expected.

When he hung up he adjusted his silver silk tie and, with a heartfelt sigh, signaled his resigned acceptance of the world and all its foibles. Then he quite forcibly suggested, "You could, should you so wish, avail yourself of a very economical weekly rate with cooking facilities."

A week! Did he know something I didn't? My return

ticket had been purchased for three days later. What the hell was going on?

"Nah, I think we'll just take it day by day."

"A most excellent method of dealing with life in general. I can offer you a very economical rate of twenty dollars for a full twenty-four hour cycle—with a one-time deposit of half that amount for use of a room phone."

He smiled when adding, "Contact with the outside world is essential nowadays, wouldn't you agree?"

I tried to remember how Cagney or Bogart would reply. Failing, I chose to maintain an enigmatic silence.

He courteously averted his eyes when I peeled off a couple of bills from the roll Jesús had given me.

"Will you need assistance with your luggage?" He and I both eyed the briefcase, and he pursed his lips as my knuckles waxed whiter.

"Nah, I'm traveling light." I flashed him a severe look to show I would be no pushover. Still my heart was pounding when I closed the glass door behind me.

Though the bed had been made, the sheets still reeked of some high-octane perfume curried by a musky odor that permeated right through to the mattress; this I discovered since I hid the briefcase between it and the springs. Still, it was a place to lie, and I loosened my tie for the first time since I had departed Decatur. Only then did it hit me how scant were my orders: I was to wait until I was contacted—but by whom and when? Would it be by phone or a knock on the door? Probably phone since the all-knowing Cuban had insisted on a deposit.

But what if I should miss my *man?* How was I supposed to eat or drink? No wonder I got the shit kicked out of me on Avenue C. This whole operation needed streamlining and a hell of a lot more attention to detail. Or was I the fool and right now the Cuban and his posse were rounding up some crowbars to smash in the door and relieve me of the briefcase?

I awoke in a lather of sweat. Though I had sensed a movement across my lips, I tallied it to imagination until I caught sight of something horrific rising over the rim of my nose and heading hell bent for leather towards my eyes. As I departed the bed shrieking, the intruder took off for a less volatile haven on the wall.

I crawled over to the window, afraid that my yelps might have brought the cops to the door, but it was business as usual: johns and ladies of the afternoon arriving and departing in a flotilla of cars and taxis. Apparently, a stray scream or two was not out of character in La Hacienda. I collapsed back on the bed, keeping a wary eye on the large black-winged moth on the wall and dozed off.

By early evening I was awake again, dripping, and wrestling with the air-conditioner whose controls I tweaked every which way before discovering that the bloody thing had been unplugged. Nightfall found me both ravenous and dying for a beer with paranoia spiking by the minute. Who was I supposed to hand the loot over to? How would they recognize me? What the hell were Jesús and Mary thinking? Jesús and Mary, my arse—sounded like the bloody holy family. And was I their idiot Joseph, fretting outside on my donkey while they carried out their immaculate deception? Or were they thinking at all and had they inadvertently delivered poor innocent Paddy into the hands of a band of cutthroat Cuban counter-revolutionaries?

The tap water was rusty and, though I doused my head in it, I didn't dare venture a swig. Pulling a chair over to the window, I turned out the lights, the tongue literally hanging out of my head. The cars now arrived even more frequently, sweeping both parking lot and windows with their headlights. I stiffened at every sound, yet prayed for a tap on the door. By midnight I could take it no more. Cursing my stupidity for neglecting to bring a change of clothes, I ran down to the motel office in my shirtsleeves, head swiveling like a marionette for fear my *man* would arrive in my absence.

To my surprise, the Cuban had been replaced by a six-foot-tall black woman in a mini-skirt, with hands the size of a couple of Dennehy's shovels.

"Honey," she squawked after she lowered her baseball bat, "don't be comin' in no doors like that. Folk might think you got badness on your mind."

Sensible advice, indeed; nor would it be her last. When I inquired about the whereabouts of the Cuban, she rolled her eyes until it seemed they might pop out of their sockets and changed the subject.

She was much more voluble concerning the location of the nearest restaurant, rattling off a litany of names, highways, and exits. Upon my informing her of my lack of wheels, she introduced me to the glories of Miami delivery cuisine. After I had feasted on the greasiest of fried chicken, she even clickety-clacked down to my room with a five dollar bottle of some licorice-tasting firewater and the news, delivered in an alarmingly deep voice, that she'd be soon off duty should I desire company.

And so began my siege: days of sweat, grease, muted TV, payments to the Cuban followed by a discreet interrogation

until it began to occur to me that perhaps he suspected I was
an FBI plant sent to infiltrate his anti-Fidelista ring.

I would return to my room and ponder all manner of such
possibilities, my paranoia running rampant, until the shadows
deepened, only to spend the interminable nights deflecting
the advances of the huge black whatever—the licorice booze
rising in price upon each spurning. With money and time
expiring, my moth-like intruder leered at me from various
walls and ceiling.

By the third day I could no longer even lie on the bed
such was my anxiety. With my plane leaving in hours and
my money running low, I was in a quandary. Should I rifle
the briefcase and purchase another ticket home? Maybe my
man had "fallen down a stairs" too and even now Miami
Vice was stalking me, with Cuban counter-revolutionaries
hot on their heels.

Then the penny dropped. Jesús had sent me to La
Hacienda for a reason. He and Mary were laughing their
arses off up in the Bronx, and here was I sitting like a clay
pigeon waiting for the big bang. The briefcase was full of
monopoly money!

I was tossing my few things in a laundry bag when a
knock on the door nailed me to the floor. Though the air-
conditioner was working again, a cold sweat oozed out of me.
Then another knock, this time more insistent. I crept over
to the bed and snuck the briefcase from beneath the mattress.
I sat there on the soggy carpet cradling its plastic in my arms.
For Christ sakes, it wasn't even leather! Should I lift the
shades and peer out? I had no idea what to do next.

Then I thought of the two of them back in the Bronx
fucking away to their hearts' content and me sitting in this

black hole of Miami with a plastic bag full of funny money. To hell with them! I cracked open the door but kept the chain latch in place.

A somewhat solemn gentleman in a crumpled seersucker suit, Panama hat pulled low over his shades, nodded formally. Like everything else, I had not been advised on the proper protocol for this pivotal moment. For all I knew it could have been Juan the bloody Ripper come a-calling. Still, I doubted the Miami Police Department would be so courteous, and the Cuban was nowhere to be seen lurking behind the fatigued palm trees, so I admitted him. My gentleman caller, on the other hand, appeared to be well versed in such procedures: handing me his briefcase, he opened mine, and after a very cursory inspection of the envelopes, departed without a word.

Only then did it occur to me that I had failed to give his offering the reciprocal once-over. I need not have worried. The briefcase was locked and there was no key. I pondered breaking it open but to what end? Elvis had already departed the building. Besides, there was some heft to it, and my plane was departing in little more than an hour. Begging Mary's forgiveness for my unfounded suspicions, I grabbed the case and ran out into the parking lot.

No taxis—just a bunch of whores strutting their stuff. I screamed and waved until I was hoarse. Finally, a large white convertible slowed down, and a handsome man in a tan fedora leaned towards me.

"Do you have need of a lady?" he graciously inquired.

"Ah no, I haven't the time right now," I waved him on.

"My cousin, Maria Delarosa, is fourteen . . ."

"That's a grand age." I smiled, scurrying around him as a lone taxicab sped by.

"Yoh!!!" I screamed New York style but had to leap backwards for the sidewalk as a truck almost took the front of my nose off.

"She has expressed interest in meeting you," Fedora confided.

"Who?"

"Maria Delarosa."

"How the hell does she know me?"

"She has watched you from afar."

"She has?" Said I, mentally noting that you never know your luck even as I tried to hail down another sight-impaired taxi driver.

"Motherfucker!" I roared in his dusty wake.

Fedora commiserated; apparently he too had little love for the purveyors of the Southern Florida livery trade. He then flipped open his wallet and showed me a picture of my admirer, a preening thirty-year-old in a Catholic girl-school uniform.

"Will you give me a fuckin' break! I don't need your sister," I howled.

"My cousin." He gravely corrected me.

"Whatever! All I want right now is a taxi to the airport."

"It is very distant," he frowned.

"How distant?"

"Forty, perhaps fifty dollars."

"You've got to be kidding me. It was only ten to get here."

"Ah, *Señor*, but, as in life, the journey home is a far greater distance."

Another fucking Latino philosopher. Must be the bloody weather. I weighed my options: a non-refundable ticket versus negotiating another night's shelter from the amorous night clerk.

"Let's go!" I barked.

Careening around corners and speeding through lights while I screamed at him to keep his eyes on the road, he quizzed me incessantly about Maria Delarosa's prospects in *Nuevo York*. To keep him concentrated, I divulged the address of Scutch's bordello and assured him that she would be in much demand with the clientele. When pressured, I reeled off the prices Irish gentlemen would be willing to pay for particular erotic services rendered. He was still drooling when I dived from his pimpmobile and raced through the terminal.

Too late! The plane had already boarded. With a useless ticket and the guts of sixty bucks in my pocket, I was instructed by a less than sympathetic porter that the only way I was ever going to see New York City was to "haul ass to the bus station and snag a ticket on a Greyhound."

"How the hell do I get to the bus station?"

"You take a bus to the bus, how do you think?" He pointed to a shuttle that was just about to take off.

"Thanks for nothin'," I snarled, galloping past his outstretched palm.

Miami Bus Terminal had one thing in its favor—it was well lit. This undoubtedly put a cap on the number of robberies, rapes, and murders. Still it reeked of poverty and fear, my own adding considerably to the mix. Shuffling towards the ticket booth, I caught a hazy reflection of myself in a dusty window: a wild-eyed, shifty looking rogue in a wrinkly suit clutching onto a briefcase as though it were an extra limb. In three days, I had become my mother's worst nightmare.

Twenty-three hours of bone rattling to New York City, I was informed, would cost thirty-nine dollars and forty cents, with the next bus departing at midnight on the dot. At least I'd be back in the comfort and security of Scutch's well before last call the following night.

I forked over the fare and set aside enough for a subway token; whereupon, I followed the parade of pilgrims to the nearest liquor store and loaded up on a pint of their cheapest vodka. At the deli next door, a quart of orange juice cleaned me out, and I returned to the bus station, a tired and hungry, but resigned man. I didn't dare speculate on what I was carrying in the briefcase, but I knew that three or four grand from its sale had my name stamped all over it; things could be worse. If nothing else, I'd be sedated on the journey home.

I gulped down half of the juice and was meticulously mixing in the vodka when five fingers of steel dug into my shoulder.

"What the hell you doin', boy?"

My heart ripped off a succession of manic triplets when I caught glimpse of a uniformed sleeve. The eagle had landed. The bloody Cuban had struck and informed on me.

"Mixin' a drink, sir."

"In a public space where the consumption of alcohol is forbidden?"

"Oh sweet Jaysus on high!"

He swung me around like a top and I gazed upon the ruddy face of a burly, ginger-haired Miami patrolman.

"Where the hell you from?" His brow puckered up.

"The Bronx, sir."

Disappointment swept across his face and his grip tightened. I scanned the other travelers for the Cuban but not a sign. There was only one thing for it.

"Oireland, your honor," I piped up like Darby O'Gill,

damn near throwing in a "faith and begorrah" for good measure.

"My people are from Kerry and Galway." His grip loosened a tad, and he stepped back for a better look at the wild Rapparee he had apprehended.

"Now isn't that the height of coincidence, officer dear? Don't I have family in Dingle and Connemara meself."

"Dingle?" It was as though he had heard mention of Shangri-La.

"Yeah, I'm there every summer for the regatta."

"My grandmother," he blessed himself, raised his eyebrows and pointed up at the dusty roof of the terminal, "God rest her soul."

He seemed somewhat distraught so I reverently raised my eyes in the direction of his finger, if not his granny, and threw in an unctuous Sign of the Cross to sweeten the pot. I would have dropped to my knees and flagellated myself if that would have helped, but for the grip he still had on my shoulder.

He nodded his appreciation. "Mary Kate Josephine O'Sullivan used to speak about the sailboats and eating sticks of Peggy's Leg on Dingle pier."

I didn't give a flying fuck if she sucked on the balls of a syphilitic bull. I kept the Kerry references flying, though my memories of Dingle were limited to the four walls of a pub jammed with German tourists on a day so wet it would have been no surprise to see Noah floating by on his ark. Through all this I clutched on firmly to the briefcase, anxiously speculating on just how many years its contents would entitle me to as a guest of Ronald Reagan in the nearest federal pen.

"What's your name?"

"Sean, sir, Sean Kelly."

The lilt of my name was apparently music to his ears, for he nodded his approval until I feared he might be having some form of spastic attack.

"Sean," he caressed the word, making every effort to approximate my accent, though he sounded like Barry Fitzgerald with hemorrhoids.

"Sean Kelly," he thereupon thundered, once more the honest cop, "had your name entered my book, we would not be having this conversation! Do you understand?"

Oh, I did explicitly and assured him a hundred times that such was the case. He finally raised his hand for silence.

"However," he intoned, "since we do share a common ancestry, I am willing to give you what amounts to a fighting Irish chance."

Given the amount of contraband in the briefcase, I was ready to drop on all fours and lick his boots at this turn of events. But no such gesture was necessary, for he regally explained, "The driver of the New York bound bus, Jeremiah Clay, is a brother in Christ. With that in mind, I intend to place your fate in his hands. Should he see fit to accept you, then you may leave Miami with no charges. Should he not . . ."

His head began to bob in sadness at the fate that awaited me.

We had by now attracted a posse of black men who were somewhat detachedly interested in this conflagration between two honkies. To a man they groaned when Officer Hogan emptied my vodka into the nearest garbage can. Many of them followed, at a respectful distance, as we set off to interview the driver.

I shuddered in the presence of this little poker-faced, fundamentalist prick as Officer Hogan documented my crimes. Jeremiah Clay shook his head in dismay at the mere thought that any Christian could need a stiff drink for the short jaunt to New York. He might just as well have been informed that I had been apprehended buggering an adolescent goat.

With the thought of a night in a Miami jail ahead of me, followed by twenty or more years in a federal penitentiary, there was only one thing for it. After a tearful unburdening of my many sins, I promised on my mother's grave to accept Lord Jesus—should he be willing to receive me back in the fold—for I had missed Him dearly during my debauched years. I further added that, regardless of their judgment, I would never even dream of demon alcohol again, leaving little doubt that I would transform myself into the most upright of Christ's warriors if they could only find it in their hearts to offer a measure of clemency.

Driver Clay and Officer Hogan exchanged knowing glances and then a couple of sanctimonious nods at the news of another grand slam for the Man from Galilee. Seizing the moment, I mounted the bus with alacrity, Jeremiah thundering in my wake that he would keep his eye upon me and, if I exhibited any deviancy, he would cast me forth on the darkest yards of the highway. As I moved to the last remaining seat, many men, black and white, winked and motioned to their own well-concealed cartons of fortified juice.

I waved goodbye to Officer Hogan, smiling even as I muttered the wish that Mary Kate Josephine burn in hell, and that he and all his progeny die roaring. Twenty-three hours later, with every bone in my body creaking, and hungry enough to eat a scabby horse through a barbed wire fence, I screamed even more graphic curses at Driver Clay while stalking him through Port Authority.

When he reported me to a bored cop, I remembered what I was carrying and hightailed it. Out on the Deuce I bought a couple of overripe bananas with my loose change and gorged myself on the train to the Bronx.

No one had even missed me in Scutch's. Still, I covered my tracks by claiming to have been out of town on an interview, to which they all nodded their understanding, some figuring that I had been on maneuvers with the IRA, others concluding that a man had a right to whatever lies he chose. Nor were any hackles raised about my lack of resources; instead many a beer was shoved my way. As it turned out, the bar was in a celebratory mood. Mrs. Thatcher had seen the light, the hunger strike in the North was over, with the prisoners' demands for political status, apparently, granted.

Within an hour I was shaking hands with myself. Scutch cut me off after my sixth pint, and it was beyond my stuttering powers to argue that the bed might not be the best place for me. I was halfway up the block when I remembered the briefcase. With the fear of both God and Jesús coursing through me, I turned on my heel and legged it back. A couple of towering Cork men had taken my place at the bar. To their consternation, I dived between their legs, but to no avail. Tears of frustration streamed from my eyes as I crawled around the sawdust.

"Looking for something, sailor?" Scutch lisped to much sniggering. He wouldn't have been such a smartarse had he known he could have done twenty for even holding the bloody thing. Nor did I bother enlightening him. I was so overcome with gratitude I never even noticed a tall thin figure scoping me out from behind the jukebox.

CHAPTER NINETEEN

I awoke in Mary's room. I had no memory of getting there, but that was the least of my problems. My old nemesis, the black-winged moth, had metastasized into a great bat-like figure and was now spread across the length of my body. As I slid from under his suffocating clamminess, I stifled my screams and eased down onto the floor. From that angle I could tell that the curtains were drawn, and the room pitch black except for a thin arc of light oozing under the door. But it wasn't until I heard Jesús' voice that I knew for sure I'd been dreaming.

"I tell you, somethin's wrong."

"Miami is always screwed up," Mary reassured him.

"No, it's everywhere now . . . even with my kid."

"That's just his mother."

"What do you know about Estela 'cept what I tell you?"

"She called me a *puta*."

"She call you worse than that."

"She should talk—the fat whore!"

The cans on the table shuddered as he threw back his chair.

"Go on! That's what you do to her, isn't it?"

I could almost see his hand raised, and the old helpless feeling swept over me. I trained my eyes in the gloom and tiptoed back to the bed. Where the hell was the briefcase? I groped frantically through the sheets before touching its cool plastic.

"Who was the guy outside the bodega?" The menace in his voice was almost palpable. "The guy my brother seen you with?"

"Oh, so your brother thinks I'm a whore too? He should know, the way he looks at me."

"Don't you never say that about my brother! You hear me?"

"But he can say it about me, right?"

I couldn't take any more. Had to get back to the sanity of Scutch's. But where the hell were my shoes? And how was I to explain sleeping in Mary's bed?

"Is important, Maria. Who was the guy?"

"Just someone from the pub."

"No! My brother don't lie!"

"There are things you don't know about your precious brother."

"That guy was with a *negrito*. You don't let them in your pub."

"How would you know? When was the last time you were there?"

"I don't go because your people spit on me."

"They're not exactly singing Halleluiah for me either."

He plopped down on a creaky kitchen chair. His voice was muffled behind his palms. "Was watchin' the cartoons with my kid yesterday and I start shiverin' and shit, my hands, they sweatin' and this feelin' that I don't see him no more."

"It's just your imagination."

"You ain't from here. Don't know like we do."

"Oh no? Well, how about if I told you I saw Our Lady

of the Bronx shimmying down Bainbridge last night. Would that make you feel any better?"

"Don't talk shit like that! Bad luck!"

A stream of water splashed in the sink, and I could tell she had stuck her head under the cold tap; the mascara would be running down her face.

"Eyes on the street, all lookin' at me."

"Just a coincidence," she dismissed him.

"No coincidence. You lose my powder!"

"I told you I'd pay you back, every penny of it."

"You get me to use the *blanquito.* He too much like Juan."

"Juan is dead!"

"Don't check white people in suits. Me in a suit, they think I'm a pimp."

"Oh, give me a break. The only reason you used Sean is because you want him out of here."

"Why you use him, Maria?"

"You're hurting my wrist!"

"Tell me."

"Because I want him away from this hell. He wouldn't be here if it wasn't for me."

The chair creaked and he stood up. I did too. For the first time since I arrived, I heard my Mary speaking—the one who cared for me.

"And you go with him, right?"

"You know I'm not going anywhere."

Had it not been for the walls, I could have touched the despair settling between them, but I didn't give a damn. I knew she still loved me. Everything else had been a mask.

"I wish you stay because you want to, Maria."

"You know what I want."

"No. Not now. You promise me!"

"He goes home tomorrow. You give him my cut."

"And what get you through tomorrow?"

"I'll find a way. But he goes."

Her concern gave me the strength. I had thrown open the door and was in the kitchen before I'd even figured what I was going to say. They both jumped—Jesús' hand darting inside his jacket.

"How's it going?" The greeting sounded dumb even to my ears.

"Where have you been?" Mary was the first to recover.

"Your *man* didn't show up in the motel until yesterday and then . . ."

"So?" Jesus cut me off and I could read his mind. What was I doing in her room—in her bed?

"Sow birdseed! You didn't give me enough money."

His face hardened and he took a deep breath.

"What happened?" Mary was bolting the locks on the front door.

I sauntered over to the fridge, fuller of myself than any bantam cock, but the iciness in his voice gave me pause. "The lady ask you a question."

"Your *man* in his Panama hat didn't show up for three days, so I had to take the damned bus back."

"The bus?" Mary reached out for the briefcase, but I wouldn't give it to her.

"What did you expect me to do, walk? And oh, by the way, I didn't appreciate you letting that fascist Cuban know I was coming."

"Cuban?" They mouthed the word together.

"Yeah, the old guy behind the desk at La Hacienda. And

not for nothing, you could have picked a better place to put
me up. I see enough hookers and transvestites down the
Bowery."

"Who was the Cuban?" Jesús' eyes narrowed and he
addressed the question to both of us.

"He's drunk. Can't you tell?" Mary almost cut him off.

"I didn't have a drink until I got to New York."

"You're not going to tell me you were bullshitting in
Scutch's and with what you were carrying too?"

"I just dropped by for a minute."

"A minute? With that smell of drink off you!"

"*Borracho!*" Jesús hissed and moved towards the door to
block my exit.

"There are people looking for this." She moved even
quicker and snatched the briefcase out of my hand.

"No one saw me!"

"You were falling down drunk. How do you know who
saw you?" She had her hand out. Jesús passed her a small key.

"No one was even looking at me, I swear."

"I put all my trust in you." With jittery fingers she turned
the key in the lock and opened the case, then flung out some
magazines and dug her thumbs into the lining. The bottom
of the case sprung up to reveal two plastic bags full of white
powder. She caressed them so reverentially I thought she
might drop to her knees and offer up a benediction. Instead,
she turned to me. "You've got to go—now!"

The note of urgency caught Jesús' attention.

"Not until I get paid," I said.

"You'll get your money."

"He go nowhere," Jesús said.

"Go on, Sean, go now!" She pointed to the door.

"No!" He slapped her on the shoulder with the back of his hand. "Someone got a big mouth."

"No, baby, he wouldn't do it." Though he still had his arm raised, she moved even closer to him. "Right, Sean, you didn't tell anyone?"

"Ain't talkin' about him," he hissed at her.

There was a long frightening silence. When she finally spoke, her eyes were wild. "How could you say that, Jesús? After all we've been through?"

He stared right through her until she cried out, "Don't look at me like that!"

She seemed to shrink beneath his stony glare. Then he spat at me, "Where the *loco* one—*pura basura?*"

I didn't know what he meant, but she quickly piped up, "Danny?"

"He say people know where to find me."

"He didn't mean anything," I said. "He just talks like that."

"Startin' to make sense."

"No, it's something totally different."

He closed the briefcase and moved towards the door. "I'm going to find that *maricón.*"

"No, I know why he's not here." I stepped in front of him. "So?"

He waited while I fought for the words to explain what had transpired between us; I knew what I should say, just didn't have the courage.

"Let me have mine," Mary interrupted.

"'Ain't got the time for that now."

"Please . . ." She begged him.

He put down the briefcase and held out his arms, but she didn't go to him. "Maria, you're all I got."

She didn't move until he took her in his arms and kissed her wet hair. Then she rested her head on his shoulder and he murmured, "Be strong, *amór.*"

When she looked up at him, he smiled. "Remember . . . Boquerón."

He kissed her on the mouth and murmured, "*Por siempre.*"

Then he picked up the briefcase. She held his hand until he opened the door, then she bolted and barred it behind him.

CHAPTER TWENTY

She leaned back against the door, eyes steely with resolve. Though staring right at me, I was of no interest to her. She was listening. His footsteps halted on the landing below. We waited so long I thought he might have moved on silently. Then we heard him skip down the last steps and pass out of our hearing. When I moved she shushed me fiercely.

I barely heard the scuffle until a shot was fired; it echoed like rippling thunder up the bare stone stairs. Racing footsteps approached, a fierce hammering and: "*Abre la puerta, Maria!*"

She swept silently across the room and grabbed on to the edge of the table.

"Open the goddamn door, Maria!" He kept pounding, his voice shrill with panic.

"For Christ sake, open it." I hissed at her and ran over, but she barred my way.

There was a fierce struggle outside, a succession of sickening thuds over a litany of multilingual curses, and then the lurching sound of too many bodies descending the narrow staircase. After an eternity, the street door slammed and all was quiet.

I was petrified. She remained tensed, her fists clenched. This time the footsteps were measured and authoritative; it was almost a relief when the knock finally came.

She put her fingers to her lips and turned to the door.
"Hello?"

"NYPD! Open up!"

"Do you have anything on you?" she hissed at me, already at the kitchen mirror applying damage control to her face.

"What?"

"Did you skim anything from the briefcase?"

"What do you take me for?"

"Are you sure?"

"Of course, I'm sure!"

"You better not be lying. Just a moment, Officer!" she called out in a very exaggerated Irish accent while fiercely brushing knots out of her hair. She grimaced at her appearance and swept aside a couple of Kate's lipsticks before settling on one. Her hand shook as she applied it, and she had to use a tissue to remove a smear from the corner of her mouth. As she rushed past she whispered, "I'll do the talking, you hear me?"

"One moment, please," she called out before opening the door. Her bog accent would have sounded hilarious in other circumstances.

The cop flashed identification. He was wearing a Yankees cap, a navy pea coat, and blue jeans. Tall and authoritative, he gripped her by the arm.

"You OK?" he rasped but stopped dead when he saw me.

"Oh, thanks be to God you're here, Officer." She was still laying it on thick, but just then there was a flurry of footsteps on the stairs. He stepped sideways to block our view of the approaching figure.

"Detective," he corrected her and raised his voice for the

approaching figure to hear. "Ryan, NYPD. You got a Maria in here?"

"Sure isn't that a Puerto Rican name, Detective. They never stop out there, day and night. Amn't I blue in the face callin' the precinct."

He glanced sharply at her, betraying a slight puzzlement, then shouted back to the landing. "I got this one covered. Check the roof."

He closed the door and stepped inside. As he warily scanned the room, Mary rattled on in her ludicrous accent. "It's the drugs, you know. That crowd was shouting all kinds of abuse, and I was afraid of me life."

He gave me the full once-over but was reluctant to make eye contact. She shadowed him when he looked inside her bedroom. "I'm Mary Ryan, Detective, same name as yourself, and this is me cousin Sean just over from Ireland. Hasn't the life been frightened out of him."

Without warning, he flung her up against the wall. I moved to help until I caught the flash of gunmetal. She was splayed against the peeling white plaster like some rag doll.

"What's he know?"

"About what?" Her confidence might have been shot but not her accent.

"Stop making a fuck of me, you little cunt!" he roared. "Get in that room, pal, and stick your fingers in your fucking ears, if you know what's good for you!"

I was already on my way when the front door slammed into the wall. He threw me aside, dropped to one knee, and leveled the gun at Kate, two six-packs of Heineken in her hands, the red wig ever so slightly askew as she sang at the top of her voice.

"I'll away home to me own wee garret,

If I can't get a man, sure I'll have to use a carrot."

"Don't move," Ryan yelled.

"Where's the opener, Sean, me flower? Isn't the tongue hangin' out of me."

"I said don't move, you dumb bitch!"

"Dumb bitch, how are you? Haven't I just had a scorching night on the tiles?"

"Are you deaf?"

"No, but I'll be as skinny as Twiggy if that little Jewish fellah doesn't give me a break."

Ryan lowered the gun, slipped it back in his pocket, and stood up. "You go kicking in doors like that, lady, you won't need to worry about your weight."

"What do you want me to do? Open it with a headbutt—and me with me arms full of the best beer that Holland has to offer?"

"So you want to play games? Let's see your green card. You too, pal."

"Ah will you sit down, like a good man, and have a drink." Kate winked at him and did a little swivel, the better to show off her figure. "Sean, *a stór,* you wouldn't believe the carry-on of that Arnold." She slammed the six-packs down on the table. "Mary, did you ever do it doggie style?"

Heavy footsteps passed by on the landing. Ryan called out, "I got it covered in here. Check out any Maria in the building."

"That slut is long gone," Kate said nonchalantly.

"You know her?"

She produced a compact and regarded herself critically in the mirror. "Officer darlin', do I look like the kind of girl who consorts with Puerto Rican prostitutes?"

"What makes you think she was a whore?"

"Well she was hardly the Virgin of Prague, seein' this used to be the best knockin' shop the far side of San Juan. Now will you sit down like a good man and have a bottle of beer."

"Listen, lady . . ." His eyes were still on the door while he listened to the receding footsteps.

"Kathleen to you. Officer."

"I'm sure you have a very active social life . . ." He appraised her figure for a long moment before cracking open the door and peering out on the landing.

"Social life is it? Sure, amn't I the belle of Bainbridge Avenue. Which reminds me, Mary. I ran into them two fellahs from Donegal down in the bodega. They'll be up here in a couple of minutes."

When Ryan closed the door, Kate thrust out her chest and sashayed over to him. "Stay with us, will you, Officer." She pleaded. "Them two boyos are fierce drunk . . ." She winked at him. ". . . in case they get out of hand like?"

Ryan glanced at Mary. She was hugging herself to control the shivering.

"Don't leave town," he cautioned her, then leered back at Kate. "Drink some coffee, Kathleen. I'll take a rain check on the drink."

"Oh, don't you love the way he says 'Kathleen,'" she cooed as she watched him open the door.

When he turned he focused on me, and all the menace returned. "Get the fuck back to Ireland if you know what's good for you."

The instant his footsteps had receded on the stairs, Kate dropped the rigmarole. "Where's Danny?"

She pointed at the white rectangle where the Connolly poster used to hang. I hadn't even noticed its absence. His corner was even more monastic than usual, the bed neatly made, guitar gone, book case empty.

"Oh for Christ sake, who cares about him?" Mary snapped. "Jesús got busted."

"Why didn't you let him in?" Kate lashed back.

"The lock stuck again."

Kate snorted in disbelief. They glowered at each other until Mary backed down. "Do you think that cop suspects anything?"

"He just wants to fuck you," Kate said. "What else is new?"

"Give me a break, will you!"

"So take off my fecking lipstick and stop using people for once in your life."

"You're just jealous about your precious Danny."

"Jealous? Look at the state of you. You're like something the cat dragged in."

Mary was hugging herself fiercely now though the room was sweltering, the steam whistling through the broken knob on the radiator.

"What did they do to Jesús?" she said in a tiny voice.

"They beat the head off him and had him over a car." Kate shot a glance at me. "They were opening his briefcase."

"What are you looking at me for? It's not my briefcase," I said.

She just shrugged that she hadn't time for such humbug.

"Was he bleeding?" Mary asked.

"You don't want to know," Kate dismissed her.

"I don't want him to be hurt."

"It's a bit late for that now."

I tried to open a bottle of Heineken, but the cap wouldn't unscrew.

"Will he talk?" I asked, dropping the bottle back in its pack.

But Kate walked past me. Over at the sink, she began rearranging her various lipsticks and mascara into precise columns.

"You're taking the next plane home," Mary said.

"With what? Yez never paid me."

"Oh God," she hugged herself even closer. "I'm dead out there without him."

"Before you go writing your obituary," Kate wheeled around on her, "what happened to Danny?"

"Why don't you ask him?" Mary pointed at me.

"Well?"

"We had a . . . bit of an argument."

"Over what?"

"One thing and another . . ."

"One thing and another what?" Kate snapped at me, and I had to turn away, such was the disgust in her glare. She waited for some moments, and when I didn't answer she just said, "I see."

I stammered for some words, something, anything that could explain what had transpired between us, but where to begin?

Mary broke the silence. "Someone ratted on Jesús, and Danny Boy disappears right before the cops arrive? How convenient."

"That's pure shite and you know it!" Kate spat out the words.

"Why? He left Belfast in a hurry too, didn't he?"

"You know damn well why he left."

"He grassed on someone. It's common knowledge."

"You little bitch! All you ever think about is yourself."

Mary was shaking like a leaf that had barely made it through the winter. She looked from one to the other of us. "You just don't understand," she said.

"I understand more than I ever wanted to—about the both of you."

A chip of plaster dropped from the wall when Mary slammed the door behind her. The bed creaked beneath her weight.

"Whatever about Belfast, you know damn well why he left here," Kate said to me. And she was right.

chapter twenty-one

The walls drew closer now, the rooms smaller, though
there should have been more space with Danny and
Kate gone. It all had to do with Mary. Edgy as all
hell, she paced the floor relentlessly except when stretched
out on the unmade bed, her eyes tracking the labyrinth of
cracks in the ceiling. I tried to coax her down to Scutch's,
but she was afraid to go out, yet even more terrified of being
left alone. She hardly ate: a cut of toast every now and then,
a thimbleful or two of anemic tea. Even those she barely
tolerated. She'd start at any sound on the landing, frozen for
minutes like Lot's wife; and if I even moved, let alone spoke,
she'd hush me as though I were some kind of moron totally
out of sync with reality. She was expecting a caller: That
much I was certain of.

I thought I might go crazy. Apart from fear of getting my
head kicked in, the sheer guilt racked me. With time to put
things in perspective, I knew Danny would never have forced
himself on me. Yet I had betrayed him. Kate knew that full
well and wanted no more part of me. There was only one
consolation: Jesús was finally out of the picture, though now
replaced by the specter of Ryan.

Danny had been right about the guitar. I was out of
touch. The calluses at the tips of my fingers had almost

disappeared, and the strings sliced new furrows at first. But that was only part of the problem—what to play? The Tinkers' repertoire, with all its baggage, cut deeper than any strings, and I could no longer get behind old staples like Strummer, Leonard, and Dylan. Their distanced certainties rang suspect in Mary's jittery presence, while their pieties evaporated like steam on the frigid streets outside.

Everything was magnified in the apartment, the very rooms alive and trembling, and it was there that I finally learned how to write songs. Over the years I had figured out how to reel in words and melodies that gelled well enough. Infusing them with life, however, was another matter. But spirit was bountiful on Decatur. I had only to strum a few chords and link them with some idea, no matter how ephemeral, and before long a finished story would waltz in front of me. There were still roadblocks; quite often a melody would suggest itself, yet the hatful of chords at my disposal would fail to give it wings. I'd sit for eons, clumsily constructing some chord whose name I hadn't a notion of, before I could go on. It was while stalled on one such impasse that Mary played her hand.

"That guitar over and over—the same bloody song!"

"It's called writing."

"Well, for your information, life isn't a collection of trite little verses and choruses."

She was standing over me, fists clenched, her brow damp and furrowed. Once upon a time I would have sat her on my knee and tried to right the world for her. Now I barely had the energy to sigh, "When you come up with something better, let me know."

"I have! I live it, I love it, and then I put it behind me."

She suddenly shuddered as though struck from within.

"What's the matter?" I grabbed onto her.

"Leave me alone!" She ripped herself away. "I wish Ryan did want to fuck me."

"Why do you say these things?"

"Oh, shut up! Sex is the last thing on my mind."

"Yeah, I'd noticed."

"All it would mean is he doesn't want to bust us. Does that hurt you too?"

She dashed over to the wall and switched out the lights. The lone sixty-watt bulb over the kitchen sink wreathed the room in shadows. "They're watching us," she whispered.

"Who?"

She didn't answer. Just gazed intently through the half-opened door into her bedroom. I followed her eyes but could only see darkness. Why was she always looking in there? What was she expecting? What was she hiding or hiding from?

Then the phone rang downstairs. And rang and rang and rang until the old Ukrainian lady picked it up and began to jabber in a stream of bald guttural sentences that routed Mary from her trance.

"That bloody thing goes right through me." She jammed her palms against her temples but spun around when a reflection of bus lights careened along the wall. "I've seen them on the street."

"Who?"

"Who do you bloody think?"

"It's all in your head, Mary."

"What do you know, sitting there pontificating like you understand everything?"

"Well, there's one thing I do know—I'm going for a drink."

She raced me across the room and barred my way. She was all fire and bone, and I had the craziest idea that she might attack me.

"You're not leaving me here on my own!"

"Then come out. You can't stay in forever."

"I wouldn't last an hour without Jesús."

"Well, you can wait here on your own for him." I tried to shove past, but she was full of a mad, feral strength.

"You haven't a clue, have you?" she sneered.

"Every time he looked at you, it killed me."

"You should put a reggae beat behind that one. Rip off Bob Marley, for a change."

"Leave me the fuck alone!"

Still she refused to move, and I knew it would take a brawl to get past her.

"We don't belong here," she murmured as I cracked open a beer. "We walk their streets, but we're just ghosts among them."

"Who are you talking about now?"

"Don't act so stupid." Her right hand was trembling.

"Are you OK?" I asked.

"A couple of years from now, Jesús will barely remember me."

"No candle-lit dinners in Bouqerón?"

"You're just like him—full of romantic notions. But neither of you has a bloody clue."

"What are you talking about?"

Someone passed on the stairs. Her eyes darted to the door. In the shadow light, she resembled a half-starved raven I'd once trapped beneath a sand riddle.

"Are you all right?"

"No, I'm not all right!" Her breathing quickened and turned shallow. Her hair, lank and sweaty, had drooped over her eyes. "Oh Sean, there's so much you don't know—even back at home."

"Yeah, with everyone laughing behind my back."

"You were the only one worth anything. There was no one else . . ."

She stopped abruptly as though her breath had run out, then suddenly snatched the can of beer out of my hand and took a mouthful. She barely made it over to the kitchen, but the vomiting was over quickly. She was shuddering, and her knuckles were whiter than the enamel she held onto. Then she steadied herself and took a deep breath. She ran the tap and washed off her face, then kept it running to clean out the sink. She was ghastly pale and narrow as the blade of a knife. I knew I should call a doctor, but I couldn't take my eyes off her.

"That night on the Lower East Side . . . they would have killed you, Sean. But I didn't know, I swear." The tears were mixing with the beads of cold water on her face.

"It's OK."

"No, it's not. I can't get it out of my head."

"It's all right, Mary, believe me."

"You don't know them."

"Listen, we got out of it alive."

"They'll be back. They never forget."

This time she shuddered as though she'd been punched.

"What's the matter?"

"Oh God, do you really not know?"

"What?"

"How can you be so stupid?" She gripped her left wrist and began rolling up her sleeve.

"Look," she said, like a child confessing some small indiscretion to an adult. Only then did it dawn on me that I hadn't seen her bare arms since I'd arrived.

"For God's sake, will you look!" She ripped at the thin shirt and winced as it rose above her elbow. Her arm was pocked and puffy.

"I haven't scored in days, Sean."

ChAPTER TWENTY-TWO

"Where's Mary?"

"Down the bodega."

"On her own?"

"Yeah. She goes out all the time now."

"And you let her?" Kate stood in the doorway scarcely believing her ears.

"She's fine . . . most of the time."

"She must be a lot better." She closed the door and tossed her coat on a chair.

"She's getting there."

That was a bit of an understatement, because every day is different in the life of a recovering junkie: every day twenty-four hours further on from the moment you yanked the very roots of your being out of the habit that had meant everything.

For all its horror, the first week was not the worst, though the night she came clean was a living nightmare as she cursed, cried, sweated, passed out, and clawed at the very walls. She held onto me like a leech, threw me away like a wet rag, puked on me, and knocked into or kicked over everything in the apartment. She loved me, hated me, blamed me, forgave me, and blasted everyone who had ever meant anything to her. She dragged me through a sewer of degradation beginning with her father who had abused her on through every poseur outside the chipper who had ever copped a feel or even smiled at her, until the night she scored her first snort of God's pure grace in London and rejoiced in the blessed relief that heroin afforded. I heard all about her search for connections back in Ireland and the muck she crawled through to keep her spike fueled. Each one of her sudden absences was explained in excruciating detail, all of it coated with the guilt she felt at betraying me. To top it all, I was made relive her flight to the Bronx, and cringe as she recalled the initial stability and love she found with Jesús.

On it went around the clock with little sleep and less to eat until I didn't know, and cared less, if it was morning, noon, or night. I was drained, claustrophobic, and paranoid, but mortally afraid to leave her alone; yet, I knew I had to score something in the downer department to reel in her skittering metabolism and give her spirit some peace. When I couldn't keep my eyes open any longer, I managed to get the word out to Arsehole. True to form, he breezed in hours later with a fistful of Quaaludes for Mary and a six-pack of tallboys to ease my own blistered brain.

Nothing would do him but to take a shift and, in that drowsy voice of his, he spun her a tale of his own habit back in London and how he'd kicked solo, but sure hadn't she the soundest of men in me and wouldn't he be there too with Valium when she'd done with the 'ludes, because there was sweet shag-all point in leaping out of the frying pan into the fire; and when the Valium had played its part, wouldn't there be sleeping pills aplenty to float her through the darkness; and when mother's little helpers had done their jobs, then there'd always be Jameson's, in its blessed legality, to dull the jagged edge of the blade. When I awoke, Mary was out like a light in the bed, with Arsehole snoring up blue thunder in the chair beside her. I was less than an ace away from kissing him, for that was the first time either of us had relaxed since Jesús had been busted.

For weeks she slept days on end and half the nights too. Still, every so often, with nails slicing her palms, she'd explode and crave a fix; but gradually the skittering lightning in her eyes softened to a dull distressing gaze that bespoke of some ongoing examination of scenes far from pleasant. As soon as those vistas were either dealt with, dulled, or beaten back into memory, we entered the long arid lap of hopelessness. What was there to live for? Was there a point? Those questions in myriad variation infected the apartment until the very walls were suffused with gloom.

Then one day I noticed her observing the pigeons squabbling on the window ledge. It was the first time she'd shown any interest in the world outside, beyond starting at every footstep on the landing. And soon after she began wearing mascara again and fretfully glancing in the mirror. But those were the good times. Other days were consumed with the search for the there that used to be there, wondering if life could ever be normal again and, by the way, what the hell was normal anyway? For once you've sealed hell's gates behind you, reality is not something you can exactly put your finger on in a hurry.

I had moved into her room, mostly lounging on the chair or dozing next to her on the bed. She was so fragile I feared she might break apart. Yet in those first days she clung to me when she woke up sweating and shivering. Then, as she got better, she had a need of warmth in the bleakness of the night. There was no thought of sex. She found her own body disgusting, especially the scars on her spindly arms. On one occasion I pleaded with her to remember our day out on the island and how healthy she had been. But that saddened her even more, for she confessed that she had almost lost her mind waiting for the boat to return so that she could get away from me, boot up, and find the vein.

But as her body began to heal, so too did some of the scars inside her head. One night I awoke to find her crying softly. I kissed her forehead, she moved closer and rested her face next to my throat like she used to when we lay in the heather back on the mountain. The old familiar yearning welled up, and I didn't care anymore, for I was empty too. What matter about Jesús or how they had touched each other? It was just the two of us now. I don't know if she felt the same, for she initiated nothing, just clung to me while I made love to her.

There were other nights when she couldn't bear to be held; the mere thought that someone might desire her was beyond her understanding. But from then on I was hers again and, when my need was bad enough, she would satisfy me in one way or another.

It was a life in limbo. Neither of us worked. I played the guitar; she stared out the window or flipped through the pages of a book. The winter was unsparing, and the wind sweeping down Decatur cut right through to the bone. There was little need to go out, except to the bodega or Scutch's. Kate visited from time to time and loaned us money. She also paid her rent in advance and insisted on covering Danny's share in case he should return. Eventually I got the call to sit in on a few gigs on Bainbridge, and Scutch suggested that Mary do a couple of day shifts to help out.

I used to drop her off around noon and pick her up at seven. The quietness of the afternoons suited her. She fit in well with the old men who had little left to look forward to but memories of Donegal or Mayo amid the tube-light company of television sets in rooming houses. She couldn't handle the hurly-burly of night shifts, although, on occasion, she gave it a try for Scutch's sake. The roughness of the clientele distressed her, their lurking despair always threatening to explode. The sheer toll of kicking smack had gnawed away any reserves of toughness; she was easily distracted and could rarely put the distance needed between herself and the roiling Paddies. She could no longer handle slagging—the currency of Irish pub communication— retreating behind a barrier of reserve, often taken for snobbishness. After a while, Scutch taught her how to place orders and check deliveries before bestowing on her the somewhat impressive title of day manager. And with that, she began to recover and even show sparks of her old self again.

I liked picking her up in the evenings and looked forward to the secret smile she saved for me. After she had counted out the till, we would sit at a back table while she counted her tips and sip a couple of beers before going home to bed. In her better moods, she would ramble on about this one or that and, if sunk inside herself, I would leave her be, for I had learned that there is no profit in delving; one never knew what demon might arise. Then one evening Noreen and her roommates arrived.

I had stopped calling her on a regular basis during my trip to Miami, usually just showing up at the Gallowglass out of the blue. I could tell she was worried about me, but she was possessed of a natural reserve. During the first weeks of

Mary's ordeal, I was preoccupied, although I was determined that as soon as things lightened up I would get back in touch.

On my first night out alone, I did call her. I'd had a couple of pints and, full to the gills with sincerity, I gushed on about missing her and insisted that I owed an explanation. It was downhill from there on. How could I tell her that Mary was kicking heroin or explain Jesús and Ryan? I did blurt out that Mary needed me; but the more I tried to waltz around the baldness of that statement, the longer the silences dangled between us. Finally, she made me promise that I would call her the next day when I was sober. But Mary had a relapse, and it took me the best part of a week to get her back on an even keel. When I finally called, one of her roommates tartly informed me that, "Noreen has gone to visit a *friend* in Boston and won't be back for some time."

It was a shock to see her, for Scutch's wasn't one of her hangouts. It was still early, but she and her roommates got the usual ebullient welcome that any three single women get in a bar full of boozed-up, horny men. Though we didn't make eye contact, I knew she knew I was there, for she was effusive and over-friendly to the morons milling around her. A deep sadness overwhelmed me. I had been happy with Noreen. Her simplicity and clear soul had been like a balm to me. In our time together, the Tinkers were kings of the avenue and I had Danny's friendship; the world was mine for the taking. Now where was I?

I must have looked away or tried to concentrate on what Mary was saying, for out of nowhere Noreen was standing next to me.

"How are you, Sean?" And I remembered how I loved the sound of her voice.

"Great, Noreen, how are you?" I replied with a lot more confidence than I felt. There was an empty chair at the table; I should have asked her to join us, introduce her. Instead I blushed to high heavens and, as the seconds passed, I knew I had hurt her more than I'd even feared. Still her natural dignity was intact. She nodded to Mary and murmured, "Excuse me."

Mary threw me a confused look but, before she could say anything, Noreen gathered herself and said, "I just wanted to make sure you were OK, Sean."

And then she was walking away. She may have been crying for she stumbled on the uneven floor and brushed against a table, knocking over a glass. She didn't even look at her two roommates but passed straight out into the street. They too were caught off guard but grabbed their purses and ran after her. One of them flashed daggers at me before she slammed the door. A murmur rippled along the bar, exacerbated by the clipped silence from the jukebox. Then there was the rumble of a familiar bass line, and Sting called out "Roxanne."

"Who was that?" Mary asked.

"Oh, just some girl . . ." I took a swig of beer to hide my burning face and hummed along.

"She didn't act like 'just some girl.'"

"She used to follow the band around. Into Shiggins big time—probably just wanted to, you know . . ."

"Hmm." Mary smiled uneasily as my voice trailed off. "I'll have to make sure I come to all your gigs from now on."

She laid her hand on mine. Her fingers were cool but far from reassuring.

CHAPTER TWENTY-THREE

It snowed that night and even Decatur looked beautiful. It had already begun on our way home, and I was glad for the diversion. I was afraid Mary might inquire in more detail about Noreen. It would have been hard to lie, as my thoughts were full of what she'd meant to me and how I'd failed her. The snow solved some of that, blurring the harsh outlines of the Bronx and some of my uncertainties.

Mary drifted off to sleep soon after we made love, but my heart hadn't been in it and I couldn't lie still. I felt aimless as the drifting flakes, though they at least were bringing peace to the troubled city. I knew I should relax, that snow signaled redemption, but I could see no clear way ahead and resented the silent white invader. Eventually, I got up and went outside.

The flurries were swirling up and down the avenue, and it was hard to see at first. I had never experienced snow of this nature. It was already settling into drifts around the doorway. And what a transformation! Battered, bawdy Decatur looked like a scene from a Christmas card. I half expected to hear sleigh bells and witness Dickensian characters come caroling down the footpaths in greatcoats and mufflers. And then I understood my black mood. Though the street was transformed, the snow merely hid what was underneath—likewise my situation with Mary.

There were no cars skidding by, and even the buses had stopped running. A bunch of kids had fashioned a thin piece of metal into a sled and were skidding down the cobbled hill. Their excited jabbering barely cut through the cloaked silence, but their brown faces leaped out in relief against the uniform whiteness. Some of their friends pelted them with snowballs. They halted the assault to let me pass. The snow, it appeared, had even bestowed manners. Had they been playing stickball in the heat of the summer, it would have been a different matter. They grinned at me and I couldn't resist; I waved my arms and shimmied. They screamed in wonder at the *cojones* of the *blanquito loco*. I bobbed and weaved around a street lamp, the snowballs whizzing around my head. Then one hit me square on the face, ending the fun and games. I sprinted through the traffic light, and they returned to their sledding.

It was already a winter wonderland. The vacant lots looked like the fields at home on the rare day they'd get a sprinkling of snow. The piles of uncollected trash had been transformed into crystal hills, while the weedy trees that had seemed skeletal only hours previously now magisterially stretched their arms to catch the drifting flakes. The junked cars, their windows smashed, had come to resemble stagecoaches, with the snow carpeting the remains of dashboards. Even the burnt-out buildings had regained some of their majesty, the charred brick camouflaged behind the swirling paleness. And what a blessed silence: no drums, horns or radios, just peace descending in a sacred veil of whiteness. I wanted to dive in the nearest drift and lose myself. Who cared that tomorrow would bring slush and discomfort. As long as the snow kept falling, the Bronx would regain its virginity and remain forever beautiful and unsullied.

I looked in on Mary when I returned. She was sleeping, her lips dry and slightly parted. Her hair had begun to grow out again, and it was splayed across the pillow. Flushed from sleep, her cheeks had lost some of their chiseled gauntness. She was another person already, and I marveled at how markedly her appearance changed with her mindset. Had she always been that way? When out of her presence I often found it hard to capture her face or hold it in freeze-frame. Now I etched each detail into memory and closed my eyes, but it was useless. Which Mary had I just stared at and which was I remembering?

As I shut the bedroom door behind me, I wondered if I ever really knew her. But such thoughts were dangerous, and I banished them as best I could. I stopped for a glance out the window. The snow was still coming down steadily, but the wind had stopped blowing. At this rate, it would be well over a foot deep in the morning.

"Snow is falling all over Ireland," I murmured to myself, and thought of my Leaving Certificate English teacher. Old Murph was a notorious drunk who often came into class with the smell of the previous night's whiskey still on him. His hand shook and he could be dangerous if provoked; but he loved books and, to our delight, would occasionally veer from the curriculum and read from his favorites. My mother had known him in her courting days and sighed that James Murphy had been disappointed in love. I used to fancy that it was over her and felt an odd connection with him.

One day when it had snowed, he locked the door of the classroom. We were quiet as flowers, for we knew a treat was at hand. He began to read a story about a man in the olden days who had attended a Christmas party in Dublin with his wife. Nothing of great interest happened, but Old Murph's voice was melodious and danced in time with the flakes outside the big windows. The man was troubled by his wife's mood; she had shed a tear for a boy whom she'd been sweet on. I couldn't figure the man's problem since the young fellah had died many years previously and was obviously no threat.

When the story ended, Old Murph closed the book and said, "We never really know anyone else, do we?"

The radiators were hissing, the classroom warm, and not even the hard chaws wished to break the spell.

Murph then sighed, "And sure how could we, when most of us will never even know ourselves?"

The bell had rung for lunch, but his words stayed with me; even back then I could tell that one day they might be important to me.

I slept on the couch that night. I never even heard Mary leaving and didn't wake until Kate shook my shoulder.

"A fine minder you are," she chided, her face grave and judgmental when she handed me a note with Mary's writing on it.

My heart dropped as I wiped the sleep from my eyes and tried to bring the swimming writing into focus.

"Gone to the Laundromat. I love you," it said.

I read it a second time just for the sheer relief. For, though Mary now came and went of her own accord, I was always on edge in her absence.

The sun was blazing and the room gleamed from the reflection of the drifts on the windowsills. Though I hadn't drunk much, my thoughts were all a-jumble. This condition was hardly helped by Kate prattling on about Arnold and her problems with his in-laws. With a sinking heart I remembered

Noreen and how badly I'd behaved the night before. I wanted to call her, to run over and try to explain, but how, what, where, when? How could I enlighten her when I couldn't make any sense of the situation myself?

There seemed no solution, and I wished Mary were back; at the worst she'd divert Kate and give my head some peace. Over at the sink, I threw some water on my face. When I turned, Kate was right there, arms folded, staring me in the eye. "You didn't hear a word I said, did you?"

She was right. Still, I knew there was something more to her observation, for she could rattle on till the cows came home if she was so inclined. I followed her eyes towards the door. She was listening for the sound of Mary lugging the laundry up the stairs. Then she shrugged haughtily. Arnold, no doubt, had his own washer and dryer; yet I knew she was feeling insecure. Her dentist might have been sweet on her, but that didn't mean that his brother and sister-in-law down on Central Park were thrilled at the thought of their Irish nanny sitting down to Seder with them.

"What's the matter?"

"Nothing!" With no wig on, she tossed back her own head of light brown curls. She looked well. Was it the regular rub of the relic or the fact that someone finally adored her? Voluptuous as ever, for once her clothes fit. They were more her own style too, whatever that was: Mayo chic curried by a dash of the Bronx.

"Everything all right with Arnold?" I ventured.

She plonked herself down at the table and tore the wrapping off a box of Parliaments.

"God damn it," she said. "Three weeks without a fag. I'm ten minutes back in this place and look at me."

She greedily sucked in the smoke. I could almost feel it caressing her lungs, while a look of sheer relief softened her face. When she finally exhaled, her eyes hazed over as if she'd just had the fuck of her life. The afterglow, however, was short-lived. "He wants me to convert."

"He what?"

"Arnold wants me to become a Jew." She stubbed the fag out with ferocity.

"Well, Jesus was a Jew."

"Yeah, but I'm not marrying him, Mister Smarty-Pants!" She snapped then fumbled for another cigarette. "I had to call me sister the nun."

"What did she say?"

"That I'd be the only Jew in Mayo," she wailed and then flung the box of Parliaments against the wall. "Oh, what do I care about me sister and the long auld Holy Mary face on her! I couldn't give a damn if I became a Jehovah's Witness and went from door to door as a tinker woman for the rest of me days!"

"Then what's annoying you?"

"Arsehole saw Danny down the Village. There's something the matter with him, Sean."

I should have guessed what was at the root of her agitation, and I wanted no part of it. But when I tried to stand up, she gripped me by the arm, "You have to go down there and get him!"

"Me?"

"I can't sleep for thinking of him, Sean."

"Well, go down and talk to him then."

"Sure they wouldn't let me next nor near one of them places."

"What places are you talking about?"

"Where the quare fellows drink—what do you think?"

"What harm would come to you?" I played for time, longing for Mary's return to put the kibosh on this talk. "At least you'd be safe. What do you think they'd do to me?"

"I don't care if they bugger you from here to Ballina. You're the only one he'll come back for!"

"I'm not getting mixed up in all that again."

"He wouldn't be down there if you hadn't screwed everything up with the band."

"Grow up, Kate! That's not the only reason he's there."

"Listen, Mister Big-Shot," she snarled, "when you were down and out, he looked after you. Do you remember the first night you came staggering through that door without an arse in your pants? Who got you your start, hah? And who stood up for you when the whole of Bainbridge was pissing themselves laughing at you?"

"No. I have Mary to look after now . . ."

"I swear to you she won't set foot out of this apartment, not if I have to strap her to that bed in there. Go on, Sean, now before she comes back. Please!"

CHAPTER TWENTY-FOUR

B ut I didn't go, and she cursed me into a knot for the ingrate that I was before storming out and swearing she'd never darken my doorstep again. Over the next couple of days, I did my best to blunt the edge of her harshness until one night down the pub Arsehole let slip that it had actually been three weeks since he'd seen Danny. I freaked out. What the hell did he mean, three weeks? Why hadn't he told me in the first place?

He came right back swinging. "Because there's no talking to you any more, man! You hadn't even the decency to speak to little Noreen when she came in here to make up with you."

I lashed back until Scutch warned that we'd both be out of there on our ears if he heard another word. Had we no consideration? Didn't we know Thatcher had reneged on her promises and Bobby Sands had gone on hunger strike, with three more prisoners waiting in the wings to follow him. The whole bar was trying to listen to the bloody news from home, not the antics of a couple of drunken bollockses the like of us.

He must have felt that he'd overstepped the mark for, in short order, he sent down a couple of shots of Bushmills. By the time we'd knocked back another three or four, we'd pledged to go down to the Crooked Man on Christopher Street and bring Danny home—with or without his consent.

The next day I waited in vain for the bastard outside the subway. I would have gone to his wreck of a room over by the Concourse, but it was pelting rain; besides it was already deep into the afternoon, and I was less than thrilled about making the night scene alone down on Christopher.

Despite a cup of coffee and a palm full of aspirin, my head pounded the whole way down to Manhattan. Although I wasn't the most political, it was hard to shake the image of Sands starving himself back in Ireland. What led a man to do such a thing? What commitment he must have, what principles and belief in his cause. When I measured myself against him, I found much wanting.

And how to face Danny? Would he even talk to me? Had I put him in danger by not explaining to Jesús that he would never grass on anyone? And yet Mary said there was a reason he left Belfast. He was obviously deeply connected: The whispers on the site, the visit to the Gallowglass and the stilted conversation with Benny left little doubt about that. What was his secret? Did he know Sands? If he'd stayed in Belfast would he too be lining up to starve himself? Why had he fled the North? And why the hell wasn't I back there doing my part—with this bitch of a British prime minister pissing all over my people?

My head was so spinning with questions I missed the West 4th Street stop and had to jump off at Broadway/Lafayette. The rain had eased, but the freezing March wind cut the face off me on Houston Street. The street lamps were coming on as I rounded Sixth Avenue and caught a glimpse of the Empire State, its beacons twinkling in the fading afternoon. Danny had told me that they decked it out in green for St. Patrick's Day. Would they tie a black armband around it this year in solidarity with Sands?

I turned my collar up against the cold and ploughed on. With ten months under my belt, I was truly a city veteran. A pride of lions could have come strolling by and I wouldn't have cast them a second glance as long as they honored my space. By the time I hit Christopher, though, my nonchalance was peeling off like sunburned skin. This was hardcore man world. No messing about and sweet damn all coquetry. Eye contact, for want of a better term, was searing, and since I had chosen to stroll down the street of dreams in black leather jacket and blue jeans, it could be safely assumed that I wasn't there soliciting pen pals. Though my eyes were set in concrete and riveted straight ahead, I was under no illusion that I had crossed a line. What the hell was Danny doing in this meat market? Was he out of his skull?

I almost missed the Crooked Man, so intent was I on avoiding the meaningful stares. The saloon was down a couple of steps. As I hesitated in front of its lurid seediness, so too did a Montgomery Clift lookalike. Having no desire to hear what this sensitive young man so obviously wished to say, I bounded down the steps.

It was warm inside but so dimly lit that I didn't notice the couple wrapped around each other in the narrow vestibule. I must have gasped, for both men pulled back to give me the once-over before resuming business.

"Excuse me, lads," I murmured and brushed sideways past them into the bar. In the far corner, a quartet of biker-looking guys slouched around a pool table. They looked up and regarded me for just a moment and then got on with the game. The music was low and pulsing, a bit like Joy Division without the vocals. Some couples were dancing in front of the bar, or more like groping to the beat. Others were strewn around tables, a foot up here, an outstretched leg there. A black light cast everything in a soft ghostly glow, especially the white undershirts that, along with leather and a fortune of glinting silver, appeared to be *de rigueur.*

There was no sight of Danny and I panicked. What an idiot to come all the way downtown without his address, just Arsehole's hazy word that he spent most of his time in this dive. Then a dancing couple stumbled off towards an alcove, and I saw him sitting at the bar, stiff-backed as ever. Even in the distance he looked thinner; shoulders that had once bulged out of the familiar leather jacket now had all the room they needed. His dark-brown hair was sculpted close to his skull and ran in a precise straight line across his neck. Even with his back turned, I could tell he was stroking his lower lip in the way that he did when he wished to be left alone with his thoughts. Still as a harvest night, he brooded away, as ever an island unto himself.

I stepped past the groping dancers and was about to lay my hand on his shoulder when he said without turning, "What about you, Paddy?"

His voice was deeper and hoarse, the Belfast accent sounding incongruous in the surroundings.

"How did you know it was me?"

He nodded at the mirror and then spoke into his drink, "You were never a one for the subtle entrance."

"You always had my number, didn't you?" I smiled, trying to thaw the frost that I could almost touch around him. He didn't answer and I wondered if he'd heard me. When he did turn, it took every fiber of my being to hide the shock. He was sick all right, the grayness in his face highlighted by little red blotches and an angry lesion on his cheek that he instantly covered with his hand; but, if anything, his eyes were more feverish, blazing away like ice on fire.

I wanted to ask him what was wrong, how could I help? But he flashed a silent warning: Back off, this was no one else's business.

"Are you havin' a drink?" Without waiting for an answer, he signaled to the bartender who had been studying me. After finishing his brazen appraisal, this slender young man yanked two Heinekens from the fridge and motioned to the top shelf. When Danny nodded, he poured three shots of Jameson's. After he had downed his, he pouted and playfully inquired, "Sean, I presume?" His point made, he giggled and pranced off to the other end of the bar.

Danny took a sip of his beer and regarded us in the mirror. That seemed to be the *modus operandi*. Men lined up alongside each other communicating in reflection. I risked a look. His gaze scorched me: I was the outsider. It was no different from on the site. There was a code of etiquette, and after you had taken the time to observe its rules and rigmarole, you might eventually be tolerated. All very well for moody fellahs like him who had cut their teeth on the British army, but I couldn't just stand there all night bloody well staring at mirrors.

"What do you think of the hunger strike?" I ventured for want of something better to say.

He raised the bottle to his lips but seemed to be only sipping on it. Finally, he shrugged, "They shouldn't have broke the first time. It'll be even harder now."

"How so?"

"There's only one thing the Brits understand." He clenched his fist on the counter. "Everything else they take for weakness."

"Do you know Sands?"

When he had satisfied himself that my question wasn't loaded, he shrugged again. "Bobby is sound. He won't break."

I was out of my league in these matters, for it could just as easily be Danny McCorley starving himself to death, while there wasn't an iceberg's chance in hell of Sean Kelly missing a meal for any cause beyond carelessness.

"Both sides picked the wrong man. Now they'll have to live with the consequences." He closed the matter and turned to me. "But I'm sure you didn't come all the way down here to discuss conditions in the Kesh. What's the good word?"

"Jesús got busted."

"No?" His sarcasm was positively dripping.

"He's blaming you for grassing on him."

"He knows where to find me."

"He'll kill you when he gets out, Danny. You know that, don't you?"

"Takes two to tango, lad." He took another slug, but the sneer fled when he studied himself in the mirror. "Anyway, how come you're so sure I did it?"

"Didn't you?"

"Yeah, I done the bastard good," he smiled grimly. "Should have sorted him out the first day I met him. Would have saved a lot of problems."

So he had grassed on Jesús. Mary was right. And what about Belfast? Was she on the money in that regard too? But I knew better than to go there.

Then he looked right at me. "I did it for you, lad. Just be glad they didn't nail you too."

"I'm out of all that. Learned my lesson."

"About bloody time. And how is my old friend, Mary?"

"Clean as a whistle."

"What happened? The well ran dry?"

"Don't be so hard on her, Danny. She went through hell."

"I never said she didn't have guts. Just discretion."

"We're back together."

He must have given some secret sign, for the barman was in front of us again; this time, he poured only two shots before strutting off. Danny tossed his down with a vengeance and was suddenly racked with a cough. As he swung away from me on the stool, he covered his mouth. The bartender looked back in concern, but Danny shook his head. When the spasm had passed, he gestured at my untouched shot. After I had downed it, he smiled wanly and gasped, "She's still running rings around you."

"She's changed, Danny."

"Take off your blinkers, kid. She's tougher than the two of us put together."

"You don't know her."

He was still not breathing right from the whiskey. It was as if something had lodged on his chest and was blocking the air from getting through.

"No, I suppose I don't." The words seemed to rattle around inside him. The bartender hurried over with a glass of water. "But I know you, lad. I know what you could be."

I waited until he had taken a couple of sips and was breathing a bit easier.

"Jesus, Danny, give me a break, will you? I've got her back. That's the only reason I came over."

"Yeah."

The mood of the music had changed too, having segued into a Donna Summer vamp, the kick drum booting a solid four on the floor. The dancing couples had stopped their groping and were now cavorting like a bunch of tinkers' colts. It reminded me of nights at the disco back home when a crowd of the lads, sick of being refused by the biddies, would form a circle and throw the most outrageously campy shapes just to get a rise out of them. But these boyos were deadly serious. Danny had even turned to observe the scene.

"Did you ever read Milton?"

"Sure." I turned away from him to hide the lie.

"There was a man who knew the score."

"That he did."

"Behold," he pointed at the dancers and roared above the music, "my kingdom."

A number of them smiled back. I was angry at myself for bullshitting; now I'd never know what he meant. Still, not much of a bloody kingdom—a crowd of prancing fairies who'd be the laughing stock of any self-respecting bar on Bainbridge.

"We're all worried about you, Danny. I mean, how are you making a living down here?"

"As long as I got me looks I'm on the pig's back." He grimaced and his hand shook when he instinctively raised it to hide the lesion on his cheek. Then, in a broad John Wayne twang, he shouted again above the music, "Hey, they even like my fucking cute accent! Right, lads?"

No one smiled this time. They'd seen this act before. He studied them, probing for some reaction, just bulling for a row. But not a one of them was keen on instant suicide. With no takers, he turned back to the mirror. Bainbridge or Christopher, whatever was eating at him wasn't affected by a change of scenery.

I had saved some money from the gigs and had rolled the bills into a tight little wad. I reached out for his hand under the counter. He started when I touched him and some of the hardness dissolved in his eyes.

"It's from the three of us," I lied as he clung to my fingers.

"Keep it!" he snarled when he felt the roll.

"Please, Danny, you never know."

He didn't speak for a while, just glared at the mirror.

"Don't do this to me, man," he finally whispered. With his fists clenched and the hurt further softening his face, he had the look of a little boy: angry and lost, but unwilling to admit it.

After I'd put the money back in my pocket, he sighed and took my hand in his. I could feel it tremble. He was exhausted, his breath coming in short sharp gasps for fear of another fit of coughing. He had to lean into my ear to be heard above the music.

"Do you recall the time we restored that building out in Flatbush?" He squeezed my fingers, desperate that I remember a weekend nixer that we pulled off on the quiet. "What was the first thing we did?"

"Jesus, I haven't a clue. I was only making the tea."

He coughed a little, then risked a deep breath. "We went in with crowbars and ripped off all the old plaster till we got down to the red brick."

He was willing me to remember. He wanted me to finish his thought, but I had no idea what he was getting at. He took another sip of water, and his breath came a little easier. "That's what I'm doin' right now," he whispered, "gettin' rid of all the shite that I brought over with me."

He reached out impulsively for his bottle and took a slug of beer. He savored it then slowly let it wash down his throat. The bartender watched apprehensively, as did I. When he was sure there was going to be no coughing, Danny's eyes sparkled again. "You'll have to do the same thing, Sean."

I nodded that I understood, but I didn't.

"There's no getting' around it," Danny added, and the bartender solemnly nodded.

I wished the little bastard would feck the hell off and leave us alone, but he stood there rooted to the other side of the bar. Finally, I whispered in Danny's ear so he wouldn't hear, "About what happened that night . . ."

"What night?"

"You know . . ."

"Oh, yeah," he sighed.

"I'm sorry."

He spread his palms in the old what-can-you-do Bronx fashion. "I had feelings for you . . . I let me guard down for a minute, and you saw the real me—the one who cared for you."

"Yeah," I blushed, but this time I held his eyes. I knew it was important.

"Yeah," he whispered back. There was a sadness to him but also an understanding: If that was the way of the world, then that's what he had to deal with. He shrugged again and turned back to the mirror. I did the same but couldn't handle the silence.

"Ah, Jaysus, Danny, c'mon back to the Bronx, will you?"

"I'm not goin' back to be something that I'm not."

"You'd be better off among your own."

"You still don't get it, do you, kid?" he said in the manner he used to on the site when I'd ask a stupid question. All was forgiven, though I knew deep down it wouldn't be forgotten.

"You don't look well, Danny."

"Don't let it fool you, boy. I'm the King of bloody Sweden . . . are you havin' another?"

"No, I have to get back."

He was relieved, for his breathing had turned erratic. He was tiring and his eyes were feverish again. He nodded at me in the mirror.

"You know somethin', kid?"

"What's that?"

"We almost did it with the Tinkers, didn't we?"

I couldn't look at him, just clenched my fists and hung on.

"Stick with the music, boy. It will always stand to you."

I handed over the bag Kate had given me. Her perfume cut through the cigarette smoke. He took out a garishly colored sweater.

"She knit it herself," I said.

The bartender leaned over for a closer look. Danny stuffed the sweater away and muttered, "Jesus, her taste was always up her arse, wasn't it?"

"Can I tell her you send your love?"

The bartender leaned forward to hear. Danny hesitated then looked him square in the eye and murmured, "Yeah. You do that, Paddy."

A multi-colored sleeve slipped out of the bag. The bartender made a face.

"What the fuck are you laughin' at, you little faggot?" Danny snarled.

The bartender raised his hands in protest and scurried off. The music had segued into a synthesized drone. An anxious bass line grew in power until it threatened to engulf the room. Even the dancers seemed befuddled; most retreated to tables or darkened alcoves.

"You'll come to the wedding, won't you?"

"And watch her throw her life away on some gobshite?" His voice was hoarse and brittle, eyes closed in concentration to control the cough.

It was the old Danny, the one who finished a sentence with a question. I stood there awkwardly shifting my weight from one foot to the other, afraid to catch his eye in the mirror.

"It's time you went back to your Mary," he finally rasped. "That song still has some verses left."

Then the music stopped, and an odd emptiness seeped through the room. I didn't want to leave him, and he sensed my pity.

"Go on, get the fuck out of here!" he snarled into the swirling silence, and everyone looked over at us. Two of the pool players stepped to the head of the table, cues in their fists. They had tolerated me thus far, but now they made it plain that I was no longer welcome. I was the outsider, and the circle had need of being closed. I stood up and put some dollars on the bar. When I laid my hand on his shoulder, Danny brushed it off like yesterday's rain.

"Good luck," I said. I knew there'd be no answer. Though the room had filled up, they cleared a path in front of me. A couple of hostile glances, but most of them understood. I was hardly a threat—just wasn't part of the program.

"Hey, kid!"

I was at the door when I heard his hoarse shout. I turned back. He was smiling, that rare old Danny smile when it was just the two of us against the world back on Decatur.

"Eyes on the prize, remember?"

Then the room closed in around him, and I walked out into the chill of the night.

chapter twenty-five

Bobby Sands was dying and Bainbridge was in turmoil. It had been over two months now of waiting, wishing, hoping, praying for some sense or sanity to prevail. People who didn't give a damn if the North of Ireland keeled over and floated off into the Atlantic were outraged at Thatcher and everything English. Even Scutch Murphy, that most apolitical of men, had organized a benefit for Republican prisoners; and during the collection, it was baldly stated that dollar bills, fives, or even tens would not be up to snuff. It was twenties and better, or don't bother your arse coming! A couple of Tyrone boys from the site dropped by to collect the takings. They hadn't noticed Danny at the protests outside the British Consulate and wondered what news there was of him. Despite "circumstances," as one of them gingerly put it, they couldn't conceive of his absence, given his ties to Sands.

Mary and I took to going down to the Consulate but caught no sight of him either. The mood was black on Third Avenue. It was obvious that the Iron Bitch had every intention of letting Bobby die just to make her point. Where would it all end, with three more strikers starving close behind him and others refusing food on a regular basis? To top it all, where was Danny and why hadn't he shown?

The toll was beginning to tell on everyone even remotely involved. One evening Mary appeared more stressed than usual. I suggested she give it a break for a night, for as the tension mounted there was always the threat that someone would snap and fling a brick through the windows—or even worse. Many of the cops sympathized with the marchers and had little love for the Brits inside or what Thatcher was up to, but they had a job to do and made no bones about the fact that there would be hell to pay if they were forced to do it.

Mary wouldn't hear of staying home for the night; indeed, it seemed as though she could barely wait to get out the door. As we were hurrying down the stairs, the old Ukrainian woman shuffled out on the landing. Mary brushed her off, but there was something about the look they exchanged that nagged at me.

The news was not good on Third Avenue. Bobby had received the last rites. The rosaries were out, and a low level hum arose from the pious. Those of us estranged from the old ways shuffled on, embarrassed by the mumbling ritual but oddly comforted by its familiarity. Where only days before relief could be found in the solidarity of the winding lines, now people averted their eyes and retreated behind the curtain of their own thoughts. It was as though each one had to face the horrible inevitability alone.

And then I saw him. Like a specter, all in black—leather jacket, jeans, and T-shirt—pale behind shades, tall and thin as a rail, proud as sin, he stood out against the murmuring lines, his collar raised to mask whatever splotches marred his face. There was no hiding his past now, no protective ambiguity. He might as well have been wearing fatigues, beret, and toting an Armalite. The same could be said for those others who had seen active service. Though moving with the throng, they kept their distance: Backs ramrod stiff, eyes hard and set, looking neither left nor right, they marched in measured steps oblivious to the rest of us. Theirs was more than symbolic protest or righteous outrage; one of their own was being wrenched from the world, and blood would be spilled in return.

When our columns passed, I was about to reach out and speak to him, but Mary laid a restraining hand on my arm. She understood: No matter how close we had been, on this night Danny and I occupied different universes. He was linked by bone and spirit to a belief that stretched back centuries. It made little matter that the desire for a free and united Ireland might be impractical; the Cause had never paid heed to the demands of fly-by-night pragmatism. Danny McCorley and his comrades had been proved right. There was only one type of reasoning the British understood, and it didn't spring from peaceful protest.

I'm sure he saw me, for we passed within yards of each other on many occasions through that long awful night, yet he betrayed no recognition or flicker of interest, and as the hours counted down, he gradually became less the friend he had been and more a symbol of the tide that was turning and the fanatic times that lay ahead.

On the train home that night, I couldn't shake his black Irish image. Something was changing, and I was now a part of it, no matter what my intention. I had grown up with no interest in politics, but I had been singed by an ancient relentless flame. Sands' fate was out of my hands, but he had sparked something visceral that had lain dormant inside me.

Unlike Danny and his comrades, I would not require a blood sacrifice in return, but neither would I ever again wear apathy as an ironic or lethargic cloak.

Mary too was detached, but I didn't concern myself. I scarcely even noticed her until we were on the stairway to the apartment. Someone else, however, was troubled by her absence and recognized her footsteps.

"He call again." The old Ukrainian lady squawked from her doorway.

Mary smiled as if humoring a crazy woman and walked on in steely silence. So, here we were, catapulted head over heels back into the web of lies and deceit again. For a moment I just stood there, stunned at the immediacy of it all. I even thought of rushing straight back down to the Consulate to keep the vigil, but knew our unfinished business would only haunt me and must be dealt with in some fashion or other. And so I followed her up the grimy stairs.

Still, if I was yanked unwillingly back into a universe I had little heart for anymore, then it was with a different level of resolve as well as a new understanding of both myself and the world. Two could play Mary's convoluted game.

I pulled myself together and acted as though nothing had happened, right down to making love. I could feel the conflict roiling her as we tossed on her unmade bed and, to turn the screw, I insisted she tell me that I was the only one she'd ever loved. And even when she lied, I insisted on hearing it all over again. Finally, she could take no more and pushed me away.

"It was him, wasn't it?" I demanded.

"No," she sobbed, and that made me even madder.

"You're nothing but a lying bitch." My fingers were digging into her arm. "You still love him, don't you?"

"Leave me alone!"

"You were thinking of him when I was fucking you, weren't you?"

"Don't speak to me like that."

"You can't get him out of your mind!"

"No, I can't!" she cried. "Is that what you want to hear?"

"At least I'm getting at the truth for once."

"You've no idea of the truth or its consequences."

"It's always the same with you—nothing can be straight and easy."

"He's in jail because of me. Is that truth enough for you?"

"He was a pusher! Just like you were a fucking junky! I'm glad Danny grassed on the bastard." When she turned away I pulled her back. "And he was good in bed too, right?"

"Who?"

"Jesús, who do you think?"

She seemed to shrink, all the fight and fury fleeing. I knew I finally had her where I wanted her.

"Yes," she said quietly, "he was."

You want the truth, beg for it, can't live without it, but when you finally hear it, you'd give anything to go back to the old uncertainty. She was staring at me with such a mixture of sorrow and pity I had to look away.

"There was more, Sean," she said. "I was special to him."

"You were never less than special to me."

"I know."

"Then why did you run away from me?"

I had never asked her, though it had rarely been off my mind. She cupped my face in her hands as though it would protect me from her answer.

"It wasn't just you. It was my father and home and . . . there was nothing for me back there."

"But why didn't you tell me?"

"What could you have done? There was no point."

She was right. I couldn't even deal with my own problems, let alone hers.

She nodded and a hint of bitterness crept into her voice. "Anyway, you had your own idea of what I should be, and it was as much of a trap as everything else."

"I could have come with you."

"What would that have solved? You had your music. What did I have? A pretty face to parade up and down the town every Saturday night?"

Those nights came floating back. The security of knowing she'd be there, the smile in her eyes when she'd see me, the smell of the mountain wind in her hair, the first taste of her lipstick.

"When I met Jesús, it was different."

"What was so different?"

"He let me be me."

"A junky?"

"I was a junky back home, Sean. I used him, not the other way around."

"Yeah, but he sold it to you."

"The first couple of times, but then when we got . . . together . . . he wanted to go away, take me with him."

"To Boquerón."

"Anywhere away from here. He knew it was just a matter of time . . ."

"Until Danny grassed on him?"

"If it hadn't been Danny, it would have been someone else."

She took my hand and kissed it. "But that's the past, love.
I'm getting well again, and everything I'm doing now is for
you."

She was stronger than me. No matter how injured, she
could compartmentalize, put things behind her, and carry on.
But could I deal with Jesús' shadow always lurking by my
shoulder? Could I be bigger than myself? She knew what was
on my mind, for she took me in her arms and clung to me
tighter than the shells on the seaweedy rocks out on the island.
We made love again, and I must have dozed off for my dreams
were full of prisons: Danny and Sands, comrades once more
in their gray Northern cells, emaciated, lanky thin hair
streaming down their hunched shoulders, waiting for some
reprieve but refusing to compromise as I was always so willing
to do. And Jesús with eyes hot as coals blazing up at me from
Rikers Island, forever threatening to return and humiliate me.

The sheets were damp with sweat, and it was a relief
when I opened my eyes; but only for a moment, for she had
been watching me and whispered across the pillow, "I want
you to know everything, Sean."

I was still groggy and far from ready for any further
disclosures, but she raced on. "That was his brother on the
phone."

"Whose brother?"

"Jesús."

"How the hell would he know the Ukrainians' number?"
She shrugged off my innocence.

"What did he want?"

"Jesús wants to marry me."

"Give me a break."

"He says I owe him."

"What are you supposed to do? Waltz out to Rikers in a wedding dress?"

"He's losing custody of his kid. But if he's married to a *blanquita* . . ."

"No judge is going to fall for that!"

"You know how he thinks. White people get all the breaks."

She had a point. That was why he sent me to Miami and why he trusted her—a junky—with his powder. She saw me weakening and took my hand. "He's got a lot on me, Sean."

"There's no way you're doin' this!"

"He's got a lot on you too," she shrugged. "Your fingerprints are all over that briefcase. And now Ryan knows where to find you. Every time I hear a footstep out on the stairs . . ."

I had thought I was in the clear. After all, I had only done one trip. Just carried a bag. I hadn't dealt any smack—and I could still end up doing twenty years.

"We've got to go home, Mary! It's our only chance."

"I'm not going back to that house."

And I could never walk down that mountain road again and leave her there with her dirty bastard of a father. For that matter, could I even go back to my mother's for more than a visit?

"We can get a flat in Dublin—just the two of us." I exuded such certainty, a gleam of hope kindled in her eyes. That gave me confidence. "It'll be OK, I'm telling you. When's the trial?"

"In a couple of months."

"With two bags full of smack, they'll lock him up and throw away the key."

"Oh God, I don't want to think about that."

"Well, you better. They might want us to testify. Supposing he says something."

"He won't. He still loves me."

"Maybe, but I don't think he's drawing cupids on the wall around my name."

What had we been doing sitting in that apartment all those months? We should have been long gone from the Bronx. It was all so clear. And then a footfall on the landing outside! Mary froze, her fingers digging into my arm. We waited and listened, each of us fearing the distinctive knock. The footsteps halted and we heard the rattle of keys, but whoever it was passed on and climbed the next flight of steps.

"We've got to get out of here, Mary, we've only got one shot."

"I don't have the strength to go back."

"Yes, you do!" I insisted. "I'll be with you. It'll be OK."

She wanted so badly to believe me. Wanted to reach out, touch me, make sure I was real and would always be there, but all she could manage was a whispered, "Promise?"

"I promise you, Mary."

CHAPTER TWENTY-SIX

Sands died a couple of days later. Bainbridge was in shock. It's one thing to expect the inevitable, quite another to deal with the anger, guilt, and inflamed emptiness over a death that could have been prevented. Men and women dotted the pubs in muttering clumps, their voices hollow without the camouflage of music, for the jukeboxes had been unplugged and stood mute and darkened. The churches were jammed at normally ill-attended masses, leaving the priests to wrestle with their words, for many disapproved of Sands' gesture and equated this latest Republican challenge to organized suicide. Yet, in their Irish hearts they knew that a great wrong had been done by a British woman who mistook steadfastness for state approved murder.

A gig of mine had been cancelled, and I was glad. This was no night for levity; too many ancient and unruly feelings were simmering skin-deep, only waiting for an errant word to set them boiling. I had thought of going down to the Consulate but couldn't deal with the pain and disappointment writ large on decent faces—all we had to show for sixty-six days of protest.

I couldn't much handle Bainbridge either. For the first time I began to really comprehend the simmering resentment of my Northern brothers and sisters. "You just don't understand;" their oft-repeated words now pulsed through my head. Bobby's sacrifice wiped away many layers of colonial and modern conditioning and not only made me aware of their corrosive effect on my personality but also exposed wounds of my own making. If I felt, on the one hand, lighter and more aware, so too did I feel a weight of oppression that I had been spared up until then.

I was brooding on such matters in the bedroom when Kate arrived. I didn't even attempt to unravel her and Mary's initial murmurs of solicitation, much less news of the latest sightings of friends on television, for all the channels were focusing on the winding lines jamming Third Avenue. Yet I sprang off the bed when I heard Mary's trill of disbelief: "Where did you get it?"

"Arnold."

By the time I made it to the kitchen, Mary was thumbing through a wad of hundred dollar bills so crisp the freshly minted smell was hopping off them.

"Fifteen hundred! Just like that?" she marveled.

"Yeah, me aunt died and I had to ship her back to Ireland."

"He surely didn't believe that?" I was as stunned as Mary.

"Well, I could hardly tell him me two drug-dealing roommates had to do a runner for fear they'd be murdered."

Mary recoiled at the edge in Kate's voice and returned to her counting.

"It's all there," Kate pouted. "Jaysus, I was lucky he didn't have me out at Kennedy tearing me hair to shreds and waving goodbye to some auld Aer Lingus jet."

Mary put away the money and took her by the hands. "Thanks, love."

Kate blushed fiercely. She pulled Mary to one side, but I could hear her whisper, "That stuff I said about you using people . . . I didn't mean it."

"I deserved worse." Mary hugged her.

I'd never known Mary to have a close girlfriend. She was far more comfortable with men. I wondered if women were better equipped to distinguish her shifting façades.

"Anyway, I'm better now. Right, Sean?"

"Yeah, right as rain."

"I tell you what," Kate said, "I'll come visit yez on me honeymoon."

"And if it doesn't work out with Arnold, you'll always have a place with us." Mary kissed her.

"Hah! Then I'll arrive in style on me alimony. Mayo girls don't come cheap—especially Jewish ones."

Mary's face turned the color of chalk when the familiar rap sounded on the door. I didn't have to read her mind—my own was throbbing with the same questions: How did he get out of Rikers, and what the hell am I going to do now? My knees began to knock but not for long; my usual cowardice was being swept away by a strange new resentment—this bastard had picked the wrong day to come home.

I shoved both of them into the bedroom and waited until they closed the door, then I moved silently. I had found an old hurling stick one night in Scutch's. The curved handle felt smooth to the touch as I tiptoed to the front door. I knew Jesús packed a knife, but I was no longer the boy around the place. I had two women to protect, and he was going to have to walk right through me. I threw open the door, the hurley held aloft.

"Tryin' out for the county team?"

A couple of the red splotches had matured into angry looking welts. Danny stooped slightly, though he made a brave effort to straighten up. Then his bag dropped to the floor and he surrendered all form of pretence.

"I'm fucked, Sean."

He staggered and I grabbed on to him, though there seemed little to hold, his frame light as a feather. But he signaled that he wished to say something in private. I stepped out into the hall and closed the door behind us. With his back resting against the wall, he recovered somewhat, though his breath came whistling out in short sharp gasps.

"Have you been to the doctor?"

"Doctors my arse!"

"But what did they say?"

"They don't have a clue."

"Well, you're home now. A couple of good meals and you'll be a new man."

"Yeah." He did his best to smile.

"The girls will fatten you up." I bent down for his bag. He was too weak to resist.

"Not a word to them about doctors, OK?" he said.

"Jesus, man, they've eyes to see."

"Just do what I'm askin' you, all right?"

I could only imagine the tears and ructions when Kate saw him. He had begun to sweat from the strain of standing, and I knew I had to get him sitting or, even better, lying down. Still, I wanted to bring him up to speed before I lost courage, so I blurted out, "Me and Mary are goin' home, Danny."

He just nodded quietly.

"You're not mad?" I had to be certain, to know everything was OK between us.

He began to cough and looked so frail I put my arm around him again. The sweat was oozing from his brow, but he pulled himself together and stepped back from me.

"You never gave me that right, did you?" The question hung there between us. I didn't have an answer for him. Couldn't even begin to deal with it. And now he was so weak, and our circumstances so changed that there was no longer any need.

"But how are you goin' to fend for yourself?"

"Kate'll look after me."

"Come home with us, man. We have money enough for another ticket."

He smiled bitterly and shook his head. "An Irish dog will never bark at my arse again."

"But why not?"

"And end up like Madam George on the back streets of Belfast or some fuckin' nancyboy slinkin' around Bartley Dunne's down in Dublin?" He spat the words out at me then coughed until the tears came to his eyes. "There's sweet fuck all for me back there, man, can't you get your thick skull around that?"

The Belfast accent ricocheted across the darkness of the landing. Someone down the hallway opened a door and fumbled for keys.

"But what's here?" I hissed. "We can't even afford a bloody light bulb."

"Remember that red brick wall?"

"What are you talkin' about?"

"The building out in Flatbush?" His eyes were glassy, his voice raspy. "I'm right down to it, lad. Just one last coat of paint . . ."

"I don't understand."

"Jaysus, they didn't call you the Wexford Einstein for nothin', did they?"

"Who didn't?"

"Ah, for Christ's sake! When are you ever goin' to catch on?"

Then the neighbor passed by, and Danny came home.

CHAPTER TWENTY-SEVEN

He did get better in the following weeks. It could have been the regular meals, the girls fussing over him, or perhaps he was just coming to terms with himself. We moved his cot over to the window where, propped up on his pillows, he'd read through the day; often as not, though, I'd find him staring out onto the street. Not poised like a hawk as in the old days, he was an idle watcher now, still interested in the drama unfolding below, but indifferent to its outcome.

His cheeks filled out and the red welts lost some of their rage. But just when he seemed to be on the mend, a new lesion would appear, and I'd catch him running his thumb over it absentmindedly. Kate would scold him unmercifully; still as soon as she'd turn her back his hand would rise again. He was never a great one for dawdling in front of mirrors, but now he avoided them like the plague. His eyes still scorched on occasion, but they were often preoccupied. He had good days and bad, but it was a rare night that I didn't wake to his wheezing and Kate's murmured solicitations; then I'd lie there studying the shadows on the ceiling until she nursed him back to sleep.

She came home every evening now and, when she left in the morning, we would find a list of tasks, and dare we not follow them to the letter! She told me, on the quiet, that after a fierce fight with Arnold, she'd laid it on the line: Take her as she was with all her obligations or call the whole thing off. She must have worked out something with her prospective in-laws too, because she always made the time to take Danny downtown for his visits to one doctor or another. According to the two of them, the diagnosis was that he had a "glandular problem made serious by a lingering pneumonia." Danny would get angry and break into a coughing fit if I pursued the matter further; so, there I let it sit. Besides, things were odd enough with the four of us again sharing the apartment.

It was good for Mary to focus on someone else's problems. Kate had appointed her assistant nurse and held her accountable for the least deviancy from matron's rules. It was around then that I began to wonder again if something of a romantic nature had indeed once transpired between Mary and Danny, for there was a brittle tension between them, and they worked like a tag team to ensure that a third party be always in the room. I had little doubt that each was counting down the days until our departure.

If Mary had at first been reluctant to return to Ireland, she now oversaw our plans with all the zeal of a drill sergeant. We would rent a cheap flat in Dublin and take any kind of jobs for the first months before moving out to Howth to be by the sea. She would attend college and take shifts in pubs, while I would keep a day job and play folk clubs by night. It all sounded great on paper; so too had the Bronx.

Much of her attention was focused on me. Whatever was empty, I had to fill; anything damaged I should repair. All fine by me, for I had a great store of untapped devotion to lavish on her. Still, something was slightly out of sync. She would disappear for hours to do errands that should only have taken minutes. Then return jumpy and distressed, occasionally worried about Ryan or Jesús' brother: Had I any sightings of them? But more often than not, she was silent and expectant. She'd anchor herself by the door, listening for footsteps. A couple of times I even found her back on her knees in front of Our Lady of the Bronx. Was she using again? Her arms had healed and I saw no signs of fresh tracks. But it all began to get to me. One day I could have sworn that I was shaded back from the pub by a black man. When I mentioned it to Scutch, he accused me of being a racist— talk about the shoe being on the other foot! I banished the notion but from then on walked home in company.

Besides, there was Danny to look after and endless loose strings to be knotted before we jetted out of Kennedy. Still, the pre-dawn hours often found me uneasy. Would I fit back in Dublin? What would my mother think of Mary and me living together? For that matter, what did I think? Was her need for me real, or was I a substitute for something or someone else? How would I measure up to that memory down all the days ahead of us?

I only had to hear Danny coughing and Kate's answering murmur before flying into a panic. How would she manage should his condition deteriorate? How could she keep her job, or Arnold for that matter? Then the cough would decline to a wheeze, and the Bronx night would settle back into its subliminal rumble, and I'd remember that Mary loved me. I'd reach out for her warmth, and she'd move against me in half-sleep until we'd drift away in each other's arms; by the time we woke, the morning light would be streaming in, and we'd be a day closer to leaving.

326   Larry Kirwan

We were an odd household, craggy and obsessive to say the least, but as the weeks rolled by we eased back into familiar roles, especially when Kate arrived home with her future mother-in-law's voluminous wedding dress. It was only then that I began to suspect that a portion of the fifteen hundred dollars might have been siphoned off from some Park Avenue seamstress; for she attacked the gown with needle, thread, and a devotion to detail as if her marriage depended on it, and it probably did.

We stayed up drinking and reminiscing the night before we were to leave. I was over the moon because Danny made a great show of wishing me the best of luck and made it clear that any begrudging was a thing of the past. We blasted our favorite records; Mary and he even smooched to Nick Drake in a familiar manner, and I was too drunk to care. It must have been five in the morning before we all staggered into bed.

Despite our hangovers, there were goodbyes to be said down the pub and drinks to be called, the afternoon crowd tearing themselves away from the Yankees to toast us with not a little envy. Addresses were exchanged and plans made to meet in Dublin should any one of a number of counties reach the All-Ireland Final. Scutch and Arsehole promised to join us for one last drink in the apartment; then, in the excitement occasioned by Reggie hitting a home run, we slipped out.

I bought a couple of six-packs in the bodega but halted on our stoop. I wanted to print a final picture on my memory of Decatur, a hodge-podge of apartment buildings and rickety houses nestling precariously over an undistinguished little street. I knew I would often resurrect its hilly insouciance down all the damp Dublin days ahead. It was an integral part of

me now, for better or worse. Would I miss it? Was I doing
the right thing?

Then Mary squeezed my hand and all doubts dissipated:
We were out of here, I had won her back, and that was all
that counted. One last climb up the pissy stairway. I was
feeling so good, had I run into him, I might have hugged
Squint Eye and invited him home for a visit at Christmas.
But when we stopped on our landing to kiss, my ears pricked
up at the brooding silence from behind the door. It seemed
odd for, when we left the Stranglers had been blazing and
Kate had been cursing up a storm while slaving away on the
wedding dress. Mary sensed the tension too and stiffened in
my arms. Even in the dim light, I could see the color drain
from her face; she wanted to bolt for the airport, but what
use of that with our passports and money inside. There was
nothing for it but to throw the door open.

I don't know what I expected, but it was hardly to see
Danny bedecked in the lacy splendor of the wedding dress,
while Kate knelt at his back, pins in mouth, stitching away
like some souped-up Irish seamstress.

"One word out of either of yez! Just one!" Danny leveled
his finger at us.

"Who's the lucky guy?" The tension drained away from
Mary in a fit of giggles.

"I'm warnin' you!"

"Jaysus, the Rev. Ian would pay big bucks for a shot of
this," I razzed him.

He yanked the dress up in a fury while Kate held on,
spitting out pins left and right.

"Stand still before you rip it to pieces."

"I should never have listened to you."

"You're tearin' the bustle."

"I'm stuck in the bloody thing! I thought you said the auld cow was gynormous?"

"She has an arse as big as a ball alley. That's why I have to tighten it!"

"Get this fuckin' thing off me. You hear me?" he roared.

Then, without any kind of warning, Kate burst into tears and flopped down on the ground. It was more the strain of the weeks looking after him than anything to do with the dress, and he knew it. She lay on the floor flooding the dusty carpet. He looked down at her, the fight draining out of him; then he let the dress be.

"It's all right, Kate." He bent over her and stroked her hair. It was the gentlest I'd ever seen him.

"Listen. Sew away to your heart's content, love, just don't cry," he said, and his voice began to crack. "It does my head in."

I'm not sure she'd ever heard such concern from a man before. She stopped moaning and sat up. He ran his finger under her smudged eyes and brushed away a Niagara of tears. She smiled and threw her arms around him. He was hesitant, at first, but hugged her tightly, the two of them wrapped around each other, oblivious of Mary and me. Then he stood up and faced towards the window and, after she'd blown her nose and wiped off some of the mascara streaks, she began stitching again. An odd quietness descended, a certain peace that I'd never experienced in the apartment before—an acceptance of what would be would be. I glanced at Mary and could tell she felt it too. All might not be right with the world, but we could now leave this house in peace and get on with our lives.

"Are yez all packed?" Kate inquired through the forest of pins she was again balancing between her lips.

"Yeah, and all our goodbyes said down the pub. Scutch and Arsehole will be up in a couple of minutes for the last drink."

"Do we have anything left in the house to offer them?"

"All present and accounted for." I pointed to the six-packs. "Besides, I doubt they'll come empty-handed."

I snapped off some caps and handed the cans around.

"Not for him!" Kate motioned to Danny.

"Oh for Christ sake, woman, it's bad enough you have me dressed like a two-buck transvestite, you expect me to die of the thirst too?"

"After what you consumed last night, Mister, there's little thirst should be on you. What am I supposed to say to that nice doctor down in St. Vincent's when he asks if you've been drinking?"

"To hell with him and his bullshit!" He grabbed one of the foaming cans.

"Don't let a drop of that fall on my good dress, if you know what's good for you!"

"You'll surely bring it to the cleaners before the big day," said Mary, trying to divert her attention, for Kate was getting teary at the thought of us leaving.

"His old cow of a mother is attending to that. And I don't want her lugging it down Park Avenue smelling like a brewery."

"Will you go easy!" Danny yelped. "That needle stuck halfway up me bloody arse."

"Oh, be quiet," Kate sniffled from behind his derriere. "What time's your car service?"

"It'll be here within the hour. We don't want to mess with the traffic."

"You'll be in Dublin in the morning, you lucky devils."

"Yeah, knocking back big dirty pints in Mulligans after a feed of rashers and sausages."

"That'll be Scutch and Arsehole." I winked at Danny when I heard their knock.

"Get this fuckin' thing off me!"

"Scutch Murphy is at the door and look at the state of me!" Kate howled.

"Ah will you relax. Sure won't he have the new girlfriend from Carlow with him."

"I don't care where she's from, she better be packin' smelling salts, if she wants an active sex life." She spat out the pins and raced over to the sink leaving Danny to wrestle with the dress.

"Don't let them in here until I get this bloody thing off. I'll never hear the end of it," Danny roared at Mary, who was over by the door relishing the commotion. She opened it with a flourish.

"*Que pasa, Maria?*" Jesús had put on some weight but looked much as he did on the night of his arrest except for a small contusion under his right eye.

He drank her in and noted the changes. When he reached out and touched her cheek I flinched. This too did not escape his notice as he stepped into the room.

He nodded civilly, though his eyes were steely, then he took in Danny. "Hey, *Señorita*, got a couple of brothers out on Rikers like to meet you . . . but I forget, they like real men—not a *puta* in a dress."

Danny would have been on him had Kate not grabbed

him by the bustle. Over the ripping sound she cried out, "Look what you've done now!"

He halted, in two minds. Jesús waited, barely tensing. He had noted Danny's moment of doubt and his haggard looks. Now he drank him in and shook his head slowly. "You fadin' away, bro, soon you be invisible."

"I've more than enough left to do a number on you."

"It's OK." Jesús said, almost in a whisper. "Is just between you and me."

"What do you want?" Mary broke the silence.

"I got tired waitin' for you, *amór.*"

"I wanted to come."

"Hey, you could have brung Sergeant Ryan for company."

She didn't move a muscle, and he never took his eyes off her.

"Never read me my rights before he bash my head in, rip off my powder, so nice judge throw out the case. Hey, let's party!" He kicked out at the table, sending bottles and cans clattering to the floor.

"All right, Zorro, you made your point," Danny said. "What do you want?"

"Come here to get a hand in marriage," Jesús smiled at him. "But hey, *señorita,* look like you the only show in town."

"As soon as I get this bloody thing off me . . ."

Jesús ignored him and pointed to our suitcases. "Goin' to Boquerón, Maria?"

"No, she's coming home with me."

He dismissed me with barely a glance. "I don't think so. Something else holdin' you here, ain't that so, Maria?"

"She's straight."

He still didn't acknowledge me. Just nodded contemptuously.

"We've got to talk," Mary said, pointing to the bedroom.

"So you can whisper in my ear like you doin' to this boy now? No, I like us all together—one big happy family." Only then did he choose to look at me. "'Cause one of you nice Irish people turn me in."

He swept us all with the cold eyes of the street, finally settling on me. "Just a boy, you don't got the balls or the brains," he sneered. "But the *maricón* in the dress?"

"Best thing I ever did," Danny spat back. "What do you want to do about it?"

I had always considered them evenly matched; now it would be no contest. Though Danny's eyes glowed with a surfeit of spirit, he seemed frail and angular next to the muscled confidence of Jesús. I moved over towards the hurling stick, but Jesús was in control. He flashed me a warning, then gestured at Danny, "It all point to you."

Danny shrugged and spread his hands in the Bronx manner: *What can a man do?*

It was hard coming to terms with this new side of him. Though I had never doubted his ruthlessness and knew he didn't like Jesús, I still had trouble thinking of him as a grass, despite the whispers on the site and Mary's insinuations.

They stared at each other, locked in mutual contempt. Danny was about to take the beating of his life, or even worse. I couldn't let it happen and stepped in front of him.

"Get out of the way, boy," Jesús hissed at me.

Danny gripped me by the shoulder and tried to push me aside, but I held my ground. When Jesús slipped his hand inside his jacket, I knew I was in trouble. His eyes hardened, and the anger was all about Mary and me, and the way things should have been. He was about to cut me, and there was little I could do about it.

Then Danny coughed and the tension broke. As he tried to control the hacking, his eyes watered and Jesús sneered, "Oh yeah, it all point to you . . . problem is—it point too much."

I could hardly hide my relief when he swung away from us.

"What are you lookin' at me for?" Kate cried indignantly.

Jesús took in her new look and the self-regard that fueled it. He smiled and bowed slightly, "No, ain't you, Mama. You always show me respect."

He didn't even glance at Mary, but it was obvious whom he was addressing.

"All them nights in that stinking cell, thinkin' 'bout you and my kid, missin' you like two holes in my heart. And then it hit me, and I want to get down on my knees, bang my head off the floor. Only thing I couldn't figure was—why, Maria, why?"

"Leave her alone."

"Shut up, boy!" He pushed me back and I lost my footing. Luckily for my dignity, I landed on a chair and managed to hold on.

"Don't hurt him," Mary cried.

"He all you ever think about, right?"

"Leave him out of this, and I'll tell you the truth."

"I know the truth! What I don't know is why you mess with me so bad I don't get to see my kid no more? They takin' him away from me. You know that?"

I could tell she was about to lie, slip back inside her junky skin, but it wasn't there for the wearing anymore. She looked at me hopelessly; then her shoulders sagged, and I had to strain to hear her voice.

"Ryan caught me carrying—just a dime bag. Said he could send me away for twenty years. He set me up that night in the East Village. But he promised there'd be no violence—just deliver once and he'd forget the charges."

Jesús nodded impatiently.

"But he wouldn't leave me alone. Always hounding me . . ."

She might as well have been talking to stone. This was old news to him and hardly worth the listening.

"That was all put on? The night Ryan came here?" Kate was incredulous.

"I was doing it for the two of you!"

"We could have gone to jail, Mary!"

"No, I was protecting you, Kate. Sean got back late—he should have been long gone. It would have been over hours before you came home."

"Just deliver the spic," Jesús whispered.

"He said you'd get off light."

"He crack my skull open!"

"I didn't give him your name, I swear. He had it already."

"But he never caught me with nothin' till you set me up."

"I didn't want to! I begged him."

"Lots of things you didn't want to, but more things you did." His nose wrinkled with disgust. "He tell me about it— every time he see me, he tell me what you do with him when you alone, *puta sucia!*"

She raised her hand to her face as if she had just been spit upon.

"Don't fuck with me, Maria. I know what you done to him in that room and all the other times!"

"I didn't want to! He would have sent Sean away too."

"I shoulda known when you lost my powder. But all I could see is that you was with this boy, you junky bitch!"

The slap was not much more than an insult, but the sting echoed around the room. His eyes were raging when he moved to really hit her, and he stuck out his other arm to fend me off. That's how Kate caught him unaware with a haunch in the back. He keeled over and she threw herself on top of him.

"Run, Mary, quick!" she shrieked as Danny, wedding dress askew, jumped in to help her.

Mary ran for the door and shouted back at me, "C'mon, for Christ sake!"

CHAPTER TWENTY-EIGHT

O ur luck was in. The car service was early. The driver had pulled an all-nighter and was passed out over the wheel, the window rolled down, salsa pumping from his battered AM radio. A thump on the shoulder and a twenty stuck in his fist brought him back to the land of the living, and we peeled out of there in a squeal of bald tires and Tito Puente flourishes. Mary was like a puppet on speed, her head twirling backwards every few seconds for sign of the yellow Cadillac. This spooked the driver who was already zig-zagging through the traffic like Mario Andretti. His own eyes popping, he never lost sight of her in the rear mirror until we cleared the Triborough Bridge. When we screeched onto the Van Wyck, I begged him to slow down, but Mary would have none of it.

We arrived at Kennedy with just the clothes on our backs, while every other Paddy hauled bulging suitcases through the Aer Lingus terminal. At least, Mary had grabbed her pocketbook with our tickets, passports, and the remains of Kate's money. But that was it: no guitar, not even my leather jacket, and sweet shag all Clash records either. A real success story! I was heading home with even less than I'd brought. Lucky I'd been wearing my boots when the commotion started.

We were first in line at the check-in. Three hours to kill with the prospect of Jesús galloping in. We had barely spoken since the apartment; in ways, we'd never left. Every footstep, opening door, or shadow set off a chain reaction. She'd swivel and I'd follow her eyes. Meanwhile, the Aer Lingus ladies, in their green suits and sensible pumps, chatted away, never even giving us the time of day while we fretted and fumed in our coatless psychosis.

Then a stream of Spanglish curses ricocheted around the terminal, and we spun in tandem, the fear of God riveting through both of us. But it was only a baggage handler stiffed by a drunken Paddy. This Killarney cowboy, suede boots and matching jacket, hastened to inform the aggrieved Dominican that he could go fuck himself from a height, and wasn't he a lucky nigger to be even allowed carry the cases of a well-bred gentleman from Kerry?

This imbroglio unleashed a chain reaction, the end result of which was the Aer Lingus ladies swung into action. One of them, a young over-lipsticked shrew with a forced smile as welcoming as a serrated blade, beckoned imperially at us to step forward. She was efficiency personified, barely casting us a glance. In fact, we were moving along on castors until she inquired in a quasi-Foxrock accent, "And how many pieces of baggage will you be checking in?"

"None." Mary replied.

"None?"

"Precisely."

"And you're going back for how long?"

"For as long as we see fit."

The shrew was less than enamored at the edge in Mary's voice. She stepped back for a better look and regarded us as she might two brass-balled supporters of Bobby Sands intent on smuggling in the wherewithal to blow the living shit out of the whole island of saints and scholars.

"Is there something the matter?" Mary inquired.

"Well," this guardian of probity sniffed, "it is rather unusual, wouldn't you say?"

"Perhaps," Mary nodded, then raising her voice some decibels beyond courtesy, she added, "but you see I've just gone beyond three months pregnant and, if it's not too much inconvenience, I have a rather pressing need to use the ladies' room."

If this was a bombshell to me, it had an equally jarring effect on the shrew, for passports were stamped, tickets taken, and we were pointed towards the gate in short order.

"You never told me," I stammered, tripping over myself to catch a sideways glimpse of her stomach.

"You never asked." Mary didn't miss a stride, nor did she avail of the ladies room. But once we had passed through the gate, all her bravado fled and she clung to me. "Oh, God, we made it, Sean. None of them can get us now."

"About that three months thing . . . ?"

But she was already preoccupied, checking passports and tickets one more time, storing them carefully in her purse.

"Jesus, you had me going."

She looked up and smiled. "Would it have been that bad, Sean?"

"No, but you know . . ."

But now she wasn't smiling, more like taking my measure. It was only for an instant; then she linked my arm and we walked on.

Almost at once, a deep lethargy took hold of me, and I

could barely keep up with her. So much had happened, and so quickly. I was being swept along in a flash flood, but where was I going? It could have been the adrenalin running out, now that the fear of Jesús and Ryan had evaporated; or maybe the sheer accumulation of stress and self-negation that I'd poured into her rehabilitation.

But she was all purpose and had moved a couple of steps ahead, homing in on the cafeteria. She seemed like two people to me now: the girl down from the mountain, fresh as the showers that used to dampen her hair, and the street-scarred young woman determined that we make a new life. With each step, these personalities swung off kilter, only to reconnect awkwardly. How many years before they'd meld? Would they ever?

Still, I could see the makings of a new Mary. What of myself? Was I just flotsam being swept along in her wake? Always improvising to keep up, never sure where my next footstep should fall until I checked out hers first.

The shadows were lengthening, and a plane was taking off. In a couple of hours we'd be banking above the city, heading north towards Labrador, then sweeping out over the Atlantic. We'd leave the Bronx and all its rough magic in our wake. To what was I returning? Oh, I'd love to see my mother, all right. Take her in my arms and ease the hurt I'd caused; but in a week or two, what would I feel? Would anything have changed or would life be even more calcified? And could I settle into my anointed slot?

I had changed, though I couldn't as yet put a face on the person I had become. I might bitch about the city, rail about its craziness, but I had begun to make a fist of New York. And there was still Manhattan to explore. Not just the

Blarney Stones and the Pig 'n' Whistles where we drowned our immigrant fantasies, but Greenwich Village and CBGBs and the museums and galleries I had once dreamed of visiting.

"Get me a cup of tea, Sean. I'll hold our places." Mary had spotted an empty table. She waved me towards the cafeteria line.

I had my orders and obediently fell into place. It all made sense. We were already fitting a pattern, adapting to our roles. Another spray of plane lights down the runway, and I thought of Dublin in the damp morning. Checking the ads in the paper. Phoning Rathmines or Ranelagh—pressing Buttons A and B, the change rattling against black metal as I furiously listened for the hint of a disembodied voice. Then begging some old bitch to let us overpay her for the pleasure of freezing the nights away in a soggy room on a lumpy bed, with the rain beating off the windows, while Mary lied that her mother's wedding ring entitled her to be called Mrs. Sean Kelly.

I bought a couple of muffins to go with the tea. Mary beckoned me over, and the urgency irritated me. Then a sudden surge of activity in the corridor—a roar of outrage and a couple of screams! I raced over towards Mary, but the passing crowds got in my way. She was already on her feet, face ashen, trembling hand covering her mouth. I pushed on, still balancing the tray, as the tumult spilled around the corner and a body went sprawling across the polished floor. Three uniformed figures dived atop it, sending travelers and bags spraying against the walls. A familiar brown head bobbed up and down amidst a sea of thrashing arms and legs. Mary looked terrified, and I was about to shout out that it was OK.

But it was over in little more than seconds. The Killarney

cowboy had crossed some line beyond mere racism. He could safely be abandoned to the stern hand of Yank justice, the Irish contingent reasoned, lowering their heads, turning to their tea, and ignoring his pleas for national solidarity as he was hauled away.

I cared less than any of them about his fate now that I knew it wasn't Jesús come barging through to say bon voyage. I continued across the cafeteria balancing the tray, while dodging bags, banjos, bodhrans, bottles of Bushmills, and all the trusted bric-a-brac that veteran immigrants lug back for the lonely nights ahead.

I felt guilty about my annoyance, but I needn't have worried. Mary had already put the disturbance behind her. As ever, she could spin on a dime and was smiling and looking better than I'd seen her in all the days since I'd arrived. A couple of Paddies were giving her the once over; she knew well, but ignored them. She had eyes only for me. My heart leaped at her strange dark beauty and at the memory of how our bodies had meshed only hours before, and I knew everything was going to be all right, and Dublin would be a hive of possibility and easily negotiated as long as she was there with me. When I put the tray down she laid her hand on mine and looked at me with more love than I'd ever hoped for.

"What's the matter, Sean?"

"Everything's fine."

"You looked very distant across the room just now. Are you sure?"

"Yeah. I'm just a bit frazzled."

"Tell me, love."

"I'm telling you, it's OK."

"Sean?"

She knew. She could identify all my moods—maybe better than myself. I had nearly stirred the flowers off the cup before I sighed, "Ah, I don't know."

"If it's about Danny and Kate, Jesús doesn't care about them. I'm the one he's after."

A jet was landing and the night was settling in. I watched its lights spray patterns on the runway. There was so much I wanted to know, and so much I didn't. She could tell that and didn't want any echo from the past trembling between us.

"Listen, love, things happened and I can't take them back, no matter how much I want to."

I didn't know what to say and returned to stirring my tea.

"I mean, what do you want me to do?" She grabbed my hand and took away the spoon.

"I don't know, Mary."

"You think I like what I did?"

"I'm not sure you think at all."

"What are you saying?"

The Paddies were craning their necks to hear us. I leaned closer to her. She touched her forehead against mine.

"All that stuff with Ryan," I whispered. She snatched back her hand.

"Do you have any idea how I feel?" She was digging her nails into her palms so fiercely I couldn't release them at first. When I did, she raised my chin so that I had to look at her.

"I have to put that behind me, Sean, else I can't go on. Do you understand?"

"I think so."

"You have to put it behind you too."

I tried to banish the memory of her coming out of that room on Avenue C, her lipstick all a mess, the figure of Ryan framing the door behind her. But all I could replace it with was the look of disgust I had seen on Jesús' face and the sound of his spat insult: *puta sucia.*

She was panicking, her hand in full tremble, when she pleaded, "With a bit of time we can work it out?"

Who was I to judge? She had been trying to protect me. Maybe if I'd never come over she'd have worked out things in her own way.

"Right?" She needed an answer.

"Yeah . . . it'll be OK."

She steadied her hand, and I laid mine upon it. She grasped my fingers, and hope flooded her face. I kissed her lips. They felt hot and sweet from the tea and so reassuring I had no doubt but that we'd cling to each other in the darkness over the Atlantic that night. She sighed and took another sip. "C'mon, let's get a drink. We'll have plenty of time to talk on the plane."

She stood up. I tried to join her, but my legs felt stiff as day-old cement.

"Sean?" She reached out her hand, and I tried to find words to explain.

Then from nowhere I blurted out, "I can't think around you, Mary. You get me all messed up."

"It'll be different from now on. I promise you."

"I used to think it was just me. But you have the same effect on everyone."

She sank down into the chair like a traveler at the end of a long journey who is informed that there are still many more miles to go. "I'm doing my best. Believe me."

"I know. That's the problem."

"Oh God, Sean, don't be so judgmental."

"Hello, eh . . . where are yez from?" It was the two Paddies, drinks in hand, just about to join us at the table.

"Fuck off!" I said with all the viciousness I could muster.

"Jaysus, that's a nice how-do-you-do, and we all goin' home together," one said. I'm not sure Mary even noticed them though they stood threateningly behind her for what seemed like minutes.

"Do you have any idea what it's like giving up dope?" she demanded, and the Paddies stepped back as though slapped in the face.

"I think so," I whispered, still trembling from fury.

"No, you don't!"

The Paddies retreated to the bar, still muttering but presenting no immediate problem. Mary was clenching and unclenching her fist, and the silence pulsed around us. "One day you're walking down the street with the power of God flowing through you. Then—this."

She waved her hand around at the munching figures of our fellow travelers, burgers and French fries in motion to and from their mouths, tables littered with leftovers, all of it bathed in full unflattering neon light. "I quit all that for you, so we could start over again."

"I'm not going back, Mary."

I don't know where it came from; but once spoken, I felt relief as though something foreign had been expelled. Just as surely, a great sorrow poured into the void.

"Just like that?"

"Danny's sick."

"You know Kate will look after him."

"Yeah."

"But it's not just that, is it?"

"Well . . ."

"Sean, this is important. If I go on this plane without you
. . ."

"I've got things to do here, Mary."

"And they don't include me?"

"They always include you. You know that."

"Why don't you say what you mean for once in your life,
instead of always hiding behind words?"

"I'm trying, Mary, believe me."

"Well, let me spell it out for you. I kick dope—you kick
me. Right?"

"You can come back in a few months. I'll make some
money, we can get an apartment down the Village."

"He'll kill me if I come back. Don't you understand that?"

"He might be killing Danny right now."

"And that's more important?"

She regretted what she said and reached out to touch my
face. "You said you'd never let me go again."

"I won't, Mary, I promise. Someday . . ." I began but she
was already checking her passport and ticket, and laying mine
out on the table.

"Someday is for other people, Sean."

She clicked her purse shut and walked off towards the
boarding area. She never even looked back.

CHAPTER TWENTY-NINE

She took all the money. I was lucky to have the guts of twenty dollars and a token in my pocket; nothing for it but hop a bus back to the city and head for the nearest Blarney Stone. Oh man, did I need those beers. Down at the end of the bar, some old men sat nursing theirs, a couple of black subway workers stood separately near the food counter, while a few strays stared blankly out the window, all presided over by a big Paddy bartender who was either mentally challenged or had little gift for conversation. That suited me just fine. I kept my head down, not even risking a glance in the mirror until nine o'clock, when I knew her plane would be taking off. I must have looked pretty mournful, for the bartender sent me down a Jameson's on the house. Later, one of the black guys included me in a round by mistake, or maybe not. Whatever, he draped his arm around me and ordered me to "enjoy." Easier said than done.

It was near eleven by the time I got on the subway. I figured she'd be well past Newfoundland by then. I didn't feel in the least drunk; in fact, all my senses were tuned to such a perfect pitch I could have guided the train through the tunnels with my eyes closed. How odd that we were both in motion, each of us, in our own way going home. The lights on the plane would be dimmed by now, the cramped space already familiar, insomniacs settling in for the movie, sleepers for the long haul to Shannon.

And there was I speeding through the bowels of Harlem, wondering if she was wondering about me. Did she understand? Had she half expected this outcome anyway? She was always one step ahead of me. That's what my mother didn't like. Or maybe Mam already suspected that she was a user? Not that she'd have known a junky from a piebald pony, but she understood there was something missing in Mary, a void I couldn't hope to fill that would one day lead to problems.

The fatigue and depression hit me like twin hammers going up the subway stairs at 205th. And as I made my way down Bainbridge, its pub lights twinkling, I realized that what had been steely clear at the airport was just illusion. I was lost without Mary. And to think I could have been nestled next to her in the warm claustrophobia of the jet. Panic-stricken at my mistake, I hurried towards Scutch's. Indeed, I almost turned in the door, but the memories of her working behind the bar got the better of me, and I kept walking.

Decatur was pulsing with drums and life, families out on their stoops drinking and basking in the perfect temperature. Summer madness was in the air and, even if there was no dancing in the street, the whores and junkies had a certain friskiness to them, for the night stretched ahead and was long on promise. A dealer offered me a toke, his eyes glassy, his body swaying to the inner groove of his Colombian. He jabbered away about Reggie this and Bucky that and Goose and Gator the other, and how Mister October would surely bring redemption to the Bronx, while I drew his reassuring fumes into my lungs. There had been a time when his baseball blabber was all a mystery. I understood every word now and slapped fives with him; but I was on remote, still in Mary's orbit as she hurtled further out across the Atlantic.

It was only when I climbed the stairs that I began to fear for what I might find behind our door. I couldn't believe that I hadn't rushed back to make sure Danny and Kate were OK. What was I thinking, drinking like an idiot in a bloody Blarney Stone? How could I have been so dumb, so uncaring for those who loved me?

And then I heard it from the landing below. Mister Cohen singing about a thin green candle and the dust from a long sleepless night, and my heart almost leaped out of my chest, for it was Mary's special song. I raced up the last flight of stairs, thanking God that one of us had sense. The door wasn't locked and I let myself in. The dim light over the sink cast everything in surreal shadow, yet it was enough to show that the apartment had been wrecked, the table upended, bottles and cans everywhere, spilt beer and quenched fags stinking up the joint. It must have been a fierce fight and at close quarters too. Kate's belongings were strewn about, her lipsticks and unguents mashed into the floor. But there was no sign of either of them. She must have brought Danny to the hospital.

Mary's door was closed. She hadn't been able to go home either, hadn't stepped aboard that jet. What was left for her in Ireland anyway? She had taken a taxi back from the airport, then dozed off to her favorite songs while waiting for me. I checked out the record player while Leonard mourned on. My suspicions were confirmed: strewn around the floor were jackets of Nick Drake, *Astral Weeks*, and the Cure, all her favorites. Then the dread hit me: She used this music for other purposes too. I prayed to God she hadn't scored and even now had a spike in her arm. I couldn't go through all that again; yet, I knew I would for her.

I turned off the light. Leonard was in his final psychotic coda when I nudged open her bedroom door. It took me moments to adjust to the darkness; still I could sense her outline in the bed. I didn't want to disturb her. I wanted to take this last moment to rejoice in her return and vow that I'd never let her out of my life again. I had tasted the despair of losing her and wanted no more part of it. I knew my destiny and was finally content with it.

She started in her sleep, stretching in an odd manner; and, for an instant, the broken bodega light flashed on to reveal two figures entwined. Then it was all darkness again.

I took a step forward and focused on the shadows. I had to confirm what my eyes refused to believe. Had all the months that I'd nursed her off the junk meant nothing? My first instinct was to storm out, go to Scutch's or to hell; but I'd done enough running for one day, and it was time I came to terms with myself. I strode over to the bed and switched on her dim nightlight.

Neither of them woke. They were lying outside the sheets. Danny had a large ugly bruise on his cheek, but other than that he didn't seem too much the worse for wear. His breathing was shallow but peaceful.

Before I even heard it, my hair stood on end. Then I sensed a movement behind me and spun around. I knew someone was out there—cloaked by Leonard's voice evaporating into the long fade out. In the unruly silence that followed, I stood still as the little statue of Our Lady that was glowing from the alcove. Finally, I plucked up courage and peeked around the door, but whatever had been was gone, leaving only a curtain trembling in the breeze.

I crept back in the bedroom and looked down on them. All at once, I felt very tired and found it hard to concentrate. Better to sleep. The pain and confusion would still be there for stoking in the morning.

Back in the sitting room, Kate's bed was broken. The legs had finally splintered beyond repair. My couch had been drenched by the bottles and cans from the upturned table, so I lay down on Danny's cot, but no matter how much I studied the cracks in the ceiling, I couldn't sleep. The weight of memory was doing my head in. I went back into the bedroom and lay down the other side of Kate. Danny was breathing in time to the flashing of the bodega light. After a while I fell in step with him and drifted off. I was still unconscious hours after Mary's plane landed in Shannon.

CHAPTER THIRTY

I barely remember the rest of the summer, or the fall for that matter, except that the Yankees blew it in the Stadium and Danny fumed away on the couch when Mister October flailed and flurried but was unable to rescue them. In a way it all seemed fitting. I was basically just going through the motions, waiting for a letter, a phone call, any sight or sign of Mary, but not a word. Nor had she shown up at home, for my mother made no mention. It was as if the ground had risen up and swallowed her. For the first four or five months, I thought of her incessantly, but the city sways to its own rhythm, and eventually she moved to the wings, though there was never a day when she didn't waltz back out, all bathed in blue, and it would often take hours before I could coerce her offstage again.

It was in such a frame of mind that the winter broke upon me. The wind whipped down Decatur like barbed wire. Some nights it was even too frigid for the drunks to venture out. Still, the bars reported no drop in business, for once ensconced in their coziness, there was little enticement to brave the black ice that lay like sheets across the glassy streets.

Most of the lads had been laid off, for cement could not be mixed, and so the nannies carried the avenue, since rich kids' butts still needed wiping, no matter the weather. This sea change upset the applecart of many the relationship. There was much nursing of beers amidst dark mutterings as the ladies, flexing their muscles, broached that very American subject of relationships and hinted about engagements and other annoyances that had been swept under the carpet in flusher times. Lads anxiously jerked heads around to watch TV weathermen jauntily prophesize more frigidity, while those with deep pockets flew home to await the thaw and lend a hand on the farm or family business. The rest of us hunkered down and prayed for better days.

I knew Jesús was watching me—I would have run into him on the avenue otherwise—but I took comfort in Mary's conviction that he was only interested in her. I heard rumors of shake-outs in the neighborhood drug hierarchies; new faces lounged on the corners. Some said they were from Harlem or Washington Heights, that change was on the way with muscle aplenty to back it up. It all added to the ripples of uncertainty swirling through the street, and I took to buying my smoke elsewhere. One night the local numbers runner stopped for a chat. After a rambling discourse, he pointedly mentioned that Jesús had lost his kid; then he strolled on without slapping his usual fives. That set me on edge for days. I even had the locks changed. But I was rarely out anyway, a gig here or there to pay the rent; most of my time was spent taking care of Danny.

And just as the cold slowed down the city, it had the same effect on our lives, one day bleeding into the next. Since I wasn't working, I took over many of Kate's duties, often accompanying Danny down to St. Vincent's Hospital. There was much murmuring amongst the doctors but little substance to any of it. Since pneumonia was still the greatest fear, I saw little point in dragging him downtown in subzero weather to hang around waiting rooms with other shallow-breathing, sunken-cheeked men. Just make him comfortable and hold on until the spring. The change in weather was bound to help.

At first, he railed at the heavens and cursed God for blighting him. For one who had been fiercely independent, it cut him to the core when he was unable to move on his own steam or look after his personal being. Every stray glance in a mirror was now a private Gethsemane to him. He was cranky and difficult to deal with, and at times I felt like screaming that if he wasn't so goddamn vain he wouldn't be going through half the hassle. Then I'd realize that I was letting it get to me and just needed time away from the hothouse that Decatur had become.

As the winter dragged on, he no longer seemed to care much anymore; with that, he became less irritated and prone to judgment. Even in his healthy days, though often compassionate, the raw edge of sarcasm had rarely been far from reach. Now his humor softened, and in the long shadowy afternoons, he took to laughing at his own follies as much as at those of others.

He opened up about some of his past: the straying father who beat his mother until Danny grew strong enough to throw him out. He spoke movingly about her life spent in the thick of the Belfast Troubles; but he was still bitter about a political estrangement from his sister, his only other close family member. He shrugged off his football glory—it was just something that he was good at, no big deal—though one evening he produced a chamois pouch lined with silver and gold medals and walked us through the various games at which they'd been won, and not without a glow of pride.

His books meant most to him, especially the dog-eared collection of Russian novels and the political tracts of Connolly that had introduced him to the notion that the world could and should be a better place. One night he even spoke about Sands and some of the other hunger strikers and of their hopes and dreams, foibles, and little vanities. It was strange to think that these martyrs were lads only a few years older than myself, obsessed with football and music, girls, and the *craic,* but who had been touched by a fire, often not of their own making. He dwelt on the stress of growing up in an embattled Catholic community: the constant surveillance and the ongoing threat of internment leading to the ultimate refusal to live as a second-class citizen in his own country. Yet whenever I tried to get him to talk about his own political involvement, it always led to a dead end where his voice would trail off and he'd stare out at the street, lost in some memory not for the sharing.

I learned how to coax him back into the present by playing some old Clash or Lennon track that would spark a debate; and if that didn't work, I'd stand behind him and read aloud a random line from Dostoyevski or Turgenev and challenge him to name the story. He rarely erred, and sometimes he'd urge me to read on; then he'd lie there, eyes closed, tangled up in the beauty of the words and the worlds that they took him to, far from our mean little rooms on Decatur.

Few came to visit; then again, he was adamant that no one know any details of his illness. Scutch and Arsehole often dropped by bringing gifts of grapes and Lucozade. They'd usually just sit in silence, reading the papers from home, or staring out the window with him and smoking fags until the room would be blue with smoke, and Kate would arrive in a fury and put the run on them.

For the most part, it was just a slow draining away of time and emotion until I was so spent it was hard to feel anything. I was sick and tired of pain, what-might-have-beens and the clatter of emptiness echoing around inside me.

When he moved to Montefiore, Kate stayed with him around the clock. I don't know how she did it, for she was worn to the bone herself. The strict hospital routine brought relief, and I stringently observed the visiting hours. Kate would have no part of such nonsense and slept in a chair, except for the nights when the nurse from Kerry would wheel in a cot. Then she'd lie next to him, smoothing his hand or holding it to her face until the drugs kicked in and he'd drift off back to the streets of Belfast and a different world from the one he was trapped in.

The apartment was so barren without them that I began to fixate full time on Mary. How come she hadn't written? Had she just closed a chapter on me and that was that? I'd get furious and argue to myself that men were the true romantics; women, for all their talk about love, were the realists, with little problem turning the page when needs must. All manner of things sprung to mind, and I pursued each one down a maze of possibilities. How could she have just walked onto the plane without even a glance backwards? Did all the years mean that little to her? And what of that penetrating, momentary glare when the issue of her pregnancy arose? Had that been a test of my maturity? Had she been entertaining doubts all along about my steadfastness? Had she actually been pregnant? When was the child due? Was it mine? Until my head would explode with sheets of feedback, and I'd run for the safety and solace of the bottle.

In the end I dreaded being alone, causing me to spend most of my time at Scutch's. So much so, that one evening the nurse from Kerry read me the riot act for my drinking and warned me not to show up in that state again. But it was no time for moderation, and I found the perfect antidote: After my alcoholic interludes, just toss back a quart of hot coffee in the diner. I'd drag a chair over to the bed, stare at the white walls, and try to ignore the thinness of Danny's breathing while my mind raced and raged at the injustice of it all.

I was in the diner when Kate called Scutch's, and so I missed the opening shots of the argument over whether he should have received last rites. I arrived to hear one of my least favorite Tyrone boys shouting at her, "You're nothing but a black Protestant bitch! The man deserved a priest."

"Danny wouldn't have wanted it!" she screamed back at him. But all the fight went out of her when she threw herself into my arms, the lines of grief and exhaustion creasing her face. I tried to console her, though I felt I might float away such was the lightness in my head. She was sobbing so hard I thought she might come apart, and she whispered over and over, "I was right, Sean, wasn't I?"

"Yes, Kate, you were," I murmured back into her ear until the fury clawed at me. I broke loose from her and stuck my face into the Tyrone boy's. "You fuck off with your religion! Where were you when Danny was lying stretched out on Decatur?"

Who knows what would have happened if the nurse from Kerry hadn't separated us? But that was only the beginning, for on the following night, Kate insisted that he wouldn't have wanted anyone viewing his emaciated body, so the coffin was closed at the funeral parlor, leading to another round of accusations about her pushiness.

If he had been a problem in life, Danny was even more of a challenge in death. I slunk into the background, except for leading scores of mourners to neighboring pubs for the ritual drowning of sorrows. But poor Kate was run off her feet dealing with issues big and small, all of them thorny. What flag was the coffin to be draped in—the Provos' Tricolor or Connolly's Starry Plough? What prayers to be said, if any? Where was he to be buried, by whom, and more importantly, who was to shoulder the costs?

But by Christ, did she rise to the occasion, though her rationale was often confusing to both political and pious. Because it was bright and colorful, Connolly's Starry Plough won by a mile over the Tricolor, whose hues, she said, were a washy auld green and orange that Danny would never be caught dead in. People could pray any damn way they pleased, she ordained, but there would be nothing official, for she never once saw him darken either the door of a church or an OTB office. But she was most adamant that he be buried back in Ireland, where he belonged, by his bitch of a sister if she ever had the decency to return a phone call. The whole kit and caboodle would be paid for out of a fundraiser to be held in Scutch Murphy's, and woe be to every last bastard on Bainbridge Avenue if there wasn't a proper turnout.

For days I felt nothing except bruised relief. But things came to a head at the fundraiser in the presence of many figures from his life. Some I knew well; others were less familiar, usually rebels like himself, young and old, socialist and revolutionary, construction worker and football player, bartender and librarian, down and out, and the occasional well-heeled. They all approached Kate and me at the bar and said how sorry they were for our trouble. We were his family, or apparently the only one he'd ever acknowledged.

As the line grew longer, it finally struck me that I'd never see him again. Then the flirty bartender from the Crooked Man stood at my stool and at his heels a black-leather, blue-jeans posse. He took me in his arms, and I felt the hot tears on his cheeks as he whispered that Danny had loved me. The bile of regret rose up and almost choked me, because I remembered only too well how badly I'd hurt him that awful night I'd gone screaming out of the apartment.

And then I was in the bathroom, with Scutch and Arsehole saying I was making a holy show of myself, what would Danny think, and I'd better grab a hold of myself because there was a long night ahead, we all had to pull as one and not let the bloody side down. Slowly, I gained strength from them, for I could tell they were equally shattered, and I knew there was a way of handling this. I'd just have to be a whole lot bigger than myself to find it.

But the Irish are past masters in the art of mourning. Soon the shots of whiskey were passed around, and Danny was toasted as though he were a cross between Cuchulainn and the Croppy Boy. At the height of the tumult, a silence began to spread slowly through the bar. I felt it as a cold rush of air from the opened door before I even noticed Dennehy, backed by a cadre of Tyrone boys in suits, and bringing up their rear, Benny from the Gallowglass. There had been mention back in the funeral parlor that the Provos had failed to make an appearance. It was suggested that Kate's choice of the Starry Plough over the Tricolor had been the reason. Others laughed off that suspicion and shrugged that the hard men would come in their own good time. Someone else remarked that the whole affair should have been run by them, and that failure to consult Belfast would have far reaching consequences.

Dennehy was dressed in a dark suit and tie, a raincoat folded over his arm. He was freshly shaved, and even from a distance I could smell the Old Spice. He swept the room in an instant. That frigid summation brought to mind a night Danny had warned me about a local smack dealer: "In the end there's only two kinds of people, Paddy, those who have killed and those who haven't."

Whatever about violence, you could tell Dennehy had a background with a shovel, for he carried his wiry frame with a slight stoop, and his hands were coarse and knotted. I had always thought of him as a taller man. Perhaps he wore boots on the site or his importance there boosted him in my mind; or maybe it was the whiskey that caused this shift in perspective. For once I wasn't in awe of him.

A space cleared and he strode over, his hand outstretched. I didn't accept it, for I wanted to show him I was no flunky bowing to his magnificence. Instead, I took his measure from the toes of his polished brown shoes to the tip of his tight-cut, graying hair.

He caught on to my game instantly and betrayed the barest glint of interest before reverting to his steely blank stare. He nodded to Kate, "I'm sorry for your trouble, Miss."

Then he murmured to me, "*Ní beidh a leithéad ann arís.*" Noting that I didn't understand the Gaelic, he tried to mask his disdain when translating, "We'll never see his like again."

With the barest flicker of his hand, he called a drink for the house while, at the same time, intimating to Scutch that no big deal should be made of it. A murmur of appreciation and "fair dues to you" rumbled around the room. None of his Tyrone entourage availed of the opportunity, although I knew that a couple of them were far from teetotalers. Benny, however, did reach out his big fist and took a tumbler of whiskey. Without waiting for the mass of mourners to get theirs, Dennehy raised his glass and, with a bare nod to me, tossed back his Jameson's.

"I take it you're in charge of getting the remains home." He spoke now for common consumption in unusually measured tones. Then again, I had only heard him barking orders on the site or occasionally whispering to Danny in a pub. There had been something troubling about their relationship, although Danny never spoke a bad word about him; yet, I could sense that he was beholden to the boss man in some shape or form.

Dennehy didn't wait for an answer but produced a white envelope and handed it to me. "Everything will be provided for."

"That won't be necessary," I said as off-handedly as I could manage.

He studied me as a scientist would some specimen of little interest that should be acknowledged, if only for form's sake.

"We look after our own." He placed a slight emphasis on the first word. Then he added, "Mister."

"Kelly," I said louder than appropriate, and a hush spread around the room again. "Sean Kelly. I used to work for you, in case you hadn't noticed."

Dennehy withdrew the envelope but held it by his side.

"As I said," he enunciated, never raising his voice, "we look after our own."

"Then where were you all those months when he was on the flat of his back on Decatur?"

"We never lost sight of him."

"You never darkened his door either." Then I looked directly at the Tyrone boys. "None of you fuckers either!"

They betrayed no hint of emotion, though I had seen Danny go to bat for a number of them.

"Mister Kelly," Dennehy still didn't raise his voice but his Northern accent cut through the smoke, "there are certain matters you don't understand."

Benny must have anticipated my reply, for he stepped lithely through the Tyrone boys and laid his big fist on my shoulder. He squeezed but I was already speaking. "Yeah, like who was Morgan?"

I felt like crying from the force of his grip but refused to show it. Any iota of compassion or understanding fled Dennehy's eyes. It was just the two of us now, and he had far more experience in this kind of situation.

Scutch understood too. He took the hurling stick down from behind the cash register while Arsehole poured the remains of his Heineken into a glass and gripped the neck of the bottle. The room stiffened as the Tyrone boys took a step forward and positioned themselves around Dennehy. I had a feeling I might soon be renewing acquaintance with the nurse from Kerry, for I had once witnessed these psychos clear a Blarney Stone over a far more trivial issue. But I was beyond caring.

"Come on, Jack, we have that social to attend." Benny,

casual to the extreme, took us all by surprise. Dennehy weighed his options: wipe the floor with me publicly or settle matters at a less delicate time. Without even a shrug, he laid three crisp one hundred-dollar bills on the counter for the drinks called.

"Thank you, Mister Murphy. It's a hard evening on us all." He handed Scutch the white envelope. "I'm putting this in your care. No doubt calmer minds will prevail in the morning."

One of the Tyrone boys already held the door open. The cold air swept into the room and carried with it a premonition of consequences to come if the money wasn't accepted. Scutch laid the hurley down on the counter and placed the envelope behind the cash register where he once had put my Clash records. Dennehy bade farewell to Kate but looked right through me. Then he walked out, followed by his entourage and others who wished to have their allegiance publicly noted.

When the door closed, a murmur arose until those remaining realized that Benny still sat at the bar. He stared glumly at the mirror, his red hair rambling down around his shoulders. Then he picked up his tumbler and drained the remains of his whiskey. He placed a ten-dollar bill on the bar and hitched up his trousers under the army jacket he was wearing.

"Come over and see me sometime," he said for all the room to hear, then bent down and hugged me while he whispered, "you little fuckin' eejit."

CHAPTER THIRTY-ONE

Danny got his military funeral. His sister never showed up to claim the body, and the comrades were waiting at the airport. Dennehy was right; the Provos did look after their own. Danny lies in Milltown Cemetery within shouting distance of Bobby Sands, each felled by very different enemies, both still awaiting a united Ireland.

He owed nothing and owned little, just some shelves of books, a guitar, a leather jacket and his football medals. Money wasn't his thing, as they say. After the funeral expenses had been settled, just over five hundred dollars remained; in the end, pragmatism had overcome pride, and Dennehy's money came in handy. Kate asked me to hold on to the balance in case any old bills came due. I placed the five fresh hundred-dollar bills behind Connolly's restored poster and bought a couple of rounds of drinks for Arsehole and myself, extravagantly tipping an astounded Scutch with the remainder. After all was said and done, I figured we three deserved it and felt certain Danny would be the last person to begrudge us.

The apartment was like a tomb. Kate couldn't bear to be there, though she paid me a couple of months' rent in advance, "just in case."

"In case of what?" I asked. The edge in my voice cut her badly, and I didn't even know why it was there. I guess I felt she was running away, but who could blame her?

I forced myself to stay in a couple of nights a week for the preservation of both money and brain cells. But the memories battered me. No matter how much I read, wrote, drank, or smoked, eventually my eyes would take to cruising the room. Even though I had banished the remains of their belongings to closets and dark corners, I could still hear their voices. I dreaded waking in the night, for I could sense Mary's presence and, in the half-dream stage, even touch her. Nor could I sleep with the bedroom door closed for fear of claustrophobia; one night I even tossed Our Lady of the Bronx under the bed to escape her black accusing eyes. But there was no respite, for Connolly glared in at me reprovingly, although he was hardly a one to talk, with Dennehy's five hundred bucks stuffed in his back pocket.

Scutch and Arsehole were very considerate but, after some weeks, they were eager to get on with life, such as it was.

"There's sweet fuck all point living in the past, mate," Scutch lectured me one night, and he was right. But I almost punched out Arsehole when he added, "And you can be sure the quare one over in Ireland is far from pining over you." He may have been right, but I didn't need to hear it.

I was stuck in a rut of my own making. To make matters worse, money was running low, and Scutch wouldn't be buying me drinks forever. I took a few gigs to keep the wolf from the door, but my heart wasn't in it. Everything sounded false, except when I was downing shots of whiskey; but one too many and I took offence at the inevitable slagging. At first, the owners cut me a bit of slack. Everyone knew I was taking Danny's passing hard, but what was understandable after a week became a nuisance after a couple of months.

The evenings were growing a little longer, and the cold air no longer whipped down Decatur. I took to accompanying Arsehole to the various buckets of blood near Fordham where the college girls hung out. Sometimes I even chatted them up—lovely innocent Irish-Americans with big hair and perfect teeth—but it was like shooting fish in a barrel, for most of them were only dying to talk to someone "from home," about parents from Leitrim, Mayo, or Donegal, and cousins whom they visited each cold and rainy summer. Nice and inviting as they were, I couldn't handle it, and invariably, to Arsehole's consternation, I'd stride away in mid-sentence and end up across the street staring over the train line at the young trees in Fordham and wondering how tall they'd be before I ever felt anything for anyone again.

I found myself often by the apartment window vacantly gazing at the drama unfolding below. A couple of gray doves had taken to landing on the sill; they reminded me of Bob Marley's "Three Little Birds" and, one day on a notion, I unpacked my guitar. The doves looked up in alarm at my first notes but after a while ignored me. From then on, I played the tune whenever I saw them. Within a week, I was playing all the time.

I had no idea where these new songs came from, nor did I wish to tempt providence by inquiring. At best, they were strange, angular, and choppy, or else moody and oblique, with words that I didn't totally understand. On some level, though, I knew that they were filling a hole that Danny and Mary had left. Never in a month of Sundays would they fit the bill on Bainbridge, nor did I bother giving them an airing even for the comatose during the graveyard shift.

I wondered why Noreen never came to see me. She must have known that I was back on the scene. A couple of nights when shuffling home from the pub, I almost rang her. But I either didn't have the change or couldn't recall her number. I figured she had to be missing me. Jesus, I missed her. Then again, I missed just about everyone when I had drink taken. The next day, of course, with a hangover pounding, it never seemed like quite the right idea to phone, and so the cycle would begin again.

Then one night the songs stopped coming. The vein had dried up, and I was at the end of the line. But what line? Connolly, as ever judgmental, was no help, and I knew Our Lady of the Bronx wouldn't have much to offer from her horizontal position under the bed. Before the walls began throbbing, I bolted for the door and took the stairs two at a time. Out on the street, I gulped in a couple of draughts of fresh air. One of the dealers headed over towards me and, for form's sake, I bought a couple of joints, though the last thing I needed was a head full of smoke driving the demons even crazier. Then I began striding along with my head down through traffic lights and stop signs; with the songs gone, there didn't seem like much point in anything.

I knew where I was going all along—just wouldn't face up to it—until I found myself parked under the Armory smoking a joint in Danny's memory while staring across the street at the Gallowglass. Little had changed, except that a new bodega had opened up the block. Slowly but surely the Latino Bronx was pushing beyond the Concourse and enveloping all before it. The old pub still held the line, cantankerous to the end, but most other things Paddy were already in flight to Woodlawn or the concrete fields of Yonkers.

I knew Noreen would be there. It was one of her nights. I had to talk to her, explain what had happened. I could do so now without hurting anyone. We could start with a clean slate. And all at once what had been foggy for months became crystal clear.

There was a spring to my step crossing the street. I positively glided between the cars and buses. Not a horn honked; I felt invisible and mighty. It would be good to sit with her, the lilac in her hair, our bodies touching, to hear her sing, and then have her slip back across the smoky room to me, and me only. Maybe Johnnie Crowley would be playing; I could tell him about the new songs. Add his magic to them. Resurrect the Tinkers and summon the King of the Fairies to beam down once more on the avenue.

Benny must have seen me coming, for he didn't betray the least surprise. He didn't take his leg down either, nor did he smile. He regarded me evenly, as though I had just stepped out to make a phone call or pick up a sandwich. I glanced down at his huge thigh, trying to mimic Danny's attitude.

"You took your time," he remarked.

I could hear the clatter of the banjo, but it took a little while to identify the fiddle. Even through the soundproofed walls, I could detect the lack of Johnnie's magic.

"Is Noreen here?"

Benny studied me for a long time. Then he shrugged with not a little world-weariness and beckoned me towards the glass panel. I leaned over his big leg and looked in. My heart lurched into a little jig at the sight of her. She looked

Larry Kirwan

fresh and lovely and still untouched by the Bronx, though she seemed a trifle somber; but that was OK, for it was only fitting that she should be missing me a little. Then Benny wheezed in my ear, and I was enveloped in his tang of stale smoke, beer, and bachelorhood. I stepped back and waited for his leg to drop.

He yawned his acceptance of the world and all its foibles, indicating that I should follow suit, but his equanimity was shaken by the smugness of my smile; with one quick motion he grabbed the scruff of my neck and dragged me back towards the clear glass. At first, I couldn't get a good view of Noreen, for she had turned to a man sitting next to her. I hadn't noticed him before. He was older than me and well dressed, a master carpenter, perhaps, or a bricklayer who had started his own business. She must have just spoken, for he smiled, then very gently drew her head to his shoulder. She rested there for a moment in the way that people do when they're beyond familiar. She couldn't see me, but I drank in every centimeter of her, for I knew she'd soon be a memory.

"Wasn't there something else?" Benny said as I headed to the door.

"Yeah. Fuck you."

"How about Captain William Morgan?" He paused to make sure he had my total attention. "Formerly of Her Majesty's Royal Irish Guards, currently an agent for MI6, until we have the pleasure of blowing his head off."

Danny might as well have been in the vestibule with us so palpable was his presence.

"Hard as nails and gay as Christmas," Benny added, choosing his next words to give the guts of the story while

betraying the least possible information. "Danny was done
for carrying a gun around the same time as Sands. He got
the usual treatment—at first. Then Billy Morgan took an
interest in him. He was separated from his comrades, and for
three months we had no word of him. Then, out of the blue,
he was released."

"So?"

"He was done for a gun in his pocket, man! Sands got
fourteen years for just being in the presence of one."

"It was a set-up. Any idiot can see that."

"Yeah, any idiot." Benny's weariness returned. "That's
what Danny said too."

"He wouldn't talk. You know that."

"Everyone talks, kid. It's just what do they say."

A couple breezed in laughing. Benny dropped his leg and
hustled them through. The music blared out, and I caught
a glimpse of Noreen. Did she see me before the door closed?
It didn't really matter.

"The Brits don't fuck around. There was a reason they
handed him over to Morgan. They shared . . . shall we say
. . . certain tastes." He spread out his palms—the old Bronx
gesture: *What are you going to do?*

"Danny had a button and Morgan knew how to push it."
He shrugged.

So that was what was on his mind, all those winter
afternoons when he lay there staring out the window. That's
what he had to put up with from the Tyrone boys on the
site—the suspicion that he had talked. That's what drove
him to distraction—the frustration of never being able to clear
his name.

"There's only one way to beat those Brit bastards—don't

give them an inch." Benny looked at me for some kind of empathy. But I didn't have it to give.

"Danny would have been a dead man if Jack Dennehy hadn't gone to the wall for him and taken him out here. But there was no earthly way we could ever let him go back."

I was already opening the street door when he called after me, "Sean!"

I didn't turn around.

"For what it's worth, I believed him too. We just couldn't take a chance."

CHAPTER THIRTY-TWO

It was late in the morning by the time I got the apartment cleared and dropped the keys off with the landlord. The previous night's party had been low-key. Arsehole had done the arranging, and the remaining Tinkers had shown up at Scutch's. Johnnie Crowley had even played a couple of tunes for good luck; that meant a lot, because he had never much acknowledged me before. Kate had come earlier in the afternoon and taken Danny's guitar. We split the football medals with the Tinkers, and I kept the leather jacket. It was way too big for me, but as she said, "Maybe you'll grow into it someday."

Yeah, right! The guitar would probably have been of more use, but I could still smell Danny from the jacket and that meant more. What remained went to the Salvation Army. Funny how you can so easily dispose of a life in a couple of garbage bags.

Arnold came too and stayed through the party. He seemed like a decent enough guy, and was way into Kate. You had to wonder, though, if he was going to be big enough to absorb all the loss bottled up inside her.

We didn't talk much about Danny. It didn't seem right. The one time his name came up, Arnold blushed and Kate rushed off to the ladies room. There was a bit of an awkward silence until Shiggins, cool as ever behind his shades, veered the subject away. Mary's name never arose, I suppose in deference to me, although I think I could have handled it. This lent an air of unreality to the affair, and before long most people drifted off, with the excuse of one thing or another to be done in the morning.

Then it was time for Kate to leave. I knew she was dreading it, for she'd been ignoring Arnold's hints and gone way over her normal quota of vodka. Much as I adored her, I was ready for her to go too. She was unsteady when stepping off her stool and almost fell into my arms.

"I love you, Sean." She clung to me.

I told her I loved her back, but I was really just trying to hold it all together. "You'll come and see me, won't you?" She sniffled into my ear. "We only have each other now."

"I will, Kate . . ."

But we both knew I wouldn't. Arnold damn near had to carry her out, the tears streaming out of her in bucketfuls.

And then it was just Scutch, Arsehole, and myself holding down the fort with one last drink, then another for the road, and a final one for the ditch. And before I knew it, I was on my feet and we were hugging and promising to stay in touch, and I'd surely be back up to do some gigs, and wouldn't they come down and see me when I finally hit the stage at CBGBs. But we all knew it was bullshit.

I went back to Decatur for one last night and, when I took Connolly down from the wall, Dennehy's five hundred fell to the ground. I thought of giving it to the Sally Army, but figured I might need it as much as the next man, for I had no idea what I was going to do beyond taking the train down to the Village and seeing where the wind blew me. If nothing else, I'd be the first singer-songwriter bankrolled by the Provisional IRA.

I had the poster under my arm as I strolled down 204th, carrying my father's suitcase, the guitar strung to my back. Not for the first time since awakening, I thought about Mary, where she was, what she was doing, was she thinking about me? And I remembered what Danny said when he sent me back to her: "That song still has some verses left." Had we come to the end of the tune, I wondered, or were there some lines left unsung? Would I ever see her again?

It was a beautiful May morning, with a hint of crispness still in the air. I savored the sights of my old haunts, the pubs and coffee shops, committing them to memory for any lean days ahead. I marveled that I didn't run into a single friend. Not one hello, nor even a goodbye. And yet I knew the only borough on the mainland would always be fair haven. The Bronx had been far from easy on me. It had pruned and tempered my expectations, and rightly so, for it was rocksteady real while I had been a crock full of dumb notions. I arrived a boy and was leaving a man, a little scarred perhaps, but a great deal wiser; yet I had no doubt that the two years spent on its bristling streets would stand to me down all the days to come.

I had actually passed the spot when I remembered. I ran back and dropped to my knees; I almost had my eye at ground level before I saw it peeking up through a crack in the concrete. The same seed, the same few grains of earth, and a year later it was back—not even the size of a respectable daisy. A couple of elderly ladies, their accents thick as the hills of Donegal, gave me a wide berth. Just another drunken Paddy on his knees, and at that time of the morning too!

But by Christ, did that little red weed give me heart! On an impulse I headed over towards Kingsbridge, retracing one of Danny's meandering routes. What was my hurry anyway? I'd no idea when I'd be back. Might as well drink in as much of the scene as possible. I paused across the park from Poe's little cottage, the rake-thin junkies shuffling about, eyes far back in their wasted heads full to the brim of vacant dreams and that all encompassing singular need, waiting for their man or, perchance, their woman? Had that been Mary's function? Her people? Her turf? Was this where Jesús first caught sight of her willowy figure and alabaster skin—scoring like an old pro? Was I still on her mind back then or just another fading Irish footnote to eventual redemption in the Bronx? Had I ever really known her? Or was I just fixated on a particular façade that suited my own purposes? So many layers of life for the taking, yet we experience so few. And then Old Murph's words struck me: "We never really know anyone else, do we? And sure how could we, when most of us will never even know ourselves."

With this caveat ricocheting around me like some electronic mantra, I hurried across the Concourse, but as the Armory loomed into view, a symphony full of memories began to swell and slither ever-so-slightly off the beat. And before I knew it I was on Jerome and standing outside the Olympia, the old sheet-rocked emporium of dreams, now sandblasted of all romance in the caustic morning glare, and all at once I knew for certain I was history on these streets and that nothing could or ever would be the same again. And then I heard a rumble in the distance and train wheels screeching, and I knew it was beyond time to go, and I wanted more than anything in the world to get aboard that graffitied downtown 4. I bounded up the steps of the El, fumbled for my token, and made it through the turnstile; but, what a disaster, it was the uptown train arriving from Manhattan across the tracks. My disappointment must have been etched in granite, for further down the platform three tough looking Dominican kids began to snigger and then laugh to high heavens. They were scarcely more than sixteen, but tall and well built with the mark of the streets already upon them. One made a crude gesture and, even in their rapid-fire Spanish, *maricón* stuck out.

The tallest gathered that I understood the insult and called it out again in a louder taunting voice. I was about to ignore them and move away, but then I noticed Danny's beam of sunlight streaming through the punctured roof, and all I could think was—that's I, Me, Mine, man, and these morons are blocking my way.

They were chanting *maricón* as I began to walk towards them. They considered this the height of hilarity and waved their bent wrists at me, blowing kisses and shoving each other, simulating in comic detail how a faggot like me would fight. I had no idea what I was going to do but pressed on regardless. They stopped clowning around as I got nearer. With the guitar and the case propelling me, I was gaining momentum; still, they showed no signs of breaking, and I was resigned to taking my lumps. The tallest was closest to the tracks, fists clenched, determination riveting him to the platform. But the middle one was confused and, just as I was about to hit him, he stepped aside and I sailed through. I clenched my teeth, expecting a punch in the back of the head. But it never came. They shouted *maricón* again, but this time there was a hollow ring to it.

At the beam of sunshine I dropped my case. With the warm halo of light bathing me, I raised the poster of Connolly and roared back at them, "Fuck you," and it echoed right through the bulletproof Bronx sky.

That put a stop to their shouting, and they edged back a discreet foot or two, though they never lost sight of my eyes. I didn't give a goddamn anymore—I was so far beyond them.

I barely noticed the approaching downtown train until it shuddered to a halt. A door opened right in front of me, and I stepped aboard.

SOME OTHER READING
from

Brandon is a leading Irish publisher of new fiction and non-fiction for an international readership. For a catalogue of new and forthcoming books, please write to Brandon/Mount Eagle, Cooleen, Dingle, Co. Kerry, Ireland. For a full listing of all our books in print, please go to

www.brandonbooks.com

ROBERT WALDRON
The Secret Dublin Diary of Gerard Manley Hopkins
A Novella

A bold exploration of the years one of England's foremost Victorian poets spent in Ireland, of his torments, ecstasies, fears and loves.

"Waldron's depth of insight makes him an author to watch." *Publishers Weekly*

Paperback original ISBN 9780863224096

MARY ROSE CALLAGHAN
A Bit of a Scandal

"In graceful, casual prose, Callaghan spins a believable story. A beautiful story of doomed love." *Kirkus*

"[S]ubtly exposes the perverse manipulations that may complicate and confound love. Callaghan is a compassionate storyteller, and her narrative talents, especially for dialog, nuanced character development, and surprising plot twists, are fully evident. Readers of Anne Enright and Maeve Binchy will discover much to admire here." *Library Journal*

Hardback ISBN 9780863223884
Paperback ISBN 9780863223969

MARION URCH
An Invitation to Dance

A thrilling epic, packed with passionate romance and incident from Ireland to India, from London to Spain, Paris and Munich, from the USA to Australia.

"A well-written and well-researched fictional biography of Lola Montez, an Irish-born woman who posed as a Spanish dancer and entertained kings (she was the mistress of Ludwig of Bavaria at one point), the Parisian glitterati, and American and Australian miners." *Historical Novels Review*

Hardback ISBN 9780863223839
Paperback ISBN 9780863223952

SAM MILLAR
Bloodstorm

A Karl Kane Novel

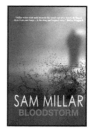

"*Bloodstorm* is the first in a powerful new crime series from Irish author Millar. Extremely original, it is a chillingly gripping book, and the consistently tough prose should help gain Millar more fans in the U.S. with a taste for the hard-boiled."
Publishers Weekly

Paperback original ISBN 9780863223754

SAM MILLAR
The Dark Place

A Karl Kane Novel

"Every now and then you stumble across a writer and when you are reading their latest offering you wonder how on earth you haven't read their books before. I was instantly gripped when I opened the cover of *The Dark Place*. In only 256 pages, Millar manages to cram in enough tension compared to most novels that apparently need double the number of pages." *Crimesquad*

Paperback original ISBN 9780863224034

EVELYN CONLON
Skin of Dreams

"Through two continents and two generations Evelyn Conlon traces the countenance of life and death and its so-called punishment, in a tale deftly told with revelation that startles with new insight." Sam Reese Sheppard, co-author of *Mockery of Justice*

"A courageous, intensely imagined and tightly focused book that asks powerful questions of authority... this is the kind of Irish novel that is all too rare." Joseph O'Connor

Paperback original ISBN 9780863223068

PAUL CHARLES
Family Life

An Inspector Starrett Mystery

The second in the new detective series set in Donegal in the west of Ireland

"The appealing Starrett, with his intuitive gifts, is a worthy addition to the ranks of contemporary police detectives." *Publishers Weekly*

Hardback ISBN 9780863224041
Paperback ISBN9780863224157

PAUL CHARLES
The Beautiful Sound of Silence

A DI Christy Kennedy Mystery

"[O]ne of the strongest in an impressive series... Veterans and newcomers alike will appreciate the smart writing and ingenious planting of clues." *Publishers Weekly*

"Paul Charles ranks up there with Peter Robinson, Stuart Pawson and Stephen Booth." *I Love a Mystery*

Hardback ISBN 9780863223778
Paperback ISBN9780863223983

BRYAN MACMAHON
Hero Town

"We hear the authentic voice of local Ireland, all its tics and phrases and catchcalls. Like Joyce, this wonderful, excellently structured book comes alive when you read it aloud... Here in New York we read of Ireland's new-found need to counter affluence with a return to roots. Begin with *Hero Town*." Frank Delaney

Hardback ISBN 9780863223228
Paperback ISBN 97808632234263

WALTER MACKEN
Sunset on the Window-Panes

Careless of the hurts he inflicts along the way, Bart O'Breen walks his own road, as proud as the devil and as lonely as hell.

"In his company, to use a fine phrase of Yeats, brightness falls from the air." *Newcastle Chronicle*

Paperback ISBN 9780863222542

TOM PHELAN
Iscariot

"This is a novel about religion, families, sex, guilt and joy – with a 'whodunnit' narrative that keeps you reading to the last page... *Iscariot* promises suspense, darkness and redemption – it delivers."
Cork Examiner

"Tom Phelan's second novel leaves us in no doubt about his talent as a keen... observer of humanity."
Sunday Tribune

"Moving... erotic... always gripping." *Irish Globe*

Paperback ISBN 9780863222467

PADRAIG O'FARRELL
Rebel Heart

"I read it in one mid-night sitting; it has the button-holing compulsion of a man met in a dark laneway. I can't wait to see the film version." Hugh Leonard

"The plot is clever and well-worked...an entertaining and thought-provoking read." *An Phoblacht*

Paperback ISBN 9780863222214

GERRY ADAMS

Before the Dawn: An Autobiography

"One thing about him is certain: Gerry Adams is a gifted writer who, if he were not at the center of the war-and-peace business, could easily make a living as an author, of fiction or fact."
New York Times

Paperback ISBN 9780863222894

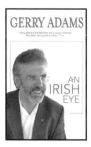

GERRY ADAMS

An Irish Eye

"Most of this book's pieces are occasioned by news items, political developments, or particularly poignant anniversaries, and as such they provide readers with a broad-spectrum view of Adams doing what he does best: arguing passionately for republicanism while reminding his audience that the Troubles are one of many social-justice challenges facing Ireland and the rest of the world. Although many pieces reveal the author's ample wit, more than a few also capture Adams in a pensive posture." *Booklist*

Paperback original ISBN 9780863223709

GERRY ADAMS

An Irish Journal

"Gerry Adams is a skillful writer with a sound intellectual foundation for his political beliefs." *Time*

"Gives an almost personal feel for the peace process as it develops, from Sinn Féin's first meeting with Britain's new prime minister Tony Blair to the build-up to the Good Friday agreement."
Sunday Tribune

Paperback original ISBN 9780863222825X

ADRIAN HOAR
In Green and Red

"The work is of a high standard, well documented, with index, a list of sources and copious notes... there is hardly a dull moment in the account from beginning to end." *Irish Independent*

"Splendid... Instead of a cardboard cutout of an Irish hero, we get a hugely complex and beautifully written portrait of a man who struggled against his own marginality." *Scotland on Sunday*

"Well researched and well written." *An Phoblacht*

Hardback ISBN 9780863223327

SEAN O'CALLAGHAN
To Hell or Barbados:
The Ethnic Cleansing of Ireland

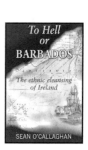

"An illuminating insight into a neglected episode in Irish history... its main achievement is to situate the story of colonialism in Ireland in the much larger context of world-wide European imperialism." *Irish World*

"A fascinating read." *Sunday Tribune*

"Essential reading." *Irish Examiner*

Paperback ISBN 9780863222870

J.J. BARRETT
Martin Ferris: Man of Kerry

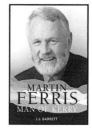

"I can recommend this story of how at least one quintessential Kerryman came to beat his sword into a ploughshare. It is a tale told in friendship and admiration by the man best qualified to do it."
Tim Pat Coogan

"An amazing insight into the world of a man on a mission." *Irish Post*

Hardback ISBN 9780863223105
Paperback ISBN 9780863223518

JAMES MONAGHAN
Colombia Jail Journal

"Through the unique perspective of James Monaghan — one of the Colombia Three — we get a fascinating account of their struggle for survival and their ultimate escape back to Ireland." *Irish Post*

"You should definitely add James Monaghan's inspiring, exciting, and perceptively-written *Colombia Jail Journal* book to the Latin American section of your bookshelf." *Toward Freedom*

Paperback original ISBN 9780863223761

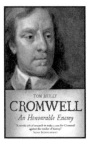

TOM REILLY
Cromwell: An Honourable Enemy

"Reilly argues in convincing detail that the conventional accounts have got it wrong." *RTÉ Guide*

"Make no mistake, this is a very important reappraisal of Cromwell's nine-month tour of Leinster and Munster." *Sunday Tribune*

"The book is very welcome, and will force historians to reappraise this remarkable man." *Books Ireland*

Paperback ISBN 9780863223907

DANNY MORRISON (ED)
Hunger Strike

"Vivid and passionate in song, poetry and good writing." *Verbal Magazine*

"Though submissions from republicans dominate the book the contributors are from diverse backgrounds, from such well-known writers as Ulick O'Connor and Edna O'Brien to hunger striker Mary Doyle, former Beirut hostage Brian Keenan, and pro-Agreement unionist William Brown." *Galway Advertiser*

Hardback ISBN 9780863223594
Paperback ISBN 9780863223600